Severed Ties

A Nick Cooper Story

DANIEL ROBINSON

ISBN: 1986794660

ISBN-13: 978-1986794664

DEDICATION

To my wife – all my love.
Thanks to all my kids and other family members – your encouragement is my
drive. Thanks to all my friends who believed in me as an author. Thanks to my
mom and dad who think all my work should win a Pulitzer…maybe someday.

And thank you Maggie, my Standard Poodle, for not eating my homework…
(manuscript)

This novel's story and characters are fictitious. Certain long-standing institutions, agencies, and public offices are mentioned, but the characters involved are wholly imaginary.

Kathy,

Thanks so much for
wanting to read my novel!
I hope you enjoy it.
Best Wishes
Daniel Roberts

Part One

Chapter 1

LIVES CHANGE IN A BLINK

Eddy's Tavern and Grill

Chicago, Illinois

1979

Dave Larson slumped on his barstool at Eddy's Tavern & Grill; his head hung low in self-induced misery. When he'd first arrived, he was inconsolable. Now, five gin and tonics later, he wallowed in an alcohol-drenched state of misery. Though he could provide no real proof for his theory, Larson was convinced his wife was cheating on him. This possibility consumed every inch of his being and tore at his heart in non-stop, chest-crushing anguish.

Larson loved his wife, Doris, and their eleven-year-old son, JJ. Though the trio occasionally struggled, he believed they were, and always had been, happy. But lately, Doris had changed, and things seemed to be spiraling out of control.

For the last three years, Doris Larson had worked in the law offices of Claiborne, Biggs, and Dawson as an executive assistant to partner, George Dawson. She put in long hours—a given in the trade. Dave had understood this. In fact, he appreciated it in the beginning as it allowed him the occasional stop at the bar on his way home from work. However, over the last few months, Doris rarely came home before 11:00 p.m. That change immediately started grating on Dave's tolerance and patience. And then she started working weekends, something she had rarely done previously. She would leave before her husband woke not returning until well into the night. Saturdays and Sundays. Because of these absences and what Dave believed was a change in his wife's demeanor, he was sure someone at the law firm was screwing his wife.

Doris denied her husband's accusations. She'd laugh and claim he was crazy. "Besides," she'd say, "I have no desire to be with anyone but you." Or, "The only man I've ever loved is you." When pushed to exasperation she would plead, "For the love of God, *no one* in my office would do such a thing."

Larson never bought her denials. There were too many signs. Tonight, he had decided to catch her in the act, certain she would step out of line. Parked down the street from her office building, he waited to see if she left with anyone. If she did? Well, he'd confront her and her *friend*, and he would put an end to this bullshit.

As the minutes dragged on, the anticipation ground away on his already tortured nerves. And then, to make the situation worse, rain began to pelt the windshield. Larson switched on the car's wipers and then rubbed the fog off the inside of the windshield. He strained to keep vigilant. The rubber blades swished back and forth, clearing away the pounding torrent, but they couldn't erase his runaway imagination—the vision of Doris kissing another man. Embraced in a naked tryst. His heartbreak shot into rage. He grabbed the steering wheel and squeezed it with all his might. He'd kill the son-of-a-bitch. Chop the bastard into a thousand pieces.

The blades ran on monotonously; Swish. Swash. Swish. Swash. The half-crazed man glared through his windshield, ready to pounce. He was sure his Doris would walk out arm and arm with *him*.

When Doris did leave the building at 9 p.m., she came out by herself, got in her Buick, and drove off. *She was meeting him somewhere else, right—had to be*! Even worse, maybe she'd already screwed him on an executive desk or on the floor of the break room. Who knew what went on in a huge law firm—especially after regular business hours!

Now, as he teetered on his barstool, booze flowing freely through his veins, Larson decided enough was enough. Her denials wore on him. He felt as though he'd been carrying the world on his shoulders. *Doris in the arms of another man.* Just the thought caused a pounding in his head and a crushing weight in his chest. He was done. He'd drive home and demand answers—finally confront her. "I'll say, "I want the fucking truth," he muttered to himself. *No, not strong enough.* "I *demand* the fucking truth." He'd look her straight in the eyes, she'd fold, and the whole sordid affair would finally bare out.

And yet. Once the matter was out in the open, Larson knew that his young son's life would be shattered. The family, ruined. That's why he'd kept his mouth shut all this time. The moment she'd confess, everything would smash into pieces. *It no longer matters. I know what she's up to and will not take it another goddamn minute.*

"Larson, get your head off the bar. No sleeping," the bartender snapped. With great effort, Dave raised his head and glanced at his watch. 11:10 p.m. His wife would surely be home by now. Bleary-eyed, he gulped down the rest of his drink then tossed his last two twenties on the bar.

As he stood, Larson caught his reflection in the mirror behind the bar. He studied his features. At forty years old, his curly, dark brown hair showed no signs of graying. With solid shoulders, muscular chest, and a good inch over six feet, he considered himself fit and appealing. Glancing down, the ex-high-school jock was proud that he had little middle-aged pooch like so many men his age. His chiseled chin was still there, something his wife Doris had adored when they'd first met. He was a damn fine-looking man. What possible reason could Doris have to cheat on him? Their sex life was great, for God's sake. *Okay, maybe not great . . . but good.*

Money!

Goddamnit that was it! This indiscretion was all about money. A frown stole his reflection's smile. *Indiscretion? Screw that shit. She was fucking the guy.*

Dave closed his eyes and tried to stay focused. He needed to keep his anger pointed at the right person. But the money? His lack of financial success stalked him like a murderous assassin. He had exhibited such promise. That's what the couple joyfully considered when they first dated.

He was smart, good looking, ambitious. Sure to be a success. But now, years later, he'd let his wife and son down. He was a financial failure. *What had he been thinking all these years*? Shit, even tonight, he sat at this bar, stewing about it, spending his last forty dollars on himself. Because of his failures, his wife was in the arms of some high-and-mighty rich fuck. "Not if *I* have anything to say about it," he growled at his image. With that, Dave staggered out of the bar.

Though the stout construction worker had knocked back enough alcohol to put a horse into a coma, he maintained sufficient reason to know driving drunk wasn't a smart move. Larson told himself that very thing as he stumbled out the door into the blackness of night. Unfortunately, his overwhelming need to challenge his wife's recent behavior overcame good judgment. A fleeting vision of a cop pulling him over and an arrest for DUI blazed through his mind. He considered it, shrugged, and groped in his pocket for his keys while staggering across the parking lot.

"Son of a bitch. Where is that piece of shit car?" Larson grumbled as he searched for his blue Chevy. The chilly night air shrouded Larson, and his breath escaped like cigarette smoke. Briefly forgetting his search, Larson pulled up and began blowing in and out, witnessing the mist as it vaporized. A childlike grin appeared on his face. After a few minutes of this inebriated amusement, a tremor of cold jerked him back to his task. He shook off the chill, regained his purpose, and lurched forward. *Shit, I'm fucking drunk*. Larson giggled at the thought.

Darkness veiled the unlit lot making it difficult for even a sober man to get around. Larson, gin infused, appeared blind as he stumbled in one direction and then the next, zigzagging and fumbling along step after wobbly step. Through unfocused eyes, he failed to see the pothole, and his right foot sank ankle-deep into water and mud that filled the crevice. He let out an animalistic shriek as a jolt of pain shot up his leg, and his key ring, which he was finally able to get out of his pocket, flew from his hand, skidded across the pavement, and landed directly under a car. It was his Malibu. Rubbing his throbbing hip, but at least still standing, Larson marveled at his luck.

"My goddamn keys found my goddamn car! Fucking perfect. My lucky night," he slurred with a sarcastic chortle. Grabbing his pants at the waist and pulling them up in triumph, he lumbered toward his car. With every other step, he shook his leg in an attempt to rid his sopping pants and foot of the soggy, muddy mess from the pot hole. As if he had an odd herky-jerky limp, he bounced up and down. Step, jerk, lift. Step, jerk, lift.

Larson weaved his way to the car, stretched out a hand, and used the passenger door as a steadying influence. He bent down, reached under the chassis, and snagged the errant set of keys. "Got 'em."

Straitening up, though with a pronounced wobble that nearly resulted in a fall, Larson began fumbling with the wad trying to find the right key. Sporting a drunken lopsided grin, he studied the metal objects with intense though hazy resolve. *Are you the one*? He stared expectantly at a single silver key, half-heartedly believing it to answer him back.

The sudden plodding of footsteps interrupted him from his frivolous stupor. Before he could grasp who or what was coming, a huge set of hands grabbed his arms at the elbows and wrenched them backward. Dave squirmed but didn't go into full panic until another unseen assailant slammed a dark bag over his head and cinched it tight around his neck.

"Hey, what the fuck?" Larson protested as an electric bolt of fear triggered a spastic attempt to wriggle free.

A punch in the gut doubled him over in agony and knocked the wind from his lungs.

"Keep your mouth shut," a menacing voice threatened.

Fighting to catch his breath, Larson dropped his keys, the jangling wad landing right where he'd just picked them up. As one attacker zip-tied his wrists, a van screeched into the lot, and a door slid open. A behemoth of a guy, foul smelling and sweaty, lifted the solid Larson and tossed him into the back as if he was weightless. The thugs climbed in next to him.

"Why are you doing this?" Larson said, his voice shaky.

"Shut it." The man barked.

The door slammed shut, and the driver sped away.

"Please! This is a mistake. I don't have a pot to piss in," Dave said, his words more sober than his brain. "I swear to God, I'm broke. My credit cards are maxed. I've got maybe $400 in my checking account. You want that? Yeah, let me get that for you guys—there's an ATM in the bar—I'll have it in a second."

"Shut the fuck up! I'll take my steel-toed boot and kick you so hard in the mouth that you'll be spitting teeth for a month," a different thug barked.

A scream raced up Larson's throat. Even addled by alcohol, he knew he was in deep shit. *Once you're in the vehicle, you're dead.* He was fucked, and he knew it. His mind raced for an answer. To get someone on the street to see him, he'd have to move toward a window. He wouldn't have much time, but if he jumped up and stuck his head in the window, scream bloody murder, maybe…But the thought of kissing a metal-toed boot kept Larson passive and unmoving.

The van bounded over the puddle-laden lot jarring Larson out of his foggy deliberations into a sudden moment of clarity. He needed to concentrate. Pay close attention to the vehicle's movements. Left. Right. Straight. He would note every stop, railroad crossings, any sounds, or smells. In movies, he'd seen detectives prodding the kidnap victim to remember each detail. The authorities would then retrace the getaway vehicle's movements and find the bad guys. Case closed. Unfortunately, the problem with this genius strategy was that after a few stops and turns, Larson couldn't remember a single move the vehicle had made.

I knew that shit was stupid, Larson thought. *Fucking Hollywood bullshit!*

After thirty minutes or so, the vehicle slowed to a stop. Larson heard two voices muttering back and forth but couldn't make out what they were saying. After more conversation, the driver made a sharp left turn, went over a bump in the road, and then went straight. Dave heard the crunch of gravel as the vehicle jostled up and down over rough terrain for a minute or two.

The van came to a jerking stop. No one spoke nor moved for several agonizing moments. The silence gnawed at Larson's already fractured nerves. Bitter bile rose in his throat, and the urge to gag overwhelmed him.

Though still terrified of a possible boot to the teeth, Larson fought back his fear and decided to get some answers. He curled into a ball as a means of protecting his face. "Why—?" Before he could get the second word out, the door slid open. Someone jerked him out by the arms and tossed him to the ground. With his body's weight as impetus, his face plowed into the rain-soaked graveled path. A searing burst of pain creased through his nose and shot down his spine. As he lay in agony, water soaked through the bag, wet his face, and caused him to cough and spew. Strong arms pulled him up to his knees and held him there. The vivid faces of his family filled his mind. JJ, Doris, the three of them together. Larson was shaking uncontrollably, and he began to weep.

"It figures you'd be a pussy," a deep voice said from somewhere in front of Larson.

"Who's there? What do you want with me? Please, I'm begging you. I have a wife and son, for God's sake," Larson pleaded through the bag.

"Yeah, well, I hope you've provided for them when you're gone. Pull the hood off," the man ordered.

The powerful goon holding Larson snatched the bag off. The cinched cord ripped at his nose and scraped his face and forehead. Blood began trickling down

12

his face. Larson didn't feel the ruptured skin or notice the blood as fear had taken over all sensation.

As his eyes adjusted, Larson instinctively tried to swivel his head back to glimpse the figure behind him. Massive hands grabbed his hair on either side of his scalp and wrenched his head straight. The assailant bent down to Dave's ear. His breath was hot and acrid smelling. In a hoarse-voice that sounded like he had gravel in his throat, the man snarled, "Try that shit again; I cut your damn throat myself."

"I'm sorry," Larson whimpered. "I won't, I won't."

The area was illuminated by the van's headlights and a large, black, four-door sedan parked in front of the van. The two vehicles pointed at each other with about twenty feet separating them. Larson and his captors were off to the side but still mostly lit.

Dave peered into the night toward the direction of the voice; an image gradually emerged from the darkness. The man—big, over six feet, broad-shouldered, and barrel-chested—was built like a linebacker. Though the lighting was poor, Larson could make out that he was wearing a striking three-piece suit. A purple handkerchief sprouted from his breast pocket matching the tie around his neck. His shoes glistened with a mirror like shine. The man reeked of money.

The shadowy form took a couple of steps closer; the light inching upward as he went. Larson desperately wanted to see his face. Know who this man was. Possibly reason with him. He cocked his head at different angles, but this maneuver gave him no more than a darkened profile of the man's head.

"You know, I don't like doing this. I mean, if I could think of any other way to work this out, well, I'd do it. But, to my deepest dismay and regret, anything I suggest always has a catch that never plays out to my satisfaction." The man tried to sound apologetic though Larson sensed no sincerity.

"What the hell's going on? Like I told your guys, I don't have shit. Nor do I have a relative or friend I can ask that would give you money. So—"

"Yeah, yeah, I am aware of that. You're a loser. I've known that for some time. Look, I'd love to sit and chat, but to be honest . . ." The figure glanced down at his watch. "I don't have time for inane banter. I'm running late."

"I don't understand? If you don't want money, what do you want?" Dave asked in confusion, and then he heard a gun cocking. "What the fuck? Are you going to shoot me? WHY? What did I do to you? Please, tell me what I've done; I'll fix it. I'm begging you," Larson pleaded through heavy sobs.

"You've done nothing to me. Not really. Unfortunately, you're in my way. An obstacle to an endgame I've planned for some time. Dave, my friend, you are the odd man out, simple as that. Look, I feel bad. Real bad. You're probably a decent guy."

Dave thought he heard compassion in the shadow's voice. *Maybe, just maybe, there was a way out of this. How can I convince this guy to let me go?*

"Nah, I don't give a rat's ass about you," the man said with a cruel laugh.

Chuckles came from the surrounding darkness. "Boys, this how you permanently sever ties between people." The man raised his hand and the night erupted with gunshots. Dave felt two streaks of fire explode in his chest, but the shot to his head brought him down and permanently erased all consciousness.

Chapter 2

FIRST CONTACT

March 9, 1997

Barnes & Noble

Chicago, Illinois

Nick Cooper sat scowling. It was an odd look since he was genuinely pleased with the day's turnout. In fact, he believed this crowd might be the largest he's had. The reason for the perpetual frown? The man loathes these events. To the much-chagrined Cooper, these signings are long, tedious, and often irritating. When the grumpy ex-cop-turned-novelist repeatedly answers the same inane questions, he wants to scream. Didn't any of his fans have an original thought or an interesting question? He doesn't want to be here, but, according to his good-intentioned agent, Reggie Harding, these regularly planned exposures to the public are vital to a book's success.

Even with his aversion to the process, the author sits behind a beat-up card table draped with a silk cloth and forces himself to be agreeable and personalize each patron's book. He matches the retail throng's ignorant views and opinions with equally mundane replies and messages before signing his name. He tries to be amicable, but each note contains the same curt edge to it.

With four published books to his credit, Nick knows he should be grateful to those shoppers willing to line up on a Saturday to buy his novels. And he is, mostly. The problem is his tolerance - or lack thereof. After fifteen years as a Chicago cop, he finds he has retained little charity to fall back on when facing a public that seems oblivious to the fictionalized world he writes about.

Cooper swallows back another urge to snap after a teen boy asks if he's "killed anyone lately." The boy's smile is idiotic, but apparently sincere, as he waits for an earnest answer.

After sighing, he considers the ridiculous question. He hasn't been a cop or carried a gun in years. Cooper says "No," before stiffly signing the kid's book. As the kid reads the message, a big grin creases his face. With a mouth full of braces, the teen clutches his prize and turns away. Cooper watches as the dim-witted youth gleefully plods toward the exit. The novelist shifts his attention past the next person who shuffles up to the table.

As he cranes his neck to glance around the blue-haired octogenarian, he realizes that at least a dozen more people are waiting for their personalized copy of his latest book. Cooper jerks his head back in irritation and abruptly spins around to check the wall clock. He moans when he realizes that only ten minutes have passed since his last check.

"I loved your new book, Nick," the woman says as if she's known the writer her entire life. "I own all your books and like every one. Maybe someday you could personalize each one for me? I would love to meet and chat about the books, share viewpoints, and find out more about the characters. I was a bit of a writer myself, back in the day. I might have some ideas you can use in your next book."

"I'm sure my agent can arrange something," Cooper says, though without sincerity. At that moment, he eyes Harding. The man is writing notes as if Cooper wants him to set up a meeting with the woman.

Cooper jots a quick cursory note in her book and signs his name on the inside page. He hands the book back to the diminutive and fragile-looking woman. She gazes at the words, and then her adoring eyes drift to the writer. She smiles widely and exposes yellow teeth that knot up Nick's already souring stomach. When she turns to go, Cooper swears under his breath in revulsion. Closing his eyes, he rubs his recently graying temples hoping the effort will alleviate a throbbing headache that has instantly materialized.

"Have I ever mentioned to you how much I hate these things," Cooper whispers not so subtly. Not hearing a response, Nick opens his eyes and glances over at Harding. What he sees seems unfathomable. His impeccably dressed agent sports a ridiculous toothy grin. Somehow, he appears to be enjoying himself. After three hours of sitting, without doing much of anything, his agent's back is board straight, legs are comfortably crossed, and his arms extend out on the table with hands clasped. The man looks - happy.

Cooper gives the conventional-looking Harding a head-to-toe once over. He is dressed in a powder blue, Brooks Brothers' blazer, devoid of the slightest piece of dust or lint. Pressed to perfection, the crease in his pants is so sharp it could cut. Then his shoes—the patent leather reflects the overhead light in a dazzling shimmer. His starched shirt is rigid, wrinkle free, and glorious.

Who dresses like that?

Cooper stares at his friend. With a demeanor of utter conflict, he then looks down at his own clothes. Starting at his feet, he pales. His tennis shoes are dirty with a broken left shoelace. "Dang," he mutters. His khakis, held up by a frayed leather belt, worn two, no, three days in a row, are wrinkled and rumpled. The polo player emblem on his blue shirt is half-gone. "Holy shit, I'm a fucking disaster."

Before he could ask himself why he dresses like a street vagrant, Reggie leans over and whispers, "Nick, please answer the nice book buyer's questions, sign their books, and smile as you hand them back. Then, when your loyal fans buy your novels, by the thousands I might add, you can cash those lovely royalty checks as they roll in. Is that so hard?"

Harding's client ignores the direction and says, "Reggie, I look like shit. Why do you let me dress like this for these things? Christ, man."

Continuing to stare straight ahead, Reggie replies with a hint of smugness, "It's part of your lovable persona. Everyone adores that rough exterior of yours. Your appearance screams that you are a regular guy. A gumshoe detective who's paid his dues. Working the mean streets and living off a pittance of a government salary. You know, stuff like that."

Although Nick's bullshit detector erupts, he straightens and feigns eagerness as he waits for the next book to be pushed under his nose.

Reggie, short for Reginald Percival Harding, of the firm of Harding, Johnson, and Clay, persuaded Cooper, once again, to attend a book signing. Cooper never wants to do these frickin' things, and Harding knows it. Though his agent is every bit as much of a friend as he is his representative, there's a simple yet finite reason he sits next to the writer—Reggie recognizes Cooper might not have shown up if he wasn't escorted.

Reggie and Nick met right after Detective Cooper retired from the Chicago Police Department. Cooper had recently finished writing Chicago Death Squad, the first Davin Ross detective novel, and needed someone to publish his manuscript. After receiving several dozen rejection notices, Cooper discovered that getting a first novel to print was a difficult task. He'd been told his writing was good, and the stories intriguing, but no one wanted to publish them.

Nick had just started dating, Margret 'Margie' Evans, a tall, leggy blonde nurse, with wealthy societal conscious parents. She persuaded the frustrated writer to dress up and accompany her to Chicago's McCormick Center for a charitable fundraising event for the homeless. That night, she introduced Nick to Reggie, a longtime friend of hers, and the guys hit it off.

Reggie Harding possessed a to-the-point directness that the ex-detective admired. As the two chatted, the agent's sincere enthusiasm for Cooper's work, both as a former law enforcement officer and novelist stoked Nick's ease and confidence, and the charity function breezed by. The two had made an instant bond. At one point, Cooper winked at Reggie and then leaned over to Margie,

"Thanks for introducing me to such a jerk." Horrified, Margie spun toward Harding who concurred with similar disparaging remarks about the novelist.

Straightening in her chair, Margie stuttered and stammered as she tried to clear the air. The two men laughed, Margie moaned, and their friendship was set.

In time, Reggie garnered the perseverance to transition his new friend from a somewhat beleaguered cop into an author of note and financial success. Some would even argue that Reggie and his wife, Danielle, did much more for the man. The couple helped Cooper through the difficulties of his writing life and his oft-times rotten personal life. This is why, when Cooper complains about doing autograph sessions, he ultimately understands that Reggie genuinely has his best interests at heart.

So, here he sits at the Barnes and Noble on Webster Avenue promoting his latest—*Davin Ross' Last Case, The Marshall Kent Story*. It's the fourth and final chapter in the fictional life of Cooper's somewhat alter ego, Detective Davin Ross. Ross's trials and travails, in the novels, were loosely based on his time spent on the Chicago Police Force, with a tad of embellishment along the way.

This signing event started at 1:00 p.m. About twenty-five people were already line up when Cooper and Reggie arrived. Cooper breezed relatively quickly through those original devotees, but a steady stream of fans kept the line constant.

"Would you mind signing my book?" the next up said as he held out a copy. The man spoke with a distinct French accent.

"Sure." Nick tilted his head down to write. "Who's it for?"

"Marshall Kent," the man answered back with confidence.

Cooper glanced up slowly, "Excuse me?"

There's a moment of hesitation. "Only kidding—the same name of the killer in your book, right. Good for a laugh," the man finally replies, yet he bears no smile to back it up. "The name's Henri, Henri Thomas. I am from Paris on holiday. I found out you are here, and I rushed right over. I must admit to being a little nervous—I guess I tried too hard to make a little joke."

"No problem." Once again, the triteness of the people that attend these signings irritates Nick. He tries to be polite by not replying like he wants to.

Up to this moment, Cooper hasn't intently looked at any of his fans, well except for that one leggy blonde, but now he takes the time to examine the figure in front of him. Maybe in his late forties or early fifties, the guy towers above the rest of the people in line. He's physically intimidating. A vision of Charles Atlas comes to Cooper's mind.

His patron's face, though somewhat drawn, appears rigidly stern with few creases, while his skin tone is paled with an almost pinkish hue. A full head of salt and pepper hair is tightly cropped and neatly maintained. He might have been just another blown-up bodybuilder except for two things: his head seems too small for his body, and two, his eyes carry a darkness unlike the narcissism in every muscleman's eyes.

As the two men size-up each other through a weird sort of staring contest, Cooper senses a vibe he hasn't felt since his retirement from the force. Something about the man was off and though he seems familiar, Nick can't pinpoint why. The two continued to eyeball each other for several moments. The odd exchange suddenly ignites Cooper's internal alarm, and hairs on the back of his neck stand on end. When he finally reaches his limit of creepiness, he starts to say something, but the stranger beats him to it.

"You know, your character Marshall Kent surprised me. *Oui*. Ingenious how he devised ways to kill his wife's murderers. I mean, he was something. I admired his inventiveness. All the planning and effort to acquire the various tools for torture. His efforts to track the men responsible for the wrongs against him. You wrote in such detail. Damn, Monsieur, you spooked me. Gave me a lot to think about."

"Yeah . . ." Cooper says somewhat hesitantly. Squirming in his seat at the oddness of the man's comments, he half-grins "I'm glad you liked it."

The woman behind the Frenchman looks at her watch. She taps her toe. Cooper seems to give this little regard, but the strange man notices the woman's attempt to move things along. The towering figure pivots toward the woman. Though neither Reggie nor Cooper can see what transpires between the two, what the man did so startles the woman she takes a quick step back. She bumps into the next in line, shakes her head in apparent revulsion, and hurries out the store.

As Cooper observes this exit, he wonders if she paid for his book stuck snuggly under arm before she dashed out. This selfish thought evaporates as the Frenchman turns back and with a tense smile says, "Please write, 'To Henri, thanks for being a fan and your exquisite autograph, *s'il vous plait.*"

"*Es kwez eet,*" Cooper unintentionally mimics under his breath, though loud enough to be heard. He nods vacantly before signing. Once Cooper's name graces the book, he hands it back. Without another word, Henri Thomas glances down at the page before closing the cover. At that moment, Cooper senses a change in the man. He had appeared tense, rigid in his demeanor when he first approached and spoke. Now, a relaxed almost satisfied look encompassed him.

"*Merci beaucoup,*" the Frenchman says with impassioned sincerity, and walks away.

The next person in line shuffles forward and places his copy of Cooper's novel on the table.

"Hello, I'm so—"

Cooper holds up a hand as he and Reggie watch the man lumber toward the store's exit. But, instead of exiting, Thomas looks back at the two as if he senses they are watching. With a stone-faced glare, he peers at the pair like a comic book villain. His back stiffens, and he raises to his full height. The man hovers in the doorway like a lurking Dr. Doom.

The look causes Reggie's mouth to droop open in bewilderment, while Cooper's brow furrows and a small, humorless smirk crosses his face. For several uncomfortable seconds, Thomas does nothing nor do the two who sit motionless at the table. The three only stare at one another.

Then, as if given a tardy prompt from some unseen stage manager, Thomas raises his bear-like hand to shoulder height with palm out. He spreads his fingers open and wide. In a slow, deliberate manner, he lowers each finger one at a time. First, his pinky, then his ring finger, and then his thick middle finger. With only his index finger and thumb still raised, Henri Thomas turns his wrist. His hand and fingers are in the shape of a gun, pointing directly at the two. Thomas jerks his hand back three times. He maintains this pose for a moment and then blows across his fingertip. A wicked smile twists across his face, and then Henri Thomas walks out.

Reggie and Nick continue to stare at the door as it closes with a clank. Then, as if they receive their own unseen aside, the two turned simultaneously toward each other.

"Wow, that was definitely disturbing," Reggie's voice cracks.

"Boy, you said it," Nick agrees, and then adds, "It's obvious that I have some entertaining and interesting fans."

"And what the hell did he mean with the whole hand-action thing? He appeared to be counting something down before shooting you," Reggie adds.

Just as curious as his friend, Nick shakes his head. Not bothering to hide his sarcasm, he mutters, "Thank God his finger wasn't loaded. Anyway, I think he was pointing at you."

"Very funny, ha, ha," Reggie scoffs, not bothering to hide his cynicism.

"You know, other than being really odd, there's something familiar about that guy."

"You think you might have met him before?"

"I don't know, maybe. But if so, he looks different," Cooper replies. His brow creases and his eyes narrow as he tried to recall when or where he could have met the man.

The next person in line, patience now depleted, plops their book down on the table with a pop. "Wow – you're a great writer. Could you…"

Chapter 3

WTF?

After the French Connection effect subsides, Cooper spends the remaining hour without incident as he signs books and makes small talk with Reggie. Occasionally, one of the two speaks in their best French accent. Cooper always sounds Jamaican, which makes them laugh even more. They chuckle about the event but skirt any mention of the gun threat. Yet the more they clown around about the Frenchman, the more the hairs on the back of Cooper's neck stand up, and his skin crawls.

The clock hits the magic hour, and the book signing ends. Their imminent and thankful departure is upon them, and the two wrap up the session by saying goodbye to the store manager. As they step outside, Reggie and Cooper discuss getting together soon, before "man hugging" and going their separate ways.

As Nick drives the forty-five minutes home, the foreigner's odd but obvious threat hangs in his mind like a noose. If people were born with an actual warning system in their head, Cooper's would be blaring. While a cop, these moments would instantly push his intuition buttons, and cause his gut to question every aspect of the interaction. It was one of Nick's most significant assets.

His partner, Derek Anderson, often sat amazed as Cooper would touch his nose in thought, and then *bam*, he'd do or say something that helped solve a case. Right now, Cooper's gut told him something was up with that French asshole.

After pulling in front of his home, Cooper gathers his briefcase, exits the car, and locks the door. He scans the neighborhood with a wary eye. Tonight isn't any different—he does this every time he parks the car, a habit. As he looks up and down the street and sees BMW's, Audi's, and a few high-end SUV's he suddenly wonders why he bothers. His car is a 1990 Chevrolet Caprice, rust-colored, though not necessarily because of the paint. The car's tan interior has seen better days, with several rips and tears from long-term wear. The odometer reads over 163,000 miles—the last time that gizmo worked was two years ago.

Cooper had possessed expensive cars. He even owned a brand-new Corvette convertible. The car was immaculate with supple black leather bucket seats, logoed floor mats, and the heads-up display system. He loved the way the Corvette sounded, rumbling deep and throaty even while idling. Problem was, he wrecked that vehicle three months after he drove it off the lot.

Cooper made a small fortune with his book sales, but he no longer cares about luxurious objects or fancy cars. The 1990 Caprice he now owns and his well-worn clothes on his back work perfectly for him.

Typically, when Cooper heads up the sidewalk to his house, the surroundings blend into his subconscious, and he breezes through the front door without a second look. This time, at the steps of the porch, he glances at his mailbox. The box reminds him of a planter with overgrown vegetation bursting out in every direction. The stuffed container overflows with mail with some scattered on the ground.

"What the—," Cooper mumbles. He shuffles over to the mailbox and pulls the lid back to gather the mass of letters and magazines as best as he can. The top of the box, which had been loose for ages, snaps off its hinges. The cover slips from his fingers and plummets toward the ground. Instinctively, he tries to cushion the lid's descent by throwing out his right foot. Instead of softening the fall, he drop kicks the top into the hedge at the far edge of the deck.

"Crap," Cooper mutters as the lid buries itself in the shrubs. "I'll have to fix that someday."

After recovering all the parcels—*Christ, there must be over thirty envelopes alone*—and tons of junk mail, he stuffs the pile under his arm and heads to the door. Once he gets the door unlocked, which proves anything but easy with the bundle sliding around in his grasp, he strides in and kicks the door closed with his foot.

Making a beeline for the fridge, he drops the stack of mail on the only clear section of his writing desk. Several pieces slide off the top of the pile and fall to the ground. And though he watches this happen, the spilling pile doesn't slow his pre-destined beer run in the slightest.

Nick reached into the fridge and retrieved an Old Style, snaps the top open, and guzzles at least half of the ice-cold brew in his first few gulps. His eyes roll back in his head as he relishes the chilled liquid. Grabbing two slices of ham—the only edible thing fresh enough to eat—he swings the fridge door closed with his elbow. He picks up the TV remote, switches on the set, and plops on the living room couch.

On TV, a man stands up in a flat bottom fishing boat speaking about a new lure he designed. He postulates how the fish can't resist its wiggle and natural swimming maneuvers. This viewing lasts five seconds, tops. Nick blows out a sighing breath and jabs at the remote to change the channel. After searching through several stations, all boring, he switches to the news before moving to his desk.

Nick sits his beer down and retrieves the fallen mail from the floor. Scanning the items with feigned interest, he catches the voice of the scrumptious Paula Jones, co-anchor of Channel 4 News. Like the rest of the male population in Chicago, Cooper's infatuation with her radiant beauty is strong. Since the first day she appeared on the station, three years earlier, that crush remains intact.

The co-anchor began the newscast reporting on President George Bush's Chicago visit. Jones rambles on about the security and precautions, yada yada, though Cooper pays no heed. He simply ogles the screen like a teenage boy staring at a poster of a lingerie-clad Elle McPherson. Jesus, Paula was not only out of his league, but she was easily twenty years younger, maybe twenty-five. *As if.*

Though Cooper assumes the news is riveting, her entire report barely seeps into his consciousness. He does hone in on a few specific facts—like she's wearing an off-white tight-fitting blouse and a light blue jacket. Like her blonde hair is in an up-do, which accentuates her sharp cheekbones and silvery blue eyes. Her desk blocks her body from the waist down, a shame, but he's seen her enough times in public to know that the woman possesses stupendous, well-toned legs. Cooper watches her a moment longer before blinking himself back to reality. He lowers the volume and turns his attention to the mail

After sorting the stack into two groups—things he will open and things he will toss—Cooper opens the first dozen pieces. The first few items are bills, which he momentarily thinks of flinging into the toss pile. Instead, he puts them in the keep stack where they belong.

He sorts a few more pieces of junk mail, grimaces at two more bills, and then came to an envelope with only his name printed across the front. No delivery address, return address, or stamp. Someone apparently had walked up his steps and stuffed the note in his mailbox.

Nick opens the envelope and peers in with slight trepidation before pulling a single page out and unfolding it. He holds the sheet up to read, but before he does he spots the spring training baseball scores scrolling across the bottom of the TV screen, and his priorities instantly change.

Snagging the remote, Cooper frantically points the gadget and turns up the volume. His full attention lands on the smartly dressed Bobby Johnson, the sports analyst. Waiting patiently through the scores of the western division of the National League, Johnson finally blows out a frustrating breath as he sees the Cubs score. His demeanor converts from ambivalent to grumpy. The Cubs have lost, again, to the Cardinals. Down go the volume and the remote.

Refocusing on the note, he immediately realizes that the computer-generated paper has no header of any kind.

Hello Nick.

Our paths have crossed. You may not remember me, but I remember you. Because of your direct interference in my life, I lost everything---my wife, my home, my friends, my career—everything dear vanished because of you. From that moment, I vowed to exact my revenge. I've had time to scheme and strategize, years, and now, the plan is perfect. The blueprint of action had to match my intense desire for vengeance. I cut no corners.

For the longest time, I couldn't devise a satisfying idea. Then, a plan emerged, and now I am ready. But before I began my quest, I felt compelled to write you. I needed you to understand where the plan came from and to make you aware of how grateful I am.

Before I explain the good, please know that I couldn't care less about your success as an author. So, don't think otherwise. Yet I must admit, if not for that success I would not have found my way.

Recently, I read the last book in your 'Davin Ross' detective series. The fourth of the group, I believe. And though I am sure the first three were grand, the truth is, I've read none of those, nor care to. The only book I needed to read, to my sincere appreciation, was your last one.

Ironically, this novel drew my attention due to a conversation with an associate. This man, an avid Davin Ross fan, told me about his favorite writer, a terrific author who brought graphic life to a character that always got his man. Now, I will admit, I'm not much of a fiction reader—frankly, the genre bores me. To humor my friend, I asked him to give me the basics of the story.

To my surprise, after a few minutes of his visual if not somewhat annoying narration, I became genuinely intrigued. I asked if he would lend me the book so I could read it, which admittedly--I did so with great voracity. (Don't let your ego get the best of you; my reasons for this avid intensity are not what you're thinking.) I couldn't put the book down as each chapter became more and more enlightening.

However, Nick, I digress. I failed to explain to you what excited me the most about the book. That would be the author's name:

NICHOLAS "NICK" COOPER!

To say I was thrilled was . . . well, let's just say it sent a favorable chill down my spine. Coincidence? I think not. This was a sign. I've been thinking about you for a long time. You have not only been on my mind through conscious effort, but I also dreamt about you. However, in both realms, my entire life balances on a single obsession—my desire to end your life while making those you love to suffer as I have suffered!

Nick, I want you to feel the pain I've endured up to the last beat of your heart. I want your final breath weighed down with misery. Before you die, I will make your life and those close to you, a living nightmare. You will struggle with the same sleepless nights and agonizing waking hours I have had to endure.

Yes, you may now take a much-needed breath, as I'm sure my note caught you by surprise. Don't trivialize the life-giving exercise of breathing, as you will not experience this practice much longer.

Starting today, I will begin a personal rewrite of your book. As they say, "The names have been changed, but the stories will remain true." Nick, if you're as *terrific* of a detective as you once thought you were, you'll know why I carried out my scheme before the new ending arrives. However, no matter what you do or how smart you think you are, the result will be the same--the "hero" will die. This time, the dead "hero" will be YOU, and not the fictional Davin Ross.

Let's get started, shall we?

Oh, and keep this in your mind—

"Numbers form a tragic end,

for all, both foe and friend.

The innocence of those close by

won't deter for they will die."

"HT"

Nick stares blankly into space. The threatening words mystify him but also trigger training honed years earlier. He sets the paper down, opens his desk drawer, and retrieves a pair of tweezers. Carefully grasping the page with the long-handled instrument, he searches the front and back. But there are no telltale signs. He lays the sheet down and picks up the envelope. Not one trace inside or out. Cooper's brow creases as he tries to understand what this means. He deliberates whether to take the message seriously. His first inclination is to toss it out as a joke. Then, after a moment more of contemplation, Cooper straightens his chair and rereads the letter, this time with more focus.

After he finishes, he leans back and peers at the television although his brain isn't registering the broadcast. Instead, he vacantly stares. The contents of the note swirl in his mind. As he dissects the last two lines, Cooper recalls a passage from the climatic ending of *Davin Ross' Last Case*:

". . . Darkness hovers like a rabid bat. Though I've lived in this house for nearly thirteen years, it's difficult to move without bumping into things. I know they're there but can't seem to avoid them. Being acutely aware that the slightest noise could spell my doom, I am as careful as I can be.

This hole in my gut—the gunshot wound is severe. And though I can't see it, I know I'm bleeding badly as I can feel the warm liquid as it oozes through my fingers in a steady stream. I'm feeling a little lightheaded, and I'm not sure how long I will last without medical attention.

I will say this—if I go, I'm taking him with me . . .

Chapter 4

DARNELL, JJ, AND GEORGE

Darnell Dorsett, a tall, skinny, one-time street ganger, was now one of North Side Chicago's most disreputable criminal kingpins. The unremorseful thug owned a long rap sheet with charges ranging from purse snatching at twelve to attempted murder at the ripe old age of nineteen. Now thirty-five and remarkably still on the streets, his newest listing of criminal activities included drug dealing, bookmaking, and competition removal. Even with multiple arrests, Darnell never actually served any time. How a thug like this remained out of jail was one of the great mysteries of the Chicago judicial system. It became evident, once again, when you owned the right people, in the right places, anything could be possible.

Dorsett amassed a small fortune through the manipulation of his various criminal ventures. Though he lived a life of luxury, spending grotesque amounts of cash on pleasantries such as fine clothes, jewelry, and cars, he maintained a keen awareness of when to invest money to further his criminal businesses. Occasionally, that meant payoffs or payouts to people of power and position. Large amounts of cash or unique favors regularly flowed to influential individuals who performed behind the scenes tasks for the criminal.

Whether Dorsett wanted someone's personal property, information, or he merely needed the removal of a person, the man never blinked an eye to calling in favors or putting his own funds to good use. Unfortunately, the latter of those maneuvers cost Darnell, and several prominent acquaintances, their respective lifestyles.

Just when it seemed that Dorsett was untouchable, and that his criminal activities were immune to prosecution, a gangly teenager walked into his bar and changed everything. The boy had boldly marched into Dorsett's bar to place a

31

wager on the day's Cubs baseball game. It was a no-brainer, as the boy had bragged that day to his friend. And, more to the point, it would be his way of getting enough money to cure his financial woes for months to come.

JJ Larson, 19, lived in his stepfather's immense but increasingly repugnant shadow. The stepfather, George Dawson, was a prominent Chicago criminal lawyer whom his mother, Doris, had worked for before marrying him after the death of his dad. JJ hated the man. Cursing him and defiling his very existence often and with relish—though he did so only behind closed doors and when there was no way he could be heard—the brute terrified him.

Though Dawson was somewhat aloof towards JJ during the courting of JJ's mom, the frail boy had no inkling of the true nature of the man until it was too late. The trouble between the two males immediately kicked into high gear the day JJ and his mother moved into Dawson's house. George cornered the unsuspecting freckle-faced thirteen-year-old in his room and explained the facts of life . . . as seen by George Dawson.

While JJ was unpacking, George slipped into his bedroom and closed the door. With a look that sent a shiver down JJ's spine Dawson let him have it. "JJ, I've only got one rule you need to be aware of. That rule is that whatever I say goes. That's it, case closed. No backtalk, no excuses, no bullshit. You try to weasel your way out of chores or responsibilities, we got a problem. You show up late for anything that I've given you a time to be there, we got a problem. You go running to your mom and crying about how tough I am, we got a problem. This is my home, not yours and you will respect that. You disrespect that, and we got a big problem."

When the one-sided conversation ended, JJ's nightmares began.

For the next six years, nothing JJ did would meet his cruel stepfather's expectations. His grades weren't good enough, his posture was poor, the boy talked back when not given permission—on and on, he and George engaged in a never-ending battle. Throw in the hormonal imbalance of the average teenager's moods and the friction between the two flamed out of control.

Though the disagreements were typically one-sided, curse-laden, verbal attacks by Dawson, the large man never laid a finger on the boy. Even so, on several occasions, he seemed one breath away from beating the kid. After overhearing his stepfather say, "If this punk-ass good-for-nothing little shit belonged to someone other than Doris, he would be missing half the teeth in his head by now, or worse," JJ realized that he was in pure hell and if not for his mom, one step away from a hospital stay.

As the years passed, things only got worse, and nothing his mother or anyone else would say or do seemed to help. Though he had only begun tiptoeing along the path toward adulthood, he knew what kind of man Dawson was, an A number 1, DICK!

Everyone remembers someone like Dawson while growing up. Gutless bullies who blind-sided someone because he didn't like the way the unwary sucker looked at his girl, his dog, his car, or whatever. Like George Dawson, these people were self-absorbed loud-mouthed assholes that used thug mentality to back up their boasts.

No question Dawson had a mean streak. But to JJ's luck, Dawson was afraid to harm the boy physically. As with most mothers, nothing meant more to her than her child. Yet, to JJ's alarm, Doris rarely stepped in unless things spiraled too far.

Sitting by the pool, George and Doris drank frozen daiquiris and soaked in the sun while JJ worked in the yard. As the temperature hit 95 degrees, JJ decided to cool off with a quick dip. All was well until a splash of water wet Dawson's towel.

"Are you kidding me?" George bellowed. "Don't you see my towel laying here? Are you blind?" JJ, knowing all too well that George's wrath was kicking in, swam as fast as he could to the other side of the pool as a means of escape. As he came up and tried to climb out of the pool, Dawson was there, hovering over JJ like a vulture waiting for its next meal to keel over and die.

"Where do you think you're going? When I'm talking to you, you better stay put and take it. How do you expect to learn anything if you're always running away? And look at these bushes. My God, a child could trim these better than you. Have you ever done a day's work that was worth a shit in your entire life?"

"George," Doris chimed in. George looked her way. He was all swelled up and heaving like a gorilla about to pounce. JJ, looking at his mom and expecting her to chastise the man, was disappointed, as she was simply holding up her husband's drink. Though it was a subtle but effective way of quelling the man's rage, JJ saw it as her taking his side. She had eased the situation, got Dawson to come back and sit down, but JJ couldn't see it. George had gone off the deep end and lit into him simply because a splash of water got his towel wet. And his mom did nothing—as usual.

Dawson believed that his wife loved him as her husband but was also keenly aware that to go too far with JJ would be the end. That became all too clear when the two had been watching the news and a story of a man that had beaten his own son to death came on. Tim Bronson, 16, had come home from school and eaten his father's leftover T-bone steak. The father had been upstairs, drunk, and decided to get his food. When it wasn't there, he went berserk.

Scouring the house for the thief, and getting madder by the second, Pete Bronson finally found his son in the garage. The gnawed bone from the steak sat on a paper plate next to him. The two got into a shouting match, and the father picked up a large monkey wrench and began beating his son. One blow to the head cracked the boy's skull. Tim Bronson died at the hospital later that day. The wife had gone to court each day supporting her husband. She told anyone that would listen that he was a good man, and she was sure he didn't mean to hurt their son.

"I don't understand people," Doris said during the report, "that woman is crazy. He killed their son for crying out loud. If anyone did that to my son, well, let's just say that they better never go to sleep around me." And George could clearly see that she meant it.

So, the adult bully reigned in any physical attack and bit his tongue as best he could while waiting for the day to rid himself of the teenage scourge.

Regrettably, time wasn't an ally to JJ. As with most teenagers, the young Larson boy questioned every authoritative directive sent his way. Regarding George Dawson, that would mean challenging every word out of the ogre's mouth. If Dawson said the sky was blue, JJ called it gray, and if Dawson asked him about his day, JJ would ask him why he cared. The relationship death-rolled into an everyday tit-for-tat bitch fest, and both loathed the other for it. And then it happened.

"Where is that son of yours?" Dawson bellowed one night after coming from the house's garage.

"Why, what's wrong," Doris said, trying to seem calm but knowing all too well that George had already gone from zero to one hundred.

"My tools are all over the place. How many times have I told JJ to stay away from my tools? Where is he?"

"George, honey, please control your anger. Listen to me. You can get him to be more considerate of your things if you offer to do some projects with him. When you finish, you can teach him the importance of putting things back where they belong. It's all a part of teaching kids to be responsible. It doesn't always come naturally. You don't understand that because you've never raised a child before," JJ's mother said as she lightly touched her husband's arm in compassion.

Dawson pulled his arm away and moved a few steps back. "That may be the biggest load of crap I've ever heard in my life. I can tell you that after one good thrashing I never forgot to put something of my father's things away."

Doris went white. "Thrashing? George Dawson, don't you dare. Never lay a hand on my son. I cannot and will not tolerate that. If you would just try to bond with JJ things would be so much bet—"

"If you ever lay a finger on one of my tools again…" he growled

JJ cowered. "I didn't.

The hell you didn't—*and* you left them out, you-good-for-nothing—"

"George, calm down," Doris said.

"Calm down, my ass. The kid stands here lying to my face, and you tell me to calm down." He pivoted toward JJ. "You will not touch *anything* of mine, you hear me? You poor excuse for— "

George took a menacing step towards the cringing boy; Doris stepped right between them and stared viciously at her husband. It stopped the red-faced and raging man in his tracks but didn't alter the inevitable course of the two men's relationship.

JJ and George were like repelling magnets. No way were things going to cool off. Caustic verbal abuses roared, souring what little ambiance the household had.

Dawson seethed through the unrest not because he didn't "understand" the kid. It was mainly because he didn't like the little prick. And for JJ it wasn't only because Dawson acted like a total asshole and treated him like shit; he could almost deal with that. What ground at JJ's soul was how the dick belittled and downplayed his real father.

In JJ's fragile mind, his stepfather acted like JJ's dad was a figment of his imagination. Often, George would chastise JJ for mentioning his birth father while in his mother's presence. George tried to play out that it was inconsiderate to bring up the man; it was too painful for his mother, and the boy should respect that. The reality was that George wanted Dave Larson forgotten.

On his father's birthday, his own birthday, and on the anniversary of the man's death, JJ grieved. These were times when the boy needed compassion and understanding from George. Sadly, his stepfather's uncaring attitude regarding anything about Dave Larson, especially the anniversary of his death, was the core reason in JJ's mind for the constant conflicts.

On those days, knowing that only pain and anguish would be felt, JJ would slink off to his room and lose himself in his world of art, specifically the art of drawing. He took to art early in his life, and his talent blossomed immediately. As a pre-teen, Doris and Dave Larson would marvel at the intricately detailed portraits JJ sketched. One night, when guests had come to their house, Doris convinced him to draw the friend's baby.

"Mom?" JJ groaned in embarrassment.

She insisted.

The nine-year-old begrudgingly trudged off and retrieved his drawing tools and pad. Whispering, his mother leaned into Gladys Hopkins, the child's mother, and said, "Watch this."

JJ sat in a chair next to the baby carrier and gazed at the cherubic child. As the little girl gazed back with playful eyes, JJ's hand moved across the pad. Deftly, he slid the pencil in arcs, dashes, and shading.

After fifteen minutes, a clone of the little girl emerged on the pad with a likeness that seemed surreal. With mother and father gawking at the drawing, JJ mused, "If I had a little more time, I think it could be better."

The parents laughed. "I have never seen such talent in someone so young. JJ, someday people will pay you to draw."

The Larson's nurtured and supported JJ's talent, realizing the joy he got from the work. They made sure their son had all the supplies he needed and provided mentors and teachers. They took him to local art showings and seminars.

As the years passed, JJ's work excelled, and he received many accolades. What amazed those who saw the young artist's drawings was his uncanny ability to see someone one time, and then, as if a camera existed in his head, he could sketch them with incredible realism.

Months could go by and then something or someone jogged a memory. JJ would then pull out his drawing pad, and in short order, a vivid picture burst from the page. The renditions would be incredible. It was as if the person sat right there posing as a model.

JJ had always been shy, but with some gentle prodding from his parents, he was convinced to display his work at local and regional art shows. The boy had barely scratched his way into his eleventh year, but over a period of a few short months, the talented artist would become somewhat of a celebrity in the Chicago art world for his incredible lifelike portraits, no matter what age of the artist. The pictures provided sinewy spectacles of physical flesh and raw emotions that radiated from the canvas.

Mrs. Larson was extremely proud of her son's drawings. Before his father's death, she had transformed their family's den into a gallery of his art. Dawson knew this and tried to avoid the same fate for his home. But the first thing the new Mrs. Dawson did when she moved in was to place several of JJ's drawings in conspicuous places throughout the house.

George Dawson despised JJ's pictures. This wasn't because he thought they were terrible. He knew they were good. It was simply that his arrogance and ego wouldn't allow him to see the value in the boy's soul-soothing endeavor. To Dawson, JJ's ability to make a living was all that mattered, and that didn't include being a loser who drew stick figures.

"Earn an education then get a real job," he would say to the cowering youth. "There is no future in these drawings. Your efforts are a waste of time."

The attorney showed blatant and deliberate ambivalence regarding the boy's passion. He never complimented JJ's artwork. If someone else admired the work, the man would rudely interject, "Not bad for an amateur." Or, he might shake his head and offer, "I've seen better." But each time he added, "It's a pipe dream if he thinks he can sell these things for anything but chump change, if at all."

The final straw between the two broke, and it was brutal. The situation occurred at one of George's annual Christmas parties held at their home. JJ walked into the kitchen to get eggnog for his mother when he overheard his stepdad talking about him to one of his lawyer friends.

During the short conversation, Dawson called JJ, "The bastard child he never wanted," before adding, "The late father was a piss-ant nobody with zero future and no way of giving JJ's mother the kind of life she deserved." These two comments alone were probably enough, but the *coup de gras* occurred when Dawson confided, "And as far as I'm concerned, Larson, was a man with no future and a waste of human life. Good riddance."

That day and *that* conversation sealed the deal for JJ Larson. The incident would prove to be the turning point in two significant ways. First, any positive relationship he and his stepfather might have had was dead, buried, and permanently dissolved. Second, the circumstances surrounding George Dawson and his father's death took on an entirely new life form in JJ's mind. The accusations he mentally suppressed now exploded into his consciousness causing him to question what was true and what wasn't.

Chapter 5

THE DEATH OF DAVE LARSON

People who knew the family spoke behind closed doors of domestic issues at the Larson home before Dave's demise. These snickering asides usually involved the late hours Mrs. Larson spent at work, plus her overly friendly relationship with her boss. Speculation and sidebar innuendos revolved around an affair between the two. Leading this charge was none other than her husband, Dave Larson.

Then, as fate would have it, and before any definitive proof could be exposed, JJ's father was shot to death. In what the police would ultimately label as a robbery gone bad, though the average person saw more, the man was found with two bullets in his chest, and one directly in his forehead. A year later, almost to the day, the names of Mr. and Mrs. George Dawson appeared on the Dawson home mailbox.

Barely into his teens at the time of his dad's death, JJ was given little information regarding the circumstances of the event. And though he was now old enough to know more, he remained unable to get anyone to really open up about it. Sure, he asked the obvious questions along the way, but the few answers received didn't satisfy his growing if not obsessive curiosity. With his speculative imagination relentlessly tearing at his every waking moment, he began an insatiable quest to get an answer from the one person he believed knew the most. His mother.

In the past, when JJ had confronted his mother, Doris would evade the topic or gloss over it with quick and vague answers. Now relentless, JJ kept up a constant attack week after week until the woman finally broke.

It was a summer afternoon when JJ's mother entered his room with a basket full of clean clothes. JJ was at his desk drawing. When his mother came in, JJ sprung up, walked past her, and closed his door.

"You can't leave until you clear up some things for me." JJ's voice was cold and edgy as he stomped back to her.

JJ's mother shrunk back at this demonstrative outburst. She knew what he wanted, and her first instinct was to flee. Nothing good could come from this type confrontation. But, against her internal objections, she obeyed and sat timidly on the side of his bed.

"Mom, I've waited long enough. I'm not a child anymore. Tell me what happened to Dad. I'm not going to stop asking, so just come clean."

With eyes darting back and forth, Doris stared up at her son. She said nothing for a few moments. JJ narrowed his gaze and scowled.

"Mom, please."

Doris winced and then sighed in resignation. "JJ, you know times were tough. Your father and I were desperately fighting severe financial problems due to a series of bad breaks. Construction jobs for your dad got scarce, and he often went weeks without work. During those times my salary barely kept us afloat."

JJ's mom scooted back on the bed and put distance between the two. "Things got so stressful that your father and I often skipped meals as our only means to satisfy household bills. Each month, we would play the 'Rob-Peter-to-pay-Paul' bill-paying game. We'd skip the water bill to pay the electric bill. Then skip a car payment to pay the past due water bill. This only delayed the inevitable. The process caught up to us and our financial situation teetered precariously."

His mother droned on about the family's struggles, and JJ experienced a pang of gut-wrenching guilt.

"Ok. So, wait a minute. How did you ever make ends meet once Dad died?" JJ asked. "I mean, you just said that when dad couldn't work you guys weren't making it. How could you manage alone after he died? How did you keep us in the house? Pay our bills? And we never missed a meal? Our struggles seemed to vanish after Dad was gone?"

Mrs. Dawson went silent for a few minutes, and she turned her gaze away. Before she could answer, a thought jolted the boy, and he stiffened. A dormant memory, pushed into the deep recesses of the boy's psyche at the time of his dad's death, came rushing back in a torrential flood—*within one month after the funeral of his dad, his mom had left her job.*

The boy knew no insurance money existed; he had heard his mother express that sad fact to his grandmother shortly after the funeral. *So, what happened? Why wasn't cash a problem for a family, who a few weeks before was almost evicted from their home?*

As if she wanted to escape, JJ's mother glanced toward the door and tried to get up. JJ put a hand on her shoulder and looked down at her. The few tears running down her face launched into an all-out sob fest.

Even so, JJ refused to let her leave. He wanted the truth, and he would not let up until he got definitive answers from her. As his mother shook with heavy sobs, his knees went weak. The weeping struck JJ hard. "Mom, you've kept the truth about dad's death from me long enough. I know he was shot . . ."

Doris looked at her son in horror. "How did you find that out?"

"Grandma told me. But she wouldn't tell me anything else. It's time to come clean. Please. Tell me what happened."

Over the next fifteen to twenty minutes, Doris Dawson choked, sobbed, and sniffled her way through enough of the story to change JJ's life—forever.

"You remember when your dad went missing and we thought he had gotten in an accident or something?"

"Yeah."

"Well, that's not what happened. Your father stopped at a bar the night he disappeared. When he didn't come home that night, I called the police. They didn't look for him for twenty-four hours. I guess that was some kind of standard thing, I don't know. But when they did start, it took them a couple of days to figure things out. They eventually found his car and car keys in the bar's parking lot, but your dad was nowhere to be found.

"We called all around. Talked to everyone we knew. But he had vanished. Then, four days later, a couple of vagrants stumbled on his . . ." JJ's mom stumbled on her next words, "on your dad in a vacant, rain-soaked lot. His body lay in a quagmire and all his valuables, including his wedding ring, were gone.

After a brief investigation, the killing was ruled a robbery-homicide, and the case was closed. No one was ever arrested or convicted of the crime. It was as if the murderous ending of your dad's life didn't happen—no one ever contacted me again about it. I even asked George to help, but he couldn't get anywhere, even with all of his connections. He said he had been stonewalled. I was beside myself, and you, well you had lost your dad, your hero. You shut down for months. I didn't know what to do for you."

Doris looked into her son's eyes. JJ was crying too. She reached over and grabbed his hands and bade him to sit next to her. She took her apron and wiped his cheeks. "After the funeral, all seemed lost. Besides both of us being heartbroken, I also knew that in no time we could be out on the streets. Your father and I owed money on everything, and soon they would come and take it all away. That's when George did help. To be honest, he stepped up when no one else would, not even family. Though the situation might appear odd to others, I had you to take care of and welcomed his kindness. And, well, the rest of the story you know."

"Yeah, your knight in shining armor became your husband and my stepdad. Though he has been far from that to me," JJ scoffed.

"JJ!" Doris gasped.

"Sorry, Mom. I know you're into George and all, but on top of the fact that he has made my life a living hell, there's something . . ." JJ started, but his voice trailed off as he turned his head.

"What?" Doris asked.

After a moment, JJ sucked in a breath and stared at his mom, his jaw set and ready to run off a tirade of self-deduced accusations. Just because the prick arrived just in time to save the day and pay their bills, didn't mean he wasn't behind Dad's death. Why hadn't the cops looked at Dawson? Someone must have suspected this guy who immediately paid their bills, and in record time married the widow.

"Never mind, Mom," JJ said as he swallowed back the indictments still lingering on the tip of his tongue. "Thanks for coming clean about Dad."

Doris stood up and kissed her son on the head. She wiped her eyes with her apron, grabbed the laundry basket, and headed toward the door. When she got there, she turned and looked back at JJ. "I know you and George are having a tough time. But if you just give him a chance, maybe the two of you two could become friends."

JJ forced a smile and watched her turn and go. He walked over and shut the door, leaning his head against it as the lock made a discernable click. He stood in this position for several moments, tears streaming down his face as he thought of his dad. He then walked over and opened the top drawer of his dresser. A picture of him and his dad from a camping trip was hidden beneath a pile of white tube socks.

"Dad, I will make it my goal in life to find out who killed you. That fucker left you in that lot. I promise I won't rest until the killer is found and justice is doled out. Even if I have to do it myself," JJ said softly, though with conviction. In his mind, he already knew who was to blame for his dad's death—directly or indirectly—and he would make the murdering scum pay.

Chapter 6

CRAP SANDWICH

George Dawson's wrath didn't begin or end with his stepson; he had already earned a reputation as a ruthless brute in the professional arena he prowled. In court, he could intimidate and coerce even the staunchest of witnesses. There were often rumors of jury tampering, or evidence mishandling, though no direct connection to Dawson was ever established.

Judges disapproved of him. Other attorneys loathed him. Even the partners at his law firm avoided confrontations with Dawson. Yet, with a reputation as a winner, he swiftly rose up the ranks until becoming a partner.

As an attorney whose physical stature alone unsettled many on the witness stand, he seemed more than eager to use his skewed but substantial intellect to make those around him miserable. It didn't matter where you sat in the stratosphere of importance. He showed no favoritism. When Dawson set his sights on menacing someone, the rare exception prevailed. If, or when, he came across someone who might have been his mental equal, something seemed to arise that riddled the foe's credibility. The lawyer was often one step from being accused of criminal behavior himself.

Though Dawson's career flourished, and success came in huge leaps and bounds, his professional accomplishments didn't satisfy his insatiable desire for dominance. Not in JJ's eyes anyway. Whether George was on top of the world because of a successful case, or grumbling when something didn't go his way, JJ seemed to receive the same ill-treatment.

When something aggravated "King" George, JJ became his psychological punching bag. Once, a jury deliberated a case Dawson thought a win. He and his client were ready to celebrate a victory when the judge announced a hung jury. George was livid.

Arriving home that night, Dawson came in the house like a raging bull and headed for his liquor cabinet. JJ had been at a local arcade with his friend Butch and arrived home an hour late for dinner. When he walked in, George, three drinks in and wine at dinner, gave the unsuspecting boy both barrels.

"Where the fuck have you been?" George demanded. Before JJ could answer, Dawson morphed into rage mode, "You have no respect for me or your mother! Dinner was an hour ago! Coming and going whenever you want like a little princess. Well, that shit's going to change.

"You do nothing around here, you're worth nothing to anyone, and you'll end up a nothing the rest of your life because you're a lazy good-for-nothing!" George bellowed.

George had taken a step in JJ's direction. The frightened boy looked around for his mom, but Doris was nowhere in sight. JJ's stepdad backed him into the wall and, no more than an inch away from his face, spewed spittle as he thundered, "It's time I stopped pussyfooting around with you and teach you the consequences of being disrespectful."

Just when JJ thought he might finally get the physical pummeling he believed George wanted to give him for years, Doris walked in. The woman was red-faced with anger and outrage of her own. She glowered at her husband, almost daring him to do bodily harm to her boy. George glared back, snarled, and snorted like a silverback gorilla, then went back to his drink, muttering as he went. JJ took advantage of the pause to race up the stairs to his room.

Though Mrs. Dawson would always step in, as she did that night, she eventually realized that throwing herself into the middle of these spats only fueled more animosity between the two combatants. So, she changed tactics. She took JJ shopping and bought him toys, art supplies, or treats. This helped for a while until the material solution backfired.

After another merciless episode between the two men occurred, George came home to find JJ, now in his mid-teens, wearing a new pair of expensive sneakers. The man was no dummy and easily surmised that his wife had coddled the boy with presents. Though Doris should have received the brunt of his attack, George turned his verbal assault on JJ. Soon, the two were in an all-out yelling war.

Normally, JJ would be shrinking away in fear and looking for an escape route, race up the stairs and hide until George had time to cool. This time, as he teetered backward on his heels, Dawson spewed, "No matter how I look at you, I'll always see you as a *big fat crap sandwich*. You're just two pieces of stale, moldy bread with nothing in between but *a huge pile of crap*."

As JJ found his footing and scurried up the stairs, Dawson yelled, "Crap sandwich, crap sandwich, CRAP SANDWICH! You're nothing but a pile of shit between two rotten pieces of bread!"

From then on "crap sandwich" became a standard insult.

Chapter 7

A THIEF IN THE NIGHT

The family lived in a big house, over five thousand square feet, with, as JJ often said, "all kinds of fancy-schmancy crap in it." One summer afternoon, after George had banished his stepson for the day, JJ and best friend, Butch Carrington, sat on the stoop of Butch's ordinary, yet cozy home. Lamenting on his life, JJ exclaimed, "How can a house that has everything be so empty?"

"What do you mean?" Butch said as he gave himself a blast from the inhaler he always carried. JJ's friend was small and sickly. Diagnosed with severe asthma at ten, the condition seemed to suck the life from him as he aged. Most kids at school avoided Butch, but not JJ. The two had been best buds since early childhood.

"We have a pool in the backyard, a billiard and card room in the basement, and a media room upstairs next to my room. George has a bunch of rifles and pistols in a big glass gun case and a shit load of signed sports memorabilia on the walls in his home office. Who has all of that and brings so much misery to everyone?" JJ scoffed. He tossed a stone across a crack in the pavement. "Of course, the billiard room with its built-in bar is off limits to me.

"On top of all that," JJ complained as he pitched a larger stone into the street, "George and my mom play golf and tennis at some expensive club. He has a membership at a downtown men's club—something Mom doesn't even know about." JJ stopped and looked at Butch. With a grin that belied the real emotion of terror in his heart, he said with a laugh, "Shit, if George knew I had that information, he'd throttle me."

"What about that car he drives? He looks like a gangster in it," Butch said.

"Yeah, the jerk always drives an obnoxious black Cadillac, a new one every year. And not one of those little Caddies. He goes for the Eldorado or Fleetwood, or whatever is the biggest most expensive car they make that year. He wears thousand-dollar suits, gets his hair and fingernails groomed, and even gets a regular pedicure. My God, what an asshole!

Someday, I'm going to have all that shit and good riddance to that dickhead," JJ said as he high fived Butch.

"Yeah, just as soon as you get out of high school, go to college, and get a real job— you'll show 'em," Butch said, and then they both laughed.

At one time, in his early teens, college for JJ was a foregone conclusion. By the time going to a university came up for consideration, he was so despondent from George's ridicule, that getting a higher education seemed more of a nightmare than a dream come true. Dawson had stuffed the notion that JJ was unfit for the world—let alone college—down JJ's throat. JJ couldn't bear the thought of failing.

But Dawson wanted his stepson gone, out of the house, period. Sure, the kid was a loser and probably would flunk out, yet *"the head of the household"* insisted JJ go to some college or university—preferably far away. George constantly brought home college brochures and pamphlets with the selected schools at least a state away.

As high school graduation approached, and discussions of college continued, so did the opportunity for new battles to erupt. JJ's stance—he wasn't going to college; Dawson's rebuttal—he sure as hell will go, or he was out on his ass. A final showdown was past the brewing stage. It stormed, roiled with murky thunderheads, darkening every moment with a cloud of animosity.

Buying things gave JJ a moment of joy. Besides drawing, it was often the only way he could sooth the constant barrage from George. Unfortunately, he lacked the motivation to get a real job—Dawson's insults had soured him on that.

So, he felt forced to look for other financial resource opportunities. That's when he took notice of the bulging wallet planted so arrogantly in his stepfather's back pocket. The huge mound looked big enough to choke a horse. JJ couldn't fathom how much could be there. What he knew was that George had plenty to share.

JJ construed a plan—he'd steal from the rich "prick" and give to the deprived and disadvantaged . . . himself. *But how?*

One evening, as he laid in bed, he contemplated his situation until it suddenly hit him. A plan so simple it amazed him that he hadn't considered it sooner. He rolled onto his side and smiled widely as he mulled over his foolproof escapade. *I'll wait for Mom and the ass-wipe to go to sleep, sneak into their room, and lift a few bills out of his wallet. It would be easy, a no-brainer. Each night, after the ogre changed into his pajamas, he heads to the bathroom and spends five minutes brushing and flossing his teeth. He washes his face and combs his hair— which is weird before sleeping, right? —then switches the light off and slides into bed. Within just a few minutes, he's sound asleep snoring and farting like the walrus he is.* And there it was, the perfect time for JJ to pilfer a few bills. No one would be the wiser.

Pure genius.

The boy contemplated the scheme, considering all angles, before drifting into sleep.

A few days passed, and though he believed he'd succeed, he hadn't acted yet. Nerves kept him from making a move. JJ needed confidence, and this finally came via the big man himself.

JJ wanted a new skateboard for his birthday. Much to his and his mom's dismay, Dawson flatly refused. "Don't think that because it's your birthday it means you get a present. You're not three years old, for God's sake. And besides, around here everything needs to be earned—and you've earned nothing," George sniped.

Maybe it was the weight of the misery that JJ had endured. Maybe one too many insults caused the tower to crumble. Whatever it was, something inside of JJ snapped. Under the table, his hands curled into tight fists. His nails bit into his palm. He wanted to jump onto the table and yell, "YOU FUCK. YOU MOTHER FUCKER!" Grab his plate and smash the food into Dawson's face. Instead, he sat squirming but silent. *Tonight's the night*, his mind screamed as he tried to contain his anger. *You fucking ass-wipe jerk, I'll clean you out!*

After *"family"* dinner ended, JJ took his plate to the kitchen sink and went to his room. Usually, no one would see him for the rest of the night, something George Dawson privately appreciated. On this night, however, JJ made an appearance around 10:00 to announce that he was tired and going to bed. Doris wished him a good night's sleep, George only grumbled something unintelligible.

Once back in his room, he turned on the small lamp above his drawing easel and grabbed his dependable Copal flip clock. Adjusting the timepiece for a one a.m. alarm, JJ stared down at the faux wood-grained timepiece in anticipation before setting it back down. Time drifted by at an excruciating pace as JJ sat watching the clock, waiting for the time to advance, one flap-flip at a time. It seemed to take forever, gnawing at his nerves and making him tense and uncomfortable.

Every so often, a bead of sweat crawled from his hairline and trickled down his neck. At one point, he heard his mom and stepdad pass his room as they headed to bed. He smiled with anticipation and looked over at the clock. Frowning at the plodding pace of time, with the last flip reading 10:41, he decided he needed something to take his mind off the wait. He turned his attention to his drawing pad.

Usually, his hand would move deftly across the paper, and images would come alive—lean, sinewy forms with shadows and highlights. Tonight though, the pictures appeared fuzzy and vague as JJ's mind honed-in on each snap of the clock's flipping plastic tabs. Minute by long minute, flip after flip—the sound of the clock's numbers dropping pierced the boy's nerves. He was jittery and excited, all at once.

JJ finally gave up on drawing, put his pad and pencils down, and laid prone on the bed. He stared at the ceiling and begged the clock to hurry. The anticipation was killing him. He wanted the money. Dollar signs spun in his mind. When the wheel finally flipped to 12:59, he reached over and turned off the alarm before it sounded on its next turn.

Moving stealthily, JJ crept to his door. The hollow-core wooden slab creaked as he pulled it open. The jagged noise amplified in the dead still of the night, and JJ froze in his tracks. *Shit.* He expected to see a heaving and puffing Dawson storm from the master bedroom, ready to defend his ground. The thief stood motionless waiting for the inevitable. Seconds seemed to stretch into minutes. The silence in the house thundered in his ears.

Still as a tree trunk, he waited.

Nothing.

JJ swallowed back his fear and slid out the door.

Pressing his back against the doorjamb, he nervously checked toward the kitchen. Quiet. He glanced down the hall toward his parents' bedroom and the financial wad that awaited him. The coast was clear in both directions. About to make his next move, he noticed the nightlight in the bathroom sent a bright halo of light in his direction. *Jesus, how much light could a little bulb give off? It's like a goddamn spotlight.*

JJ got an eerie feeling he was being watched. Heart thumping, the burglar recoiled, turned his head, and saw him--the darkened figure staring back at him. He almost peed his pajamas as he gasped and shot backward, stumbling against the wall with a thud. He turned his head, closed his eyes shut like a vice, and prepared for the worst.

The heart-stopping stalemate dragged on for an interminable time as neither he nor his challenger flinched. As the boy's eyes squinted open and focused, he scoffed at the sight. The shadowy image was merely his reflection in the hall mirror. A thin, nervous smile crossed his face. *So much for being a tough mother-fucking outlaw.*

The length of the hallway from his room to the L-shaped corner that led to the master bedroom was about twenty feet. Creeping on tiptoes, he made his way down the hall into pitch-black darkness. He thought he could hear the echo of his heart slamming in his chest—the sound as eerie as a jungle drumbeat. It unnerved him. The hall had never seemed so long. With each step, JJ sucked in a deep breath. He used his hands and arms to guide him along the wall. The harrowing drumming of his heart seemed to ricochet down the hall into the master bedroom. As he reached the door that led to the fat wallet, a different noise threatened— a heavy, nasal-clogged snoring that sounded like a massive beached walrus taking its last breaths of life.

At one moment, there would be deep throaty inhales of air, something of a half-choke and half-gag, and then a floppy flatulent exhale waffled and wheezed on the way out. Every couple of breaths, the process stopped, and there would be several seconds of silence before a choke-filled gasping sound erupted. It was as if George's breath got caught on something before violently escaping in a brutal life-saving fashion.

He only heard the sound for a minute or two, but the rattling cacophony only exacerbated JJ's fractured nerves. *Jesus Christ. How does Mom fucking stand it?* He relaxed his fists, which were clenched into vise-like grips.

A bead of sweat rolled down JJ's face culminating in a drop that hung on his nose. He wiped the sweat away and then dropped down to his hands and knees. He moved forward, creeping along. That obnoxious snoring—in then out. In then out—it seemed to be taunting. Part of him wanted to jump up, scream, "You're fucking dead," and choke the fucking life out of this monster of a stepfather. His fists clenched again in reaction, balling up for a beating. For a moment, the room looked as if a darkroom light highlighted George in its red glow. *The fucking, despicable George. I could kill him. Stuff a pillow over his whale-like face and snuff the life from the fat fuck.*

JJ shook off the urge to pounce and calmed himself with slow deep breaths. He moved along the foot of the bed in a crawl. Stopping halfway across the room, he listened for any indication that either of the two sleeping adults knew of his presence. George's gurgling mess continued, and there was no movement from his mom. Clenching his teeth in determination, JJ moved on.

Once at the corner of the bed, he saw that the fortress of cash stood only a few feet away. He could almost touch it with his hand. JJ tried to will himself over to it, but he felt cemented to the floor. George, the swine, stormed into his mind. Visions of the brute sitting up, turning on the lamp, and bull-rushing him to the ground filled his now reeling mind. He could almost feel George's feet as he kicked and stomped on his body. Trembling out of control, JJ thought to jump up and run back to his room. Probably the smart move. Just as he turned, his real dad's flickering image, though blurry, stood tall in front of him.

"Dad?" JJ stuttered.

The man looked haggard and withdrawn, a gaping wound burrowed into his forehead. As he stared down at JJ, thick fluid seeped out in a slow rivulet and slid down his face like a minature serpent, squirming and wiggling in jittery movements. Dave Larson peered at his son in a blaze of agony. He slowly raised his arms with palms up, in a beckoning gesture. JJ, unable to move seconds before, inched forward. *Dad? Dad! His dad was there, he didn't know how, but he was there! God, Dad. I've missed you so much.* JJ longed to hug his father, but as he went to throw his arms around the man, his dad's sad image dissolved.

JJ felt defeated and deflated. His stomach turned in anguish. It took everything he had to keep from calling out, scream for his dad to return. He swallowed hard trying to hold back the onslaught of tears now filling his eyes.

Just when things seemed to be at their worst, things spiraled even more out of control.

"She was fucking George while she was married to your father," a voice echoed from the darkness.

"She might have been pregnant with a bastard boy, and that's why she married the rich guy," muttered another.

JJ tried to squeeze the voices out of his mind. Instead, the declarations got louder, taunting him with insinuations while tangling into knots of reasonless accusations.

"I heard the poor husband knew."

"Murder. Assassination."

"That interloper hates her kid."

"You're a goddamn loser."

"He's a crap sandwich, a lazy, good-for-nothing crap sandwich. No wonder the man killed himself."

JJ lifted from his knees to a squat. He slammed his hands against his ears. *Stop it. Stop it. Stop it!*

Louder and louder, the voices jabbed at him like ravaging vultures pecking and stabbing at him with their beaks of indictments.

He fell back down to his knees. *That son of a bitch*, his mind screamed, *that fucking son of a bitch!*

He hated Dawson with every fiber of his being.

"Fuck the money," the infuriated boy blurted. Defiant, he walked over to his stepdad's side of the bed. Grabbing one of the loose pillows, he raised the laced cushion above George's face and held it there briefly as he stared down at the man. Rage branded his mind, burning a permanent revulsion that couldn't be quelled. *I hate you. I hate you. I hate you. I hate you!*

With that, he crammed the foam pillow down on Dawson's face putting every ounce of his 140 pounds behind the thrust. His feet lifted to tiptoes as he pressed down with a force that seemed superhuman. George began to struggle, but JJ wouldn't let him loose. The more the monster wrestled to get free, the harder JJ pushed. George was big and robust, almost twice as big as JJ. He heaved, shook, and made an exhaustive effort to break free, but JJ's adrenaline-filled rage kept the ogre pinned in place.

As the seconds passed, JJ howled—hysterical, crazed, and out of control. He would finally be rid of this beast, and he was giddy with delight. The teenager pushed, pushed, and pushed, laughing like a madman. After hearing a loud yet muffled last gasp for air, the struggling stopped. Dawson no longer breathed—and JJ was gloriously happy. He had never been so happy. He dropped the pillow back down to the floor and raised his hands in triumph. *"YES, YES, YES!"* The boy screamed as he danced in victory.

JJ, smiling and boisterous with triumph, looked down at the dead rat bastard. He saw that the man's face was cherry red and covered in sweaty moisture. A noticeable pall of death hung around the still figure. JJ had the urge to punch him, get one last bit of satisfaction when suddenly, his stepdad's eyes popped open.

With the leer of a demented clown, eyes bulging and crazed, Dawson, started to chant. It was a whisper at first with his voice barely audible, and then the tirade got louder. Stronger. "Crap Sandwich. Crap Sandwich. CRAP SANDWICH!"

JJ jumped back in terror, tripped over his stepfather's slippers and lost his balance. The terrified boy went flailing backward and slamming hard to the ground. Instinctively, JJ balled up into a fetal position. He covered his head with his arms and waited for the inevitable beating.

Chapter 8

JACKPOT

JJ lay waiting for a kick to the head or a punch in the stomach. Or maybe the enraged man had a gun under his pillow and would shoot him. As he waited for the first blow, he cringed—his body as tense as a steel girder.

But nothing happened.

Still tightly wound in a ball, he heard a ringing sound; low at first but increasing in volume as the seconds passed.

The quivering boy pulled his arms away from his head and slowly opened his eyes. As his vision cleared, he realized he was still in his bed, his alarm blaring. He squinted at the clock. 1:00 a.m.

"Jesus, that was fricking freaky," he muttered.

JJ got up and without hesitation made his way straight to the bedroom down the hall. Crouching down at their doorway, he slinked and shuffled past the footboard of his parents' bed. From there, JJ moved on his belly like a commando. He made it to the bottom of his stepdad's dresser, reached his hand up and groped for the wallet, found it, and brought it down. After removing three bills from the middle of the wad, JJ carefully put the wallet back. He nimbly retraced his path out of the room, down the hall, and back to his room.

Once there, he closed the door, turned on the small reading lamp, and examined his prize.

Jackpot! He fist-pumped the air in celebration. Three twenties. "A sixty-dollar haul on my first heist." Giddy, he congratulated himself. He reflected back on his nightmare and then brushed away the vision. "This was way cooler and much easier than I thought it would be."

He put the cash in the back of his sock drawer and waited a few days to see if his stepdad would say anything. George said nothing. Neither did his mom.

Spending the money felt good. *One small victory for the oppressed*, JJ thought as he handed the cashier cash for a favorite comic book.

Three "Bank of George" withdrawals later, JJ figured out that his stepdad had a system for keeping cash in his wallet. He arranged the dollar bills in front followed by the fives, the tens, and then the twenties. Next came a few fifties and last, the hundreds. Once JJ figured this out, he took the precise bills he wanted, no matter how dark it was in the room.

For the first few months, he filched money only from George once every other week, though not on any specific day. Soon, however, he noticed another of George's patterns. His stepdad's wallet appeared thicker on Fridays. Payday, JJ guessed. So, he stole the bills on Fridays, or maybe Saturday nights if his parents were out late the night before.

As time went by, JJ realized it was pointless to take the small-valued bills, so a collection of Ben Franklins filled his coffers. *Who needs to waste time on the twenties when there were fifties and hundreds ready to pluck from the wallet?*

Chapter 9

UH OH!

George Dawson always went to the bank on Friday to cash a check for the weekend's activities. On this particular Friday, George went to the bank, forgetting it was a holiday. He glanced through his wallet and confirmed there was enough cash for Saturday's dinner with the Franks—five hundred and sixty-five dollars. Usually, George would get $2400 from the bank. This would assure him he would have enough cash no matter what he and Doris did.

That night, JJ, with the utmost confidence, made his usual 1:00 a.m. withdrawal from Bank of George. He didn't notice that the wallet was thinner than normal. He took his bounty of two crisp one-hundred-dollar bills and stashed them in the back of his sock drawer, snuggled up to several others. He went to bed. When he awoke on Saturday, he took one of the hundred-dollar bills and spent the day at Pluto's Fun Arcade using thirty dollars. He stashed the change in his pants pocket. Once home, he put the remaining money back in the drawer and then watched television. A glorious day.

His mother microwaved him a frozen dinner and explained that she and George were going out with clients and would be home late. For JJ, this news was pure heaven, a vacation of sorts from the beast. JJ would have the house to himself, the big twenty-seven-inch Zenith console TV in the front room, and no loud-mouthed arrogant stepfather breathing down his neck.

As JJ luxuriated in his world of solitude, Dawson, Doris, and two other couples sat down to dinner at Gene and Georgetti's, Dawson's favorite Chicago restaurant. Appetizers and salads came first. For the main dish, George had G&G's famous pepper steak with all the trimmings. Doris, a light eater, had a salad with grilled salmon on top. The others had steak, T-bones, and ribeyes.

As usual, the meal hit the mark. All meats were cooked to perfection. The sharable vegetables were steaming hot and delicious. After the main course was finished, everyone ate a dessert and sipped after-dinner drinks. The atmosphere soothed and entertained, and for George, the guests rated bearable.

As soon as they finished the last Tawny port wine, the server set the bill next to George on the table. Robert, the only waiter George would tolerate, or that would tolerate him, totaled the check after adding the pre-arranged agreement of a twenty-percent tip to the bill.

Dawson donned his black reading glasses, read the bill, four hundred and twenty-five dollars, and pulled out his wallet to pay. He opened the billfold, counted out the bills, and hesitated. Another recount brought him to the same conclusion. The color in his cheeks drained away.

This change in appearance caught the eye of his wife. "Are you feeling okay, dear? You look peaked."

"I had five hundred and sixty-five dollars in my wallet yesterday, and now I only have three hundred and sixty-five," George said through gritted teeth.

"Are you sure?" his wife asked innocently.

George's burning glare met his wife's calm gaze; no words passed between them as no words were needed.

"What's the matter, George, a little light with the funds?" James Franks joked.

He also got the stare.

"How much do you need, George?" Doris asked as she opened her purse.

"Sixty Dollars."

Doris rummaged through her large bag and retrieved her wallet. She pulled out sixty dollars and handed the bills to her husband. George dropped the wad on the table, got up, and stormed off. Everyone at the table was speechless.

The ice storm in the car kept Doris quiet. George stared straight ahead as his mind rummaged through possibilities. Maybe he didn't have as much as he thought? No, he'd counted his cash before he left work and then after he left the bank's parking lot. How had he lost two hundred dollars? It was impossible—they were safely tucked in his wallet, and he had stopped nowhere or spent any money since leaving the bank.

This left one glaring option.

Could that little shit . . . No. Impossible. That cowardly prick didn't have the guts. Or did he? A cruel grin crossed the lawyer's face. *Oh, I'll find out soon enough. That little bastard. I'll make him confess to his thievery. Once he does, and he will, I'll beat the shit out of him. I may finally do what he's needed for a long time.* No, wait. He had an even better idea . . . The rest of the way home George whistled, and Doris stared.

From that day on, George counted the cash in his wallet before he went to bed on Friday nights and again each weekend morning. He soon realized the money usually was gone on Saturday or Sunday morning, and sometimes both. Now, he was sure of his suspicions. It was time to catch a thief.

He couldn't wait.

The following Friday night, after bragging to JJ that his wallet was as fat as a pregnant sow, *'something that happens when you work for a living,'* Dawson went to his bedroom. He performed all of his regular bedtime procedures and then climbed into bed, just as he always did. However, once he was satisfied Doris was asleep, he slid silently out of bed and hid in the master bathroom. The distance from the bathroom door to his dresser was less than four feet. Like a lion in wait for his prey, he stood motionless and ready. Less than fifteen minutes later, he heard the rat skitter in.

From his vantage point, George could see the insufferable prick crawling across the floor. Excitement and outrage raced through his mind. Eyes adjusted to the dark, he was still, waiting for the perfect moment. Just as JJ's arm lifted to snag the wallet, Dawson grabbed it and jerked the kid roughly to his feet—practically ripped the boy's arm from its socket.

JJ, panicked by this attack, screamed as if harpooned. George snapped the lamp on, prize in hand. Doris bolted upright in bed. A slight screeching sound escaped her lips as she realized two things: one, that her husband held up her son like a hunting trophy; and two, she was flashing the boy with her bare breast.

Grabbing the bed sheet, she snatched them up and covered her top. "George, JJ, what the hell is going on," Doris demanded.

No verbal response—George ignored her, and JJ couldn't speak as George's grip throttled his voice. Holding him by the nape of the neck, the burly man dragged JJ out of the bedroom and down the hall. By the time Doris had gotten on her robe, Dawson was bodily throwing JJ out the front door like someone tossing slop to the hogs.

"No good-for-nothing Crap Sandwich is going to steal from George Dawson," the man bellowed at the top of his voice. He slammed the door, locked it, and stormed past his wife without a word.

Doris went into mother mode and ran to the kitchen to make a fast phone call. Afterward, she checked her robe and then dashed barefoot outside. She found JJ sitting on the curb, crying and rubbing his shoulder. His mother didn't ask why or what happened. She merely put her arm around her son and let him sob. They sat in silence in the darkness until Doris told JJ she had arranged for him to stay with the Carrington's for a couple of days. Once she worked things out with George, he could come home, and all would be well.

For the next week, Doris said nothing to her husband—not a single word. Not just regarding JJ, but no conversation about anything. At first, George played the game and did the same. He ignored his wife and her mood and went about his daily routines. By day five of her silent treatment, George couldn't take it anymore and caved. Even though he could best most men in a mental or physical challenge, he couldn't handle this mute ambivalence from his wife.

Sucking up his rather enormous ego, he approached Doris and asked for forgiveness. After talking out the situation for several hours, and with him having to bite his tongue to keep from exploding, Dawson eventually agreed to let JJ come home with no strings attached.

At least that's what he said.

Although Doris acted happy, even elated, she knew her victory was hollow and would be short-lived. The relationship between her two men, something she fought hard to discount for most of her marriage with George, now blistered and festered like a boil. What she had always known, deep in her soul, she could no longer keep contained. The relationship with George and her son was so toxic that the poison had seeped into her.

Chapter 10

JJ THE GAMBLER

Summer of 1987

Forced to accept that his in-home ATM no longer existed, JJ's desire and need for money stayed insatiable. He had gotten a taste of financial freedom, and nothing would repress the urge.

Dawson, the asshole, repeatedly taunted him, mainly when Doris wasn't around. "You'll never get a red cent from me ever, for anything. You hear that Crap Sandwich? Not one thin dime!"

"Hey, shit-faced thief. Must be tough with no cash coming in. It's a real shame—you've got your father's loser genes; I have no doubts you'll soon be living on the streets. Where you now stand in life, there's nowhere to fall. You're already on the bottom, Crap Sandwich. Just like your pussy father was."

Things appeared hopeless until JJ stumbled onto something that held exciting possibilities. Oddly, and once again, he had George Dawson to thank for it. While staying at the Carrington family home during his short-lived eviction from *Chez* Dawson, Daryl Davis, the boyfriend of Butch's sister and three years his senior, took JJ out for a local poker night with some friends. JJ didn't play; he didn't know how, but he watched . . . and learned.

JJ was not clever, cagey, or crafty. Nor did he have much of a poker face. He wasn't considered bright yet was not condemned as dumb. The truth? The boy retained no overt signs of long-term prosperity. But, one thing he *did* possess that gave him an edge over almost everyone else—his photographic memory. This unusual mental talent, which he used since he was a young boy for his art, was now a reliable gambling instrument. His recollection of what cards had been played gave him a significant advantage over the other players. "Card counting," was frowned upon in poker games, but shit, no one knew. In small local games, he could get away with it, and he did.

When he finally returned home from his expulsion from the Dawson estate, he gathered the few hundred dollars still hidden from his trips to George's wallet and set out to rebuild his cache through poker.

The games were on Friday and Saturday nights within a few miles of his house. The hosts of the games held the events in their basements or the back rooms of small businesses. Maintained betting caps kept wagering reasonable and set up perfect scenarios for gambling newcomers like JJ.

Though he tried to pay close attention to the strategies of poker, he first lost more than he won. In time, he not only learned the finer points of the game, he excelled at them. Each night, he became more comfortable with his memory talent, and soon, he could predict the cards before the opposing players laid them down. Though his card counting offered no foolproof system, he won regularly.

Several weeks passed with little or no additional blow-ups between George and JJ. This lack of friction hadn't occurred because the two men mended their differences, far from it. The toxicity of hate, loathing, and despair hovered over the pair like a canopy of sludge. Things calmed because JJ made a conscious effort to stay away from home as much as possible. He hoped this strategy might keep things at bay and save his mom unnecessary grief.

To JJ's dismay, the opposite occurred as this plan merely fueled Dawson's dire outlook on the boy's future. While JJ stayed away, George fumed and the war, stymied by the frail peace accord that Doris had arranged, crumbled at an alarming rate. JJ's effort provided a bizarre and unexplainable outcome, one the young teenager couldn't understand.

George's mind concluded that JJ's absence meant the boy was up to no good, and he believed that whatever JJ was doing would come back to bite George in the ass. Dawson could not internally manage the oncoming storm he sensed on the horizon.

JJ reasoned that nothing his mother did or said would save him forever, and he needed to be out of the house soon. After many sleepless nights, he concluded that the only way to accomplish emancipation was to have the funds to live on his own. For this, he required cash . . . and lots of it.

The next day, JJ sat with Butch and pulled out his stash of money. Sadly, even after several months of doing well at the local poker games, JJ could only count out twelve hundred dollars in savings. He'd been spending his winnings almost as fast as he made them. He and Butch bought whatever they wanted. JJ had no perspective on the real value of of his stash.

This shortfall revelation showed how Larson's small-time gambling activity wasn't enough, so the two boys brainstormed to find new ways to increase their capital. Nothing short of getting jobs came to mind—and that idea seemed ludicrous. No way would JJ work for minimum wage.

They had no choice.

They had to go back to an old source, Daryl Davis, for help. He didn't disappoint.

"If you want to make big money," Daryl said as smooth as a used car salesman, "A guy downtown will cover almost any bet." Daryl leaned back, balancing on two legs of the chair. "He specializes in sporting events of all kinds, but mostly covers the Chicago teams. Butch frowned, but JJ's eyes brightened. After all, JJ lived and breathed the Cubs. He possessed an intimate knowledge of all stats and figures. What better way to win *real* money than to bet on a team like his hometown Cubbies? Even though the team remained near the bottom of their division, he believed this new scheme was a no-brainer.

"The betting takes place in a small bar on Addison Street, directly across from Wrigley Field." Daryl puffed on a thin cigar. "The Strike Zone Tavern. Easy to find--a large red awning runs the length of the bar, and the windows have hand-painted baseballs and bats on them."

"Sure as shit," JJ said all cool and gangster style." We know that place, right Butch?"

Butch nodded but kept quiet.

Daryl inhaled and shot the smoke out of the corner of his mouth. JJ thought it was cool. Maybe he might just start smoking those cigars. He imagined himself with money-filled pockets and a thin cigar hanging from his mouth.

"Go on in, and ask for Louie, one of the bouncers, and tell him Daryl Davis sent you. Louie gonna take you to a guy called Darnell. "*Shhe-it*—that mother fucker will take the bet.

Later that night, while downing two Big Macs and fries, Butch and JJ talked things through. JJ would do most of the heavy lifting—gather all the information they'd need to make a bet. After an hour of planning, JJ slapped Butch on the back. "Butch my boy, we're going to be rich. Once we win this bet, we will make another. We'll win that one and do it again, and again."

"We're gonna be rich, sure as shit," Butch boasted in unison.

The 1987 Cubs team consisted of several power hitters including two league leaders in homers with Jody Davis and Leon Durham. They also had perennial gold-glover Ryne "Ryno" Sandberg helming second base. The rest of the team were not all-stars, but on any day, they were pretty good. Though the team scored plenty of runs, as their offense was solid, especially at home, they still didn't win often. Their pitching and defense rarely gelled with the offense simultaneously.

One of their glaring pluses was home runs. The team seemed to hit multiple home runs almost daily, particularly when playing in the friendly confines of Wrigley. If the right pitcher was on the mound, and the wind blew out, the Cubs chances of winning were very good.

He checked the *Tribune* for weather information on the upcoming Saturday game, two days away. The skies would be sunny with a high of eighty-four. The wind would be northeasterly, about fifteen to twenty miles an hour with occasional gusts to thirty. The perfect formula for a Cubs win. And to make the victory even more of a no-brainer, the Cubs were playing the light hitting Astros.

Bingo! *Bye, bye fat ass George Dawson*, JJ thought as he tossed the paper in the air. *This is a sure thing.* He did his best Rocky Balboa impersonation, danced in place, arms raised in victory. Everyone knew when the wind blew out at Wrigley, a hitter just needed to lift the ball into the air, and the wind would do the rest. Even if the ball didn't leave the park, the wind could play havoc with even routine flies. Throw in a brilliant sun, for good measure, and many errors could happen.

Then, there was the enemy of the day. The Houston Astros were the opposite of the Cubs. Sitting in the cellar of their division, they were last in runs scored, last in extra base hits, especially home runs, and their defense was suspect. When they scored, it was the old-fashioned way: single base hits, stealing bases, and line drives—good ole' heads-up baseball, to be sure. Unfortunately, the team rarely scored enough runs to win consistently. More important, when runners did cross the plate, the tallies seldom came from the long ball.

The Cubs were sure to whack the ball into the air, the wind would carry it forever, and the Astros would fall. A crushing victory. He had it all figured out. JJ picked up the phone and called Butch. "Hey, man."

"Hey, JJ. Whatcha got for me?" Butch shot back. It was his standard line when the two boys crossed paths.

"The Astros number one power hitter, Glenn Davis, leads the Astros in home runs with thirteen at the midpoint of the season. No one else in the club is close. Hell, Jody Davis for the Cubs has already whacked twenty-nine bombs, almost more than the entire Astros' team combined." His words came out so fast he had to take a moment to breathe. "Man, this game *can't* be lost!" He saw dollar signs and lots of them. "We gotta make a bet— "

"Hell, yeah," Butch roared back.

When Saturday arrived, the forecasters were dead on. The sky radiated crystal blue with an air temperature that seemed to caress and soothe. Around the stadium, the smell of peanuts and popcorn wafted through the streets as the faithful Cubs fans milled about in mindless reverence of the sport. This was going to be a beautiful day in Chicago.

Scheduled as an afternoon affair—the norm for the Cubs in the 80's—all seemed right in the world. JJ embraced the sensation as he readied his play to make his bet. With Butch by his side, the two walked into the Strike Zone tavern. It was a gloomy place, dark and foreboding, but it didn't deter the headstrong Larson. With Butch practically attached at his hip, JJ headed to the bar and motioned for the bartender. JJ's eyes bulged as the man approached. *This goliath got to be one of the biggest people on the planet.* Maybe six-foot or six-foot-one— he must have tipped the scales at well over four hundred pounds. Large-jawed and loose-skinned, he looked like a two-legged walking hippo. The aisle behind the bar was just barely wide enough to allow him to move.

"What can I do for ya?" The mound of a man asked.

"Yeah . . . uh . . . I was instructed to ask for Louie. Daryl sent me," JJ's voice cracked, and his words came out a murmur.

"Wha'ya talkin' 'bout kid?"

JJ straightened his shoulders. "I'm looking for Louie," he said louder. "Daryl sent me."

"Daryl who?" the big galoot growled.

"Sorry, um, uh," JJ mumbled. *Daryl's last name? Shit. What the hell was it?*

"Davis!" Butch blurted, trying to help his friend out. "Daryl Davis."

The man stared at the two through bloodshot eyes for several moments before making an almost inhuman grunting sound. He nodded toward the back of the bar. JJ glanced in that direction, a wall of people blocked his view, but after standing on his tip-toes he could see what appeared to be the entrance to a hallway.

JJ tilted his head in thanks before he and Butch wound their way through the crowded tavern. After passing by the end of a row of booths, they rounded the seating and saw another colossal man sitting on a stool next to the hallway.

"Are you Louie?" JJ's voice held a slight tremble.

The man gave JJ and Butch the once-over and then stood up. When he reached his full height, he towered over the boys in every sense. Unlike the bartender, this man appeared to be at least six and a half feet tall. With his broad shoulders and V-shaped build, he could have easily been a starting linebacker for the Chicago Bears. The hulking man stared down at JJ and Butch, not saying a word. He just peered at them through threatening, dark eyes.

After what seemed like too many minutes, the guy on the stool snarled defensively, "Who wants to know?"

"We were sent by Darryl Davis, he said to ask for Louie," JJ said.

Butch felt his chest tighten. He pulled out his inhaler and gave himself two quick blasts.

"Daryl huh. Well, yeah, I'm Louie. So what?"

"Our friend told us this might be a place to make a wager on today's game," JJ's voice strained. "We were told we should ask for Louie and say that Daryl Davis sent us."

The man stared again at the two and then shook his head in apparent disgust. He held up a hand, and then turned and walked down the hall. He stopped at the door about ten feet away. After glancing back at the boys, he disappeared into the room. Several minutes passed, and nothing happened.

"What do you think is taking so long?" Butch asked

"Not sure," JJ said, debating whether they should forget this scheme and push back through the crowd and out the front door.

Butch must have been thinking the same. "Maybe we should get outta here. *Now*."

JJ nodded his head in approval and was about to make a dash for it when the hall door opened, and the behemoth emerged and motioned to them. JJ and Butch, an instant from bolting away, instead inched hesitantly down the hall, one slow step after the other.

The two stopped in the doorway. With great effort, they peered in but didn't enter. The room was dark. So dark it was difficult to see what was going on. *"Fuck, no way I'm walking in there,"* JJ thought.

Butch, still itching to run out, took a small step backward. The doorman made up their minds for them and gave them each a little shove into the room. Once in, the door closed, sealing them in. That's when they saw the man sitting behind a desk at the back of the room. The position of the small lamp with its green shade cast an eerie pallid glow on the man's face.

As the two inched their way in, JJ nervously scanned the room. In one corner, the sparsely furnished office contained a small, round card table with four metal folding chairs. Against another wall sat a brown leather couch that had seen better days. Several tears and rips cut into the back and armrests. The middle of the sofa sagged like a soggy diaper. Against the back wall stood three tall filing cabinets and next to them was the beat-up wooden desk that looked ready for the garbage heap.

Sitting at the desk was a thin black man. He had an Afro haircut that stood out a good eight to ten inches from his head. His face was taut with his cheekbones prominent below hollow eyes.

"Ah, come in, come in. Wow, Louie said you were a couple of fine-looking young men, and dang if he wasn't right—yes, indeed," Darnell boasted while beckoning the boys to sit down in two chairs facing his desk. "Louie tells me that my dear friend, Daryl Davis, sent you. Nice boy, that Daryl. Am I right?"

JJ and Butch nodded like two bobble heads.

"I'll have to thank him for sending me such swell-looking customers . . . next time I see 'em, I surely will."

Over the next ten minutes, Darnell bullshitted with the boys. Where did they live? What they did for fun? Did they have girlfriends? Blah, blah, and more blah. The teenagers loosened up a little bit, their confidence building with each passing moment.

"Well, let's get to it," the man finally said. "What can Darnell Dorsett do for the two of you today?"

JJ, who now brimmed with conviction, sat up straight in his chair and answered, "We want to make a bet on today's Cubs game."

Darnell, who had been smiling the whole time, turned the fake emotion off like someone turns off a light switch. He studied the boy for a minute and then in a low growl said, "Ok, whatcha got in mind? And don't be wasting my fucking time cause Daryl Davis or no Daryl Dickhead Davis, you waste my time and somebody's going to have a bad day. Know what I mean?"

JJ's eyes bulged as he slunk down in his chair. He was scared before he entered Darnell's office, and then bolstered with newfound confidence as the trio talked. Now, he raced past scared and run smack dab into terrified. The man had instantaneously morphed from Southern gentleman to street-brawling thug. JJ sat petrified with fright. Butch looked like he just shit his pants. The trio stared at one another—one side waiting for the other to make a move.

Finally, JJ attempted to speak, but his throat was constricted, and he could only make a slight squeak. He swallowed hard before trying again. In a strained, pubescent voice, he stuttered, "I'd . . . li . . . like to bet f . . . f . . . five thousand dollars on the Cubs to w . . . w . . . win their game today."

Darnell leaned forward and glowered at JJ then focused on Butch who trembled from head to toe. Back to JJ again. As if he could see right through him.

JJ sat frozen. If he could have moved, perhaps he would have stood, backed out of the room, and ran. Instead, he sat as if cemented to the chair. He wondered if Butch was as frightened as he was. If Butch could move his legs. If Butch was even breathing.

Both boys sat silent and motionless. Fear grasped them by the throat, and neither boy knew what to do nor what would happen. After several seconds of nothing, JJ thought he might throw up,

Darnell flopped back into his chair and laughed—roared and hooted, banged on his desk—and then looked directly at JJ, "Wager five grand! I bet you would!" He laughed again, turned toward Louie, shook his head, and said to his man, "They want to bet five grand on the Cubs. Did you hear that?"

"Yeah boss, loud and clear. I sure did," the linebacker replied in between deep throated chuckles.

Darnell gazed back at JJ and said sarcastically, "You don't look like you're old enough to have an allowance, let alone have five thousand dollars." He chortled and chuckled. "Five grand? Man, you must be crazy coming in here trying to pull one over on Darnell." The thug continued laughing and shaking his head for a couple more moments.

JJ said nothing; he could only stare at the bookie. Butch thought that if he opened his mouth, his breakfast would fly out. Then the laughing stopped, and Darnell rose up from his chair and put his fists on the desk. With eyes blazing, he ripped into the two teenagers, "So you two limp-dick little motherfuckers think you can waltz in here and fuck with Darnell? Well, I'm about to convince you how bad of a decision—"

Suddenly, from a place that even JJ couldn't fathom, he cut Darnell off mid-sentence. "Listen, my stepdad is a very famous attorney. His name is George Dawson, and he's rich. He's got plenty of money, and I can get it. Do you want to take the bet or not?" This was a defining moment. The kind that can turn sour grapes to raisins or plums into shriveled prunes.

Louie took a menacing move toward the boys, but Darnell swung a hand up and stopped him mid-step. Then, like a magician who makes a rabbit disappear, Darnell's anger evaporated, and a huge smile seemed to engulf his entire face. He flopped down in the big leather chair, leaned back, and stared at the ceiling. JJ didn't know what to think. He looked at Butch; saw he was just as baffled, and then looked back at Darnell.

The gangster sat like that for a moment and then leaned forward while raising his hands to his face. Then, with hands clasped and fingers intertwined, he steepled his pointer fingers and began bouncing them off his chin.

"I'll say one thing for ya, ya got big balls, really big balls," Darnell said with what seemed like genuine admiration. "Tell ya what I'm gonna do, and I'm sure you better believe I don't do this every day, but I'm gonna take your bet. Now, give Louie here your money, and let's put this little introduction issue behind us."

"Well, that's a bit of a problem," JJ muttered. "I don't actually have all the money. I hoped I could give you five hundred dollars and be good for the rest."

Darnell's veins started to pop from his neck. He glanced up at Louie, face contorted. stunned by the nerve of the idiot sitting in front of him. He turned back towards JJ, but no words came from the bookie for several tense moments. The gangster looked over at his drawer. There was a gun hidden there, and he thought about grabbing it and shoving the barrel into the kid's mouth. Then, as if the man had an epiphany, he took in a deep breath and eerily became calm.

The bookie smiled, easily a forced one, and said, "I'll take your bet, but you keep your five hundred dollars. We'll go all or nothing. How's that?" In a gesture that screamed surprise, Louie's brow scrunched together until it looked like he had only one eyebrow.

Darnell got up and motioned to the boys to do the same. The teens jumped up, and they all headed toward the office door. JJ stopped and turned back toward Darnell, "I'll be back right after the game."

"I *know* you will," Darnell shot back, now with a smirk on his face. "And sure as shit, I'll be waiting for ya. By the way, where are your seats?"

"Oh, we're not going to the game, we didn't buy tickets," JJ answered.

Once again, like a toggled light switch, the bookie's demeanor changed. "No tickets." He forced surprise. "Why that's no damn good, anyone putting that much money on the Cubs ought to be sitting in the front row. Tell ya what—I got two beauties right behind the Cubbies dugout, and I'm giving them to you. They're my personal season passes, and I want you to take 'em. Have a blast." Again, Louie appeared mystified.

Darnell moved to his desk and pulled out a packet of tickets; he retrieved two from the package and handed them to JJ. He put his hand on the boy's back, gave it a couple of whacks, and then escorted the two out of his office, down the hallway, and out the front door of the bar. Stopping at the entryway, Darnell motioned toward the sky. "It's a beautiful day, and the Cubbies are on a roll. You boys enjoy yourselves and good luck."

Darnell waved at Butch and JJ and watched as they headed toward the entry gate. Walking back in the bar, Darnell glanced over to where two of his guys were having a beer. He waved them over and spoke quietly to them. The men listened intently and then made a beeline for the front door.

Louie ambled over to his boss and with a perplexed expression asked, "You let them bet 5 Gs with no cash? Boss, I don't get it, you never did that shit before."

"Louie, sometimes, when it feels right, you gotta take a chance on people. And this feels *oh so right*!" Darnell paused for effect before adding, "Plus, I think I'm finally gonna get the goods on a certain someone that's needed to get his for a long time." At that, Darnell winked and headed back to his office, laughing the whole way.

Chapter 11

THE BIG GAME

JJ and Butch walked to the appropriate Wriggly Field entry gate and handed their passes to the ticket taker. Once in, they headed straight to the concession stand. While standing in line, Butch glanced at JJ and said, "JJ, I've never been so scared in my life. Never, ever, ever, ever!"

"Yeah, me too. I thought I was going to piss my pants," JJ replied. "George Dawson ain't got nothing on that dude!"

The boys purchased two hot dogs and a couple of cokes plus a bag of peanuts. "Best peanuts on the planet," JJ gushed, and they headed for their seats.

"Wow," Butch mouthed as he marveled at the scene on the field. Both teams were warming up, running around, playing catch, and having fun. This was heaven for two young fans. They headed down the stairs in search of their seats.

"Yeah, this is awesome." JJ looked at the ticket and then at the stadium. "And look at where our seats are. Holy shit this is our lucky day!"

The boys stood for the national anthem and then the home field Cubbies took the field. Sutcliff went through his warm-ups and then took his spot on the mound. In the opening half of the first inning, the big right hander mowed down the Astros—one, two, three—with two strikeouts and a pop-up. Sutcliff would go eighteen and ten that year and would be the ace of the staff. No blood in the bottom half of the inning either as the Cubs hitters all failed to reach base. The score stayed the same after the Astros' next at-bat.

"The winds blowing out like crazy," JJ remarked. "Look at the pennants on top of the stadium; they're standing straight out; this is nuts. All we got to do is pop one up, and it's fucking out of here." He tossed a handful of peanuts into his mouth and chewed them feverously.

"Yeah," replied Butch. "This is nuts."

Batting in the bottom half of the second for the Cubs would be Andre Dawson, Leon Durham, and then Dave Martinez. Dawson gave the crowd a thrill as he laced a ball that looked to be a goner until the ball was caught at the warning track. Durham struck out, something he excelled at, and then Martinez stepped into the batter's box. On the first pitch, Martinez, a left hander not known as a power hitter, hit a high fly ball to deep left field. The wind caught the lifting drive, and the ball kept going, right out of the park and onto Waverly Avenue. It was a monster home run, and just like that, the Cubs led one to nothing. The crowd went crazy with the boys right in on the delirium.

"Here we go," JJ screamed.

"Yeah, here we fucking go," Butch gushed.

Fired up and ready for a rout, the two high-fived and waited for the next big bomb. They were sadly disappointed; however, as the game went inning after inning with neither team producing anything close to a scoring threat. When the scorekeeper placed a zero in the bottom of the eighth, the score still read one to nothing.

Right after Martinez's home run, the wind mysteriously changed directions and from that point on blew in toward home plate at what seemed like gale force gusts. No ball would be leaving the stadium now; no matter how hard the little white sphere got smashed.

Butch stared at JJ and in an almost pleading tone said, "JJ, the score is one nothing, and the Astros have one more at-bat. What if they tie it or worse? What if they score two and go ahead? What are we going to do?"

JJ recognized fear in his trembling friend's eyes.

"Don't sweat it," JJ said with a wave of his arm, "Sutcliff's pitching a jewel. The Astros only have three hits, and with the wind blowing in we have nothing to worry about."

JJ made a point to sound confident and assured, for Butch's sake, but inside the lanky boy's body, his gut churned like a county fair ice cream grinder. Even worse, he needed to pee for over an hour but was afraid to leave his seat. He glanced at Butch and smiled. Butch pulled out his inhaler and gave himself three blasts.

"Christ, Butch, how many times can you do that to yourself?' JJ asked, but Butch said nothing and turned back to the game.

The Astro's Billy Hatcher, hitless in three at-bats, strode up to the plate and settled in as the first batter of the final inning. The first pitch was called ball one from Sutcliff, low and outside. After rubbing the ball with his hands, the six-foot seven-inch 215-pound pitcher went through his windup and hurled a hard slider that Hatcher laced up the middle, just missing the pitcher's head. It was a clean base hit. Both boys, praying internally for a quick ending to the inning up to this point, now prayed aloud. Jose Cruz stepped up to the plate. Butch couldn't watch and lowered his head.

A lifetime .280 plus hitter, Cruz struggled in '87 with only a .243 batting average. Sutcliff appeared calm and in control as he set up to hold the runner on at first. Before he even put his foot on the rubber, quick as a cat, he turned and fired toward first. The lightning move seemed to catch Hatcher napping. Though the throw to Leon Durham looked perfect, the umpire called the base runner safe, pointing at the bag, and gesturing that Hatcher's hand touched the bag before the tag. The crowd went wild with boos pouring onto the field in deafening waves.

Butch and JJ jumped to their feet and hurled a slew of abuses at the umpire. "YOU'RE BLIND AS A BAT," JJ yelled. Butch followed up with, "WHAT THE HECK WERE YOU LOOKING AT? IT WASN'T THE TAG—THAT'S FOR SURE!"

The umpire ignored the crowd and resumed his usual position, ready for the next pitch.

Having stepped out of the batter's box, Cruz looked at his third base coach for a sign. The coach tapped his nose, tugged on one ear then the other, and brushed his right forearm before finally touching the brill of his hat. The result of his postulations was "hit away." Cruz returned to the box and dug in. Sutcliff positioned his foot against the pitching rubber. The tall right-hander stared intensely at his catcher and received the desired pitch. Sutcliff smoothly went through his hold motion, glanced at Hatcher, and then fired to the plate. Cruz swung hitting a broken-bat liner towards second base.

The moment seemed to freeze time for Hatcher. He couldn't decide whether to risk going to second or stay at first. If Sandberg caught the soft blooper, he would double him up at first, and there would be two outs. He was in no-man's land. The ball narrowly eluded Sandberg's outstretched glove and headed into right center with Hatcher scrambling safely to second, and Cruz rounding first with a single.

Terry Puhl was scheduled to hit next, but the Astros' manager pulled him for switch hitting Ken Caminiti. Caminiti, their regular third baseman, was given the day off from playing the field—minor injury issues. After swinging the bat a few times to get loose, he stepped in for Puhl as a pinch-hitter. With a history of Caminiti being a giant killer against Sutcliff, Hal Lanier, the Astro's manager, loved the matchup.

JJ and Butch watched in suspense as the batter strode to the plate. It felt like a David and Goliath moment. Moving to the right side of the plate, the batter took the end of his bat and tapped his left foot, and then the right, to clear any clay from his cleats. He turned, glanced at his third base coach for instructions, nodded his understanding, and stepped up to battle.

The two boys unwittingly held hands. They prayed to each other and to anyone else that would listen, "Please do not let him get a hit."

After the first three agonizing pitches, the count sat at one ball and two strikes. "Christ, we only need one more strike. Please, God," JJ muttered under his breath.

Sutcliff went through his routine and then flung the pitch toward home plate, a fastball low and inside. It would have been called a ball, but Caminiti crushed the offering toward the hole between first and second.

The ball rocketed toward the outfield and looked to be a sure hit, which would have easily scored Hatcher. But Leon Durham, the Cubs first baseman, made a spectacular play— diving to his right and snagging the sharp grounder. Throwing from his knees, he fired a strike to second to force out Cruz. Shawn Dunston, who possessed an arm like a howitzer cannon, then rifled back to Sutcliff covering first. Instead of a single for Caminiti and a sure run scored, Hatcher stood on third as the sole survivor of the play.

The famous Wrigley Field wind, blowing in for almost eight straight innings, began to swirl. There was no telling which way it would be blowing from pitch to pitch. The entire sell-out crowd of over 41,000 people rose as one, stomped, and screamed. The place went crazy with the Cubs one out from winning the game.

The fans at Wrigley are like no others. Even when the Cubs are in the cellar, losing game after game, the stadium stays packed, and the crowd foaming out the mouth. An outsider, if they didn't know better, would think the last out of the World Series was on the line. The Cubbies' fans were diehard baseball fanatics.

JJ and Butch clapped wildly. The crowd around them was on their feet. Allen Ashby was at the plate and appeared zeroed in. As the tough-hitting Astro catcher dug in and Sutcliff strolled to the rubber to face his foe, the Cubs bench asked for a timeout.

Stunned, JJ gasped, "*What? What? We called timeout? NO, please don't tell me that they're taking Sutcliff out?*"

The Cubs called timeout, and they removed their starter.

"Smith," Butch hollered, "They're bringing in Lee Smith! Thank God, they are bringing in Lee Fucking Smith."

Lee Smith was a highly reliable Cub closer for the past five years. Yet now, after hundreds of innings on the mound in some of the most intense situations, the pitcher provided more drama than dependable performances. When hot, you still couldn't hit 'em, no matter whom he faced. However, when Smith labored, well . . . big fat watermelons come to mind.

The imposing relief pitcher, all six feet-six and 264 pounds of him, took several warm-up tosses before motioning to his catcher he was ready. The fans remained at a fever's pitch with the noise staying as deafening as a jet engine at takeoff. JJ and Butch eyed every twitch and gyration that Smith made as he prepared to deliver his first offering. As he stepped on the rubber, Butch took a moment to scan the crowd.

JJ's sidekick took all the breath his inhibited lungs could take as he relished in the electrifying scene. His chest heaved, and adrenaline raced through his body—the timid, often-sickly boy loved the moment. Just as he turned his head back toward the action, he noticed a man glaring down in his direction—no directly at *him*. The guy stared at Butch with a big gratifying grin creasing his face. He winked and then lifted his hand to his neck and pulled it across the exposed skin in a throat cutting motion.

"STRIKE ONE," the umpire yelled. JJ grabbed Butch's arm and spun his friend back toward the field. "What are you looking at? Two more strikes and we win, for crying out loud!" JJ screamed.

Butch quickly glanced back over his shoulder at the man, but the area now stood empty.

"STRIKE TWO," the umpire bellowed while pulling his hand back and forth in a wild piston-like movement. Time seemed to stop with the crowd entranced but still going nuts. JJ and Butch jumped up and down, screaming for a final strike to end the game.

The right-hander bore down on the batter before going through his motion to hold the runner at third. Hatcher jumped back and forth, and Lee stole a quick glance. But the seasoned vet didn't take the bait as the synapse in his brain fired the signal to go. The pitcher hurled the ball homeward, and the ball rocketed at ninety-six miles per hour straight toward the middle of home plate. Alan Ashby, with eyes trained on his target, took a ferocious cut. As implausible as the moment seemed, the sound of the bat hitting the ball almost drowned out the titanic noise from the crowd. The leather-bound sphere jettisoned away, streaking at the wall in dead-away center field.

Dave Martinez, a gifted if not spectacular outfielder, instinctively bolted toward the fence racing at breakneck speed. The ball and the fielder both headed in the same direction.

Everyone in the stands stared in disbelief. Lee Smith hopped up and down moving toward the Cubs dugout trying to will the ball to land in his teammate's mitt. Both benches were on their feet and at the edges of their separate dugouts. One group waved as they tried to will the ball to leave the field. The other team pleaded with their teammate, "CATCH IT. CATCH IT!"

Now at the edge of the warning track, Martinez extended his hand toward the wall. He tried to sense his distance to the ivy-covered structure. He knew contact was imminent, but his eyes remained steadfast on the arcing projectile. Knowing he was mere feet away from the barrier, Martinez planted his left foot and propelled himself high into the air with his glove hand extended as far as humanly possible.

As if scripted by the Baseball Gods themselves, the ball landed with a thwack into the top part of his mitt with half the ball in and half out of the leather glove. Martinez crashed into the wall and fell to the ground.

At first, the crowd was uncertain whether the player made the catch or not. Martinez laid on the turf, not moving. Seconds before, the fans in the stadium and all along the rooftop seating were screaming at the top of their lungs. Now, the silence deafened every man, woman, and child. Like a defendant waiting for the judge to render a death-sentence verdict, no one moved or spoke as they awaited the decision. Martinez jumped back to his feet and showed the crowd, the umpires, and the world he caught the ball. Just like that, the game was over.

The fans lost their minds. Everyone hugged everyone, and JJ and Butch jumped up and down, high fiving and hugging, delirious with joy. Even though he hadn't been the man he was since his stroke, you could still hear Harry Caray's famous, "Cubs win, Cubs win, Cubs win!" over the loudspeaker.

JJ and Butch stayed in their seats for some time after that last catch to savor their two sweet victories. The Cubs winning and JJ's five-thousand-dollar wager. With all that cash, he would finally have that bastard stepfather of his off his back.

At one point, JJ looked down at a dark ring near his crotch—the stain formed when he peed himself during the action of that last inning.

Looking over at Butch, he said without embarrassment, "I pissed my pants. I couldn't help myself. I needed to go so bad in the 7th inning but was afraid to leave my seat in case something happened. When Martinez caught that ball, I peed and didn't even try to stop."

The boys stared at each other for a second and then burst out laughing. The two, still patting themselves on the back for their great luck, started up the stairs. When they looked up, two men stood on the walkway above . . . and they weren't ushers.

"That was one hell of a game. I love it when the Cubs win, how 'bout you, Earl?" one guy said to the other while giving him a little poke with his elbow.

"Oh yeah, causes a tear in a man's eye when the hometown team brings home the victory."

"Hey Earl, you know what would have made this Cub win even sweeter?"

"What's that Vic?"

"If the Cubbies would have covered the spread and won by two, then these two young men would really have something to cheer about."

Chapter 12

RUN!

JJ and Butch, now at the top of the steps, stopped dead in their tracks, "What the hell are you talking about? What spread? The Cubs won, that's all I bet on," JJ said as a wave of nausea washed over him.

Vic, one of Darnell's thugs and the apparent spokesman of the two, replied, "Well, well, if it isn't JJ. It's JJ, right? Anyway, the thing is my man, the Cubs gotta win by two runs to cover the spread, or you lose. So, guess what? You lose!"

"Maybe you shoulda read the fine print, dumb ass," Earl chimed in, and then the thugs laughed and jabbed each other over the intended levity.

"Time to settle up with the boss; hope you brought your checkbook," Vic said, again a burst of laughter from the two.

A stadium usher came out of an exit a few feet from where the four men stood and walked up before stopping behind Vic.

"Games over gentlemen, time to move to the exit. Crews got to get in to clean up. We have another game tomorrow, you know," the man said while setting down a broom and garbage bag. Startled, Darnell's guys swung around in the sweeper's direction, and that's when JJ screamed to Butch, "RUN!"

In what was literally a heartbeat reaction, Butch and JJ took off. The two headed down the walkway as fast as their legs could carry them. At the first exit they came to, JJ, with Butch on his heels, made a hard left down the ramp and then a sharp right into the interior of the stadium. They ran past the concession areas and food kiosks and tore up the pavement into large chunks—not even looking to see if Vic and Earl were behind them.

Regardless, there was no question that they were.

"Here's an exit," JJ yelled. "After we go through, take a left, and we'll head for the subway."

Racing through the gate, the boys made the turn and headed down the sidewalk along North Clark Street toward the subway and what they hoped would be freedom. At a full sprint, they rounded the corner at Addison and headed toward Sheffield.

Butch stumbled, almost falling to the ground. Legs and arms flailed as he tried to maintain his balance. JJ, seeing his pal in trouble, slowed, grabbed Butch by the arm and helped him regain his footing. The incident happened in mere seconds, but Vic and Earl used the lapse to gain at least ten feet on the fleeing boys. JJ glanced back in their direction and gasped. The two men followed no more than forty feet away.

"Holy shit," JJ screamed and shot like a rocket toward the subway entrance. The two darted and weaved their way through the remaining celebrating Cubs fans often bumping and banging the unsuspecting revelers.

When they neared the corner of Fletcher, JJ realized that the nearest gate to the train was clogged with a large crowd of people. Everyone was trying to make their way up to the platform and the trains above.

"Forget it," JJ screamed to Butch. "Follow me."

Not missing a step, JJ changed directions and sprinted across Addison Street. He headed south on Sheffield before racing down the sidewalk. Neither he nor Butch had a clue where they were going. There was no time to think.

Just run!

After traveling about a hundred feet down the block, JJ chanced a quick glance back at their pursuers and thankfully realized that some distance was gained. Yet something else had changed; JJ only saw one of the two thugs still pursuing them.

"One of them gave up! If we keep running, the other one's bound to get tired. We're way younger than they are," JJ shouted over his shoulder.

He turned his head back around at the very moment that a small group of people stepped out of a building from his right. He tried to bypass them by going to the left onto the street, but one man in the group caught his approach and mirrored his move thinking it to be the best way to avoid a collision. JJ ran full force into the guy.

The collision sent JJ sailing as a shockwave of pain raced through his slender body. He hit the unforgiving pavement, skidding his knees and elbows and tearing his pants. Ignoring the screaming person on the ground a few feet away, JJ bounced up and took off running again. He felt terrible about the guy but didn't look back as any additional delay would allow Darnell's man to pounce on him.

Vic and Earl were gang bangers and understood how to work the streets, at any speed. When they witnessed JJ and Butch cross Addison and head toward Sheffield, they intuitively split up. Earl remained in direct pursuit with Vic passing over Addison and running between two buildings, through a parking lot, and down an alley that ran parallel to Sheffield. As Vic approached the end of the narrow lane, he used a path that cut on a diagonal heading back on a straight line to Sheffield.

When JJ ran into the crowd and fell, Earl watched him get up and head across the street and down the sidewalk on the opposite side. He also noticed that Butch hadn't slowed for his comrade and kept racing straight ahead toward the intersection of Sheffield and North Clark. The older pursuer smiled. Whatever way JJ went now wouldn't matter, because Butch was going exactly where they wanted him to go.

Butch had avoided the group that JJ ran into. He raced around them onto the street, and then back up on the sidewalk before going all out straight down Sheffield. He ran blindly, with no idea where he should go. After a few minutes, he could see the intersection of Sheffield and Clark a half block away. If he could only make it to that intersection, he'd probably get away.

Even though adrenalin raced through Butch's veins, the hormonal rush couldn't stop his weakened air passages from the inevitable asthma attack. Drenched with sweat, the frightened teenager felt the chest-contracting symptoms he knew all too well. He would need a shot or two of his inhaler or risk a massive, breathtaking spasm. Yet, stopping now for the fix would mean certain doom.

After running another twenty seconds at full gallop, Butch neared the intersection. He decided to dash to the other side of the street and looked over his shoulder to check for traffic before he crossed when he realized a few things. First, there was no traffic, thank God, and second, and something he couldn't understand, there was no JJ.

As Butch crossed the street, he caught a quick blur out of the corner of his eye. Before he could even react, he was hurtling, out of control, through the air. Running all out, Vic came directly at the fleeing boy from the side alley and blindsided him with a crushing blow.

The force of the impact sent Butch sailing across the road and to the ground with his body skidding and rolling along the rough pavement before crashing into the street curb on the opposite side of the road. Butch's inhaler, seconds before snuggly in his pocket, popped out from the impact and flew unseen into a sewer drain, clanging and pinging off the concrete walls. Bloodied and dazed, the boy looked up through blurry eyes. Seeing his pursuers hovering over him like vultures ready to feast, Butch simultaneously wheezed, coughed, and cried.

Chapter 13

CAPTURED

After regaining his feet, JJ had run straight down the middle of Sheffield for a half block before crossing over to the opposite side of the road from Butch. He sprinted flat out for another one hundred feet and then took a hard left down an alleyway heading for Wilton Avenue. Once he got to the end of the alley, he glanced over his shoulder, and to his great surprise and relief, no one followed him.

JJ slid to a stop before making his way to the corner of the building on his right. Standing behind the barrier, he kept all but a small portion of his head hidden. He panted like an exhausted dog, and his sides stabbed at him. Sweat poured into his eyes, which burned as if doused with battery acid. However, through all his body's physical ailments, only the terror of the chase prevailed in his consciousness.

JJ waited a few minutes while keeping a vigilant eye down the alley. He expected to see at least one of his assailants—at any moment—no one came. His mind raced, and his head felt as if it contained a huge timer banging the seconds away at an interminable pace—tick . . . tick . . . tick . . .

The anticipation of what, or more precisely who might appear terrified him. Then another fear hit. *Where was Butch?* The image of his friend's face burned in his mind. Not physically or emotionally as strong as JJ, the thought of those freaks catching his best friend made his blood go cold. He decided that he needed to go back to the other end of the alley to see if he could find him.

With nervous anxiety, JJ made his way back in the direction he came. When he arrived at Sheffield, he stopped at the corner and scanned the area.

Nothing appeared to his right, but to his left, about a half block away, what he saw made his stomach twist into a knot. Darnell's bangers were dragging Butch down the road. JJ didn't know what to do—his lip quivered, and tears streamed down his face.

By the time Vic and Earl returned Butch back to the Strike Zone Tavern, the broken boy was sobbing like a baby. Several people along their return asked if the boy needed help, noticing his tattered clothes and injuries. The thugs tightened their grips to vice-like pressure, which sent an unspoken reminder to Butch to keep his mouth shut. He did.

The trio reached the rear-entry delivery gate of the Strike Zone and Vic rang the bell, waited a moment, and then went in when a buzzer sounded. They made for a covered walkway lined with boxes and a mixture of bar and restaurant items. From there they went up an inclined path to the door that led to a storeroom.

The bar's backroom storage area smelled of old beer and even older tobacco, both of which caused Butch to gag.

"You puke on my shoes, and I'm gonna break your nose," Vic said with an insincere chuckle. The brutish men pushed their way through a door on the opposite end of the room and headed toward a long hallway that led to the bar. Three doors stood on the left-hand side of the hall and two on the right. They passed all before reaching the third door on the left. They knocked, waited, and then went in.

Like the last time he and JJ graced his presence, Darnell sat behind his beat-up wooden desk. The room hung thick with smoke. Butch's already swollen eyes burned as the acrid air tore at his eyes' inflamed blood vessels. He ached all over and bled from several cuts and abrasions. These injuries, however, paled compared to the fact this straight-laced boy from the suburbs of Chicago was so scared that he thought he might shit his pants at any moment—if he hadn't already.

"What do we have here?" Darnell asked as he leaned back in his chair.

Vic and Earl took Butch to the couch when Darnell snapped, "I know you're not gonna put that bleedin' fool on my couch and mess up my fine leather. Tell me you boys aren't that fuckin' stupid." The two thugs stopped and looked at each other, glanced toward Darnell, and then dropped Butch to the ground as if he was radioactive.

"What we got here boss is a mother-fuckin' runner," Vic said and then kicked Butch in the ribs, which automatically induced a spray of blood-filled spit to spew out of the boy's mouth. "That's for making me run after yo' ass!"

Darnell stood up and walked over to the boy. He squatted down next to him and shook his head from side to side. After looking over the boy's injuries, a Cheshire cat smile crossed his face. "Boy, I bet that hurt," the foul-breathed man mocked. He looked up at Vic and then back to Butch. "And to think that I went out on a limb to trust you two boys. Man, that cuts me to the quick. You know, thinking about it, I gotta admit that this doesn't make Darnell very happy. We don't much like runners 'round here, do we boys?"

Vic and Earl made "tsking" sounds and shook their heads.

Darnell stood up and leaned against his desk. "What happened?" he demanded of his men, all levity gone.

Vic circled Butch and began his tale. "We cornered this one near North Clark when the other one went toward Wilton. Earl chased this little shit down Sheffield, and I cut through the block down the delivery alley and waited for him. You should have seen it, boss, I imagined myself as Dick-fucking-Butkus as I blind-sided his punk ass. Took him out like a rookie running back.

Earl and me figured that catchin' this one was as good as getting both, so we brought this pussy back with us as a hostage." At that, the two thugs chuckled before high fiving each other.

Darnell leaned forward and peered down at Butch. A pathetic sight, Butch sat on his butt with his legs pulled up, head bent, and arms wrapped around his bruised ribs.

"What was your name again, kid?" he asked sounding almost sympathetic.

"Butch," the boy moaned.

"Well Butch, you wanna get outta here on two working legs?"

Lips trembling and tears pouring down his cheeks, Butch lifted his head and focused on Darnell. Pure terror had hijacked Butch's entire being. "*Wh . . . Wh . . . What*?" he managed to say. "What do you mean on two working legs? What'd *I* do? I wasn't even the one who made the bet!"

"Crazy how that works, huh," Darnell said sarcastically. "I guess you oughta choose your friends a little better next time."

Darnell smiled a cartoon villain's half-grin and then tilted his head back as if pondering the situation. After a few agonizing moments of silence and several rubs of his stubby chin, the lifelong criminal leaned forward. "Let me tell you what's gonna happen. You're gonna give me your friend's phone number. You do that, and I don't break your left leg. Then, I'm gonna call that little bastard and remind him of his debt. If he shows up, then I don't break your right leg. When he pays me my ten grand, you boys get to go on your merry way, and everyone's happy. How's that sound?"

"Ten grand?" Butch gasped. "But JJ only bet five."

"Yeah, but that was before the two of you decided to try out for the Olympics and go cross-country on us. You wore my boys out, caused them some embarrassment, and, well, that raised the stakes a bit," Darnell snarled, "So unless you have no desire to use those legs again, give me that little fucker's number."

Scared shitless, Butch rattled off JJ's home phone in staccato fashion, "444-7769."

Darnell eyed Vic and Earl and gave them a nod. They walked toward the cowering boy, picked him up off the floor, and carried him to a door at the back of the office. It appeared to be an old meat locker door, several inches thick, with large steel hinges and door handle. In another day, the bar operated as a local butcher shop, and the room behind the door was the cutting room.

As they were about to cross the threshold, Darnell said, matter-of-fact, "Now you gonna learn that you shouldn't fuck with Darnell Dorsett."

Butch's head snapped around. "I thought you said that if I told you what you wanted to know, you wouldn't hurt me?"

"No, my fine friend. What I said was that I wouldn't break your legs. I didn't say nothing 'bout any of your other body parts.

Butch's face bore a look of horror, and he tried to scream but nothing came out but a throat-clogging croak. The nineteen-year-old's terrified face disappeared as the door swung closed. Any sound he made or would make faded into muffled silence.

Chapter 14

BUSTED

The phone rang incessantly at the Dawson house. Mrs. Dawson, who had been glued to the TV, did a frantic search for the phone; it was never in its cradle like it should be. She dug around the couch cushion, "Ah, here it is," she said in a cry of victory. "Hello," she answered politely.

"May I speak to Mr. JJ, please?" the gravel voice on the other end said.

"He's not here. Is there something I can do for you? I'm his mother."

"Oh, tha'd be fine. If you'd tell him that his good ole' buddy Darnell Dorsett from the Zone called, and to call me back? The number is 444-6121. Oh, yeah, please tell him that thing he lost is here—it's a bit damaged, but if he hurries back, it should be ok. Any delays or he forgets to contact me, well, I can't say for sure what could happen to it."

"Oh dear, well, I could come and get it."

"No, don't bother yourself, Ma'am. Just have JJ ring me up."

The line went dead. *What a strange phone call,* she thought, and then her maternal instinct kicked in. Doris immediately worried. *That boy better not bring home some stray animal. God only knows what would happen if he did that.* She carried the phone back to its cradle.

As it always seems to occur when JJ least needed, he and George arrived home simultaneously. JJ saw his stepdad but ignored him as he jogged across the lawn and headed straight for the front door.

George spotted JJ and noticed the boy's odd gate and disheveled look. As he parked the car, a frown creased his face as his internal alert ignited. The lumbering man reached the entrance just as JJ shut the door from inside. Reaching out with his hand and blocking the swinging door, Dawson stepped into the house and pounced.

"So, JJ, what completely worthless thing did you do today? The lawn isn't mowed like you were supposed to do." George placed his briefcase on the floor, itching to tangle. "Gee, what else is new?"

JJ ignored the tirade and darted up the stairs.

"I'm talking to you boy," Dawson shouted.

As if his ears were plugged, JJ kept moving.

"Stop right there young man. Do not go another step! If I have to chase you up those stairs, this will not end well."

JJ came to a jerking stop and like a rusted robot turned in one rigid motion. The two glowered at one another as if they might spring through the air like wild animals. Thankfully, Mrs. Dawson chose that moment to walk through the kitchen door with a drink in her hand.

"Why do you two constantly bicker with one another?" Doris, in the most calming voice she could muster, said. "JJ, go upstairs, and wash up for dinner," she continued trying to prevent any additional shouting. "And honey, take your jacket off. I've fixed you a nice bourbon and soda, just the way you like it."

JJ took his mom's cue. He spun around and, like lightning, moved up the stairs toward his room, two and three steps at a time.

"Oh, and by the way," his mother added in a glance upward. "Your friend Darnell from some Zone place called. He's got something of yours and wants you to pick it up, right away."

JJ froze at the top of the stairs. With great effort, he turned and faced both George and his mother. Darnell's message crashed through him like a hurtling meteor. "What did you say?" he asked.

"He said you lost something, or he had something you wanted. I don't remember exactly, but I wrote the name and number down in the kitchen." Doris carried the drink over to George who had removed his jacket.

Though his wife had done her best to distract him, Dawson's blazing eyes never left JJ. Something was up, and he knew it. His hands tightened into white knuckled fists as he glared at JJ.

In a moment of startled recognition, George turned to Doris. "What did you say the man's name was?"

"Darnell or Donny I think, no, definitely Darnell. He sounded like a black man. Why, do you know a black man named Darnell from some placed called the Zone?" she asked her husband. She looked back and forth from JJ to George before adding, "Like I said, the name and number are written down if you want me to get it?"

"That won't be necessary Doris," George sneered through gritted teeth. A pinkish hue raced up the big man's neck before turning his face an angry red. He turned back to JJ, and in a tone that could peel wallpaper growled, "What the fuck have you done?"

Chapter 15

THE CONFESSION

Moving halfway down the flight of stairs, JJ finally plopped down. Tears dropped from his eyes as he tried to relate what had happened. He gasped and choked through sobs of guilt as he described the event, from start to finish.

"So, let me understand this whole thing," Mr. Dawson began in a clipped tone. "You bet five grand on a baseball game using money you didn't have. You made the bet with a stranger; someone you *had* to know would take advantage of two complete idiots from the suburbs. On top of that, you weren't even aware that a spread existed when gambling. *What in the hell were you thinking?*" Mr. Dawson's face contorted like some freakish carnie at a state fair.

In complete mental shambles, JJ searched his mind for a response, but nothing his mixed-up brain came up with made sense. When he did finally open his mouth to speak, no words came out. After several miserable attempts failed, the boy finally raised his hands as if begging for someone, anyone, to help him with this nightmare. With no answers, he began to bawl like a baby.

JJ's mother had a look of complete bewilderment, and with a tilted head, she said, "I don't understand what's happened."

George turned on his wife. "I'll tell you what's happened," he shouted, looking at her like the last intelligent brain cell had escaped from her head. "Your imbecile son bet five thousand dollars on a baseball game—*five thousand dollars that he didn't have mind you*—and couldn't pay off when he lost. And now Darnell Dorsett—it is Dorsett, isn't it?"

JJ nodded as if he just received the death sentence.

"And his hoods are holding his stupid friend hostage until JJ pays them. Does that about sum it up, you little moron?" A spray of spit flew from Dawson's mouth and flew past Doris' shoulder.

"You say 'Darnell' like you know him," Mrs. Dawson said while looking at her husband with a questioning expression "Is JJ in danger? Oh, my God," she gasped. "He's in danger. *He's in danger!*" The woman's chest began to heave as if she couldn't get air into her lungs?"

Dawson froze. He stared wild-eyed at his wife and then, in what seemed like one of the most incredible impressions of Mr. Hyde morphing into Dr. Jekyll, he suddenly calmed. He realized he needed to take control of this situation.

"Here's what we're going to do," George said, his voice steady and monotone. "JJ, you're going to go upstairs to your room to think about what you've done and how upset your mother is because of it. You're going to ponder how your friend could be hurt or worse. Then tomorrow, after this whole mess straightens out, we are going to sit down, the three of us, and we are going to settle a few issues in this house, once and for all. Believe me when I say this, things are going to change around here. In the meantime, I am going to go down to this Strike Zone Tavern place and see if I can somehow get Butch out of trouble."

"Shouldn't you phone the police?" Mrs. Dawson's eyes were wide and her words, staccato.

"You don't dial up 'officer friendly' on these guys," Dawson snapped. "The situation is dangerous enough as it is.

Without another word, George grabbed a coat and opened the door. Before walking out, he turned toward the still blubbering boy. The two male's eyes met. Dawson, the predator. JJ, the prey. No words were spoken, but JJ Larson knew that all was lost.

Chapter 16

JOE AND MARIA TO THE RESCUE

"Officer," a man shouted as he and a woman scurried toward a uniformed patrolman. Chicago beat cop Nick Cooper turned to see the couple racing his way.

"What can I do for you?" Cooper asked.

Officer Nick Cooper, at a couple of inches over six feet, was a dark-haired man with boyish good looks that betrayed his age. His toned physique gave him an athletic shape, with broad shoulders and a vee-shaped back. Though not chiseled, his high cheekbones were well defined, and he sported a solid chin and jawline. Almond-shaped blue eyes finished the dashing look of a man born to wear a uniform.

"Officer . . ." The man stopped mid-sentence and squinted at Cooper's name badge. ". . . Cooper. We witnessed something that concerns us."

"Yeah, what's that?" Cooper replied not bothering to hide his indifference.

"Well, we'd just come out of the stadium, traveled here all the way from Madison, Wisconsin, you know, to catch a Cubbies game."

Tourists with an inconsequential disaster, Cooper immediately surmised. He ground a lit cigarette butt into the cement. "Yeah, go on."

"We're kind of sure they didn't realize we were watching, but we were." The words now flew out of both their mouths in simultaneously rapid fashion.

"Hold on," Cooper said as he held his hands up. "Slow down. Now, start from the beginning. What happened? Tell me step by step."

"This boy," the man said, "Probably late teens. We saw him running down Sheffield Street. I mean really flying like he was being chased or something."

"He *was* being chased Joe, you know that," the woman blurted.

The man frowned and then said, "I know that now, but I didn't know it then, now did I?"

"Go on, Joe." She gave him a nudge, ignoring his explanation.

"So, the kid started to cross from one side of the street to the other and—WHAM!" With this, Joe the tourist slammed one fist into the other producing a loud smacking sound. "This huge guy comes from nowhere and smashes into the boy. I mean WHAMO SLAMMO. The kid goes skidding across the street."

The woman chimed in not missing a beat, "The boy looked hurt. He rolled back and forth on the road and sobbed something terrible. I wanted to see if he needed help when a different man ran up. He, and the one that smacked into the boy, picked him up by the arms and dragged him away."

Silence hung in the air for a moment as the woman's head bent slightly down. Her eyes darted from side to side as if she was searching the ground for what to say next. In a distinct moment of unease, she added, "We were going to say something to the two men, but the look in their eyes . . . well, we thought better of it. If you understand my meaning."

"Yes, of course," Cooper said coolly.

The husband brushed past the awkward moment and said, "The boy bled from several places. But honestly, I think that might be the least of his worries."

"How so?"

"Well, that child was frightened. I mean, he looked scared to death. Wouldn't you say, Maria?"

At that, the woman began vigorously nodding her head up and down like a bobble headed-toy.

Not sure whose turn it was, Cooper asked, "Which way did they go after that?"

"Which way did they go?" the woman said quickly. "We know exactly which way they went because we followed them."

Before the short and round sixty-something woman from Wisconsin could take her next breath, the man pointed in a direction before blurting, "They went up the street back toward the stadium before going through the delivery entrance of that bar."

Cooper looked over and realized that he had indicated The Strike Zone Tavern.

"We didn't follow any further at that point, because, well, because it seemed like we should find help first."

"Get some backup?" Cooper offered.

"Yeah, exactly, get some backup," the man agreed, his tone caustic. "They've been in the bar for about thirty minutes." He paused here for effect. "We know that because we needed that much time to find you."

Cooper glanced at the tavern again, grimaced, and then shook his head. In the short time he patrolled this beat, he had already sparred with the bar's owner, Darnell Dorsett, several times. Those instances involved mainly bullshit stuff like patron fistfights or complaints from unknowing tourists that got ripped off in the bar. However, Cooper's issues with Dorsett seemed small compared to some things that went on before he arrived on that beat. The man had apparently been a pain in the ass and a blight on the neighborhood for years. Several accusations, though never successfully prosecuted, were for severe crimes.

"Ok, can the two of you please follow me across the street? There's a covered area by the stadium. You'll be safe there while we figure this thing out. I'll call my precinct to advise them of the situation. While we're waiting for our 'back up,' I'd like the two of you to stay put—just in case we have other questions."

The two concerned citizens looked at each other as if they suddenly realized that they might have made a mistake getting involved. After a short moment of reflection, they turned back toward Cooper and in perfect unison nodded their heads in uncertain agreement.

Cooper took a few notes while waiting for the call from his dispatch. He jotted down their names, address, and phone number. He asked a few more questions—how long they would be staying in town, whether they would be going directly home from Chicago. By the time Cooper's call came back, he discovered that Joseph and Maria Pendleton from Madison, Wisconsin, came to the big city to visit their children and to see a Cubs game. They were returning home in two days.

Thankfully, at the moment the Wisconsin vacationers prattled on about their kids, grandkids, plus Peter, their great-grandchild, Officer Patrick O'Leary arrived. The patrolman had been on the other side of the stadium moving down Waverly when he got the call.

A big burly Irish cop, O'Leary bore the scars and reputation of holding his own in a scrap. Once, the man single-handily dealt with a group of excited Cubs and Phillies fans that mixed it up after a game. The boisterous fans had raced past the usual shouts and taunts that started inside the park and threw fists, elbows, and legs when they got outside of the stadium.

No more than an earshot from the altercation, O'Leary raced over to intervene. He quashed the melee within seconds. The two Phillies fans laid face down on the pavement crying like little girls, and the two Cubs fans were up against the wall, moaning, with faces smashed tightly against the bricks. O'Leary was the guy you wanted on your side if a skirmish came up.

O'Leary and Cooper positioned themselves on the west side of the stadium to talk over strategy. Nick explained the situation to Jim. He told him of his concern, and that though they possessed a clear sight line to the tavern entrance; they wouldn't be able to see the rear door where the boy had been taken in.

The two agreed that O'Leary would go to the back of the building while Cooper would go into the bar through the front. If Cooper needed help, he would radio O'Leary, and the cop could surprise the occupants from the back.

Cooper gave O'Leary a few minutes to make his way into position, and then he headed toward the bar's entrance. As he walked, the patrolman radioed into headquarters and briefed the desk sergeant of the plan. As he reached the door, Nick did a 360-degree spin to check the area. Except for a large man window-shopping to his left, the coast was clear. He took in a deep breath, opened the bar door, and went in.

Chapter 17

THE LAWYER

The adage that it's often better to be lucky than good was never more apropos than when it came to George Dawson becoming a lawyer. Dawson had been a middle-of-the-pack high school student, not because he wasn't smart but more so because he put most of his efforts into football. Known as Geronimo by his team, due to him diving head first at anyone carrying the ball, the hulking teenager was always big, and he was certain that the sport would take him to the Promised Land.

He had planned to get an athletic scholarship to a college of his choice, but, due to injuries, he never excelled enough as a linebacker to be noticed. Once graduated from high school, Dawson applied at several colleges, but his grades held him back from acceptance to the ones he wanted. Finally, with an assist from a friend of his father's, John Marshall Law School admitted him as a student.

Law wasn't his first choice, but once he saw what lawyers made and how much power the career could provide, he set all of his efforts on getting to the top of his class. His dreams of wealth and power were driven by an ego with few equals. Since football wouldn't give him what he wanted, being a high-priced lawyer would. Unfortunately, the most prominent and best law firms went after the elite of the graduates. George wasn't there and needed a boost. If he would rise to his own expectations, he had to double down.

He got tutoring and volunteered to stay after classes for additional activities. He stopped going out with the few friends he had and spent every waking hour studying. Even those efforts weren't getting him where he needed to be. Then, something happened that set the tone for the rest of his life.

Waiting for a meeting to discuss his progress, Dawson sat alone in his professor's office. Indifferently, he scanned the room and noticed a briefcase on the floor next to the desk. He looked at his watch and then to the briefcase. *Ten minutes early.* George tapped his foot. Checked his watch. *Eight minutes early.* The briefcase was only a few feet from where George sat. *A simple case of curiosity,* George reasoned. Still sitting, he leaned forward and tried the lock. *Well, I'll be goddamn; it's unlocked.* He opened the briefcase and rummaged through it. Seven minutes early. He lifted several folders. None had his name on them. Good. A magnifying glass, two pens, a rubber band—and then, as if the heaven's opened, George found a picture. It was a selfie of Professor Krieger with Professor Linda Scott. They were naked and in a very compromising position. The two were married, but not to each other. George grimaced in disgust and then smiled.

After that meeting and frank conversation with Professor Krieger, George's grades dramatically improved. His externship at Claiborne Law offices in downtown Chicago arrived mid-year with great fanfare, and upon graduation, his job and path to eminence were secured. Over the following years, through guile, cleverness, and back-door treachery, Dawson became a well-known, successful, high-powered defense attorney. As his nickname suggested, Geronimo Dawson would dive headlong into even the most difficult of cases, and more than not, he would win.

Along that journey, he made it his mission to garner as many "friendships" as possible. Those that found themselves roped into his inner circle found they could rarely get out. He was good at controlling, manipulating, and stockpiling favors.

Now, because of the utter stupidity of his stepson, George was nervous and on edge. A man who rarely lost his cool and composure now found himself in an out-of-control situation.

"Dorsett. This is Dawson. I've been calling you for the last twenty-five minutes. For God's sake, what's happening? My stupid-ass stepson told me his friend is at your bar. I'm here to pick him up, make things right. Just as I arrived, I see a cop go in. I went around the block to kill a few minutes. Now, I see another cop next to your delivery door. *What the fuck is going on in there*? Is the kid ok?" George Dawson stammered into his cell phone.

"Well, G e r o n i m o," Darnell stretched out the lawyer's nickname sarcastically. "Things are under control here, thanks so much for asking." With protest in his voice, he added, "And yeah, that punk-ass kid is alright. Maybe a scratch or two, but fine, for the time being. Don't get any asinine ideas, I got him stashed where no one's gonna find 'em till I'm ready to let him be found. I hope you brought cash."

"I'm outside. Came here to pick that little shit up and take him home. Regarding JJ's bet, my past services for you should forego any bad debts that my moron stepson may have with you." He paused for effect. "Especially, if you think you might need my extraordinary talents in the future, which you will. And let me remind you, our mutual friends would be somewhat pissed if they found out that you even took that bet from my wife's kid."

"You can think what you want, Mr. Big-Shot Lawyer. I ain't afraid of those pig ass friends of yours, and more importantly, if you ain't got the cash, you ain't getting the brat. And one more thing, if you ever talk to Darnell like that again, I will have your balls cut off and stuffed in your big fat mouth. Are we clear on that?"

Dawson wasn't scared of this scrawny punk and wanted to reach through the phone and rip the shit's throat out. If George Dawson had his way, he'd shove this fucker's head so far up his ass he wouldn't be able to tell where his ass started, or his shoulders ended. Dawson stifled his urge to verbally throttle the man and in a restrained voice asked, "Is the cop there?"

"Yeah," Darnell stated indignantly. "I'm about to take care of *that* situation right now."

"You've got my number. Call me as soon as he's gone, and we'll settle things," George said, and then hung up.

Chapter 18

THE STRIKE ZONE TAVERN

When Officer Nick Cooper walked into the bar, the contrast between the bright sunshine outside and the dark, almost dungeon-like atmosphere inside was harsh. The beat cop stood in place for a moment while his eyes acclimated to the gloom. Once he established his bearings, he glanced around and saw that the place hadn't changed since the last time he was there. It was still the same crappy dump it had been. If not for the photos of past and present Cubs players on the walls, there would be no correlation between The Strike Zone Tavern and baseball of any kind.

Suddenly, the stale and smoky air of the hundred-plus-year-old drinking establishment invaded Cooper's nose, and he swallowed back a gag. He couldn't grasp the reason anyone would want to patronize the place. The bar smelled like a mixture of old cigars, vomit, and cheap ammonia-based cleaning liquids. The stench snatched at his breath, forcing him to breathe through his mouth.

Nothing that a few dozen drinks couldn't hide, Cooper guessed as he took a couple more steps inside. His eyes now in focus, he scanned the interior. The bar sat to his right, some twenty feet away. Back in the day, the long wooden structure would have been a spectacle of carpentry excellence. Today, the wood was battered and nondescript. Fifteen, maybe twenty, barstools guarded the patron's side, with no more than three stools of the same design.

A small dining area with tables of various shapes and sizes was to Cooper's left. Between those tables and the bar were several dilapidated booths lined up against a dividing wall. As Cooper took in the whole scene, he tried to figure out how this shit-hole business could even stay open. The place had to violate at least a dozen health-related codes. However, upon further review, it became abundantly clear that his opinion meant little as the stools were crammed full of customers, as were most booths and tables.

Behind the counter roamed two bartenders. Well, Cooper assumed they were bartenders. The hesitation in his description wasn't due to whether or not they worked behind the bar serving drinks to their patrons. The thing was—neither looked like any bartenders he'd ever seen. As he gawked at the two, the depiction "giant-ass grizzly bears" came to mind.

As Cooper made his way over to the bar, a man sitting on a stool at the back by the entrance to a hallway caught his eye. Two signs indicating the way to the bathrooms and an exit sign hung above the hall entry. At the end of the corridor stood a large metal door with another exit sign. Cooper assumed that door led to the area that O'Leary guarded.

Making his way to the bar for a chat with the behemoth brothers, Cooper observed that the man on the stool rose up and made his way over to the first door in the hallway. He saw the man knock twice before going in. Cooper made a mental note and then walked to the long wooden counter.

The patrolman stood in a space reserved for servers to get drinks waiting for a bartender to greet. Each Goliath glanced his way at least twice; neither attempted to acknowledge him. Growing increasingly impatient, Cooper realized these two oak trees weren't the only ones ignoring him. Not a single person in the bar paid him any regard. This was not a regular phenomenon. When a cop entered an establishment like this—or any place he walked into—the typical reaction was for people to take notice. It was as if the officer had a flashing strobe light on his head. People would look; it was simply a natural response. Yet, not one patron turned in his direction.

As the seconds ticked by, Cooper continued to be snubbed. The officer felt the urge to jump over the mahogany countertop and give Jabba the Hutt's offspring a throttling. Thankfully, someone saved the agitated cop from that insane action by tapping him on the shoulder. Cooper turned, finding himself face to face with the man himself, Darnell Dorsett.

"Officer . . ." Darnell glanced at Cooper's name badge like he had never seen the man before. ". . . Cooper," he finished. "Come in for a little heat relief, have we?" He shot the cop a wink. "How 'bout an ice-cold draft beer? Eddie?" Darnell nodded toward one of the behemoths behind the bar. "Give Officer Cooper one on the house."

"No thanks," Cooper said, "I'm on duty."

"Well, if you're on duty, and you're in my house, you must need something from Darnell. What can I do for you?"

The entire bar, which had been ignoring Cooper, now stared at the two men.

"I'm here because a young man was brought in here about an hour ago, and he didn't appear to be in too good of shape."

"Well, you have been advised correctly," Dorsett confessed with a huge grin. "That boy was in an awful way. Fortunately, my compassionate people here at The Strike Zone gave him a little TLC and sent him on his way. Hell, the whole scene happened mere minutes before you got here. Ain't that right, Eddie," Darnell said nodding again toward the bartender who now towered opposite Cooper on the other side of the bar.

Right boss," the man grunted back in an almost unintelligible manner. Eddie stared down at Cooper as if he was on a stepladder. Standing at about six feet, six inches, the broad-shouldered thug had a beard big enough to house a family of chipmunks. His bloodshot eyes were too small for his head, and his two top front teeth were gold.

Unfortunately, Cooper's smart-ass sense of humor—something he'd been told his whole life to be an acquired taste—suddenly and without regard, awoke.

Cooper nodded at Eddie and inquired with a straight face, "What the hell do you feed him? Your food bill must be outrageous! And you got two of them!"

Darnell's face darkened. The smile disappeared as his brow contorted, and his cheeks shook. Yet, the gangster controlled his temper, and after a moment or two, one side of his lips rose ever so slightly.

"Your humor and its timing are, let's say, a bit curious Officer Cooper," Darnell snarled.

The next verbal dagger to shoot from Cooper's lips got stuck there when the second mountain of a man came up behind Darnell. Peering up at the glowering man and then back to Dorsett, Cooper said, "Yeah, so I've been told." Cooper took out a notepad and pencil from his back pocket, "Let me have the boy's name and who treated him."

"Man, ain't that the shits?" Darnell raised his hands in an apparent motion of asking for forgiveness. "We didn't even get his name. That's just plain crazy ain't it? My bookkeeper, Wanda, she did the ER work on 'em. I paid little attention to the scrawny little runt."

"What did she do to him? Can you explain his injuries?"

"From what my boys told me, he had a few scrapes and bruises, something caused by him falling while running across the street. The boy got his knees and elbows all banged up. Thankfully, two of my guys were walking by, saw the whole sordid mess, and helped the boy up. We brought him here for some repair work. That's about all there is to say. We did the good deed, and the kid took off."

Cooper looked around the room before turning back to Darnell. "Yeah, lucky for him your guys rallied to his rescue. I need to talk to Wanda."

"Oh," groaned Darnell in a shallow attempt to appear distressed. Reaching his hand up to his chin, he began to scratch his small goatee before adding,

"Wanda's gone for the day. Dang, if you didn't just miss her. She'll be back in a few days. If you wanna come back to see her, I can schedule you an appointment."

Cooper frowned at Darnell knowing all too well he was full of shit, the skinny little prick. This situation was going nowhere fast. "I'll need her address and phone number," Cooper said.

Darnell eyed his bartender and spoke, "Eddie, go on back and get Wanda's number and address for Officer Cooper."

Eddie, moving at the speed of a sloth, lumbered around the bar toward the hall and office. After arriving at the same door, the hall monitor had entered, he went in. After no more than a couple of minutes, he came out with a piece of paper in his hand. He returned at the same interminable pace and handed the folded item to Darnell.

"Here ya go, officer. Let me know if I can help in any other way."

Cooper took it, glanced at the number and address, and then looked at Darnell. "What's in those back rooms?" Cooper probed as he nodded toward the doors down the hallway.

Darnell answered, looking Cooper straight in the face, "Offices, storage, stuff like that."

"I'd like to have a look."

"Well, no offense, but that's gonna take a search warrant. Got one of those?"

The two men glared at each other for several uncomfortable seconds before victory flashed in Darnell's eyes. "I guess not. So, we're done here." With that, he made a tipping of a hat gesture, spun around, and headed toward the very room Cooper wanted to check out. "Come back anytime," he offered over his shoulder. "And if you ever need tickets for a Cubs or Bears game, Darnell will hook you up."

Cooper watched the smug jerk strut back to his office, the towering Eddie in tow. Scanning the bar, Cooper noticed that the bar patrons now scrutinized his every move. He felt like a bad comic doing his stand-up routine in a room full of hecklers. *Jerks*, Cooper thought and turned to walk out. As he reached the exit, King Kong number two was already there. Cooper walked toward the massive man while putting away his pad and pencil. He knew the professional play here was to be respectful and say nothing as he left, but *that* wouldn't be Nick Cooper.

"Something has been really bothering me?" Cooper muttered. "When you had Princess Leah chained up in that sexy halter thing in Star Wars, what did you think could happen? I mean, sex was obviously out of the question, so what then?"

The big man showed no sign of understanding, or maybe he just didn't give a shit. Instead, he simply stared at the cop with vacant, bloodshot eyes. Cooper, who was wearing a hat, touched two fingers to its brill, smiled his best smart-ass smile, and ambled out of the bar.

Once outside, he dashed across the street and radioed O'Leary. "It was all bullshit," he barked into the mike, "The kid is still in the building, I'm sure of it." He further explained that he would phone into dispatch. "Stay put. If anyone comes out the rear, radio immediately, and I'll haul my ass to you."

As he called into the station for instructions, Cooper hurried toward where he left Mr. and Mrs. Pendleton. Desk Sergeant Flint advised Cooper that the captain was leaving. He was told to find a safe location and wait.

Cooper found a secluded spot that allowed him a straight-line vigil on the front door of the tavern. After only a few moments, a tall, stocky, square-shaped man headed toward the tavern entrance. His feet moved in rapid stutter-step fashion, odd for a man his size, and reminded Cooper of a man that needed to pee—badly. The cop frowned but knew he couldn't stop patrons from coming and going without possibly alerting someone of his surveillance. *There's something familiar about that guy.* Cooper squinted in concentration as he tried to put it together, but the recollection wavered just outside of his memory. Then it hit him.

This was the window shopper he saw before going into The Strike Zone earlier. But there was something more.

Cooper took a moment to consider. *Yeah, I knew I recognized him. He's that big-shot attorney. Shit, what was his name?* Cooper shook his head. The name was on the tip of his tongue, but he couldn't quite grasp it. Then he remembered that the guy had a ridiculous nickname—an Indian reference, something like Tonto, Cochise, or Crazy Horse.

The more Cooper thought about the man, the more he recalled. The papers had featured the lawyer countless times. He'd never faced him in court himself, but if he remembered correctly, his clients had one common connection—money. They were swimming in it.

Cooper scrutinized the lawyer. Every step the big man took retained a nervous almost unbalanced look to it. *Why the hell was that attorney rushing into this tavern? No way this guy belongs in a place like this.*

"Cooper?" his radio squawked.

"Here, Sergeant."

Captain Lewis took the radio phone from the desk sergeant "Nick, this is Captain Lewis. What's happening?"

"Things have just gone from strange to stranger, Captain." Cooper reported the events from the time Maria and Joe Pendleton approached him until the attorney's arrival seconds ago. "The lawyer just went into the bar—looked like a cat shitting razor blades, all herky-jerky and tense. I'd bet my right you-know-what he's got something to do with this whole mess."

"Do you think the boy's still inside?"

"I can't say for sure. But based on Mr. and Mrs. Pendleton story, I believe so."

"Ok. I've reached out to Judge Taylor for a search warrant. Stay put, don't take your eyes off the place, and keep O'Leary in check. He's pretty much a bull in a china shop. I've called in for additional backup. They should be arriving in fifteen minutes. I'll have them set up a couple blocks away. Once we have the proper documentation, we'll move in."

"Yes, sir. We'll be waiting . . ."

Chapter 19

THE PROHIBITION STOREROOM

Dawson raced into The Strike Zone and headed straight to Darnell's office. He didn't knock; he just crashed in unannounced. Darnell's head jerked up and, from years of criminal anticipation, his hand automatically went to the gun on his desk.

"Man, you're gonna get your ass shot off if you do that shit again. You damn near gave me a frickin' heart attack. Ain't you got no sense? Me seeing a fat-fuck white man like you come barreling through that door—I'm going to shoot first and ask questions later. Good thing my forty-four's safety was on, or we'd be crushing your ass up in that old meat grinder we got out back," Darnell blasted.

"Sorry," said Dawson, not meaning it, "I'm a bit freaked out with all of this."

Darnell didn't hesitate and asked, "Got my money?"

"This whole thing is bullshit, and you know it. You should have kicked my ass-wipe stepson out of this shithole the minute he walked in. Since when do you take a bet from anyone without the cash up front? Unless—" Dawson stopped and stared directly at Darnell. With his head slightly cocked, he added, "Unless you're using him to get something on me."

"Oh Geronimo, you are *so* mistrusting. Darnell would never do anything like that. I will confess that your boy did admit to being your stepson. Why else would I take a bet from that skinny little shit unless I knew you were good for it? I thought I was doing you a favor, chumming up to your boy and all. The one thing I didn't figure was that little RJ would try to run out on me. But hey, things are gonna work out ok in the end."

"JJ."

"Whatever."

Dawson pulled out his checkbook from his inside coat pocket. "I'm writing this check but the whole thing is fucking bullshit, and you know it. Five thousand dollars is a lot of money! You wouldn't take that bet from anyone else. You're screwing with me, and that's fucking bullshit," Dawson shouted.

"That's ten thousand," Darnell stated with conviction while smiling from ear to ear. Dawson's head shot up so fast it seemed as if it might fly off and slam into the ceiling.

"What the fuck are you talking about? JJ told me he bet five thousand. What kind of crap are you trying to pull?"

"Well, here's the thing," Darnell said leaning back in his chair. "We had us a runner. Anytime we got a runner, the debt doubles. It's Darnell's company policy; can't do anything about it. Wouldn't look good to my other patrons, if you know what I mean. However, if you only want to give me five grand, I guess I can give you back half the boy I got tied up back in the storage room—your call."

George Dawson trembled with anger. If he thought he could escape that place without Darnell's men attacking him, he would race over to that skinny son of a bitch and strangle the life out of him. Even though Dawson was an ex-linebacker and still a rock-solid brut, this bar belonged to Darnell. If things got messy, he had no chance of getting out in one piece, especially if he intended to take Butch with him. With cheeks quivering and turning a bright red hue, he reached down and ripped up the first check and then made out another for ten thousand dollars and tossed it on Darnell's desk.

"Now retrieve the boy, and let me get the hell out of here," Dawson demanded.

Darnell gawked at the check as if it was a nude shot of Halle Berry and then smiled broadly. He gave a nod to Louie, and the bodyguard plodded over to the room where they held the boy. Louie pulled the massive swinging door open with the hinges squealing in resistance.

A few minutes went by. "What's taking so long," the lawyer said.

At that very moment, they heard Louie yell, "Holy shit." Both men shot their focus to the open door. "Boss, you better get in here! We got us a big fucking problem."

Darnell bolted up from his chair and ran through the door with Dawson right on his heels. As they went through the opening, Dawson realized there were two inner rooms past Darnell's office. The first space was small and empty with a second bigger room hidden behind a movable cabinet along the back wall. The faux structure was pulled away from the wall exposing a sizeable rough-hewn brick lined storage area. Bootleggers used spaces like this during Prohibition to hide cases of illegal booze.

The two men hurried in and saw Louie leaning over Butch. The boy was dead.

"Oh my God! You stupid son of a bitch! You fucking killed him?" Dawson barely got the words out of his throat.

"What the fuck man?" Darnell screamed at Louie as he stared down at the kid's lifeless body. "I wanted those guys to teach him a lesson, rough em' up a little, not to kill the little prick. Take that tape off his mouth man. Shit! What the Fuck!"

Louie, panic in his movements, ripped the tape from Butch's mouth. The boy's skin possessed a blue tinge. Lifeless eyes bulged from their sockets, and dried mucus hung from his nose.

"You idiots," Dawson continued screaming at the two men, "This kid suffers from bad asthma. You stupid, dumb motherfuckers."

Whether intentional or not, Darnell and Louie appeared to ignore Dawson's rant. They stood frozen, staring down at the pasty, blue-hued boy. A twisted blend of horror and fear washed over Darnell. They were about to face a shit storm. The crime boss's verbal rage reignited as he turned back toward Louie and a new barrage of expletives bounced around the room. The giant tree of a man backpeddled until he was flat against the wall.

This new attack seemed to have a similar effect on Dawson. Though the tirade wasn't directed at him, his feet also shuffled backward. Something inside him caught on that he was sitting on a volcano ready to erupt.

Self-preservation took over.

Dawson's mind said to run, but the shock of the moment zapped the strength in his legs rendering them almost useless. He stumbled and lurched before tripping over his own feet. He was headed for a fall, but right before he plummeted face down, he slammed his hand against the wall, regaining not only his balance but to some extent, his senses. He turned and ran. He remembered none of his surroundings, but his feet never stopped until he made it back to his car.

Once there, he jammed his hand into his pocket, pulled out his keys, and—*shit, shit, shit*—dropped them in a green puddle of antifreeze that had leaked from a parked car. "God damn it," he shouted, frustration and fear gripping him by the throat. The generally unflappable lawyer shuddered uncontrollably. Unlike earlier, when he trembled out of anger, this bodily reaction resulted from pure panic. Dawson believed he'd seen it all, done most of it too, and he always came out smelling like a rose. This time though, he saw a big pile of shit and was neck deep in it.

If Darnell went down for this, it wouldn't take much arm-twisting to get him to rat out anyone close to him that might help his situation. Darnell Dorsett had his tentacles around many prominent people, Dawson being one. It was time to act.

Chapter 20

WE GOT OURSELVES A RUNNER, PART 2

"Drag his ass over here," Darnell said to Louie, desperation in his voice. "And for Christ's sake, tie that bag at the top. We gotta make sure no one can see anything while we're carrying him. Do you still have the car keys?"

Louie nodded, produced the keys, and then pulled the bag to Darnell. Once there, he searched around some empty produce boxes until he found a small piece of wire on the ground. He snatched it up and half-assed wound the wire around the top of the bag.

They had stuffed Butch's body into two black fifty-five-gallon plastic bags and then drug it out of Darnell's office, down the hallway, and into the loading dock area. Though they were noticed as they made their way toward the back exit, those eating and drinking in the bar paid little attention.

"I still have that dumb ass Farnsworth's boat keys—it's moored at the Belmont Yacht Club. We'll take the body out on Lake Michigan, tie some cinder blocks around its ankles, and dump it into open water," Darnell said.

"Ok," Louie said securing the bag.

"Check outside to see if anyone's there."

Louie raced to the door that led to the street, looked through the security hole, and then inched the door open. He glanced in both directions, saw nothing, wedged the door, and scurried back inside.

"The area's clear except for your car and a couple of other cars parked in the lot on the other side of the alley," Louie said as he grabbed his end of the improvised body bag. As they approached the exit door, Louie stopped and pulled out a pistol he'd stuffed in the back of his pants. Holding the gun up, he looked at a concerned Darnell. "You never know, man. I ain't takin' no fucking chances. I've been to prison before, and I ain't going back—not without a fight."

"Just don't fucking shoot me," Darnell snapped. "Once we get this loaded, grab a couple of those cement blocks." He pointed to a stack along the outside wall.

"Patrick, come in. Are you there?" Officer Cooper radioed O'Leary.

"I'm here, what's up?"

"That lawyer I told you about just slammed out of the bar looking like he was being chased by aliens. White as a ghost, man, and terrorized. Keep an eye on the loading area and rear door and call me if anything happens. I'll check in to ask for permission to make a move."

By now, roadblocks designed to stop traffic flow during the Cubs game were down, and cars moved steadily up and down the streets around the stadium. Cooper waited until traffic cleared then crossed Addison. He headed in the direction the attorney went hoping to see if he was still in the area.

Once he got to the corner of Sheffield and Addison, Cooper stopped. He didn't want to lose sight of the bar's entrance. He took a quick glance back toward the bar and then turned his head back down Sheffield just in time to catch sight of a big black Cadillac come to a screeching halt at the stop sign. In that moment, the driver and Officer Nick Cooper locked eyes. During that split second, both participants knew two things: that the driver saw the officer and more critically, that the officer saw the driver. Then, in a flash of squealing tires, the car turned right and raced away.

Turning back toward the bar, Cooper returned to his original surveillance position. As he crossed the street, his radio signaled.

"Nick?" Captain Lewis said.

"Yes, sir,"

"I have the search warrant. Oddly, I got a lot of verbal heat from the judge when he heard the name, but I got it. We'll arrive in twenty. Your back up is getting into position. Sargent Carson will be heading your way shortly to take over."

"Sir, I think you better find a way to get here quicker. Something tells me—" A gunshot rang out, another, and then another. "Shots fired," Cooper yelled into the microphone.

"O'Leary . . . Patrick? Patrick, are you there? What's going on?" Cooper pulled his gun from its holster, released the safety, and squatted low next to a blue sedan parked on the street.

"Nick, I'm here. The rear delivery door opened. Two guys came out. One was Dorsett; I didn't know the other. They carried something in a large black bag. I started toward them as they neared the gate leading out to the street, but before I could even identify myself, the other guy aimed a gun and started shooting. I don't know how he missed me. I couldn't have been more than twenty feet away."

O'Leary swallowed hard before continuing, "I got a shot off before diving headfirst behind a parked car near the south side of the door. The guy with the gun dropped his end of the bag and ran back into the bar forcing Darnell to drag the bag himself. Right now, I'm not sure exactly where they are. But if I were to guess, I'd say they're heading your way."

"Ok, stay put. I'm across the street from the front entrance. There's a dark blue Chevy Impala right in front. I'm behind the right corner. Shouldn't be more than five minutes before help arrives," Cooper said and then clicked off.

Two more gunshots broke the tension-filled moment. This time, however, Cooper knew where the shots came from—inside the bar. He swung around the front of the Impala and set himself up into a crouched firing position. The front door of the Tavern popped open, and a throng of people poured out. Cooper's heart thumped so hard that if he didn't know better, he would have sworn he was having a heart attack.

Chapter 21

DEATH LOOKS LOUIE IN THE EYE

"Man, we are screwed big time," Louie shouted while walking in circles. He still carried the gun, swinging it back in forth and pacing like a madman.

"Be careful with that thing, man! You're gonna shoot yourself in the foot, or worse, shoot me," Darnell barked. "And why'd you have to shoot at that cop?"

"I'm sorry boss, I panicked. When I saw him coming at us, I just panicked and started firing." Louie nervously raced back over to the rear exit and looked through the security hole. He eyed Officer O'Leary crouched down behind a car. "God damn it!" he jerked back. "We gotta get the fuck out of here. *Now!*"

Darnell stepped up and scanned the area through the portal. The tavern's big garbage dumpster stood about thirty feet away. It was slightly to the right and would give them cover. *That will have to do.* He grabbed the top of the bag, "Louie, come help me. We gotta toss the kid, and then we're outta here!"

Louie ran over, and the two men picked up the bag and went through the rear door and over to the dumpster. Just as they lifted the bundle shoulder height, the bag opened, and Butch's head popped out. This caused the bag to move slightly and forced Louie to adjust his grip. As he turned his head to pull the bag up and over his shoulder, Butch's face stared back at him, not more than an inch away. With his eyes wide open, bloodshot, and eerily vacant, the now-deceased Butch retained the classic look of the living dead.

Louie freaked. The big thug dropped his end of the bag and made an agile leap backward. The weight of the body was now on Darnell, and he reflectively dropped his end. Butch's body thudded to the ground in a heap.

"Fuck this shit, man," Louie screamed. "Let's get the hell out of here, NOW!"

Darnell thought of protesting but followed Louie as he ran back through the rear door and down the hallway with the intentions of going out the front. On the way, Darnell ducked into his office and headed straight to his desk. He grabbed his forty-four, sitting right where he had left it moments before, and a box of shells out of the bottom drawer. He slammed the drawer closed with his foot and raced out of his office.

Knocking over several chairs and a table, Louie made a rumbling dash to the main door. Darnell met him there seconds later. Though the tavern remained full with game-day guests, most patrons only observed as the two raced through. The unaware crowd hadn't heard the three gunshots, the music in the bar was too loud, nor did they know that there was a teenager's dead body laid in the back of the bar.

A blackened window next to the entrance contained a small section of paint scraped away. Darnell peered out the small patch and saw another police officer crouching behind a parked car on the opposite side of the street.

"Son of a bitch, it's that pain in the ass Cooper," Darnell said under his breath. Beads of panic generated sweat streamed down his face as he bent his head down in thought. After a moment, he jerked upright and motioned to Louie to follow him to the bar. With Darnell's huge bartenders looking on, he opened the cash register, pulled out all the fives, tens, and twenties, and shoved them in his pockets. He lifted the internal tray and grabbed the few fifties and hundreds stashed there and stuffed those in his pockets too.

"Here's what we're going to do," Darnell said, spittle flying from his mouth. "We're going to the middle of the room. I'm going to squeeze off two shots into the ceiling to grab everyone's attention. That's when I want you to convince every motherfucker in here to get the fuck out of the bar. Take your gun and wave it around if you have to. When these assholes go rushing out the door, we'll blend in and use them as shields to escape. We'll make our way to Bobby Johnson's place, and then I'll call the man. He'll figure out what to do. You ready?"

Louie nodded his head, and they worked their way around the bar toward the center of the packed tavern.

Chapter 22

DARNELL AND LOUIE CHOOSE POORLY

"Patrick," Cooper shouted into his radio.

"I'm here!"

"People are piling out of the bar like a stampede. Our guys might come out with the crowd. I'll cross back over Addison. You stay where you are. If they head your way, I'll follow them down the alley. If they come my way, I'll signal you, and you come from behind them. One way or the other, one of us should be able to surprise them."

Cooper clicked off and moved into the middle of the street. As the bar's patrons raced by screaming, a potential problem crossed his mind. He radioed O'Leary; "They're coming out the door and going right. If our guys go left, I'll let you know. If they get to the end of the building, go down the alley, turn left on Clark and head your way, you'll be ready for them. Be careful!"

Cooper ran across the street toward a building to the left of the bar's entrance. His hiding spot's entryway slanted inwards about six feet and gave the officer an excellent vantage point. Moving about halfway in, Cooper crouched and tried to catch his breath and calm his nerves. The next few minutes would determine the outcome, and he needed to be ready, both mentally and physically.

"Cooper?" a voice said over his com.

"Cooper here."

"It's Sergeant Carson. What's going on?"

"Shots fired. Three from the rear of the building, and two from inside. The bar's patrons are pouring out in a mass of hysteria. I've positioned myself in an alcove on the same side of the street as the bar. O'Leary is in the back. I've instructed him to stay put and if the perps turn and head his way, I will notify him and follow them," Cooper reported, his breath coming in short bursts.

"Roger. I've got officers still getting in position around all other points of possible escape, including the stadium. We will need a few minutes more to be set. Stay put, and I'll let you know when we are ready. If they come out, don't make a move toward them. I've got a loud speaker coming and I'll get myself in a position to alert them to our presence and to surrender."

"Yes sir. The only thing I'm worried about is if they try to use someone as a hostage."

"If they do, don't try to take them yourself."

"Copy that."

Cooper stuck his head around the corner. The escaping crowd was thinning, and no Dorsett yet. At that moment, three college-aged men came out followed by a woman with curly brunette hair, long spindly legs, and a look of utter terror on her face. To Cooper, she looked in her mid to late twenties. She stumbled over the threshold and almost fell, but quickly regained her balance and prepared to run. Two men simultaneously bolted out of the door and came rushing up behind her. It was Darnell and one of the other men Cooper had seen earlier— both with guns in their hands.

The terrified woman ran directly toward Cooper's hiding spot. Her arms and legs seemed to go in every direction, a runaway windmill. Cooper surmised she would pass him within seconds with Darnell and his man right behind her. He shifted to the inside of the entryway, giving him the best position to move in behind them once they passed. He knew he was supposed to stay clear and to not engage, but he wanted to be ready for any contingency.

Getting louder and louder, the woman's footfalls slammed against the pavement. Cooper tensed. She would pass at any moment. Time seemed to stand still. His adrenaline sped through his body. And then, as if a switch shut down all conscious sensation, Cooper felt nothing.

Cops train for this moment, but not until one is in this situation does he know how he'll react. Cooper prepared for the worst when he heard Darnell yell at the top of his lungs, "Get back here you fucking bitch, or I'll blow your Goddamn head off."

The woman screamed in hysteria. Cooper jumped back to the other side of the entryway. She was almost close enough for him to touch her. Then, as if she believed she could shield herself from a hail of bullets, she instinctively threw her arms and hands up by her head, and that's when disaster struck.

Instead of continuing down the sidewalk toward Cooper's position and hopeful safety, she made a sharp turn heading out onto Addison and, to his horror, into the path of an oncoming car. In what seemed like slow motion, the car rammed into her, throwing her body high into the air. Cooper, stunned by the spectacle, watched helplessly as her crushed figure sailed past him, coming to rest only a few feet beyond his hiding spot. The bloodied woman lay in the middle of the road, a mound of crumpled and broken body parts.

At that split second, Darnell and his man shot past Cooper. With their heads turned toward the woman, neither caught sight of the hidden cop. Though stunned by the horrific accident, Cooper snapped out of his trance and back into action when he saw the two men with guns race past. He raised his pistol and jumped out of the hiding spot, down to one knee, and into a firing position.

"Stop! Police!" he yelled. "Darnell Dorsett, my gun is leveled right in the middle your back. Drop your weapon, get to your knees, and put your hands behind your head!"

Stunned by this command, the two criminals came to a stop and spun around in Cooper's direction. Darnell, realizing that he was staring down the barrel of a gun, instantly dropped his weapon.

The gun in his henchman's hand hung down by his side, non-threatening, but not on the ground as instructed. When Darnell's gun hit the pavement, the clanging noise seemed to trigger something in the large man next to him. Not saying a word or even changing his expression, he raised his weapon and aimed it at the officer. Cooper didn't wait. He fired. A round seared the middle of the thug's chest.

The man jerked back with the impact, but instead of going down, his large frame simply absorbed the shot. The wounded man looked down in shocked horror as blood formed around the hole in his shirt. His head came up, his eyes met Cooper's. The gun dropped from his hand and landed with a clank at Darnell's feet. The shot man went down to his knees and then fell flat on his face; dead before the sound of flesh meeting sidewalk could be heard.

Darnell's eyes bulged as the goon's head smacked the cement with a sickening thud. "Get to your knees, hands behind your head. NOW!' Cooper shouted, gun aimed directly at Dorsett's chest. The lifelong criminal just stood there looking at his fallen man. Darnell's eyes shifted from Louie's dead form to the guns lying at his feet. The stunned gangster slowly reached down.

Chapter 23

THE BEGINNING OF THE END

Darnell never had a chance. An officer had made his way behind the criminal and when he saw Darnell bend toward the gun, the officer tackled him. In seconds, Darnell Dorsett was handcuffed and having his rights read to him.

Two other detectives came rushing up once the all clear sign was given and moved Darnell off to the other side of the street. After a few minutes of conversations, they walked the handcuffed bookie to a squad car and put him in the back seat.

The car crept toward Cooper. As it passed, Darnell's face emerged in the rear side window. With a Cheshire cat's grin, the bastard dared to wink. An overwhelming urge to race after the car, stop it, drag Darnell out by the hair, and beat him to a pulp overwhelmed Cooper. Fists clenched, he considered pulling his gun and shooting the prick. The appearance of Captain Lewis and Patrick O'Leary in front of the bar jerked him from his fantasy and back to reality.

In dazed silence, he eyed O'Leary rapidly moving his hands as he spoke. Cooper made a move toward the two but stopped in his tracks as something tugged at his conscious. Realizing the magnitude of what had just occurred the officer stood there for a moment breathing in deep breaths through his nose. He turned and walked to where the dead woman's body still lay.

Bending next to her, Cooper reached down and grabbed the edge of a tarp that one of the other officers had draped over her body. As he did, he hesitated for a moment, anticipating the worst. After pulling back the plastic material, the youthful cop was surprised to see a face and head that seemed unharmed. In fact, she looked serene, peaceful even.

As Cooper brushed back a few strands of hair that crossed her face, he realized that she was attractive, not in a beauty queen kind of way, but a lovely young woman. Nick wasn't a father, nor did he have a sister, but he overcome by emotion. He would never forget this moment.

As he studied her, he suddenly comprehended that he was staring down at someone's daughter or wife, or maybe she was a mother. *How in the hell is this woman laying here and not Darnell Dorsett?* Cooper gritted his teeth as the veins in his neck pulsed with rage. He felt the urge to yell, scream out his anger. He shut his eyes, took a deep breath, and did his best to bring his emotions under control.

"Darnell better fucking burn for this one," Nick spat out, and then pulled the cover back over her face.

Captain Lewis headed toward his patrolman knowing that the events of the day would affect his man. But even he wasn't prepared for the statement shouted from the tavern door.

"Captain, we found the boy's body, and there's something else as well."

Lewis and Cooper followed the detective inside and through the hall leading to the loading dock area. Several officers hovered around the green dumpster. One man squatted next to a large plastic black bag while the rest stood around him.

"It's a crying shame," one officer said as he moved away to give the two arriving men room.

The sight of the boy's head sticking out of the bag immediately struck Nick. Butch's face seemed to be etched in fear and suffering—the vision made his stomach lurch. Cooper wanted to turn away, run away even. It was bad enough seeing the dead woman, but this, well; the sight of the youth's face became unbearable.

"You said you found something else?" the captain asked with a tone of anguish.

The detective nodded and led the captain to Darnell's office and then to the room where they determined that Butch had been beaten. By the looks of things, this wasn't the first time the area was used for the brutality that Butch endured.

"Captain, you need to see this," the officer said pointing to a small two-drawer filing cabinet. One drawer was open, and a forensic detective held a folder in his hand. He gave the file to Lewis who then grabbed a pair of glasses from his shirt pocket and read. Cooper watched with curiosity as the man's eyes scanned the paper back and forth. After a moment or two, he lifted his head, "Holy shit!"

Chapter 24

JJ AND HIS MOM HAVE QUESTIONS

JJ was in his room doing the only thing that consoled him whenever he was upset o angry; he was drawing. His hands moved around the page, and the face of his best friend appeared. Within minutes, Butch stared up at JJ. A tear rolled down the artist's face and landed on the picture. *God, how did things get so screwed up?*

JJ's plan was designed to provide him some financial freedom from his stepdad. With everything that had taken place, things would be worse than ever. From that moment on, George Dawson would control every single aspect of his life. Hell, he'd probably have to ask permission to take a crap. Who knows if he'd be allowed to hang out with Butch anymore.

"Butch," JJ murmured to himself. What was taking George so long to get back? At that moment, there was a knock at his door.

"JJ," his mother called softly. "Can I come in?"

"Sure, Mom," he said although he wasn't in the mood to talk.

Doris walked in and sat next to him on the bed. She looked down at the picture and stared at the sketch in awe.

"My god, this drawing is like a photograph," she said while shaking her head slowly back and forth in amazement. The two sat, staring at his work, until Doris looked at her son.

"Honey," she murmured. "Things look pretty bad right now, but they'll get better. Your stepdad is angry, but in time, he'll get over it."

Tears rolled down JJ's face. He took his shirt sleeve and attempted to wipe them away, but the flow wouldn't stop. "Mom, I'm scared of what he'll do when he gets back," JJ said, hopelessness in his voice. His mom laid her head on his shoulder and rubbed his back. She used to do this when he was a little boy; the touch comforted him then as it did now.

"He's not going to do anything to you. Didn't you see the change in your stepdad when he left? I mean, he was still upset, of course, but he seemed to calm down within minutes. I think he realized that things have been pretty bad between the two of you and maybe sees that it's his fault." She brushed strands of hair out of her son's eyes.

"Yeah, he did go from ballistic to almost dead calm, didn't he?" JJ said, not asking a question as much as making a statement. He sat with a dull expression in his eyes when suddenly, an odd question popped into his mind.

"Mom, I was thinking about what you just said to George just before he left." At the mention of her husband's name, his mother tensed; a frown crawled across her face. Doris' husband didn't like JJ to use his first name, and George had programmed her to admonish her son when he spoke it. JJ ignored the look and continued. "Do you remember, just before he went from crazy to calm, we were talking about the guy that, you know, the guy I did the whole betting thing with?" he asked, though he struggled to admit to the deed. "Anyway, George asked you what the man's name was, and you said, 'Darnell.' Then, a few seconds later, he said, 'That Darnell Dorsett and his hoods, blah, blah, blah . . .' Mom, you never said the guy's last name, and I didn't either. So how did he know?"

His mother lifted her head from his shoulder and looked him in the eye. She hesitated and shook her head, "I'm not sure. That is very odd. Maybe he's a client, though I've never heard him mention the name."

"And then he said he would go down to the Strike Zone Tavern and get him. You never said the entire bar's name either?"

139

The two looked at each other for a few seconds, and JJ was about to ask another question when he heard the front door open and close in a slam. JJ shrank back from his mom, and then they both stared at his door in frozen anticipation. When nothing happened, Mrs. Dawson turned to her son, "Stay up here. I'll bring you some dinner later. That'll give George some time to calm down and for me to find out what's going on."

Chapter 25

REVELATIONS

Doris Dawson came downstairs to find her husband standing at the bar—a glass of bourbon, easily four fingers, straight with no ice, in his hand.

"George," Doris called gently to her husband. "Is everything ok? How's the boy?"

"I couldn't find him," the man answered brusquely, and with that, he drank down at least half of his drink in one gulp. He let out a booze laced gasp and then set the glass down. He added more bourbon, brushed by his wife, and headed for the stairs. Though his wife tried to grab his arm, Dawson brushed her away without speaking.

Things were quiet at the Dawson house that night. To JJ's utter elation, George didn't come to his room nor talk to him. Doris made her husband a light dinner and a sandwich for JJ, but nothing for herself. She could not eat for fear that the food would come straight back up. Something was wrong. *Terribly wrong.* The conversation with JJ was so disturbing she couldn't eat, and she feared speaking to her husband or even getting close. He sensed this.

"What's your problem?" Dawson asked his wife. "You haven't said two sentences to me all night."

"Yes," she said, "And you haven't said one word about Butch . . . or your friend Darnell Dorsett."

Doris Dawson could feel her eyes bulge as the words flew from her lips.

Dawson froze, if only for a moment, but his many years of training as an attorney, plus the fact that he was a sleazebag, allowed him to sidestep his wife's accusatory declarations.

"Well, as I said, I couldn't find the boy. I went to the bar and searched, but he wasn't there nor was the man that JJ so stupidly got involved with. I left my card with the person at the podium inside and then got in my car and searched the neighborhood. After an hour or so of not finding him, I came home," Dawson said in his best defense attorney's directive. "And what makes you think that piece of gutter garbage, Darnell, is a friend of mine?"

"You used the man's last name, Dorsett I believe, when we were talking. Neither JJ nor I told you what his last name was. So, how did you know?"

"Are you kidding me? You of all people know the kind of vermin I'm around all day. I'm always exposed to guys like this asshole. As soon as you said Darnell and the bar, I put two and two together."

Mrs. Dawson stared at him not knowing whether he was telling the truth or straight out lying to her face, but his comments did have some merit to them.

"So, you're saying that you don't know this man and where he hangs his hat—some tavern of some sorts?"

"I don't *know* him, but I certainly know of him. And I have never been to his bar but know it's near the stadium. I am shocked and very disappointed in what you are insinuating," Mr. Dawson said knowing that he had her right where he wanted her. He sensed his opening to sidetrack her implications that he knew more than he was letting on, when he noticed the expression on his wife's face go from a perplexed demeanor to complete horror. George Dawson turned to see the ten o'clock news running on the small black and white TV in the kitchen. Though there was no sound, there was a picture of her son's friend, Butch Carrington.

"Turn it up," Mrs. Dawson said, her hands going slowly up to her cheeks.

Within twenty minutes of watching the news about Butch, George Dawson emptied close to a hundred and fifty thousand dollars from his safe into an overnight bag along with his passport and several other necessary documents. He filled a larger case with clothes and toiletries. He grabbed a few other miscellaneous items of value, he added two Rolexes, several pairs of gold and diamond cufflinks, and jeweled tie tacks, and tossed those into a bag. As an afterthought, he threw in a few of his wife's more valuable jewels.

Just as George closed the suitcase, Doris barged into the bedroom. Her eyes were red and swollen from crying. The news of Butch's death overwhelmed her, and she sensed the world coming to an end for her son. *How could she tell him? He will be devasta*—She stopped in her tracks when she saw the bags on the king-size bed.

"Where are you going?" she demanded.

"I've got to take a short trip. I can't explain at the moment, but as soon as I get settled, I'll call and let you know what to do." He lifted the bags and headed into the hall.

"What do you mean you're going on a trip? That's insane. Your leaving has something to do with Butch's death doesn't it?" she asked, her words iced with indignation.

George stopped, turned toward his wife, and for the first time in their marriage, he thought of striking her. "Doris, because I love you I am going to exit this house without responding. Believe me, you're better off because of it. I'm going, and that's that—nothing else to be said. Be smart and leave this be."

The rage radiating from his eyes terrified her. Even if she wanted to say more, his rabid demeanor encouraged her silence. Without another word between them, George Dawson turned and left.

Chapter 26

PREPARATION IS THE KEY

As a means of possible blackmail opportunities, Darnell Dorsett meticulously detailed any deal he made with his contacts. Dozens of people were implicated, with several names from the political arena and police sector included. In George Dawson's case, Darnell had described the place, time, and circumstances of Dave Larson's murder. It was all there, in black and white. Darnell had been there when George bragged "Boys, this how you permanently sever ties between people," right before killing Dave Larson. He had documented it in detail.

The police department issued an All-Points-Bulletin with several teams of detectives and officers staking out his home and office. Air, train, and bus terminals were alerted, and the man's license plate number was distributed to several law enforcement agencies.

Four days after the discovery of his body at the Tavern, Butch Carrington was laid to rest. To that point, George Dawson remained a wanted fugitive. Both Patrick O'Leary and Nick Cooper attended the Carrington funeral. They came out of respect for Butch's parents, and, though they doubted he would show, they were there to see if George Dawson made an appearance.

At the funeral, the ever-repugnant superintendent of the Chicago Police Department, Big Bob Champion, showed with his regular entourage in tow. A veritable who's who of politicians and law enforcement also attended, as well a conglomerate of media. The boy's murder was front-page news, and people of prominence didn't miss the chance to show their concern. Yet, there were no sightings of George "Geronimo" Dawson.

Tears flowed, and cries of despair ran rampant and continual throughout the service. JJ could not be consoled nor any of Butch's immediate family. Big Bob, however, attempted to make the event about himself. He even tried to get a photo op with the grieving family. Thankfully, they ignored the arrogant egotist and walked away before anyone from the media could arrange the moment.

After the ceremony, when Doris reached her car, two detectives were waiting. It was the first time Dawson's wife was in public with or without her husband since the murder. O'Leary and Cooper observed the conversation from a short distance and then saw the two detectives dash to their car and speed away.

Doris Dawson had confided to the police that her husband had gathered a significant amount of money from their home, packed bags with clothing and other personal items, and left. She hadn't heard from him since. The police tried to tighten the search web, but slippery and resilient George Dawson had influential friends from all lifestyles, and he called in favors. The now-wanted defense attorney escaped capture with most believing he had eventually skipped the country.

In the following days, the police assembled a task force to determine how to handle the other pieces of information the police discovered in Dorsett's secret files. Several members of their own department appeared on Dorsett's ledgers as well as a few select civil servants. Therefore, secrecy was imperative.

The task force tirelessly worked for weeks putting together a strategy. They knew that once the arrests began, the news would spread like wildfire. The group needed to be ready for those who try to flee. Finally, at six a.m. on Sunday, August 19th, the first arrest took place—and it was a big one.

Chapter 27

CLOSE YOUR EYES BEFORE IT'S TOO LATE

"You are phenomenal," Big Bob moaned as the young woman pleasured him orally.

Bob Champion's wife was visiting their children and grandchildren and, as he often did, Bob was taking full advantage of her absence. As part of his arrangement with Darnell Dorsett, he had access to the criminal's harem of prostitutes. A petite little blonde who called herself "Lady Victoria," was his favorite. Barely five-foot tall and weighing one hundred pounds soaking wet, she mesmerized the rotund mound of a man.

Lady Victoria moaned seductively in response to Bob's comment. She feigned the emotions to convince him of her own excitement, when in fact she loathed the fat man. He disgusted her in every way. The flatulent flabby man was grotesque not only by his girth but in his mannerisms. He would make ridiculous comments as a means to be macho, with unabashed remarks about his sexual prowess, enduring appetite, and performance.

Champion paid the girl five hundred dollars to give him a blowjob, and since that took all of about two minutes, the two hundred and fifty dollars per sixty seconds was worth it. Once he delivered his goods, he would be done for the night and pass out. She would leave with her money, and sometimes a few other things, and rarely needed to remove a single article of clothing.

The magical moment for Champion rapidly approached as he huffed and puffed in orgasmic rhythm with the woman's head bobbing up and down. He watched in delight as his penis disappeared in and out of her mouth and could feel the sensation building toward his inevitable climax. Suddenly, and without warning, a man yelled "POLICE," and the bedroom double doors crashed open. High-powered beams of light bobbed and weaved around the room as four battle-dressed members of the police force stormed in.

The woman jerked back and off the bed, landing flat on her back at the precise moment of Big Bob's eruption. He bolted upright with his body contorting in unstoppable convulsions as he tried unsuccessfully to cover his massive mound of flesh, and bodily functions, from the intruders.

The SWAT team that came through the door had seen just about everything. Few things surprised them. The sight before them may have been the most amusing, if not the most disgusting arrest ever made. Each man attempted, to no avail, not to laugh. After a few moments, one guy threw the blubbery man a robe and said, almost pleadingly, "Please, for the love of God, put this on!"

Camera crews stood at the ready as Big Bob Champion exited his home, handcuffed and clothed only in his silk robe, which barely covered his girth. Twice the wind blew the thin silky material open revealing things no family viewers should witness. The once-dapper man had seen his last double-breasted suit for a long while.

In the next few months, revelations of Bob's cover-ups, abuses of power, and involvement in criminal activities, mainly with Darnell Dorsett and George Dawson, would bring his reign to a crashing end as well as those he cavorted with. Even Dawson's honest yet naïve partners weren't spared from the fallout. Clients and businesses evaporated, and the firm almost went under.

The entire takedown of Darnell's list took a mere ten days. Many arrested, including one judge and several politicians, had no idea that Darnell retained records of their involvement with him, which meant the courtrooms stayed busy with shocked and embarrassed people for months. Final sentences ranged from house arrest for the small-time gamblers, loss of positions and careers for several public figures, and finally, life in prison for Darnell Dorsett. Dorsett tried to call in a final last-ditch favor to get his sentence reduced. Unfortunately, one of the few thugs still willing to help the lifelong criminal was caught trying to bribe the presiding judge. This revelation sealed the deal for Darnell Dorset. He would never see life on the streets again.

Big Bob Champion received a ten-year sentence for his crimes. Like Dorsett, he initially looked for help to spare him from a lengthy incarceration. He too found no takers able or willing to help. Unfortunately, the corpulent man would only serve three of his ten-year sentence due to life-threatening health issues. He went directly from prison to a correctional-assisted living facility. Two years after that, Big Bob Champion was dead from liver cancer. Just sixty-two years old, the ex-lawman passed as a mere image of his one-time "bigger than life" persona.

JJ's mom, after much legalese, managed to end up with most of George Dawson's remaining assets not taken by George when he fled or confiscated by the judicial system as recompense. She and JJ sold Dawson's home and moved to Florida. JJ eventually went to college and excelled in graphic arts. Doris never came to terms with the fact that George Dawson was a monster. Though she and JJ were better off without his menace, her life and health suffered. The one time robust and curvy woman shrank in stature because of internal mental anguish. As the years passed, the woman became a mere glimpse of her one-time bubbly and fit self.

PART 2

Chapter 1

THE THOMAS CASE

February 12, 1990

The saying that "timing is everything" couldn't have been more accurate than Patrolman Nick Cooper's situation during the Darnell Dorsett case. Only a beat cop at the time, the high-profile capture of the criminal and eventual fall of his web of associates allowed Nick to be fast-tracked through the detective enrollment process. In a relatively short time, he graduated and became a successful investigator.

During his tenure on the force, Cooper handled a myriad of cases. Most of those would be run-of-the-mill, if homicide could be called that, with a select few ending up on the front-page of newspapers around the country. One case, however, changed more than just his stature as a detective.

"Please state your full name," the bailiff instructed.

"Nicholas James Cooper."

The courtroom officer swore in the Detective, and Cooper's testimony session in the murder and illegal drug trial of Benjamin Houseman began.

Houseman had been arrested for the beating death of his business associate and drug-related charges stemming from the discovery of several pounds of cocaine found at the murder scene. Cooper's involvement in the case arose when he and his partner, Detective Derek Anderson, were following up on a lead involving an unrelated crime. The two stumbled across Houseman shortly after his deadly altercation with his business partner, a coincidence, but one with significant consequences.

The defendant pled "not guilty", claiming self-defense regarding the altercation with his ex-partner, and "not guilty" to the drug charges. "The cache of illegal substances belonged to my dead partner," he proclaimed. "I made some mistakes, I readily admit to that, but drug dealing wasn't one of them."

Opening statements were made with Houseman's defense attorney, the stunning Nancy Louise Bradshaw, painting a picture suggesting that the DA's evidence would be circumstantial. And more to the point, her client was merely in the wrong place at the wrong time, period.

Prosecutor Brian Adamson had built his case around Cooper's arrest affidavit and the excellent investigative work by the crime scene forensic team. He spoke definitively to the jury and explained that the evidence would point to one person and one person only, Ben Houseman.

After several defense witnesses came and went, the prosecutor's turn came. His first witness was his key witness, Detective Nick Cooper. Adamson questioned the detective intensely for over thirty-five minutes, hitting every conceivable angle to make his case. With Cooper's testimony, Adamson weaved an intricately detailed recounting of multiple motives—greed, deception, and revenge—leading to the evening of the murder. Once he concluded with the officer, most in the courtroom believed the defendant was guilty.

After a ten-minute recess, Nick returned to the witness stand for Ms. Bradshaw's cross-examination. Bradshaw gathered paperwork from the defendant's table, scanned a few pages, and then headed in Cooper's direction. As she approached, the Chicago lawman studied her every move. The stride in her gait and her intense focus showed a serious and purposeful attitude toward her job—she wasn't messing around. But more to the point in Cooper's mind, she had to be the hottest female lawyer on the planet.

Bradshaw glanced once toward the jury, making eye contact with each one, and then addressed Cooper, "So, Officer Cooper, you have quite the reputation as a straight and narrow by-the-book cop—"

"It's Detective Cooper. And let me also say that I've heard great things about you as well."

The defense attorney hesitated for a moment, smiled with a somewhat lopsided grin, and then looked Cooper straight in the eye. "I wasn't serious."

"Neither was I," Cooper replied, and he wasn't smiling.

A few small chuckles could be heard coming from the jury and the people in the back of the courtroom.

The judge eyed the two combatants in displeasure and moved to say something when Bradshaw began again. "*Detective* Cooper. In my hand is your sworn deposition that on December 14, at 2:30 in the morning, you arrived at Mr. Houseman's place of business, Two Guys Moving Company. Once there, and without a warrant, you proceeded to bust through the building's locked door. The statement reads that you gained access to the interior of the building and chased Mr. Houseman through the facility. Once you caught up with him, you tackled him to the ground and handcuffed him. Would that be a fairly accurate account of what occurred that day?"

Cooper was a pro, but even so, he could feel his blood pressure rise. He kept his gaze on hers and answered matter-of-factly, "Well, I'd say that *some* of the details you mentioned are correct. Unfortunately, you left out several key facts of my deposition."

"Enlighten us, Detective."

"In my statement, I said that when I arrived, I found the door to Two Guy's Moving locked. I made my presence known by knocking on the door and announcing that I was the police. While waiting for a response, my partner and I heard what we believed was a fight or at the least someone in distress. Banging on the door at that point, I said, again, that we were the police. Loud crashing noises came from inside. It sounded as if the place was being torn apart. Only then did I feel I had probable cause, and my partner and I broke through the door. When we got in, the defendant was standing over the victim with fists clenched and chest heaving like he'd just gone ten rounds with Mike Tyson."

"Your Honor," Ms. Bradshaw sniped, not even attempting to make a formal objection

"Detective, please answer the question and leave the embellishing for someone else's courtroom," Judge Greer directed.

Cooper nodded, an apologetic look on his face.

"So, what happened next?" Bradshaw asked.

"As soon as the defendant saw me, he took off running. I chased him until I apprehended him."

"I see," the defense attorney said. "Detective, what were the conditions in the building that night?"

"Could you be more specific?"

"Of course, fair enough. Were the lights on in the building when you entered?"

"No, but I could see fairly well," Cooper stated with conviction.

"Really? Would that be because you possess excellent night vision or were you wearing some form of night time vision aide?"

Again, Cooper saw red but tried to ignore her blatant attempts at discrediting him. "The room was well lit by a full moon. The light was bright—shining through a large bank of windows at the top rear of the building. I could clearly see the defendant."

"So, no interior lights were on?"

"Asked and answered," Adamson barked.

"Sustained"

Cooper answered anyway, though he did so with a tone of victory, "As I said, no. The lights were off."

Bradshaw ignored the tenor of his response and went on, "Do you think that Mr. Houseman could see you as well as you could see him? Because of the moonlight, I mean?"

"Speculation," Adamson interrupted again.

"Miss Bradshaw?" the judge inquired.

"Your honor, the line of questioning is pertinent to presenting a distinct picture of the conditions at the warehouse," Bradshaw pleaded.

"I'll let you go a little more, but make sure you provide a clear direction."

"Thank you, your honor." Turning back to Cooper, she looked at the man and nodded.

"I can't be sure if the defendant could see as well as me, but I would imagine so."

"Where you were standing? Were the windows in front of you or behind?"

Cooper considered the question for a moment and then responded, "Behind."

"Detective Cooper, please bear with me as I set up my next question."

In response, Cooper stared at her and waited. Unfortunately, the man's eyes drifted down the woman's figure in an unintended amount of unprofessional covetousness. He cleared his throat as he realized what he was doing and made a conscious effort to avert his eyes.

The attorney paused a second—her eyes narrowed, and her lips tightened. She saw something in Cooper's gaze she didn't like, considered admonishing him right there in court, but after a moment thought better of it and continued. "When driving a car at night, with the lights on, of course, images in front of the car are illuminated by the car's lights making them easy for the driver to see. Would you agree with that?" she asked.

"Yes, of course," Cooper replied, shifting slightly in his chair.

"Now, would you also agree that if you stood in front of that car facing the vehicle with its lights on, you would find it difficult to see anything except the car's lights?"

"I suppose so, yes."

"Thank you. I'd think everyone in this room has experienced this at some point." She turned and took a few steps closer to the jury, scanning the group and nodding for their agreement. "With that in mind, and with the fact that you testified earlier that the room was well lit by the moonlight that came into the building from behind you, would you agree that it's possible that Mr. Houseman's sight would have been at least diminished because the light was shining into his face?"

Cooper gazed at the defense attorney for a long moment. A slight smile formed as he realized what she was attempting to do. "The illumination of the interior came from moonlight. I doubt this strength of light could have affected his eyesight very much," Cooper answered with a full grin now crossing his face.

"But you are admitting that it *could* have affected his vision somewhat. And if so, it would be possible that Mr. Houseman may not have been able to tell if you were friend or foe, yes?"

Cooper looked at Adamson for some psychic help but received nothing. "I guess that your hypothetical explanation is somewhat possible."

"Thank you," Bradshaw said, this time with her own broad smile. "Now, when you came crashing through the door, what did you say?" she asked, changing directions with little or no hesitation.

"At first nothing. I used my shoulder against the door to gain entrance. When I came through, I stumbled and fell. I landed on my side but rolled over and popped back to my feet. After acclimating myself to the interior of the building, I saw the defendant standing over a body. When Houseman saw me, he took off running."

"At that point, you started after him?"

"Yes."

"Did you pull your weapon?"

"I had already removed my pistol right before I came through the door."

"Ok. Oh, one thing here, just so we all understand the situation correctly. After you *acclimated* yourself to your surroundings, did you advise Mr. Houseman that you were the police and to stay put?"

"No, not at first. As soon as he ran, my pursuit instincts kicked in. I immediately gave chase. However, after having run about thirty feet or so, I yelled to the defendant that I was the police and for him to stop running. He didn't, so I continued the pursuit until I caught him," Cooper said confidently.

Bradshaw walked back up to the witness stand and firmly stated, "I think we both can agree that Mr. Houseman's vision was possibly impaired due to the lighting conditions. So, it would have been difficult for him to see that you were a police officer and out of survival instincts, he fled? For all he knew, you could have been the one that had attacked his partner."

"Objection your Honor," Mr. Adamson chimed in.

"Sustained," Judge Greer said, frustration in his voice.

Cooper quickly chimed in, "So you're saying that as the possible attacker, I left the scene of the assault and then broke back into the building I'd just left which caused your client to run? Hmm . . . Yes, makes perfect sense."

"Your Honor!" Ms. Bradshaw snapped. "I would like you to instruct the jury to disregard that statement, and would you please advise Officer Cooper to respond only when questioned and not to adlib any answers spontaneously?"

Cooper raised his hands in a defensive posture, but the judge merely studied the detective for a moment and then pointed his finger and said, "Detective, you've been here many times before and know how I run my proceedings. I am advising you now, and this is a courtesy warning, to behave yourself, respect your position, and most importantly, respect my courtroom. This is the only warning you'll get. Only answer when you're asked a question. The jury will disregard Detective Cooper's last statement."

They may have been told to disregard, but at least Cooper had them thinking how preposterous the possibility was.

"Thank you, Your Honor," Ms. Bradshaw said. The woman stared at the witness, her eyes like ice. She didn't like Cooper and didn't hold back the demeanor that expressed it.

Cooper guessed the wheels in her head moved at lightning speed as she considered a way to mitigate his last statement or to find a way strangle him without anyone seeing.

She stepped closer, almost too close. "Detective, why were you at Mr. Houseman's place of business in the first place?"

"I received an anonymous call that a person of interest in one of my cases was at that address," Cooper answered.

"Hmm, let me see if I understand. You get an anonymous call about an unconnected criminal from another case you were working on. Due to this call, you went to Mr. Houseman's business. While standing at the very door that gave you the closest access to Mr. Houseman, you heard a disturbance and decided to smash through the door and rescue whoever was in trouble. Once inside, you saw my client standing over a body."

"That is correct."

"Mr.—I mean, *Detective* Cooper, did you actually witness Mr. Houseman engage in any physical contact with the victim?"

"No, as I said, it took me a moment to right myself, and that's when I noticed him standing over the victim. As soon as he saw me, he started to run."

"So, suffice it to say, you never actually saw any physical contact between the two? Correct?"

"We found a steel pipe that forensics matched to the wounds on the victim. They pulled a fingerprint that matched your client's," Cooper responded in an attempt to gain some momentum.

"That's not the question I asked," she said. Her voice showing signs of exasperation as she looked at the judge.

"No, I did not see the defendant in physical contact with the deceased," Cooper said in response.

Miss Bradshaw nodded then turned her back away from the witness stand and walked over to the evidence table. She picked up a steel bar from the table and turned back toward Cooper. She made her way back and stopped directly in front of the investigator. "Detective, is this the pipe from the scene of the incident?" she asked handing Cooper the pipe.

"Based on its appearance and the fact that the pipe has an evidence tag on it saying this is the object in question, I would say yes." At that, Cooper could feel the corners of his mouth rise again. He made a conscious effort to suppress the smile but only stifled it.

"Yes . . ." Bradshaw said vacantly. Refocusing on the objective, she began again, "What would a piece of pipe like this be used for at a business like Mr. Houseman's . . . in your opinion?"

"Objection, speculation," Adamson blurted.

Not waiting for the judge, Bradshaw offered, "Well, let me ask you this way. Would you consider this pipe to be out of place in this type of business?" she said, altering her direction.

Adamson started to object, but Cooper answered first. "Not necessarily."

"So, it *is* possible?" she shoots back.

"Yes, I guess the possibility exists."

"So, if an item, such as the pipe in question, could be found in this type of business, wouldn't it be plausible that my client may have had this pipe in his hand at any time for an ordinary activity involved within the realm of his business?"

"Yes, I suppose so," Cooper answered as he turned slightly in his chair.

"So, finding Mr. Houseman's fingerprint on the bar could easily be explained, correct?" she said; a smile of victory formed at the corners of her mouth.

"It's possible that was the reason the pipe was there, though it wouldn't account for the blood splatters and skin on the pipe and on your client's shirt."

"Your Honor." Bradshaw spun away from the witness stand and threw her hands in the air. It seemed like a desperate attempt to have the judge execute Cooper on the spot. He half-expected her to whirl around and yell, "Off with his head!"

Cooper was lost in his own self-satisfying gloat when Judge Greer woke him with, "And that's five hundred dollars, Detective Cooper. Would you like to try for the bonus round and spend a night in lockup?"

"Crap," Cooper said under his breath. "Sorry, Your Honor."

The Chicago homicide detective turned his attention toward the defense attorney, noting an interesting fact. Until this moment, her hair had been up in a neat, professional bun. Now, large sections had broken free from their bindings and hung loosely around her face.

She must have realized this as she frantically tried to return them back into the bun. The threads rebelled and rebuffed her efforts. The annoying tufts kept falling down and covering her right eye.

Cooper watched in amusement as she made several attempts to correct this, but as he did, he realized that she was more gorgeous than he already thought. Trained to spot and retain details, he couldn't help but notice every beautiful detail about Ms. Nancy Louise Bradshaw. If he were honest with himself, he'd have to admit that her features, her walk, the tone of her voice, the attitude she possessed would forever be etched in his mind. She entranced not only him but just about everyone in the room.

"No more questions at this time, Your Honor. However, I'd like to reserve the right to recall this witness if needed."

Her words brought him out of his trance. *Steady there Coop, stay focused, eyes up where they belong.*

The Houseman case went on for two more days, and Cooper returned to the stand once more. Bradshaw questioned him about the drugs and made numerous arguments about illegal searching. The prosecutors came back with forensic proof that Houseman's fingerprints, *and only his fingerprints*, were on the drugs, and Bradshaw pulled out every trick in the book to discredit the evidence.

Circumstantial, possibly, but large amounts of cash were uncovered in the company safe. That vault also harbored her client's fingerprints. Even with this evidence piling up on Houseman, Bradshaw never wavered. She argued that her client unexpectedly found the drugs hidden in the building and that, in fact, was what started the whole altercation. When her client went to his partner and showed him the drugs, an argument ensued, which turned into a physical fight. Her client, fearing for his life, defended himself with the pipe. The portrayal was compelling, and she hammered home the message with fervor and conviction.

Regarding the money, Bradshaw explained how her client routinely kept significant cash on hand for major business purchases as his poor credit rating made charging purchases difficult. She did a credible job of showing how most evidence was circumstantial—except for one problem. Houseman's knuckles were chewed up pretty good, and a test on dried blood taken from his hands and around the wounds on his partners face, matched the deceased. That's when a plea deal of manslaughter came up. To the detectives involved, the defense's entire case was rank with bullshit, and Houseman should have been sent away forever.

You had to give Bradshaw credit; she made the plea bargain happen.

Chapter 2

THE FAMOUS PUMP ROOM

February 23, 1990

As luck would have it, Cooper was at the courthouse on an unrelated matter on the day that the Houseman case ended in a disposition. Standing on the opposite side of a large vestibule, the detective saw attorney Bradshaw near the courtroom doors chatting with a man. After a few moments, the two shook hands and she turned and walked down the hall heading toward the far exit. This woman intrigued Cooper, and he felt a strong need to confront her . . . sort of.

"Excuse me, Counselor, hold on a minute," Cooper called as he hustled in her direction.

Bradshaw turned around. Even from that distance, he could see her eyes roll in that, "Oh brother," kind of expression.

"What can I do for you, *Officer* Cooper?" she asked with apparent disdain.

Cooper made his way to her and stopped a couple of feet away.

"So, Lou, though I know your client to be as guilty as OJ, you did one hell of a job."

"You can call me Miss Bradshaw, and thanks. Anything else?" She stared at the detective as if he suffered from leprosy, needed some spare change or was about to implode.

"Well yes, there is something else. Could I buy you a cup of coffee? I'd love a chance to discuss the case in detail—if you've got a few minutes."

"No thanks," she said and turned to walk away.

The response was the ultimate cold shoulder, but it did not deter, "Ah, come on Lou, don't be that way. You can't hold that whole courtroom thing over my head. Listen, if you don't drink coffee, how about an adult beverage break? Do you like wine? I know a great spot not far from here. They even pour the wine out of a bottle," he said, sarcasm beginning to spike his comments. "And if not that, how about dinner? Even lawyers occasionally need to eat, right? Though you are a bit thin so maybe not so often?"

Cooper waited for a response that he knew wasn't coming, and then he threw one more zinger at her, "And you can call me *Detective* Cooper!"

The smirking detective believed he spotted a slight hesitation in her step, and then she turned back in his direction. Cooper recognized *that* look in her eyes; all men have witnessed what he knew was coming, and he expected horns and fangs to slowly sprout out of her head.

"Look, *Detective*," she said so it easily matched Cooper's cynicism, "Don't ever call me Lou again. That's number one. Second, I make it a point not to date cops. Even if I didn't follow that currently convenient rule, I still wouldn't go out with you. I don't like you. You're arrogant, flippant, and your sarcasm is demeaning and unflattering."

"But I'm cute, right? At least that's something." Cooper smiled.

"Boy, you're a piece of work. You may have luck with that kind of witty banter at your local pub, but your rather lame attempt at boyish charm doesn't interest me. Now, leave me alone. Am I clear? Or should my secretary send you something in writing—like a court-issued restraining order?" She pointed a finger at Cooper.

"Wow, no wonder you're so good at what you do. You verbally abused me without any charts, or memos, or visual aids of any kind—very impressive. I'm sure, with such a seductive repertoire as that, you must have to beat the boys off

162

with a stick at the local lawyer's watering hole," Cooper said, and with a fast turn, walked away.

Bradshaw shook her head in utter loathing of the man's audacity. She started to leave when Cooper said over his shoulder, "Lou, since we've hit it off so well, I'll meet you Friday night in the Pump Room at the Ambassador Hotel around 7p.m. It'll be super fun; you're going to love it—and me! Until seven on Friday, *ciao*."

Cooper expected a shoe in the back, but none came. Once at the parking garage door, he glanced back hoping she might be looking his way. She wasn't, in fact, she was already out the door. Not surprised, though a little disappointed, Nick smiled.

Being in the right place at the right time often indicates that someone has guided and positioned a person to the desired end game in life. In Nancy Louise Bradshaw's case, it was her father, Walter, who had painstakingly planned and guided her destiny.

The elder Bradshaw intended to have his daughter run his firm at some point in her life, so he prompted her to attend certain schools, participate in specific activities, and let her date those individuals he felt qualified—and frankly, those intimate opportunities were far and few between—by design.

The closest the woman ever got to a meaningful relationship was a lawyer in her father's firm. Attorney Robert Henry Frazier was the ideal man for Walter's daughter. Intelligent, handsome, and successful, Frazier met all the proper standards and criteria for a permanent relationship with his daughter. Her father made several overtures on the two getting together going out of his way so that the two crossed paths on many private and professional events. Tired of her father's ongoing meddling, persistence, and borderline compulsive matchmaking efforts, Nancy finally dated the man out of sheer exhaustion. However, in short order, Robert's condescending nature and attempts to placate irritated Nancy. The man would outwardly concede to her every whim, as a means to impress and ingratiate, but in reality, Robert only followed through on what *he* decided was important, or what he wanted. Eventually, she ended the relationship. After that she road-blocked all of her father's matchmaking efforts.

Unfortunately for Nancy, her father's influence and authority left many eligible men hesitant to date or even approach her. No one wanted the wrath of Walter Bradshaw. If he didn't arrange or approve of the connection, well, why bother? Consequently, Nancy seldom dated and was often lonely.

***

Friday rolled around, and at seven p.m., Detective Nick Cooper sat on a barstool at the Pump Room, but sans the lovely Nancy *"Louise"* Bradshaw. Not surprising and no matter, as Cooper would have been there anyway. After moving to the area a few years earlier, this bar had become his favorite haunt.

Named after the famous Bath Room of eighteenth-century England, the Pump Room was in the Ambassador East Hotel on State Street. Established in the late 1930s, the hotel overflowed with a fascinating history. It had hosted people from all lifestyles and occupations. Occasionally, politicians and big-shot industry executive showed up, but the A-list of celebrities gave the place its true luster.

Past greats like John Barrymore bellowed for more champagne. Humphrey Bogart and Lauren Bacall celebrated their wedding in Booth one, as did Robert Wagner and Natalie Wood. Judy Garland was often seen there and later on her daughter, Liza Minnelli. Ms. Garland even immortalized the restaurant in the lyrics for the play *Chicago*, with the words "We'll eat at The Pump Room/Ambassador East, to say the least." Frank Sinatra often held court in Booth one as well.

The in-crowd of future generations also came to hang out at the Pump Room. Eddie Murphy and John Belushi made appearances there in the 1980's. Director Mel Brooks was spotted greeting other patrons like a maître d'. Paul Newman and Robert Redford visited when they were in town. Dozens of signed pictures of the stars graced the Pump Room walls giving the place a life of its own.

Although the meals were pricey, Cooper sometimes indulged himself and dined there. That Friday, as thoughts of the curvaceous Bradshaw filled his mind, he treated himself with the works. A few glasses of the house's excellent pinot noir helped wash down the grilled veal chops, sautéed asparagus, and pan-fried red-skinned potatoes. After paying the bill and tipping his server—the lovable, attractive, and highly efficient Tiffany Rae Johnson—he headed to the bar and perched himself on a corner seat. The barstool provided a perfect spot to view the band while allowing him instant access to replenishing his drink of the night, Maker's Mark bourbon and water on the rocks.

That night's three-piece jazz group was tight. The trio consisted of a drummer, organist, and guitarist who also contributed as their lead vocalist. The goateed hipster revealed nimble fingers and an even silkier smooth voice. He reminded Cooper of those old-time crooners whose vocal tones were hypnotic.

Around midnight, the detective finished his fourth drink of the night, expertly formulated by bartender Eddy O'Dair. Deciding to call it a night, he fished in his pants pocket for his wallet when he vaguely caught the sound of a sultry voice say, "Bourbon on the rocks, Evan Williams, please. If you added a splash of water that would be great." Cooper thought he recognized the voice but before he could sneak a peek at the face that went the voice, she spoke again. This time, the woman seemed to whisper in his ear, "Better late than never, right Detective?"

Cooper clumsily jerked his chair around, and to his utter shock, standing mere inches away, was the striking Ms. Bradshaw. He gave her a not so subtle head-to-toe review. She wore a black, sheer, long-sleeved blouse, a mid-length hip-hugging red silk skirt, and high heels that would have given the average women a nosebleed. Her eyes—for some insane reason he'd disregarded these gems previously—were a milky chocolate brown with hints of gold streaks.

Though Cooper was easily three sheets to the wind, those velvet eyes drew him in with an allure that made him want to beg for forgiveness for all his past sins.

The woman's lips were full, almost pouty, highlighted with a shade of lipstick that made him lean forward in an insane momentary thought of putting his mouth to hers. He thankfully restrained. And, unlike at the trial, her hair was down. It fell in soft waves just past her shoulders. A set of pearls hung in perfect length down her neck while flirting with a full if not sensational cleavage.

"You don't have x-ray vision, do you?" Bradshaw said with a lopsided frown.

"Uh, no, huh?"

"Well, you're ogling me like you're seeing me naked."

"Oh, um, sorry," he said. "I thought I was being subtle." Trying to recover, he shot his focus back to her face and eyes and said, "What took you so long? I was getting tired of waiting."

The two stared at each other for a few seconds with neither of them blinking or showing any emotion. Her brow furrowed. "You know *Officer* Cooper, if my drink were in my hand right now, you'd be wearing it."

"Well, we better order you two so that I can wear one, and you'll have the other to drink," Cooper replied matter of fact.

"Do you think your thick, suffocating approach at humor shows confidence, or are you just that cocky?" Bradshaw asked, her left eyebrow rising ever so slightly.

"Well, time will tell, I guess."

The attorney gazed at Cooper, once again studying his face with eyes that blinked annoyance. Nick, fortunately, realized that he was walking along a precipice. If he went one way, she wouldn't wait for the drink and would slap him and storm off. Or, he could take advantage of an opportunity to be with a knockout that also had a brain. Sanity finally won out.

"Sorry," Cooper said sincerely as he stood up from his bar stool. "Look, maybe we got off on the wrong foot. How about we start over, put the past behind us, and try to get to know each another without throwing any drinks. What do you say?" At that, he offered his hand.

Bradshaw stared at his hand for too long, causing Nick to contemplate stepping back in self-preservation. With bourbon clouding his mind, he imagined that if she had a knife, she'd probably cut off one of his fingers and send it to him through the mail as her answer. Instead, she slowly reached out her hand.

"Hello, *Detective*, my name's Nancy Bradshaw." Her hand slipped into his.

The lava-hot intensity of pleasure that rushed through him was startling, and he took a moment to gather his wits.

"I'm very, *very* pleased to meet you. My name is Nick Cooper," Cooper said, the words catching a little as he spoke. The two nodded slighted and then Nick led Bradshaw to the empty seat next to his. As she moved past him, he caught a hint of her perfume. A wave of sensations made his knees weak and clouded his already hazy mind. As she sat she looked down and with a wry smile said softly, "Um, do you intend on returning that, or are you going to hang on to it for the rest of the night?"

"Huh, oh, sorry," Nick replied as he looked down and realized he was still holding her hand.

Eddy arrived right on cue and delivered Bradshaw's Evan Williams and water. The bartender gave Cooper a knowing wink, saving the cop from any additional embarrassing comments.

"Put her drink on my tab, Eddy."

No, I'll pay for my—" Bradshaw started to say in rebuke.

"Hey, I asked you out for a drink, remember?" Cooper smiled. "Next time we'll go for dinner. Then you can pay."

"Yeah, that's going to happen." Bradshaw laughed.

Before she could take her first sip, Cooper raised his glass to hers and the two delicately tapped them together.

"First, I must warn you that I've consumed a few cocktails. So, as a disclaimer and out of professional and personal courtesy, I want to apologize now because I very likely will say a few things that might cross the line," Cooper admitted.

Bradshaw laughed before staring him in the eyes, "Listen, sailor, the chances of me coming to a bar alone to meet you without drinking my own share of alcohol are slim to none. So, if anyone should worry about saying something wrong tonight, it's me."

"I'm not sure how to take that," Cooper replied in mock resentment.

Bradshaw laughed again and then as if on cue, the two brought their drinks to their lips. Cooper raised his hand stopping her once again. "Here's to at least one night of not wearing each other's cocktail."

"Or each other's clothes," Bradshaw blurted without thinking. "Oh, crap," she gasped and then took a long pull on her drink. Cooper smiled, prepared a phenomenal retort, but then thought better of it.

The two turned their attention to the band who played their latest set. When the singer performed a jazzy rendition of a favorite Frank Sinatra tune, Cooper chanced a glance toward his companion and found her staring at him. The two lock eyes for a defining moment, and then Bradshaw's eyes softened, and she smiled. This sweet gesture had an immediate impact on several areas of Cooper's anatomy.

The detective dated his share of women over the last few years and knew that alcohol was a guilty stimulus of lust. This time, though desire certainly played a large part, Cooper felt something different. The defense attorney had intrigued him from the moment he saw her in the courtroom. She was intelligent, talented, and not easily swayed or influenced. He liked her mannerisms, the way she held herself, and her walk. She had a classy, reserved aura at times and then at others, showed fire and emotion. Add all of that to the fact that she was a knockout, and she was the full package. Nancy Bradshaw stimulated a part of himself that he didn't even know existed.

As the band finished their last song, and the house music came on, Nick swiveled his chair and faced Bradshaw. "So what, exactly, don't you like about cops?"

Taken aback, Bradshaw's eyelashes fluttered together several times in slight embarrassment, but she soon recovered by responding, "I never said I didn't like cops. In fact, I have a few very close cop friends. I just said I maintain a rule against dating them."

"I stand corrected. Why the rule then?"

Bradshaw gazed at Cooper as if she was searching his soul. Her chocolate-diamond eyes seemed to swallow him in, and his body immediately sucker punched him. *Oh Shit,* Cooper thought. *If I were standing up right now, those eyes would melt me like a candle in a fireplace. Get a damn grip on yourself.*

"I don't know . . ." Bradshaw answered still considering his question.

"Not a legitimate answer," Nick responded with a slight shake of his head.

"Ok, but you may not like what you hear."

"I'll take my chances. But before you go on, let me take a quick drink to bolster my constitution." Cooper slammed a gulp. "Shoot!"

"You asked for it." Bradshaw pointed a finger in his direction. "In my opinion, when it comes to relationships, cops are not dependable. The stress of the job makes them moody. You guys often internalize your problems, which make cops poor communicators with their spouses or significant others. The last thing any woman wants is a moody son of a bitch who won't share his issues."

Bradshaw turned her chair to face the bar and then played with the straw in her drink. "Their hours can be awful, unpredictable and . . ." She paused for a second and looked at Cooper. "To be quite honest, the fact that they can be in the line of fire at any given moment is something I'm not prepared to deal with."

"Oh, I see. Well, that *is* a problem."

"Besides," she added as she turned her attention back to her straw. "My dad expects me to marry a lawyer, or CEO, or president of some foreign country, or someone like that. If I became involved with a cop, well, it wouldn't be a fucking pretty picture." Her hand shoots up to her mouth in an embarrassing gesture. "Shit, I said fucking."

"Shit, you said it twice," Cooper retorted in rapid response. He looked her directly in the eye. "So, Dad's the real problem then."

Bradshaw shook her head a little too vigorously and spouted, "*No.* I told you how *I* felt about dating cops." Her voice was firm. "He's only part of the problem . . . a *big* part, yes but . . ." She stared at her drink.

Now, it was Cooper's turn to pay attention to the straw in his drink, "Yeah, maybe. What I'm getting here is that Dad designed a plan for you, and you involved with a lowly cop is obviously not a part of those plans. We're just not good enough for his daughter, I get that."

Bradshaw glanced over at the slightly chagrinned Cooper for a moment and then, with no warning, reached over and grabbed him by the front of his shirt and tugged. Cooper lifted his head, and their eyes meet. The two stayed that way for a long, satisfying moment. He wanted to kiss her. The desire had him by the throat. Then, in a surprising move, she gently pulled him to her and kissed him as if the two had done it a hundred times before.

When they finish, she sat back in apparent satisfaction, at which point Cooper said, "Well that'll show him," before turning his attention back to his drink.

Bradshaw shook her head, "Are you always a prick, or have you just been saving it up for me?"

"Sorry. To be perfectly honest, I think I'm a little off because," Cooper hesitated for the briefest of moments before saying, "Well, I like what I'm feeling. But it would suck if you're in it solely to piss your dad off. Listen, Lou—"

"Detective, the name's Nancy," Bradshaw blurted but not with any real spite.

"Yeah, well, Lou suits you, so you're Lou for me." He stirs his drink. "Anyway, you wouldn't have come here tonight if you weren't interested in me, at least a little. In fact, you're still here after two hours and haven't thrown a drink, yet."

"There's still time," she chimed in.

Cooper smiled slightly, "I'm thinking that maybe you feel the same way I do. So, I say, fuck your old man, and let's throw caution to the wind." Cooper raised his glass, and Bradshaw did too. *Whew.*

"Fuck 'em," she agreed, and they both downed what was left in their glasses.

The two chatted, with Bradshaw doing most of the talking until the band packed up their gear and headed behind the curtain. The mood between Cooper and Bradshaw felt comfortable, even pleasurable-- the early sarcasm and tension now evaporated.

"Hey, almost three a.m., and the bar is closing. You ready to get out of here?" Nick tried to stand.

"*It's what time?*"

Cooper looked at his watch again. "Yep, almost three."

"No shit. Wow," she said and stood. Bradshaw, all five foot eleven in heels, wobbled a little, and Cooper grabbed her arm to steady her. The detective wasn't in much better shape, and his first step was unbalanced, which caused both to teeter as if they were trying to stand up during a Disneyland Teacup ride.

Cooper clutched the bar rail with his right hand, still holding on to Bradshaw's arm with his left. With Eddy shaking his head in apprehension, the two patrons proceeded toward the exit.

"You didn't drive here did you?" Cooper asked as the two staggered through the front door of the building.

"Are you kidding? No way . . . cab'd it."

"Well, there probably won't be any cabs sitting by the curb this late, so we'll have to call you one," Cooper slurred.

"Or we could just go to your place," Nancy said as she stared down the street.

Surprised, Cooper went quiet. *Did I really hear her say that?* Bradshaw's expression conveyed no telltale sign. "Are you sure?"

"Don't look a gift horse in the puss, buddy."

"Well, my place is about 6 blocks that way," Nick said as he pointed down the street. "Are you up for an early morning stroll?"

"Absooolutellly!" Bradshaw drew the words out in alcohol-induced exaggeration.

Arm in arm, the pair headed down the sidewalk. The twenty-minute walk took thirty-five, but the two laughed and enjoyed each other the entire way. They were like two teens walking home from school—well, two drunk teens. Cooper and Bradshaw finally arrived at the front stoop of his house. As he fumbled for the key, Bradshaw grabbed his arm and spun him around.

"Nick," she cooed.

"Yes," he whispered back.

"I'd like you to kiss me, but kiss me like you want me, sort of like how I kissed you earlier but better."

Cooper blinked at the request but didn't want to miss the chance to kiss her again. He moved closer and raised his hand to her cheek. Stroking her velvety skin along her face, he slowly leaned in, and with a gentleness he didn't know he possessed, he touched his lips to hers in a light kiss. Bradshaw gave out a soft moan as she savored the moment.

Their breathing deepened as the passion of the moment intensified. Cooper continued to kiss her lips, but as he did, he became more fervent moving in and around her mouth. Bradshaw welcomed his actions matching his advances and offering her tongue to his when he occasionally slipped it into her mouth. They kissed for several moments, deep, passionate, and without bounds, and then Cooper pulled back to look in her eyes.

"How was that?"

"Practice makes perfect," Bradshaw said with a smile and then threw her arms around him. The two made out for several minutes—this time like two drunken adults.

Chapter 3

MR. BRADSHAW'S GOING TO BE MAD

With great effort, Cooper forced his eyes open, though one at a time. "Oh God," he mumbled. It took a moment or two, but he finally cleared his vision and focus. Staring at his ceiling, the aching man squinted in agony as his head screamed to the rest of his body. This misery could only mean that the previous night's alcohol intake had shriveled his brain to the size of a small sponge. Then, it dawned on him. Someone else was there too. Nancy Bradshaw lying next to him.

As he took in her figure, he saw that the sleeping woman's blouse was on, though barely, and appeared held in place by one remaining button. That button was fastened midway down her stomach but in the wrong buttonhole. Though the sheer black shirt might still be technically in place, her bra was missing, and her breasts were clearly visible. Cooper couldn't see below her waist, as a sheet covered her from the hips down, but he knew that she must be close to naked as he spotted her skirt hanging from the corner of his dresser.

The suffering man lay there for a moment and closed his eyes. He tried to erase the crushing fog from his head. The effort proved futile. He took in a deep breath before sneaking another quick peek. Still gorgeous, and now, in the morning light . . . dang, if she didn't have the most beautiful breasts. He grasped his moment of indiscretion and decided it would be best to cover her. Without averting his eyes, he gradually raised the sheet to her shoulders. Bradshaw stirred but didn't wake.

Nick needed something for his pounding head, and to pee. He swung his legs out of bed and was amused to see that his pants were still on, kind of. Oddly, his left leg was out of the pants, though the foot on that leg possessed a sock.

Conversely, his right leg had his pants bunched around the ankle, but the foot on that leg had no sock. It made him chuckle, causing his head to throb. He winced.

The vague memory of a crazy stripping of garments episode compelled Nick to take a mental inventory of the rest of the attire worn the night before. As he scanned the room, he rapidly concluded that he, and everything else, was a mess. One sock and both shoes were gone and nowhere to be seen. His boxer briefs were on, though wildly askew, and he wore no shirt.

Wow, what happened last night? Still intoxicated, Cooper attempted to inch his body to a standing position. Once up, which was no easy task, he wobbled his way to the bathroom, shuffling and dragging his pants with him.

When Cooper opened the bathroom door, the ceiling light blasted his swollen eyes. *Jesus, it was like staring at the sun.* Nick jerked his head down while slamming his eyes closed. He fumbled along the wall with his hand. When he found the light switch, he flipped it off. Feeling instant relief, he felt his way to the toilet. Once in position, the teetering man did what he needed to do and then headed to the medicine cabinet.

After swallowing two Excedrin Migraine tablets, Nick wove his way back toward the bed. After a few steps, he realized that his pants were still dragging along the floor. With great effort, he kicked them off—the crumpled mess flew across the room, landing in a bunch at the foot of the bed. As the garment settled, he saw a pair of women's tiny black panties.

"Hmm . . ." Cooper murmured, and then looked down at his own underwear, which was now snuggly and properly positioned on his body. "That's interesting." Nick shook his head in bemusement and then made his way back to the bed. Doing his best not to jostle the sleeping Bradshaw, Cooper slid under the sheet and settled in. The figure next to him stirred before rolling over and moaning in agony.

"Yeah, I know exactly how you feel," Cooper said as he carefully repositioned his head on the pillow.

These words seemed to have an electrifying effect on Bradshaw as she shot straight up before wheeling in his direction. Her hair was a mass of confusion, and it covered most of her face. What she could see through that tangled mess, Nick couldn't imagine, but he recognized what happened next; that horrible feeling of a toe to head rush of alcohol-laden blood as it tidal waves to a shrieking, screeching halt into the brain.

It took a second or two for this phenomenon to reach its full effect, but when it did, Bradshaw brought both hands up to her head. Grabbing it, she groaned through parched lips, "Oh God, oh my God, OH MY GOD! I think my head's going to explode. What happened?"

"Bourbon and water—and lots of them," Cooper croaked.

Nick watched Bradshaw slowly survey the room. By her expressions, he knew that she was trying to figure out what had happened. After scanning the room, she lowered her head as if investigating herself. Her shoulders slumped as she realized her shirt was open, her bra was gone, and her breasts were exposed.

Cooper watched in total amusement as Bradshaw lowered her hands from her head to her waist and hesitantly lifted the white linen. In anticipation, she grimaced as she peered down. As if the sheet contained radioactive threads, she dropped it in a frantic movement of embarrassment.

"Oh my God," she said again, this time with pure indignation. Bradshaw collapsed back down on the bed, hands covering her face.

"If it makes you feel any better, I woke up with mine still on," Nick said trying to allay her fears, whatever they may have been. At that, Bradshaw pulled up the sheet covering him to see if he was telling the truth.

"What if I had lied," Cooper said quizzically.

In a scene filled with déjà-vu ramifications, Bradshaw frantically released the sheet. Covering her eyes again with her hands she said, "I'm sorry! I don't know why I did that. I have no idea what I'm doing right now. My head is a spinning top. What time did we get here? If we didn't do anything, why am I naked?"

"You're not; you still have your shirt on."

"Ha, ha, funny man. You know what I mean."

"Well, frankly, the last thing I remember was the two of us stumbling through my front door, kissing crazily, and pulling on each other's clothes. After that, I remember falling onto the bed like a tied pretzel and, well, the rest is a bit blurry."

"Yeah, that does somewhat ring a bell," Bradshaw said in a hushed tone before adding more urgently, "I can't believe I let you bring me here. And on our first date."

"Wait just a minute. I don't quite remember it that way. As I recall, the bar closed, and I tried to get you a cab. *You* were the one that suggested we come here—not that I regret it for an instant."

Bradshaw seemed to think about this for a moment and then said, "Oh yeah, that also kind of rings a bell." She turned to Cooper. "Can you *please* get me something for my head? Maybe a new one?" Her voice was soft and pleading.

"I'll get you something. Unfortunately, my cache of heads in the closet wouldn't do you justice," Cooper answered, and then proceeded to get back up, but with precautionary slowness. Once convinced that his spinal cord would stay intact with his brain, Nick hobbled back into the bathroom and found the pain reliever bottle. *Damn,* he'd consumed the last two Excedrin.

He made his way through the bedroom toward the kitchen. As he passed the bed, he looked down at Nancy. She was looking back at him through one slightly opened eye. He grinned and waved as he went by; she puffed out an exasperated breath and closed her eye. When Nick walked into the kitchen, he found a bottle of Tylenol on the counter. *How did that get there? Preventive measures*, he reasoned while he filled a glass with water.

As he headed back, he discovered his shirt hanging on a lampshade in the living room, his shoes and missing sock thrown in multiple directions around the floor, and on the chandelier above the dining room table was a lacy black bra. *Jesus!* Cooper's brow furrowed, and he shook his head as he tried to remember all that had happened. With a lopsided grin, he headed back into the bedroom and handed Nancy her salvation.

Bradshaw sighed in relief when he handed her the two pills. She swallowed and then plopped back down on the bed with a groan.

"Are you alright?" Cooper asked, though he already knew the answer.

"No, but I will be after the pain meds kick in . . . and I get about a week of sleep. If I had any degree of self-worth, I'd get up, get dressed, and go home to suffer. But honestly, I don't think I'm capable of doing that right now. So, if you don't mind, can I sleep a bit more here?"

Cooper smiled, before saying, "Sure, I'd like to sleep a little more as well."

Chapter 4

DID I MENTION THAT MR. BRADSHAW'S GOING TO BE MAD?

Cooper didn't know how long they were out, but when he awoke, his captivating companion was snug against him with her arm around his waist. Her breasts, now bare, were soft against his back and one of her legs was draped over his.

Trying not to disturb her sleep, Cooper brought his hand up and rubbed his eyes to clear away the cobwebs from last night's . . . *whatever the hell happened.* His movements elicited a sigh of what sounded like contentment from behind him. Then, as if his actions started a chain reaction, Bradshaw's hand began to caress his chest.

She stroked him with a light touch for a few moments, her fingers soft and tender on his skin. Her movements were slow and deliberate as she traced down his chest and along his tightened stomach to the top of his hip.

My God, Cooper thought. The stirring inside lit him up as if she was tracing his skin with electrically charged fingertips. Bradshaw moved her hand down to his thigh, skimming her fingers up and down, her touch ever so nimble. As though it was unintentional, she brushed between his legs causing him to harden like a first-time teenager.

After a few moments, she inched her hand over his boxer briefs to his waist. She hesitated as if she was trying to determine what to do next, or if she should, and then slipped her hand into his briefs. Moaning slightly, she tickled her fingertips along the length of his now swollen manhood. A roiling rush of blood streamed into the area, and Cooper plunged into the sensations of his youth— those times when even the scent of a girl's perfume made him rock hard.

Cooper rolled over and as smoothly as he could, removed his briefs. He then moved half his body on top of hers. Leaning in, he kissed her neck along its length until he reached her ear. "You are an incredible woman," Cooper whispered in her ear.

"Hmmm," Nancy purred. She pulled Cooper tighter to her.

Nick could feel her heartbeat against his chest. He leaned away and traced his finger along her jawline before touching his lips to hers. At first, his lips merely brushed hers. She instinctively raised her mouth to his, and he left a trail of tender kisses across her lips and along her cheek. He moved the rest of his body onto hers.

Cooper's attention moved back to her neck, kissing softly until reaching the top of her shoulder. At that moment, she reached for his hand and brought it to her lips. She kissed his fingers, one at a time, and then caressed the tip of his middle finger with her tongue. After several kisses, she gradually sucked his entire finger into her mouth. The movement was as sensual as Nick could imagine. She licked it slowly and seductively as if she was enjoying a sweet and delicious lollipop.

Nerve endings throughout his body snapped and sparked. Enveloped by Nancy's essence, his physical and mental meters shot to extraordinary sensitivities—unlike anything he could remember experiencing. He showered her breasts with whisper kisses. Each time he made contact, her body arched toward him.

"I can't take any more." Bradshaw moaned, and she grabbed Nick's shoulders and beckoned him between her legs.

Chapter 5

THE AFTERMATH

As they lay together in what Cooper hoped was gratifying silence, the spent man sensed small yet noticeable tremors that occasionally ran through Nancy's body. He tried to think of something appropriately witty to say, but before he formed the words, she spoke.

"Excuse my language, but that was, um . . . well, fucking fantastic," she said with a devilish little chuckle. "It's been a long, long time."

"You mean you're not a virgin," Cooper said, feigning horror.

"Very funny," Bradshaw replied, giving him a small pinch on his behind.

The two stayed like that until Cooper raised up on his elbows and made a grimaced face, "I think your dad's gonna be pissed."

Over the following months, the Bradshaw/Cooper bond buzzed at a feverish pace. Though their relationship mainly consisted of work during the day and sex at night, they found time for the random date night outside of the bedroom. Yet, even those scarce escapades were filled with fraught on Bradshaw's part. She knew of her father's far-reaching tentacles within Chicago's social circles. Though the pair discussed telling him about their relationship from the start, the potential for disaster, as Nancy often put it, made the timing never quite right.

The pair went to the occasional movie or frequented out of the way restaurants, which they always relished and then scurried home to enjoy a night of exhilarating sex. The two likened it to a clandestine affair--an affair that fate was about to screw with.

One Friday evening, the pair rendezvoused at Ristorante Giuseppe, a chic Italian restaurant a few blocks from Cooper's place. The pair shared the house specialty, *osso buco milanese*, with a side of saffron risotto and a bottle of Chianti, hand selected by Chef Giuseppe himself.

The night temperature had dropped, hovering near fifty degrees, as they prepared to leave the restaurant. As they stood on the curb waiting for a cab, Nick wrapped his arms around Nancy. Nancy relished the strength and comfort of his embrace. She closed her eyes and smiled, soaking in the night and his touch.

Feeling the wine and thinking of marvelous things to come, Cooper gently spun her around and stole a quick but passionate kiss. As their lips parted, a yellow taxi pulled up to where they stood. Being the gentleman, Nick stooped down to open the door. As he did, he simultaneously made one mindless glance across the street. Standing on the opposite sidewalk, Cooper glimpsed another couple about to get into a cab of their own. Though the image didn't at first register—he'd seen them only in pictures—it sank in as soon as Nancy's fingernails dug deeply into his arm.

Gazing down at the ground, genuinely afraid to look up, Cooper began to comprehend—though slowly and with trepidation. His brain finally registered who the two people were even before he looked back in their direction. Mr. and Mrs. Bradshaw. Nancy, with her hands up to her mouth like someone who'd just witnessed a horrific accident, and Nick, staring back like a five-year-old caught writing his name in crayon on his parent's living room wall, both went rigid.

Before her next breath, Nancy's phone rang. She sat silent for a moment as Nick slid in next to her. He watched as her brow furrowed, and he could see anger beginning to flare as the one-sided conversation progressed. To Nancy's credit, and with a definite confirmation of her feelings for Cooper, she defiantly dug in her heels keeping her father at bay.

"Dad, this is neither the place nor time. We will have this discussion tomorrow in your office." And with that, she hung up.

The night didn't go quite as planned as Nancy couldn't cool down. Nick, though filled with sexual thoughts right before the incident, could sense the tension and gave her time to relax.

"What are you thinking?" He asked as the two lay in bed later that night. Even in the darkened room, he could see that her eyes were wide open.

"That I knew this day was coming. You know, tomorrow isn't going to be pretty."

"So I gather."

"He's going to try to *reason* with me. In other words, once he finds out who, or more to the point, what you are, he's going to tell me I'm making a mistake, and he doesn't approve. That I should stop things now before our relationship gets out of hand."

"And you will say . . ."

"To mind his business. That I make my own decisions on who I date."

"Sounds like sound reasoning. I'm sure he'll buy into it," Nick said with the intended gentle sarcasm it was intended to be.

"Not funny. Coop, don't worry about this. I can handle it. I'll convince him that we are a good thing, no, a great thing. And that he and Mom will have to accept us."

"I know. Things will be fine," Nick said, and then kissed her on the cheek. "Try to get some sleep.

The best laid plans, as they say. Nancy's father wouldn't listen to reason, and the two bickered for over an hour. The outcome, however, was that Nancy stood her ground and stormed out of his office with the proclamation that she would make her own decisions about men, period. Nick Cooper was her choice whether her dad and mom liked it or not.

Though it weighed heavy on her mind, the argument resolved one thing; the two no longer had to hide the relationship from anyone. From then on, they flowed into a zone that flourished. Their connection transcended any love relationship Cooper had ever had. Sure, they had their issues. She hated his work, and he disliked her dad's constant interference as Nancy's workload seemed to magically increase. Yet they always seemed to manage the drama.

Then something changed. Although Nick hadn't considered himself to be the marrying kind, something within his soul unexpectedly evolved, and love showed him the way to a new relationship level. As the pair approached that magical three-year plateau, Cooper set in motion a scheme to ask Nancy to be his wife. It took time to arrange things, as he wanted all to be perfect, but eventually, the moment arrived.

Chapter 6

TWO DATES WITH DESTINY

"Your father is on line two," Nancy's assistant rang in.

Nancy picked up the phone, "Hey Dad, what's up?"

"Hey, honey. Can you have lunch with me today? I'd like to get your take on an idea I have. I'd rather not do it at the office though, prying eyes and all," Mr. Bradshaw said.

"Sure," Nancy agreed, though it seemed an odd explanation, "I'll meet you downstairs at noon?"

"No, meet me at Benny's at noon. I've got a few errands to run."

"Ok, do I need to bring anything?" Nancy said, trying to get a read on the reason for the meeting. The conversation felt clandestine if not a little weird and had her natural curiosity instinct buzzing.

"No, it's not anything formal; just want to run a few things past you. See you at noon,"

Nancy tried to decipher the call. It was not like her father to set up last minute lunches. She was about to call her mother, but another call came in that lasted well over a half hour. Bradshaw didn't give it another thought until pulling up to the restaurant in the cab. Only when she saw her father and mother together at the table did she get worried.

"Mom? Is everything ok?" Nancy asked as she sat.

"Everything will be fine, in time," her father answered before her mother could. "I've ordered you iced tea," he said. The waiter brought the drinks right on cue.

"Thank you, Jimmy," Nancy said as she smiled at her father's favorite waiter.

Nancy took a quick sip of the raspberry flavored drink. "Ok, what's happening here, and don't try to sugarcoat it."

"Right to the point, just like I taught you," Mr. Bradshaw said with a smile. "I don't want you to be alarmed, but I've got a bit of an issue." He looked at his wife and then shifted his focus to the table. "I've got cancer."

"*What*? What kind of cancer? Are you going to be alright?" Nancy gasped, barely able to get the words out.

Mr. Bradshaw held his hand up as he looked at his daughter, "It's called Adenocarcinoma. But they've caught it early, and my prognosis is good."

"But?"

"Well, it's going to take a bit of the wind out of my sails for a while. Maybe a few months," Mr. Bradshaw said with apparent reluctance.

"Honey," Nancy's mom said softly. "It's not just cancer that we wanted to talk to you about. You know, your father's not getting any younger, and well, to be quite honest, we want to do some traveling over the next few years. This cancer thing has made us realize that if we're going to see the world like we've talked about, we need to do it now."

"Which means?" Nancy asked, now looking her father squarely in the eyes.

"Which means that we have to move your timeline up, a bit."

"A bit? You mean now."

Mr. Bradshaw nodded. "And, I'm afraid there's more.

"Great, what other awesome news do you have," Nancy said as she took another drink of tea, wishing it was something much stronger.

"Harder to talk about than even cancer, I'm afraid. It's your relationship with this man. This police-man, Rick, is it?" Mrs. Bradshaw offered.

"You *know* his name is Nick. And what's the problem with him?"

"You have never had a relationship that has lasted this long. From the outside, it looks as if it is getting rather serious. And, that may end up being problematic," Mr. Bradshaw said.

"Problematic? Why, and for who?" Nancy replied, anger replacing the concern for her father's health.

"Well, for both of you. The next two to three years are going to be grueling for you. As you maneuver through the learning curve, you'll be spending more hours than ever before, often times well into the night. You will be managing the team as well as handling some of our biggest cases. Your life, your personal life anyway, will be non-existent. You can ask your mother. I was absent for the first ten years of our marriage because of what we do."

"Nick and I are doing fine, and we can handle it. You guys did."

"Oh, *really*. So, how much time do you spend together now? He's a detective and must spend hours on his cases. You're a lawyer that is about to have her hours go into overdrive. You'll see each other when? On holidays? Maybe. And what if he asks you to marry him?"

Nancy burst out laughing. "You don't know Nick Cooper. Marriage is the last thing on his mind."

"Don't be so sure. In any case, you owe it to him to break it off now before you have to start making excuses every night for not be able to see each other."

"If you did that, you and Mom would have never stayed married, and I wouldn't even be around?" Nancy shot back in retort.

"Times were different. Our cases were smaller. Yes, we worked hard. Put in many hours. Even so, we didn't have the exposure to big cases like we have now. As CEO, you'll be responsible for *all* of them, our people, and the day in and day out business decisions. It is a formula for relationship disaster. Trust me, I'm right on this." He put his hand on his daughter's hand. Nancy pulled it away and stared at her two parents.

"Dad, let's get to the real issue. You don't like that he's a cop, so don't give me this crap about my workload."

"I'd be lying if I said it didn't matter, but it does. Cops, well, to be honest cops die. Especially ones that do what he does."

Mrs. Bradshaw took over, "Honey, you remember Betty Allison, our neighbor when you were around 10? Well, she had two small children when her husband was killed in the line of duty. Do you want that to happen to you? Your children without a father? You without a husband? And us? We couldn't bear to watch you and our grandchildren suffer that loss."

Jimmy showed up to take their order. "I've lost my appetite," Nancy said as she stood.

"Nancy, please," Mr. Bradshaw begged.

"Dad, I will do all I can while you are going through your treatment, and I will work my ass off for the company in my new role. I'm adult enough to make a decision on who or when I date someone. I'm sorry, but I need to leave," Nancy said. She kissed her mom on the cheek, stared at her dad with a mixture of pain and frustration, and then left the restaurant.

The rest of the day was a complete fog for Bradshaw. Her father's illness had hit her hard, but the pushback on Nick had her reeling. The thought of marriage had come to mind, on a few occasions, but she always rebuffed the notion. She and Nick were great as they were. *But marriage, now, no that seemed out of the question. Anyway, Nick's not the marrying kind.*

Nancy's phone rang, "Nancy Bradshaw," she answered.

"Hey, it's Peg. You want to head to The Pump Room for drinks tonight? This week's been crazy, and I could use a bit of a diversion."

Peg Henderson was one of the junior partners at the firm and a friend of both Nancy and Nick. She and Bradshaw often went to the Ambassador together, but it was Nancy that usually did the inviting. This request seemed innocent, yet something in Peg's voice sounded . . . off.

It was a Thursday night, and she had a full workload, but Nancy needed to wash away the bad taste from lunch. She wanted to let Nick know about lunch know what had happened, but he was busy on a case and would be late getting home. She agreed to go.

Bradshaw was an expert at reading people, especially if she had them cornered with nowhere to run. She had sensed something on the phone, but once they were in the cab, she immediately felt nervous unease eminating from her friend. Nancy stared at Peg, but the woman wouldn't look her in the eye. It was time for a cross-examining

"So, Peg, what's happening? And don't try to lie cause you're not as good of a lawyer as I am," Nancy said as she tapped her friend on the knee.

Peg said nothing, not at first, she just kept her head turned and stared out the window.

"I'm waiting for an answer. If you know what's good for you, you'll confess now cause you know I can make your life miserable. She gave Peg a wink.

"Nick's setting up a surprise for you," Peg blurted, though she continued to stare out the window. "He's going to propose. Damn it!"

"Jesus," Nancy muttered.

Peg looked at the horror stricken look on her friend's face. After a second, she hesitantly offered, "This is good news, right? I mean, you guys are so in love. It's wonderful...isn't it?"

Nancy shook her head. "The timing is atrocious. Are you sure? Wait, Nick wouldn't, I mean, he's not the marrying kind. Shit. This can't really be happening."

"You're going to say no?" Peg finally turned toward her friend. "But you're crazy about Nick."

Nancy's eyes welled up, and she held back the urge to cry. "I, uh, Christ, why now?"

"What's going on?" Peg said with concern for her friend and not because of Nick.

Nancy told Peg all that had occurred with her parents. "Ever since I walked out of the restaurant I've been arguing with myself. At one point, I decided that no matter what my parents said, I wasn't going to give up Nick. No matter what. I'd give up my position in the company first. Then it hit me like a rock that what I had spent my entire life trying to accomplish was staring me in the face. The time had come. It's the place I've dreamed of and want to be.

Peg, I simply cannot give up everything now. I'd eventually resent my relationship with Coop if I did. No, I'll convince him that I'm just not ready for marriage. Not now, anyway. It doesn't mean I'm throwing in the towel on us. Just delaying . . ." Nancy looked Peg in the eye. She shook her head at her own realization. "I know Nick. If I say no, no matter my reason, he is not going to be able to wrap his head around it. He'll think that I don't love him enough to marry him. What the hell am I going to do?"

The two women sat in silence the rest of the way until the cab pulled up to the Ambassador.

"So?" Peg asked.

"I…I'm not ready. I'm not ready for this to happen," Nancy said, tears now running down her face in a torrent.

Chapter 7

DON'T SHOOT THE MESSENGER

Peg walked into the designated scene arranged by Nick, shoulders slumped, and her head hung low. When Nick saw her walk in her face seemed made of fallen dough. Peg looked at Cooper with wet eyes.

"Where is she?" Cooper said with concern as he looked past Peg.

"She's waiting outside. You need to go to her."

Anxious, Nick exited the hotel. Dressed in an outfit that reminded Cooper of the one she wore the night they first got together, Nancy stood by the taxi stand. Gorgeous as always, but the distressed look on her face weakened his knees. Her eyes were wet, and her mascara had left a darkened ring.

"What's up, baby? Why didn't you come in?"

"Nick, don't blame her, but I grilled Peg, and she confessed your plan. I have to talk to you and I didn't want to do it in front our friends. "I . . ." She faltered here for a moment and forced her next words to come out, "I met with my father today, and he told me he's sick. He has cancer."

"Oh honey, I'm so sorry," Nick said as he reached out toward Nancy.

Bradshaw stepped back, "I love you. You know that. But marriage? I just can't commit to that right now. With dad sick, I'm going to have to step in and take on a huge role in the firm. It . . . I'm . . . Nick, marriage would be a disaster for me, I mean us, right now," Nancy said.

Nick's whole body seemed to collapse. He was a rough and tumble no-nonsense man, but he felt himself wilting. "Can't we talk about this? It's not as if we have to get married tomorrow. I mean, if you love me, wouldn't you want to be engaged? We can always get married when the time is right."

"This is all too much. I just can't talk about it right now," Nancy said through a stifled gasp. The cab she came in was still at the curb. As if she were Cinderella at midnight, she dashed to the awaiting vehicle. She stopped, turned back to Nick and said, "I thought . . ." But then there was nothing. Nancy got into the cab and closed the door.

The conversation blindsided Cooper, crushing his heart and sucking the life out of him. He hadn't even gotten the chance to propose. Sure, she'd be busier at work; he understood that. She would have to deal with the emotions of her dad's sickness, he realized that too. They could work those things out. Something wasn't right, and he knew it.

For the next couple of weeks, Nancy used her courtroom persona to dance around the conversation the two had in front of the Ambassador. Though she hadn't ended the relationship, not formally anyway, she had gone tepid. They had slept together every possible night since that first date, but lately, she made excuses to keep them apart. Finally, Nick was finished with the irrationality of her behavior. It was time for a showdown. He'd either get the answer or end the relationship himself.

Chapter 8

THE PUMP ROOM, TAKE 2

January 14, 1993

"Evan Williams and water for the two of us."

The waiter dutifully nodded and returned moments later with the drinks.

Nick and Nancy sat quietly for a long while. Neither looked at the other in the eyes. Nick had decided this was the night to get things on the table. He had his questions laid out in his mind. Unfortunately, he couldn't seem to start things.

Regarding Nancy, the detective knew when she's not talking, she' thinking. If she's thinking, she's focused on that subject and that subject only. Those moments when she would fade in and out of their conversations typically happened when she had an important case. However, Cooper didn't believe her state of mind had anything to do with work.

Cooper finally forced himself to ask. "What's going on? You've been quiet since we arrived?"

An awkward moment between the two hung like a black widow's web. Nancy stared at her hands. Finally, she looked up. Her eyes, though still beautiful, were tired and sad. "Nick, the thing is, well, you know that I have dreamt of being a lawyer since I was a kid. I've told you that many times. I've also said that my goal was to head up my dad's firm. I never intended to fall in love with you, with anyone for that matter. But I did. And, well, it got me sidetracked.

My dad's sickness snapped me out of our dream world and back to the reality of the life I was set out to have. I must fulfill the destiny that I've had since

I was a little girl. And to do that, do it right, I need all my attention pointed in the right direction. That means I can't be married, or . . ."

"Or even in a relationship of any kind?"

"It's better for you. I mean, we'd have no life. You'd have no woman, not really. You could never count on me being there for you."

"That's the biggest load of shit I've ever heard. A real cop-out, if you ask me," Nick said indignantly. "We've been doing pretty damn well for three years. Both of us have been busy with our careers, but we have still been there for each other."

Bradshaw didn't lift her head or respond.

"Look at me, damn it," Cooper said through gritted teeth.

Nancy slowly raised her head, and he could see her eyes were swollen and damp with tears. Her bottom lip quivered, but she somehow found words, "I just believe adjusting our time together is for the best. Yes, we've done okay, but now I'm going to be even busier than before. And, well, I need some time to decide what I need in my life right now."

A searing pain shot through Cooper. He'd rather have two root canals at once than face what she was implying. *Shit, she's trying to end what's left of us.* "I think I understand what's going on here," he said before she could say anything more. "You're *still* freaked out because I wanted to take our relationship to the next level, and you didn't. The idea scared you. Jesus, you'd rather walk away than to deal with the situation. *Really*, Lou?" Cooper took a quick swig of his drink. "This is horse shit!"

"That's not true, not at all . . . well, maybe a little, I guess," Nancy said with exasperation. She let out a long sigh, "Listen Coop, I've spent my whole life dreaming that one day I'd run my father's firm. And whether the timing is good or right, that time has come. And damn it, if I'm going to do the job right . . . well, having a relationship simultaneously will not work. Not for a while anyway."

Tears began streaming down her face. Her porcelain skin turned red and blotchy around her doe-like eyes and delicate nose. Cooper reached into his pocket for his handkerchief. Though he'd rather shove the cotton cloth in her mouth to stop her from saying more, he handed it to her. Nancy wiped her eyes, blew her nose, and put the hanky in her lap.

Without thinking of the consequences, Cooper blurted, "Your father put you up to this, didn't he?"

Nancy's eyes turned to slits. Nick was certain that deep inside of her, stored venom was building, and she could strike at any moment. Yet, she surprised him and didn't respond to the accusation. Instead, she turned her head away for a moment, and the two sat in silence until she looked back at him. "My father made no demands; this is my decision."

"One you have apparently already made."

"You're not making this very easy."

"Oh, you want me to do *that* too? Roll over like an obedient dog? Make it simple for you?"

Bradshaw lowered her head and scrunched a cocktail napkin. Cooper stared at her trying to think of something profound to say, but nothing came to mind. Nothing. He tried to take a deep breath. *Fuck, I can't breathe.* Any comeback faded with each shallow breath.

"Ok, how about this," she said, still not looking his way. "Let's say we slow down a bit, I mean because of everything that's going on in our lives. Then, as time goes on, we can re-evaluate our commitment. What do you think?"

Nick motioned for Eddy to bring another round of drinks.

Nancy meant the offer to sound sincere. Unfortunately, the statement seemed shallow and halfhearted, and they both knew it. Cooper contemplated a new round of demonstrative retorts when Eddy broke is concentration.

"Nick, there's a call at the front desk; it's your partner."

As the beaten man stood, he looked back at his swollen-eyed beauty and just like that, the night and their relationship ended.

Chapter 9

LESTER NEEDS A BUTT

February 1993

Lester Jenkins, a tall, bag-of-bones slug, was a brainiac that, when given the option, would rather stick a needle in his arm or shove powder up his nose rather than eat. To make matters worse, his sole motivation for life seemed to revolve around his inherent ability to avoid doing anything for anyone—other than himself.

Though raised in a home filled with love, inspiration, and personal perseverance, Lester had retained no positive attributes from this environment. In fact, Jenkins disinterest and dishonesty were exceeded only by his family's constant efforts to keep him on the straight and narrow. As for guidance, the boy preferred the streets and its people rather than the wisdom of a caring and responsible family.

By the time Jenkins became a teen, his internal path had been mapped out. Lacking any semblance of drive or focus, he decided early on that school "wasn't his bag." His mother and siblings tried to get him to go, but he fought them every step of the way until they just gave up. Once they let go of their demands, Lester stopped going altogether.

Jenkins' brothers and sisters had embraced the opportunity for a better life through education, but Lester demonstrated no ambition to be or do anything positive or productive. As Lester grew into a young adult, time—and too much of it—became his enemy. With no school or any other regular societal activity to keep him off the streets, he became a prime candidate for the gangs on the South Side. But even the gangs couldn't lure him into their fold. Lester had no stomach for the gang life, so he became a routine drug and alcohol customer instead of a member of their thuggery. This decision ultimately brought up another obstacle— Lester didn't want to work, which caused no consistent source of income for his habits.

Lester's only reliable options for obtaining funds were to steal, and since his ambitions were wafer thin, this thievery mainly with his mom, affectionately known as Mother Jenkins. This pilfering occurred whenever he ran dry of his mind-altering agents. Though he randomly sold drugs, he did so with little effort or success. In either case, he never stole enough money to keep cash in his pockets. Uneventful life rolled by for the hazy loner, one dull year after another— until one fateful day in February 1993.

Lester was high on a mixture of heroin and weed, a combination that typically put him in a comatose-like state. When he was loaded, just the thought of standing up was enough to cause him to pass out. This time, somewhere during his drug-induced stupor, Jenkins became overwhelmed with an unquenchable desire for a cigarette. This simple need would be the catalyst for a catastrophe of epic proportions.

"Just one cigarette," he mumbled, certain this would satisfy his insatiable craving. He pulled himself up, wobbling from side to side before steadying himself on the wall next to his bed. "Okay, step one is a rousing success . . ." He forgot what he was doing. Stopped. Concentrated. "Oh yeah, that ciggie. Come on legs cooperate. Let's go."

Lester kept his cigarettes hidden. If Mother Jenkins found one, she'd dispose of it without a care. She despised them. The two had a constant hide-and-go-seek game of find the smokes. Once, to no avail, Lester even dipped his hand in the toilet to retrieve a swirling group of smokes that his mother had sent to their watery graves.

Mother Jenkins wasn't a big woman. Compared to her children, she was tiny. However, what she lacked in size, she more than made up for in her bold and undying convictions. God stood as number one in the faithful woman's life. Her family ranked a close second, and she grouped everything else at a distant third. Six days after her husband, Peter, turned forty-four, he took a bullet meant for someone else. A drive-by shooter killed him in a case of mistaken identity. This terrible and senseless act forced Mother Jenkins to raise her four offspring on her own. As the grief of her lost spouse inched further and further away, she fought and won almost every obstacle thrown in her path. She was a successful, caring, and loving parent when things could have easily fallen apart.

Mother Jenkins made giving her children "a life they could be proud of" her all-consuming priority. Unfortunately, she succeeded with only three of her four offspring.

Unlike Lester, his siblings believed in and followed the route their lone parent paved. She had a simple code of faith, for her kids to become "contributing, law-abiding citizens." Lester didn't feel this code of conduct applied to him. More to the point, he lacked the determination to become a member of that fraternity.

"That child will be the death of me," she often commented when discussing Lester.

The matriarch's constant efforts to help, goad, then guilt her son toward the "right direction" bounced off him like a ball smacked from a baseball bat. With little choice, she resigned herself to the fact that her baby boy was going nowhere fast. He couldn't keep a job when he got one, wouldn't volunteer at the church, didn't like going and rarely contributed around the house. The bleary-eyed boy came home at all hours of the night or sometimes not at all. His mother was a constant nervous wreck. She would be frantic until he would finally come stumbling in. Then she would get angry and lose her temper.

"No God-fearing contributing citizen would do what *you* do to your mother," the woman would constantly scold.

"I don't mean to worry you. But if you just went to bed, you wouldn't know I was still out," Lester said.

"Don't you use that smart tone with me, Lester James Jenkins," Mother Jenkins reprimanded. And so it went, on and on.

Before his death, Peter Jenkins had worked long and hard to provide his family with a good home. His wife was proud of this and tried to keep it in pristine condition. The woman spent hours on weekends cleaning her house and tending to her garden. It was the pride of the neighborhood. She would often remind Lester, "While you live under my roof, you will follow my rules and the rules of the Lord above!"

Lester could recite that tag line in his sleep.

Although Lester *tried* to avoid real criminal activities, like being in gangs or robbing people, he couldn't avoid situations that kept him from his mother's wrath. The boy continually darted in and out of Mother Jenkins' doghouse—never straying too far. And yet, with all the tomfoolery and shenanigans, there was *one* rule that even Lester wouldn't dare to break. No smoking his "ciggies" in the house. If she found even one in Lester's possession, the woman would go into a fit of rage. She believed that smoking was an evil created by the devil and perpetuated by his disciples, the tobacco manufacturers. Mother Jenkins' father died of lung cancer at forty-nine. She never forgot his suffering, and the suffering of his family during his illness. On the day he died, she vowed to go to any length to prevent her children from following that path.

If Lester was careless, and he'd leave a butt laying around, his mother would grab him by the ear, march him into the bathroom, and make him watch her flush the obscene remnant down the toilet. "I'll save your life one butt at a time if I'm forced to," she'd proclaim in *that* voice when reprimanding Lester

Usually, the boy was too high to put up much of a verbal fight about cigarettes, which he would lose anyway. Once the woman started up about the offending butts, Lester would stick his tail between his legs and shuffle quietly off to his room, his mom still postulating as he went. Once there, he would go to a stash in one of his many hiding spots, grab his smoke, and then scurry outside to light up. Even in a fog, he was smart enough to stay far from the house—his mother could barge into the yard with a broom in hand.

The drug-addled boy's cravings that ill-fated day in February were now at a fevered pitch. He was determined to have a ciggie, no matter what. He grabbed his jacket, intending to head out once he got one from his stash, and struggled to put it on. It was like watching someone wrestle an octopus. After finally winning the match and getting the coat on, he then headed toward his door. The boy moved like a rubber slinky to the door frame and ran his hand along the top. Shit.

Nothing.

The hiding place was bare.

A smoker's instinct seized him as he looped out of his room down to the hall bathroom. The wobbly Jenkins pulled on the medicine cabinet door, almost ripping the mirrored flange from its hinges, and grabbed an old suppository box off the upper shelf. The paper container had been empty for years except for the occasional cig Lester stashed there. Now in a complete panic, he ripped the top open. "Jesus Christ," he moaned. "Fucking empty. Who the hell smoked all my butts?"

Steadying his teetering body on the porcelain sink, he squeezed his eyes shut and concentrated for a long moment. He racked his impaired and limited working brain cells trying to decide what to do. Then brilliance hit him—his bedroom's heating vent! Lester spun around, bounced off the bathroom doorjamb, and then made his way back to his room. He lunged to the floor next to his bed. It was an unsteady journey, but he made it.

The concealed gem of tobacco, probably over a year old, should be in the vent next to his bed. An old, stale ciggie is still a ciggie, and that's all that mattered. Up 'til that moment, he'd forgotten this stash. "Shit, I must have secret stashes all around the room—if only I could remember where they are," he said to no one as he scanned the room through blood-shot eyes.

He bent down and peered into the vent. His body wobbled, and his balance skewed, but so far, so good. Four screws secured the vent. They were too small to grab, but he tried to turn them by hand with no success.

Lester leaned over to his bedside table and opened a drawer. As he rummaged through, he found a small screwdriver in the back. He marveled at his good fortune, and then attacked the task. The four screws came out easily. "Praise the Lord," Jenkins said in a mocking tone. He pulled the cover up and *voila*, the perfect hiding spot. God, he needed that cig. Making a mental note not to forget this perfect hiding spot—he congratulated himself on his good fortune. His problem solved.

Jittering with anticipation, he thrust his hand into the vent teetered and lost his balance. Before he could stop his momentum, his head plowed straight down, hitting the floor with a loud thwack. He didn't move. It was as if he had fallen face-first into quicksand.

With one arm in the vent and the other along his body and behind him, Lester found himself wedged facedown between the wall and his bed with his ass sticking up like a bicycle rack. One entering his room might think he had fallen asleep on his knees. His eyes had instinctively closed as his head hit the floor and seemed glued shut. He also couldn't get his motor functions to engage correctly and remained in this position for several minutes. After a few seconds, though it seemed much longer, Lester reasoned, *maybe, I'll just sleep it off here.* Normally, he might do just that. But, man, he wanted that cig, bad, bad, bad.

Finally, when he worked up the ability to react to the situation, Lester forced his eyes open. He blinked away the haze and then concentrated on getting out of the wedge. The boy repositioned himself, took in a deep breath, and raised up his head.

A line of drool hung from his lower lip like a swinging trapeze. He tried opening and closing his mouth to get rid of the swaying spit, but the drool just swayed and wiggled like an overcooked string of spaghetti. Lester couldn't understand why. After a moment of wasted thought, he blinked away the distraction and left it hanging. There were other, more critical tasks to be completed.

With a Herculean effort, Lester got his hands beneath his body then pushed himself up into a sitting position. At last, the vent sat directly in his line of sight. In eager anticipation and with the drool now hanging in a fine line from his chin to the floor, Lester reached into the vent. He felt around touched something hard. Didn't feel like a cigarette. He touched the object again, *Holy shit*! He jerked his hand back in alarm.

Grimacing, he stared at the opening, gathered his nerve, and reached back in and fingered the object. *That can't be what I think it is, can it?* Maybe he had put some ciggies in a container. A cool, metal container to keep his ciggies fresh. Convinced of this theory, he smiled in victory and pulled the object out. *What the fuck?* Through bleary eyes, he realized that it was only a black rock, a stupid fucking black rock. Why on God's earth had he hidden a rock in his vent? He reached in once more. Nothing.

Leaning back against the wall, Lester dropped the rock into his jacket pocket in defeat. He rubbed his palms up and down his face trying to pump blood to his brain. He needed a new idea. After a few moments, which may have been as much as five minutes—time distorted when Lester was high—Jenkins realized it was useless. If there were any ciggies in his room, he sure as hell would not find them. Not today, anyway.

The desperate boy resigned himself to initiate his last resort. He would walk to the store and buy some butts. God, he didn't want to do it. It was far. He was too messed up. What choice did he have? It took a massive effort, but somehow, he raised himself off the floor, spun toward his dresser, and in one staggering move, grabbed his wallet and dropped it into his jacket pocket.

Heading for the front door, he stopped only long enough to yell goodbye to Mother Jenkins. Engrossed in *The Wheel* with Vanna and Pat, Mother's favorite, Lester couldn't be sure she heard him. *Just as well.* He plunged through the door to the streets.

Singing, though not remembering the words to any particular song, Lester stumbled the approximate half mile to Miller's Liquor Store. By this point, the boy experienced no pain. The heroin tap he injected and the four or five hits he took off Jamaican weed brought on stoner's eyes, which were mere slits. The cold air caused snot to run from his nose, though he paid it no mind. Lester was undeterred.

Walking to Miller's, which should have taken a mere fifteen minutes, took almost forty-five. The full moon made it easier to see, but at one point he ended up on a side street, heading the wrong way. It baffled him at first, but he soon backtracked and found his way back in the direction he needed.

Finally, Lester strolled through the front door of the liquor store, oblivious to whether other patrons were shopping or not, and went right up to the attendant. "Gimme a pack of Marlboro's," he said. The words seemed to drag out, thick on his tongue. As the attendant turned toward the cigarette rack, Lester reached into his jacket for his wallet. He pulled out two items stashed there and stared at them. He sat the wallet down and looked at the black rock. *What the hell? What was a rock doing in his pocket?* But was it a rock? He gaped with unfocused eyes at the object, concentrating all his intensity on the thing. Gawking in surprise, he finally realized he was holding a small handgun.

He stared at the gun in total confusion. He'd put a rock in his pocket, hadn't he? While the attendant searched for the Marlboro's, Lester studied the twenty-two-caliber firearm in bafflement, turning it over in his hands. With complete incomprehension to his actions, Lester pointed the gun toward the attendant and pulled the trigger. The small caliber projectile rocketed unseen into the man's back, and as if his skeleton had instantly dissolved, he dropped like in a crumpled heap on the floor.

"Hey, what are you doing? Give me my Marlboro's man," Lester muttered as he leaned over to see where the man had gone.

Though the clerk was half hidden by the counter, Lester could see he wasn't moving.

The drug-laden kid caught site of a bright red splotch forming in the middle the man's back, but even then, it wasn't registering. Lester shrugged his shoulders. He was confused. "Hey man, what are you doing down there? And what about my cigarettes?" Lester begged. A few seconds more of silence was all he could take. Fed up, he decided to walk around the counter for a better look. When he cleared the corner, he noticed that the cash register was open, and the till was loaded with green.

This seemed bizarre and too strange to be true. But that fucking cash was right there. It stared at him, beckoning as if alive and alluring. He stepped over the dead clerk's legs, not even realizing what they were, and reached into the till. After fumbling with the spring-loaded clips, he removed all the money from each slot. Closing the drawer, he moved from around the counter and slowly strolled out of the store not even bothering to retrieve the pack of Marlboro's he'd come for.

A few minutes after Lester left, David Smith, a neighborhood resident and frequenter of Millers, walked in. The man headed straight to the refrigerated beer section, not even glancing toward the counter, and grabbed two eighteen packs of Bud Light. This was a customary weekend purchase for the somewhat pudgy, slightly balding, single man of forty.

On Smith's way to pay, he tossed two bags of chips on the beer before winding his way toward the cash register. Not seeing Larry the clerk, he slid his purchase on the counter. After waiting a few seconds, he scanned the store and called out, "Hey Larry? Dude, where the hell are you? Hey man, it's me Dave. Larry?"

After waiting several moments, Smith walked around the counter and gasped—Larry Bishop lay sprawled on the floor with a blood-stained bullet hole in his back.

It took all of ten minutes for a patrol car to show, followed by paramedics less than a 5 minutes later. Unfortunately, this quick arrival was far too late; the bullet had severed the man's spine, and he had probably died during his plummet to the floor.

Chapter 10

A PICTURE IS WORTH A THOUSAND WORDS

Around 8:30 on the night of the clerk's shooting, Detective Nick Cooper received a message regarding the robbery and the store worker's fatality. Cooper's first call went out to his partner, Derek Anderson, who Cooper instructed to meet at the liquor store.

Anderson, first at the scene, provided Cooper with a recap upon his arrival. "You're not going to believe it. According to the uniform, the perp was not only caught on film by the store's camera, but he left his wallet and ID on the counter."

"No shit," Cooper said as he followed Anderson into the store.

After viewing the victim's body, they headed to the office to check the security tapes.

"He's fucking blitzed," the officer running the tape said.

"Sure looks like it. I'm not even sure he knows he killed someone. Watch his reaction after the gun goes off. He seems oblivious and confused as he watches the clerk fall," Anderson said.

"Let me see the wallet," Cooper asked. The street cop lifted up an evidence bag with the wallet and offered a list of items found inside the worn-out leather billfold, including the man's ID. Another cop knew the neighborhood and other surrounding areas. He informed Cooper that three uniformed cops went to a location near the house to keep an eye on open, but far enough away from the kid's home as not to arouse suspicion.

Cooper and his team pulled up to the end of the block just north of the address, right before 9:44 p.m. Officers Johnson, Burns, and Dardin were at an excellent vantage point. The most experienced of the three, Officer Carl Dardin, told the group that the house remained quiet, and no one came or left since they'd arrived. There was a light on but no movement.

Cooper and Anderson surveyed the area before instructing the men as to their plan to move forward. After donning protective body armor, the team made their way up the block toward the Jenkins' house. Taking it slow, they walked up the opposite side of the street. They kept a low profile, hiding behind a line of cars parked next to the curb. About halfway to their quarry, the sound of rushing footsteps startled the team. They spun around, guns drawn.

Dardin, with a shotgun from his trunk, aimed the weapon into the darkness, finger tensed on the trigger. A six-foot chain-link fence stood about ten feet from where they hunkered down. Though none of the men could make out what headed their way, they could hear that whatever was behind that fence was coming toward them fast.

In a flash, a massive German Shepherd charged the fence, growling and snarling—white teeth snapping. The dog barked like an animal gone mad with rabies. Burns jumped back and rammed into Johnson. "Mother Fucker," Burns groaned through gritted teeth. He glanced apologetically at Johnson and then looked at the rest of the team. Each man had noticeably tensed and likely thinking the same thing—shoot the fucking mutt. They moved on.

Continuing down the sidewalk, they arrived in front of Lester Jenkins' house. From here, the group crouched behind an old blue Buick. Huddled in a small circle, they scanned the house and the surrounding properties. All seemed quiet.

"Derek, I'm going to make my way around the left side of the house to the backyard. I'll survey the situation, and if all is well, I'll circle to the right side," Cooper said. "If Lester is in the house, realizes that he left his wallet at the scene, he may try to run. When we knock on the door and announce that we are the police, he may try to run. Whatever; I'll be ready for him."

Cooper appraised the street. He marveled at the well-kept house. Way more presentable than the other homes on the block. The streetlight on the corner of their property cast a glow on the lawn, which was as plush as an elegant carpet. On the property, a few trees grew tall and statuesque. Manicured flower beds, on either side of the front door, added a nice transition to the porch. Someone apparently took a lot of pride in this small but immaculate home. The team reasoned that person probably wasn't Lester Jenkins, which meant that someone else probably resided there too.

An ornate wrought iron screen door protected the wooden front door. The main entry door painted fire-engine red, looked to be a solid structure. It contained a conventional doorknob and deadbolt. Four wide steps led to a landing area with several large bushes bordering each side.

The team's strategy was straightforward. Cooper would position himself with a direct sightline of the back door. One uniform would flank him at the left rear corner and one at the right front of the house. If Jenkins tried to climb out of a window, this positioning would allow the two men a clear view of each side of the house. Derek would walk up to the door. Officer Dardin would cover him by the bushes next to the porch. All areas of escape—covered.

Once confident of their assignments, the rear and side teams set out. Not wanting to alert Jenkins, if he was watching from a window, each man used his small tactical flashlight as little as possible. Cooper and Johnson made their way down the left side of the house. Burns dashed over to his assigned location on the right.

When Cooper and Johnson arrived at the rear of the building, they surveyed the backyard. The area looked empty except for a well-used wooden picnic table and two lawn chairs. Cooper nodded at Johnson and then made an ample arc path toward a large shrub next to a chain-link fence surrounding the backyard. The fence stood about four feet tall with no gate or exit that Cooper could see. He looked at his watch and then gave the predetermined flashlight signal to Burns who then signaled Anderson and Dardin.

When Anderson reached the bottom of the front steps, Dardin moved down behind the bush at the left. This position gave him the best view of the door. Anderson glanced around. All clear. Feeling confident, he headed up the stairs and knocked on the door.

Chapter 11

REALITY REALLY IS A BITCH

Having arrived home just moments before the three uniforms, and still in a drugged fog, though the drugs were losing their purpose, Lester walked into the house and straight to his room. As if he hadn't already lived the previous efforts earlier that day, he reached up and checked the top of the doorframe. Nothing. Started for the bathroom, took two steps when *it* crashed into his mind. The fragment of a thought—from a dream? A scene in a movie? *A déjà vu?*

Stopped in his tracks, he vigorously rubbed his face. He thought for a moment. A memory materialized. He cautiously slipped his hand into his jacket pocket as if a poisonous snake resided there. He plucked the contents out. A wad of cash. Several bills fell to the ground. *Where did I get all this money? Where is my wallet? And the rock?*

Lester reached into his other pocket. He pulled out the metal object. His eyes went wide, and he began to tremble.

It was a gun.

And.

He had a bad feeling that he'd done something terrible.

In the inner recesses of his mind, he caught the sound of a dog barking, but it didn't register loud enough to grab the boy's attention. He dropped the entire wad and backed away as if the bills were radioactive. He banged up against the doorjamb and almost fell. After regaining his balance, he stood still and stared at the gun in horror. Lester Jenkins began to cry.

"What the fuck have I done?" he sobbed. An image, like smoke, was there then gone. The clerk, lifeless, on the floor. "Oh God no—please," Lester moaned.

He stayed in place—for what seemed an eternity—trying to figure out what happened and what he should do. His mind raced. The air seemed flat, heavy. It was getting harder to breathe. What would mother Jenkins say? He thought about calling for her. She would fix things. Lester's heart throbbed like a drummer on speed. *No, I should run. Pack clothes. Take off. But where?*

Lester's head spun. It was challenging to stay focused. *Where the hell can I go?* Uncle Jack lived in Florida. *Yeah, I could go to his house! Shit, I've hated the bastard ever since he didn't show for Dad's funeral.* Every time Uncle Jack's name came up, Mother Jenkins would say, "The man's a worthless piece of human trash. Wouldn't even come to his only brother's funeral."

She despised him.

"Nope, not going to that dick's house," Lester said in a throttled sob.

He considered the option of Aunt Ida's house. He liked her all right, and she liked him, at least he believed she did. She lived only two blocks away, crap, that wasn't far enough. For sure, the cops would find him hiding out with his mother's sister.

"I've got it! Pure genius," Lester said with a snap of his fingers.

That's when he heard the hammering on the front door.

"Lester? Someone's banging on the door. It's late. Who is it?" Mother Jenkins called, her voice dreamy. "It better not be that Donny Johnson. I told you he's not welcome here." She was in her bed watching QVC. Sleep kept pawing at her as she floated in and out of consciousness.

Lester didn't answer her. He couldn't. His voice had vanished, and his feet felt packed in cement. Tears filled his eyes, and his vision went blurry. The boy thought he might be having a heart attack.

Another thudding on the door, louder this time.

"POLICE!"

The word hit like a Taser, jolting him almost straight. Lester's legs loosened from the concrete bindings. He stumbled into the living room, through the kitchen, and toward the back door.

Cooper stood ready. This kid was going to be a runner. He could feel it in his bones.

Lester didn't disappoint.

The back door burst open, and Jenkins flew out, stumbled over the steps, and crashed to the ground.

"POLICE," Derek yelled again from the front porch, his voice echoing through the small wood framed house.

Lester landed only a few yards from where Cooper hid, giving the detective the chance to jump out and subdue Jenkins before he rose back to his feet. Raising his revolver, Cooper hollered, "THIS IS THE POLICE, DON'T MOVE. I HAVE A GUN AIMED AT YOUR FUCKING HEAD!"

Lester would have none of it. As if he hadn't heard a word, he made a bold, if not clumsy, attempt to stand up and flee. Half-crawling, half-lurching, the now sobering Jenkins tried to head toward the fence and hopefully freedom. Cooper holstered his pistol and ran at the staggering man. Leaving his feet as he dove, he tackled Lester with little effort. But once he got the lithe boy to the ground, Lester began to struggle. The tall and stringy man, a good fifty pounds lighter than Cooper, was unbelievably strong.

After several seconds of maneuvering, Cooper finally got the advantage and rolled Jenkins on his stomach. The detective positioned himself on top of the wriggling man's back with the full weight of his body holding him firmly in place.

Cooper pulled his cuffs from his belt and got Jenkins' hands in position to secure him. As he closed the shackle, a noise came from behind.

Chapter 12

THE SHOOTOUT

Derek banged on the door a third time. No answer. "I'm pretty sure I heard someone inside scream something," the officer said. Dardin understood the inference and joined Anderson on the porch. The two men leaned in and readied their shoulders for the charge when a gunshot rang out from the rear of the house, and then another.

In an effort that rivaled a choreographed dance move, Derek spun to his right, ran down the porch, and sprang on to the lawn in full stride. He yelled at Dardin to stay in place in case Jenkins came out the front and to call for additional backup and an ambulance. He met Officer Burns at his position, and the two raced toward the backyard.

At the rear of the house, Derek stopped, readied his pistol, and peered around the corner. Sprawled on the ground about twenty feet apart, he could make out two bodies.

"POLICE! DON'T MOVE," Derek yelled.

"Derek, it's me, Coop . . . I've been shot."

"The other body?"

"Not sure of their condition, pretty sure they're dead."

"You, there on the ground. Don't move. I've got a gun trained on you," Derek yelled. There was no reply and no movement.

Crouching and with his gun pulled, Derek called out to the others for their status and got an all clear from both Burns and Dardin. He made his way over to

Cooper while keeping his gun aimed at the guy laying close by. The other cops went to the body.

"What happened? Are you all right? Jesus Christ, what the fuck happened? Where'd Lester get you?"

"First, Lester didn't shoot me," Cooper groaned. "I had him on the ground. Was cuffing him when I got shot. I rolled off Lester, and the kid jumped up and scooted over the fence. He ran off somewhere to the left, I think." Nick nodded in the direction he believed Jenkins fled.

"After he came out of the house, I tackled him to the ground. I heard movement behind me, thought it might be you or one of the others. By the time I realized it wasn't, it was too late, a bullet had hit me.

"I fell off of Lester and pulled my gun. The light from behind the shooter made it impossible for me to tell who it was, but I could tell that they were still aiming at me. I fired back."

"Where'd he get you?"

"Squarely in my right ass cheek. The whole right side of my leg is numb, and I can't get up."

"Stay still. Help will be here soon."

Johnson and Burns stood over the body laying a few feet away. The two were just standing there not moving.

"Derek, go find out what's going on," Cooper said.

Anderson walked purposely toward the others. At the same moment, Dardin came through the back door. Stopping at the top of the steps, he stared at the body on the ground.

The detective turned back to Cooper and in a small, somewhat strained voice said, "The victim is a woman. I'd say in her sixties. You shot her dead center in the chest. This isn't good, not good at all."

Two hours after his tussle with Cooper, the cops nabbed Lester asleep under a trampoline in a neighbor's backyard. The family dog had been barking like mad, and one of the children looked out and saw Lester curled into a ball on the ground. The little girl, maybe four or five years old, calmly walked into her parent's bedroom. "Mama, a man is sleeping under our trampoline."

The father didn't believe her at first, but because the dog was barking out of control, he checked it out. The father spotted the intruder; called the cops, and then kept an eye on the sleeping man. Lester didn't wake until the cops pulled him from his makeshift bed some fifteen minutes later. Cooper's handcuffs dangled from one wrist, the gun he used to shoot the liquor store attendant was still in his pocket.

They pronounced Mother Jenkins dead at the scene. Cooper went by ambulance to the hospital where they extracted a bullet from his right butt cheek. The doctor reported that he would be okay in time, but that he might end up with a small limp. Cooper did, for a while anyway, and with the bad press from the case, the two issues would be his ticket to retirement—whether he wanted it or not.

The official story went like this. The investigative team surmised that Lester's mother watched as Lester ran past her bedroom and headed for the back door. The loud banging on the front door startled the woman, and she grabbed a loaded twenty-two pistol from a drawer near her bed stand. She kept the weapon at hand ever since her husband's killing several years earlier.

After retrieving the gun, she rushed in the direction her son went. Once she got to the door, she saw Lester fighting with a man. Thinking her boy was under attack, she aimed the pistol and pulled the trigger. Blind as she was, she made a lucky shot hitting Cooper and not her boy. Not so fortunate in the long run, the woman now lay dead, and Detective Nick Cooper of the Chicago Police had killed her.

The media had a field day with accusatory headlines, and the NAACP blanketed the department with complaints and protest while asking for the offending detective's badge. The headlines read, "Officer Kills Woman in Wild Shootout." In the eyes of the world, Cooper shot a "defenseless" old black woman. Although he was also wounded, the fallout from ongoing racial tension in the city made Cooper a scapegoat.

Superintendent Armstrong gave Cooper a desk position hoping things would pass. Nick knew that things would never be the same, and it was only a matter of time before the decision to move on became the right one.

Chapter 13

LOU'S PHONE CALL

March 16, 1997

The cab pulled up to the curb in front of the Ambassador. Cooper paid the driver, got out, and let out a deep, stress-relieving exhale. The hot and sticky air reminded the ex-cop of the last time he and Lou were here, which didn't make the moment any more pleasant.

"Great, part two of the *Final Days of our Lives* show picks up right where we left off," Cooper groaned to no one.

Cooper eyed the entrance and considered catching another cab home. "What am I doing to myself? I might as well be diving into an alligator-infested pond. Stupid, stupid, stupid."

"Coop, you look as if you're having second thoughts." a voice called from the top of the steps.

Nancy Bradshaw emerged from the shadows. The moment felt eerily reminiscent of a 1940's film *noir* movie set as the lighting gave her a gray-toned appearance. Even her pace as she came down the steps seemed celluloid and her strides—slow motion. "I'm in a goddamn detective movie," he muttered. "Any minute now Humphrey Bogart and Sydney Greenstreet are going to pop out asking for the Maltese Falcon."

Clad in black, Bradshaw wore three-inch spiked heels, dark stockings, and a black fedora. As she came into the light, Nick fell into those same mesmerizing eyes he loved. After a moment of dumbstruck hesitation, he realized she was even more striking than the ingrained image in his mind remembered.

"The single life agrees with you," he said not thinking before speaking.

"Ouch, that didn't take long." She greeted him with a surprise kiss on the lips. Nothing extravagant, only a peck, but even *that* sent an electric current through his veins. "Thanks for coming; I wouldn't have called you . . ." She hesitated for a moment. The look on her face made it clear that she didn't mean it the way it sounded. "What I mean is, something weird is happening, and I needed to discuss it with you in person." Bradshaw grimaced then said, "Can we go inside? The humidity is awful."

"Sure, of course." Nick agreed, and they headed up the steps to the hotel entrance. They went through the doors and climbed the few stairs up to the landing area where the reservation desk stood. As they turned into the hallway, he glanced at the photographs of famous people hanging on the wall. Humphrey Bogart and Lauren Bacall's picture was there. *Weird,* Cooper thought as he reminisced about his Bogart thoughts moments earlier.

I should get the hell out of here. The urge to run made his knees ache. All his many murder cases and investigations were a breeze compared to this.

As the two entered the Pump Room, the first thing he noticed was Eddy behind the bar in the same style of uniform he'd always worn.

"Well, if it isn't two of my all-time favorites. Where have you two been? Can I assume we will see you as regulars again?" Eddy asked, a genuine expression of fondness on his face.

Both Bradshaw and Cooper stared at him, not answering.

"Oh-kay . . ." Eddy said in a singsong voice. With an exaggerated grimace, he returned to cleaning the bar top.

Cooper made his way over to the maître d' of hôtel who sat them within minutes. Sammy Franks, the Pump Room *sommelier*, came to the table and said, "Oh, not you two again! I assumed I ran you off a long time ago."

"We've been going through withdrawals without you too. Lou and I simply had to come back one more time. It's been terrible. We've missed that lovable personality of yours," Cooper asserted as he rolled his eyes.

"Yes, of course," Sammy replied with the same inflection, "I have that effect on people. I'll send a waitress over to take your order. Enjoy." With that, he walked away. After he traveled a few feet, he stopped and turned back, cocked his head in thought, and smiled. Then off he went.

"Strangely enough, I do miss that crotchety old geezer," Nancy said to Nick who grinned and nodded.

After ordering cocktails, both still bourbon and water fans, Cooper broke the ice, "So, something must be really bugging you for you to set up a meeting."

"Nick, this isn't a meeting," she said, with hurt in her tone. "Yes, something is disturbing me, but I also wanted to see you. Too much time has passed and, well, I've missed you."

As she finished her last statement, Cooper stared at her. Her eyes seemed to confirm it, and he had missed her too.

"*Nick*, huh? . . ." he drew the word out. "That may be the first time you've used "Nick" and not "Coop" or "Cooper" since the first time we met. What's *really* going on here?"

"Sorry, I'm nervous. I don't know why I called you that." She tapped her scarlet-painted fingernails on the table. "I suppose it's because this is so weird. You know, us seeing each other after so long, and I guess I got flustered and...

Was she pleading? Jesus, it seemed so.

Come on, don't make this any harder than it is," Nancy implored.

"Ok. Sorry. Tell me what's going on," Cooper said as he took a sip of his newly delivered drink.

"I got this call a couple of days ago from a guy who told my assistant that his name was Marshall Kent and that he was a friend of yours. He said you'd asked him to phone me because of an urgent personal matter. Jill explained the caller's message, so I told her to ring him through."

"Did you know—?" Cooper asked.

"Not at first. I didn't figure it out until after I hung up. After I mulled over the conversation for a few minutes, I realized the caller used one of your character's names as an alias."

"So, you read my latest book," Cooper asked in mocked surprise.

"I've read them all," she confessed. "And you knew I would." Nancy stuck out her tongue at Cooper with that comment before going on. "The fact that I recognized the fake name was why I didn't contact you in the first place. I blew it off thinking the guy was some crackpot.

And then yesterday, a man walked up behind me while I stood in line at Starbucks and in the same voice and accent as the man on the call, tells me that 'number one' would happen in two days and to be ready because I'm 'number four.' I turned around, and this hulking broad-shouldered man was heading toward the exit. He kept his back toward me, so I didn't catch his face. When he reached the door . . . and this scared me . . . he raised his hand and opened one finger at a time until all five were showing. And then he vanished out the door."

"What do you mean the same voice and accent?"

"Well, the voice was deep in tone with a French accent."

"No kidding? That's interesting."

"Why?"

"I was recently at a book signing and a man with a deep voice and a French accent approached me and introduced himself as Marshall Kent."

Cooper related the whole encounter including the hand gestures and then added, "This has to be the same guy . . . you didn't see his face at all?"

"No, he never turned around."

"What did he say on the phone call?"

"Well after a five-minute line of bullshit regarding his relationship with you, he stopped mid-sentence and said, 'Well, this is boring. Let's cut the crap so I can tell you why I called. Seven years ago, Nick Cooper ruined my life. I lost my career, my home life, and my money. Now, I'm going to return the favor. After I've killed everyone important to him, I will erase his life.

Number one has been advised of their fate, but he is not taking my warning seriously. Don't make that same mistake. I'll be informing the other two when the time is right. I'm telling you now because our party will be special. I wanted you to be thinking about our rendezvous starting today.

The line went silent for a second, and then he finished by saying, 'Don't forget, you're number four,' and then he hung up.

Like I said, I blew the call off, but as I went over his comments in my head, and the fact he used Marshall Kent as his name, well . . . the whole thing began to unnerve me. Then, after the coffee shop meeting and the five-finger thing, I realized in your most recent book that the killer numbered his victims. Victims knew where they stood in the numerical pecking order. Then he killed each one in succession. At that point, I admitted to being freaked out and needed to talk with you."

"Did he say anything else? Any other names, time frames, or places, anything at all?"

Nancy looked at Cooper and realized that he was taking her concerns seriously.

"Coop, am I in danger?"

PART 3

Chapter 1

NUMBER ONE

March 17, 1997

"Honey, I'm home." Derek Anderson came through the door expecting a tornado of activity. "The kid's bikes are in the yard again, and there's a pile of toys on the front porch. I thought we decided those two monsters would start to clean up after themselves.

The house was silent. *That's odd.*

"Honey?"

Where the heck is everyone? He went to the fridge and grabbed a saran-wrapped chicken leg from last night's dinner. "Beautiful," he said under his breath as he absconded with the fried delicacy. He unwrapped the leg and took a bite before grabbing the container of iced tea from the fridge door. *Red plastic cups stacked on the counter—that'll work.* He filled one to the brim.

His wife made her famous fresh-brewed tea a few times a week. She would take a gallon glass container and fill it with filtered water, drop four large tea bags in, and place the pitcher on the front porch. In the direct searing sunlight, the tea brewed naturally. Did this process make any difference in the flavor? His wife believed so. "That's how the essence of the tea is enhanced," she'd say. But to him, tea was tea.

He ate his snack and lost himself in the events of the day.

The Chicago Police Department repeatedly decorated Anderson, a twenty-year veteran, for his work and bravery. The detective rarely stepped over the line with anyone and his peers liked and respected the man for it. The affection and loyalty shown to Anderson were never more apparent than the day of his retirement party. A veritable who's who from the city showed up, and law enforcement personnel from many districts and positions crowded the room.

The precinct gang prepared an impromptu roasting for him and collected a fat going-away envelope. Twenty-eight hundred bucks. Some guys close to him even brought along some excellent parting gifts. A whoopee cushion, hanging dice for his car mirror, and a fake mustache with glasses from John Elkland, the Medical Examiner. To the delight of all, Anderson donned the mustache and glasses for the rest of the celebration.

Anderson opened a double-boxed and triple-tapped container of gag gifts from Captain Lewis. After finally wrestling the package open, he pulled out a bottle of Geritol, jet-black hair dye, and a box of Depends. The presents brought tons of laughs, especially since Lewis outdated Anderson by at least ten years and probably possessed at least two of the items at home anyway. The two funniest things he received were the cane and portable potty seat that Detective Bob Johnson supplied. That they belonged to his grandfather and were "slightly" used gave everyone a moan and a great laugh. The day was a fitting and almost perfect way to say goodbye except for one glaring question—where was Nick Cooper?

Anderson enjoyed his partnership with Cooper. Coop, as everyone on the force called his ex-partner, was the main reason he'd become the cop he was. The ex-detective-turned-author taught him the most essential thing in police work; *trust your instincts.* "You've got the nose of a goddamn bloodhound," Anderson used to say to Coop. Whenever Anderson second-guessed himself on a case, Coop would put his finger on his own nose and tap the side gently a few times. This subtle reminder was a simple nod for Anderson to believe in his instincts. It took time to garner that internal faith, but when he finally did, the practice made him a highly efficient cop—fair but determined.

If Cooper hadn't been caught up in that shit-storm after shooting the widow Jenkins, Anderson believed that his friend would be running the department today. If that had happened, he wouldn't be leaving the force until they both retired at a ripe old age. The legal hierarchy had hung Coop out to dry. The departmental wrangling to distance itself after the shooting was hard for Coop to get past. Anger ricocheted through him. He quit. Vowed he'd never step back into that office again. Not as a cop.

Now, Anderson had retired. Though he was still relatively young, he believed he was doing the right thing. The real decision boiled down to which family to support, his own or the team at the force. The choice wasn't hard. Right after the birth of his second child, a suspect pulled a knife on Anderson. He had only suffered minor wounds. His wife, however, pitched a fit.

In Barb Anderson's mind, the father of her children faced perilous situations every time he walked out their front door. That fear drove her crazy. "This is my job," he'd argue. "You knew the perils of the occupation when we got married. Nothing has changed."

"I remember the man who claimed that his family would always come first," she'd shoot back. Tell me, who comes first now? When that next knife or bullet comes your way and kills you, what then? What would you like me to tell your children when we visit your grave each week?"

Eventually, the two came together and decided that he would retire as soon as he became eligible for a decent pension, and he could find another job.

From that day forward, the Andersons stashed away money—as much as they could—and planned for the day he could start a new career. That day had come. They had a decent savings account, in case of a "rainy day," and Derek had found a new gig.

During the latter part of his career, Anderson befriended two private detectives who also used to work in the department. The men now operated a company that offered security services to individuals and corporations. With new high-profile clients on board, the firm started looking for additional staff, and Detective Anderson topped their list. They knew he wanted to leave the public sector and offered him a deal he couldn't refuse.

With all the arrangements made, he looked forward to entering the next chapter of his life. With three days left on the force, he'd take it nice and easy. Once he walked out of his precinct, he'd no longer be a cop. It seemed surreal.

He'd planned for a much-deserved vacation. The family was heading to Disney World in Orlando. When he returned, he would jump headfirst into the new job. The memories of his time on the force? They'd come in fond but remote daydreams.

Coming out of the haze of his contemplation, Anderson looked at his watch. "Barb, are you home?" No answer. *She must be home. What the hell is going on? The front door was unlocked. His wife never left without locking all the doors—never.* "Barb?" he shouted. A noise upstairs caught his attention. Dinner with the family was at six p.m. Antonio's for pasta and pizza. He was taking Barb and the kids to celebrate his retirement. They must be getting ready and couldn't hear him. That had to be it.

He tossed the chicken leg bone in the trash and headed upstairs. Whistling, he slid first into his bedroom and removed his gun and holster. He stashed the gun in his safe and hung the holster on a hook attached to the closet door.

A shuffling noise came from his son's room. Smiling at the thought of surprising his nine-year-old, Anderson snuck down the hall to his son's bedroom and popped into the room. "Boo!" Anderson barked, hands raised in a claw like fashion. Oddly, no one was there. He frowned and began to turn when something slammed into the back of his head. Anderson's world went black and he crumpled to the floor in a heap.

Derek's eyes flittered open some forty-five minutes later, though begrudgingly. At first, he had no idea where he was. The room he was in was dark with only the slightest amount of light allowing him any vision at all. As the cobwebs cleared and his eyes adjusted to the dimness, he looked down and realized he was tied to one of his kitchen chairs. He also saw that he was naked except for his boxers. *What the fuck was going on?* He peered into the darkness and made out the kitchen table and the plant that hung in front of the kitchen window. Other than that, it was nearly impossible to see anything but outlines of objects in the room.

His head pounded. He tried to wiggle out of the chair to no avail. He was about to call out when the small light above the stove clicked on. Anderson blinked at the sudden brightness and then focused on a man hovering near the light. He seemed to be a tad taller than six feet, looked to be around forty-five or fifty years old with patches of gray at his temples, and age wrinkles at his eyes. The man was dressed in black from head to toe.

"Bonjour, Detective Anderson. Thanks for being home on time. It's always nice when a plan starts on schedule," the man with a French accent said.

"Who the hell are you, and what the fuck is going on? Where are my wife and kids?" Anderson shot back.

"Tsk, tsk, Officer Anderson. Is that any way to talk to a house guest?" the man replied, his attitude smug, though not exactly threatening. "You should be politer, especially in your current circumstances."

"Fuck you," Anderson said. "AGAIN, where is my family? I promise you, if you've harmed them in any way, you will regret it!"

The man approached Derek, a thin smile parading across his face. The grin made his face look unworldly, crazy even. He stood close and stared down at the bound cop. Anderson could feel the light waft of his breath on his face. Without warning, the man swung his enormous hand across the detective's face. Derek never saw it coming. Anderson's head snapped to the left, and he let out a cry of agony at the crushing blow. Just as quickly, his adrenaline kicked in. Anderson swung his head back toward the hovering man, glaring up at his attacker with a look of rage enveloping his face.

The Frenchman showed no emotion. His breathing remained steady and smooth. "Monsieur, perhaps we should start over, *n'est pas?*" he said in a matter-of-fact tone. "First, your family is fine, I assure you of that. Your wife received a call that you were running late and, per your instructions, grabbed little Tommy and Alice and headed to Antonio's Restaurant. You would meet them there. She seemed a little confused that you weren't calling but knows how the cop business works, right? She said to tell you they would see you there. She's a very trusting woman. Sounded quite pleasant on the phone too. Much more polite than you; you should take a lesson."

"Again, fuck you," Anderson yelled as he strained against the ropes. Another rush of adrenaline raced through his system with the veins in his neck bulging in response. The bonds remained securely fastened. His efforts, fruitless. Anderson took in a deep breath of resignation before saying through clenched teeth, "What do you want, and why am I tied up? What the hell is this all about?"

"What I want is revenge. You're tied up so that I retain your full cooperation in helping me achieve that revenge. You know, you made a mistake by not heeding my warning a few days ago. Because you ignored me, this will be way too easy—no challenge at all, a pity in fact."

The intruder walked into the darkness, vanishing like a specter. After a moment that seemed to last for several nerve-grinding minutes, he reemerged into the light. Like a plotting villain about to tie his victim to the tracks, he moved in and out of the light several more times, making the scene even more surreal. With his sly, shit-eating grin and glazed glassy-eyed look, the man appeared to revel in the activities. Anderson's experience with sociopaths told him that what lay behind those eyes was an evil emptiness. He knew he was in trouble and needed to find a way out of this man's insane plan, whatever it was.

After a few more paces, the assailant stopped and made a slow turn. He tilted his head slightly and then leaned in toward Anderson. With that unholy grin still plastered across his face, he said in a low tone, "I like a challenge. It makes everything more interesting, don't you think?"

At that, the man jerked back up, smiled broadly—bearing large upper front teeth. "But hey, you had your chance."

Anderson thought for a moment. The realization of the warning finally dawning on him. It was like being smashed in the head with a brick.

"Wait a minute! You're the one who called and told me I was number one on your list and to be ready. You hung up before I had an opportunity to respond," he said.

The man nodded in agreement.

"Who in their right mind would take anything about that message seriously? How was I supposed to understand something so cryptic? Can't you explain what it is that you're so upset about?"

The figure thought for a minute, contemplation evident. With a crease of acknowledgment on his lips, he sighed and said, "I will try to explain as best as I can. You see, a while back your ex-partner, Nicolas Cooper, ruined my life. He took everything I possessed and left me with nothing. I had to flee, escape the country; leave everything behind. From that moment on, I swore to destroy his life in equal proportions.

"Unfortunately, *you* are caught in the middle. Derek, my good man, because Nick stuck his nose into someone else's business, I am now faced with some tough tasks. I mean, he must pay. You can understand that," the man said emphatically.

Standing straight and folding his arms in defiance, he added, "Nick's actions forced me to leave my wife and my career, not to mention all my friends and practically all my money. A man that I knew for twenty-five years had his life ruined and died in shame. Honestly, none of these things sat well with me. Call me sentimental."

The Frenchman faded into the darkness for a moment. While hidden from view, Derek could hear the unintelligible mumbling of several words. The man appeared to have a conversation with himself. Then, the intruder reemerged into the light. He stepped a few inches from Derek's bound legs. Stooping down into a semi-squatting position, his head almost even with Derek's, he said, "Detective Anderson, you and I see things a little different. Unfortunate, but true. Therefore, since you are Nick Cooper's best friend, you are step one in my seven-year quest for revenge; number one on my list, as it were. Do you understand now?"

"No, I really don't. Nothing Nick did has any bearing on my family or me," Anderson said firmly as he stared straight into his assailant's eyes. "This is insane." Derek made a herculean effort to stay calm but found the task increasingly difficult, "You can't do this. Please. I'm begging you. Surely, you understand what this will do to my wife and kids."

"Yes, in fact, I do. You see Derek. You know, I like calling you Derek, makes this much more personal," the man said feigning sincerity. He smiled with that same sinister look in his eyes. "Your friend Nick erased the last seven years of my life. Since then, I've had to spend those years in exile in another country, never being able to show my face to anyone I knew or loved. So yes, *I do know*; and now, so will he. I swore to get my revenge, and today is day one of that promise."

The shadowy man grabbed a roll of duct tape from his jacket. He unwound the spool about five inches before tearing the piece off. With the taped outstretched, he came toward Anderson's face. Anderson jerked away, moving his head from side to side, trying his best to avoid the inevitable.

"Wait, please! Tell me your name. At least give me that so I can try to remember—something, anything, about what Nick might have done. Maybe I can fix it," Anderson begged.

"My name is irrelevant, to you anyway. And fix it?" the man said with a sarcastic laugh. He moved his face within an inch of Anderson's, his breath, soured with evil, accosted Derek's nose. "*Fix it*? That, Monsieur, is what we're doing right now."

The man released one hand away from the tape, smiled at Anderson, and then punched the bound man hard in the stomach. Anderson gasped while a low sound of pain hummed deep within. His attacker waited a few moments to allow the detective to regain his breath, and then he gripped the tape in both hands and headed back to his original target. This time Derek didn't move. The adhesive material sealed firmly across his mouth.

Once the tape was in place, the assailant stepped away and moved about the room. The dimly lit area prevented Derek from seeing much of what was going on, and thank goodness for that—a terror beyond any he had ever experienced would have engulfed him if he could see what was in store. As he frantically scanned the void, he caught an odd noise. It sounded almost like someone scratching a fireplace match across an even larger matchbox.

Just then, a spark ignited, and his accoster's face became illuminated with a bizarre ghost-like eminence. This eerie image was distressing but isn't what scared the bound-up Anderson. He'd stared down plenty of malicious criminals before, so the face above the light had little effect. What snatched at the cop's breath, even more so than the sucker punch, was what gave off the glow.

The focused flame of a butane torch.

A muffled scream of epic proportions gushed from Anderson as his assailant moved in. The blue and yellow flame seared the skin at Derek's shoulder before bubbling and peeling back the soft tissue. Anderson's eyes bulged and sweat poured down his face in unrelenting streams. The undeniable realization slammed him He was going to die in an unbearable and agonizing way.

Chapter 2

THE REAL MARSHALL KENT

After dinner at the Pump Room, Nick walked Nancy to a waiting cab, but before she stepped in, he gently grabbed her arm, turned her around, and gave her a small but purposeful goodbye kiss. She didn't resist but also didn't linger.

Once their lips separated, she got into the sedan and closed the door. As Nick watched the vehicle disappear into the night, he realized that even though the story about "Frenchie" was worrisome, the couple of hours spent with Nancy were wonderful—almost as if the last few years apart hadn't happened. Almost.

Nick went home, pulled out his latest Davin Ross novel from the shelving in his bedroom. He then rummaged through his office closet and gathered the notes and research he used for the book. For several hours into the night and part of the early morning, he reviewed them. Even though he could recall almost every detail of the book and his fictional protagonist, Marshall Kent, Cooper wanted to reacquaint himself with the real-life Marshall Kent—Peter Thomas—and the infamous "Hit List Killings" he'd carried out.

Motivated by pure rage over the murder of his wife, Thomas channeled his out-of-control emotions into heinous acts of revenge. His case remained in the news for weeks—the methods he used to torture his captured victims, the clues left behind—induced national conversations and speculation of what was coming next.

It started on one of those breezy afternoon day in mid-August that Chicago is known for. Five heavily armed men stormed into the First National Trust Bank intent on robbery. Each man wore black army fatigues, body armor, and ski masks. Their guns pulled and at the ready

"Everyone down on the goddamn floor now!"

One thief stood guard at the front entrance, while two others raced over to a door that led to the tellers. The shorter of the two punched in a code on a pad next to the door, and they raced through and over to the tellers. The last two men, seemingly the leaders, went straight to the bank's offices in the rear of the building. Thomas was the branch president, and as fate would have it, his wife, Emily, was in his office visiting.

One robber working the tellers appeared hopped-up on drugs. He barked orders in staccato fashion to the point that it was difficult for the tellers to understand. His shoulder's jerked and twitched as he swiveled his gun around the teller cage. At one point, bouncing up and down on his toes, he lost it when he didn't think one of the bank employees was moving fast enough.

"You're fucking with me bitch," he yelled at the teller filling the bag. With no warning, he used the butt end of his handgun and smashed it in her face. The young blonde woman, and mother of two, wailed in pain before crumpling to the ground with a broken jaw and two knocked out teeth. The woman's attacker laughed like an excited hyena with a fresh kill.

"You son of a bitch," a male customer on the floor yelled out after the unprovoked attack on the teller. He began to rise fully intending on shoving the brutish thief through the bank's plate glass window. The robber's guard at the door saw the bank patron's movement. Without a word of warning, he took aim and fired. Whether he purposely intended to kill or only wanted to fire a warning shot, the bullet only missed the man's head by millimeters.

Someone in a back workspace, at first unaware of the commotion, heard the gunshot and hit the silent alarm. This action triggered a blinking red light in Thomas' office—an unintentional though devastating alert to the two thieves standing in front of him.

One robber was giving Thomas explicit directions regarding getting into the banks main vault. It was at that moment that the blinking light from the alarm illuminated Thomas' pants, painting them with a red glow of warning.

"Are you kidding me? You stupid . . ." the other robber in Thomas' office snarled. Before Thomas could say anything in defense, the masked intruder took his shotgun and jammed the butt end straight into the banker's face. The blow connected with his forehead and knocked the bank president to the ground and out cold.

Thomas' wife, sitting in a chair in the corner of the office, began screaming. She attempted to go to his aid when her husband's assailant grabbed her arm, swung her around, and slapped her hard across the face.

"Hey man, knock that shit off. There was no call to do that," the man who had been instructing Thomas complained.

Ignoring the protests from his cohort, the man pulled the crying woman out into the main lobby. "We gotta go! The alarm's been activated," the robber yelled as he pushed the woman toward the bank's exit.

The teller in the corner of the teller's box, saw the two men running from the back offices with Emily in tow. In utter panic, she called out the woman's name and moved a step in her direction. The hopped-up robber, with one victim down and bleeding, grabbed the clerk by the hair and roughly threw her to the ground. Giggling like a rabid animal, he kicked her once in the head, and once in the stomach, before he and the other man raced out the teller cage's door. The five robbers then left the bank. Their take? About six thousand dollars in cash—and a hostage.

Though he didn't divulge this bit of information to the police, Thomas believed he recognized one of the two men in his office. Paul McAlister, the branch's ex-Vice President. The company fired McAlister three months earlier for his involvement in a sexual harassment charge. Thomas gauged the man to be the same height and build as McAllister, and though his voice was muffled, the president believed he recognized it. Several other employees told the police that on the day of McAlister's firing, he vowed to make Thomas pay.

Police found McAlister at his home the night after the robbery, but his alibi put him in a restaurant during the holdup surrounded by witnesses. No immediate charges were filed. Thomas, however, privately remained convinced of McAlister's involvement.

The police worked with Thomas—set up a kidnap task force in his house and waited for a ransom note or call. No request ever came. Four days later, a couple of homeless guys were rummaging through a garbage dumpster in the back end of an alley and found Mrs. Emily Grant Thomas rolled up in a carpet and thrown in a heap. After an autopsy, it was discovered that the woman had repeatedly been raped and then strangled.

Cooper and Anderson got the call to investigate.

Many weeks of investigations followed, and though the detectives felt they were close to discovering one of the kidnappers, no arrests came. That's when victim number one surfaced.

Police found Jesse Buford Haines' body bound to a chair and tortured. But not just tortured, the man had been brutally mutilated with a butane torch, flesh-charring burns covering seventy-five percent of his body. Some wounds ran so deep they almost passed clean through. The scene bombarded the detective's psyche. They'd seen much while on the force, but this act of savagery brought them to a repugnance they had never experienced before.

Though the killer was meticulous in his efforts, he did not attempt to destroy the evidence. Among several clues discovered were about a dozen damp rags lying in a pile a few feet away from the body. Each rag contained multiple burn holes throughout the cloth.

The killer appeared to have moistened several dozen clothes and draped them over body parts as he worked on them. It was determined that this process prevented the flesh from actually igniting and burning while allowing him to continue to work on his quarry. The pain of the torment must have been excruciating.

The method of torture wasn't the only thing that set this crime apart from other murders. Haines' penis was gone. Burnt off. The skin around his groin was a seared crispy mess. Thankfully, no one ever found the appendage . . . no one wanted to. The killer had carved a large number "one" into the dead man's forehead. The M.E. believed the torturer took his time with the etching, as the cutting was symmetrical from top to bottom. Anderson gritted his teeth, grimaced, and rubbed his own forehead as the doctor detailed the process. He couldn't imagine how bad that hurt.

One more clue would tie this murder to others forthcoming. Dozens of pieces of paper of various sizes and from many different media formats, with a number one to four printed on each, were tossed around the floor and onto the victim. At Haines' crime scene, all number one pieces contained his hand-written name, while numbers two through four contained only the numbers. As each new body surfaced, the corresponding rank of the murderer's victims had their names written on them.

After police finished a background check on Haines, they discovered a criminal record consisting of dozens of arrests including two for bank robbery.

The second murder victim turned up in the storage room of a vacant strip mall store. The torture scene was similar in scope to the first murder except instead of a torch, the killer used several types of serrated knives to remove most of the man's skin. This victim had been "filleted like a fish," someone had said. The M.E. confessed that the burning of victim number one probably would have been more painful than being filleted. Cooper and Anderson looked at each other. Neither wanted to know which would be worse.

Like the first victim, this man's penis was removed, seemingly sawed off as evidenced by serrated cut marks at the groin. Carved into his forehead was the number, two. Like the first murder, the killer spread numbers, now two through four, across the floor. Each "two" had the name of Bobby Joe Blake hand-written on it.

Investigations found that Blake and Haines possessed almost identical criminal records and allegedly worked jobs together, including bank robbery.

Feeling more and more curious about a connection, Nick questioned McAlister again. The ex-bank employee remained adamant he knew nothing. However, during this latest round of questioning, Cooper began to see holes in McAllister's story. One question kept bothering the detective. *How did the robbers know the code to get into the teller's cage?*

Cooper and Anderson went back to the bank. They wanted to know who had the codes, how often they were changed, and who kept track of the changes. When they arrived, they found that Thomas had taken a leave of absence and hadn't been seen at the bank since the robbery. Peter Thomas instantly became the primary suspect in the "Hit List" killings.

Before Thomas could be located, the bodies continued to mount. Victim three showed up two weeks later in an abandoned warehouse. Two vagrants had stumbled upon the corpse while they were looking for a dry place to sleep for the night. The mutilated victim's lone ID, a warehouse club card from Tampa Florida, identified the dead man as twenty-seven-year-old Carl Flanders.

In Flanders' case, the murderer used dozens of sixteen penny nails driven into all parts of his body. Seventy-five nails in total. The killing blow apparently being the nail directly between his eyes. However, unlike victims one and two, Flanders' penis was not missing. Three rusty nails driven into a one-foot-long piece of two-by-four lumber held the penis in place. The body possessed the number three, clearly etched into his forehead, and the same telltale numbers were strewn all around, with the number three having Flanders' name added.

Flanders had no criminal record. In fact, other than the obvious clues at the scene, the authorities could find nothing that connected the three men, nor could they initially locate any relatives to ask questions of, or to retrieve the body.

Not until just before Flanders' scheduled cremation did a family member come forward. The club store ID picture had been flashed on the various national news channels and his uncle in Wausau, Wisconsin, saw it and came to Chicago to bring him home. After talking to the uncle, the investigators discovered that Flanders had runaway at sixteen, and had been missing for years and presumed dead, or at the least a homeless vagabond. This latest evidence still left a gaping hole—how was Flanders connected to the first two slayings? Was he a bank robber too? Had the guys worked together on other crimes?

With this latest discovery came a public outcry demanding that the police find the killer. People were scared. The killings seemed random. To make things even worse, the public was terrified of the methods used in the slayings. *Who would be next? Why was this happening? What sadistic method would the killer use on his next victim?*

Within a week of this latest victim, a visit from Paul McAlister changed the game. McAlister arrived at the precinct with an envelope.

"This came for me in today's mail. I wanted you to see it," McAlister muttered, eyes averted as he handed over a white envelope.

Inside, the investigators found a large five cut from a magazine and a printed note stapled to it: "You fucked with the wrong man. Now *you* will suffer. PAUL MCALISTER—I AM COMING FOR YOU!"

Anderson and Cooper pressured McAlister to come clean. What did he know? They spent over an hour grilling him, ultimately accusing him of being in on the robbery. The stubborn man refused to confess and maintained the position he did not do the bank job nor murder Thomas' wife. Unlike previous interrogations, McAlister's rigid demeanor seemed to falter and fade. The man was frightened, and it showed.

Anderson and Cooper needed to find Thomas, and right away. If McAlister were number five, number four would show up. Soon. They needed a break, something that could lead them to the man before he killed again.

On a hunch, Nick did an extensive background check on Peter Thomas. It didn't take long to find out compelling information regarding their theory of him being the killer. Thomas had been a highly decorated Marine trained in counter-intelligence. He married his wife during his time in the military, and though her family frowned on the union—Thomas was a gruff sort—they soon grew to accept and love him.

After retiring from active duty, his wife's father hired Thomas as security director for his bank sites. The safety measures that Thomas initiated around the branches saved the banks thousands. Within a few years, after showing undying loyalty and hard work, his father-in-law promoted him to branch president. Until this branch's robbery, none of the banks had been successfully robbed, and no one had ever been injured during an incident. All the more reason to believe that this robbery was an inside job.

With the information gathered, Anderson and Cooper contacted Thomas' most recent commanding officer, hoping to get an insider's view on Thomas. Though the soldier couldn't discuss specifics, due to national security issues, the detectives discovered the murderers of Thomas' wife had messed with the wrong guy.

Though Peter Thomas seemed mild-mannered and appeared to have found a peaceful place in life, this was an individual capable of things that until this case, they couldn't have imagined. Thomas' commander explained that the ex-Marine possessed a single purpose mentality and wouldn't stop until he finished whatever task he set out to do. If that means getting revenge on his wife's killers, then drag out the coffins 'cause they were as good as dead.

Cooper immediately advised the department to put out an All-Points Bulletin on Peter Thomas while requesting that all law enforcement segments be involved in his capture. With the rising body count, the FBI came to assist with profiling and incident research data. Then, three months to the day of the bank job, victim number four turned up.

The man's name was Peter Barton, and all other crime scenes paled compared to his. The killer strapped Barton's naked body to a piece of plywood just wide enough to hold his frame. Upon first glance, Number four's demise was similar to Number one. The victim's body contained dozens of burn holes. Some that went deep into his flesh, others that barely marred the skin's surface.

Cooper noticed these marks didn't possess the same charring associated with the flame-type injuries seen with Number one. He also commented on the intense odor that seared at his nostrils. Once forensics arrived, the investigators would understand why. The team determined that the injuries on this body were from using a very corrosive acid. This man's penis was missing, though not cut off. Apparently, the assailant burned most of the appendage away with the acid. The M.E. believed this was done first, before going to other parts of the body.

Another issue involved the eyes. The two orbs were gone with the area's surrounding skin horribly mutilated. Barton's mouth remained open, frozen at death, with the orifice caked with dried blood. A red stream of the fluid had rolled down his face before pooling onto the floor.

Detective Anderson discovered the source of this blood. He had been the first to glance into the slain man's mouth and gagged at his discovery. The corpse had no tongue, which would turn anyone's stomach, but to make it worse the muscle was not just gone—the fleshy membrane had been ripped out.

"Pick up McAlister and bring him to the station," Cooper ordered. "I'd don't want him released until he tells us about his involvement."

Officers arrived at McAlister's work around 4:30 p.m., with instructions that if he tried to resist, they were to keep him there until a judge issued an arrest warrant. When they requested McAlister's presence, they were told that he had left the building earlier "for personal reasons" and had not returned. The manager of the retail electronics store where McAllister worked said that he drove off around two p.m. to pick up a prescription. One of the other employees said McAlister had not been sleeping well and was picking up Ativan to help with anxiety and sleep.

The first four murders occurred over seven weeks. With McAlister's disappearance, on the day that Number four was found, it appeared that the executioner was preparing to end his revenge plans on that very day. If investigators were going to save McAlister, they would have to figure out the killer's next move, *now*. They didn't have days or maybe even hours.

Cooper heeded a gut feeling that Thomas might want to end this where the horror all began. He phoned the manager at Thomas' branch. Had any security measures changed since Thomas left his job? The new manager said that generally, it was policy to do so. However, those changes hadn't occurred because Thomas' father-in-law hoped the man would come back to his job.

Cooper hung up the phone and told his partner he believed they'd find Thomas and McAlister at Thomas' old bank branch. It was a mere thirty to forty-minute drive to the location, which would be closed by then. Cooper believed they needed to race there as he didn't think Thomas would waste a minute finishing his task.

As the two investigators arrived at the bank, Anderson spotted a red sedan parked near the rear exit of the building. He checked the license plate—the vehicle belonged to McAlister. Cooper parked their car about a half block away and radioed in for back up.

Time was of the essence. As the first squad car appeared, Cooper instructed one officer to guard the front entrance, and the other to keep an eye on the back. If Thomas came out alone, they were to arrest him. After those two were in place, the detectives moved in. They hurried down the alley, ran behind the bank, and reached the rear entrance of the building. Cooper grabbed the handle of the door and checked to see if the door was unlocked—it was. With caution, he turned the knob and pulled the door open just enough to peek inside.

The place seemed empty. The lights were low, and no shadows bore the telltale signs of movement. Cooper grimaced and shook his head toward Anderson before peering back in. He put his ear to the opening and listened for several moments before catching the sound of two men talking. One man pleaded for his life while the other shushing him like a child being admonished for wanting another piece of candy.

Cooper didn't hesitate. He pulled his weapon with Anderson doing the same, and the two crept inside. With slow anticipation, they inched their way toward the front of the building, passing several offices along the way. All the rooms were empty. The end of the hall was about ten feet past the last office. Cooper stopped there while holding his hand up as a signal to Anderson.

From this position, Nick could see the entire lobby area of the bank. In front of him, and slightly to his right, he saw McAllister. Thomas had him tied up in an office chair and stood in front of him, razor-knife hovering no more than an inch from McAlister's sweat-covered face. McAllister had a swollen lip and right eye, and there was a tear in the skin on his cheekbone. Apparently, there had been a one-sided struggle.

Cooper pointed toward a desk to their left, then to himself, and back to the desk. He motioned for Anderson to move to the other side of the hall. Once Anderson was in position, Cooper slid along the ground and made his way over to the desk. Getting to that spot put him slightly to the left and behind where Thomas and his victim were.

About five feet away from the front of the desk stood a counter where deposit slips and other forms were stored. The kiosk looked to be about six feet long, maybe two feet wide, and about four feet high. Cooper crab-crawled his way there. Now, he was in an excellent flanking position to where Thomas stood. From here, he would only be about eight feet away. Close enough, he hoped, to stop Thomas before he could fatally harm his victim.

The two detectives maintained direct sight of each other. Cooper held a hand up for Anderson to hold and wait.

McAllister begged for mercy. Thomas ignored him. The former Marine seemed calm and in control. He positioned the knife blade just above McAlister's forehead. Cooper reasoned that the Number five was about to become the number of the day. He raised his right hand toward Anderson, gestured his intention to go to the front of the counter, and for Anderson to remain behind the man.

Cooper slipped around to his left and then stood, gun aimed at Thomas. He didn't want to startle Thomas into overreacting with the razor, so he tried to keep his voice steady. The adrenaline rushed through his system like a freight train at full throttle.

"Peter Thomas, this is the police. Drop your weapon, and step away from McAlister," Cooper said in a firm voice.

Thomas raised his hands, seemingly in an act of surrender. And then, in a movement that was startling in its quickness, he moved to the back of his intended victim and bent down so McAlister's body shielded him. Putting the razor to his victim's throat, he said, "Officer, please remain where you are, and advise your man behind the desk that advancing means a new ear to ear smile for Mr. McAlister."

Anderson emerged from his hiding spot with his gun aimed. "Don't move. I've got you dead," the detective stated as he moved to a side flanking position.

"Oh, thank God!" McAlister bawled. "Please, save me from this madman!" The pleading man's face contorted in gleeful exuberance as he continued to sob and wail.

"No one can save you now," Thomas whispered, and then made what seemed just a shrug of a move. A slight almost unnoticeable flinch. But the action produced a shriek out of McAlister that seemed to shake the building. Thomas had nicked the man ever so slightly, opening a minor wound on the man's throat. But the effect of the cut was intense. Still sobbing but in a muffled tone, McAlister stared at Cooper in terror. His eyes bulged horrifically, and his face trembled like a man watching as the warden grabbed the electric chair switch.

"Mr. McAlister," Thomas said, now in slightly more than a whisper, "Confess your sins. Tell these officers it was you and your band of thugs that raped and killed my wife. Do it now, or I'll slit your throat from ear to ear."

With the blade still sitting near his Adam's apple, McAllister closed his eyes and then, through pulsating sobs, recounted the events leading to that moment.

"After I was fired, I met a man in a bar. I talked, he listened."

"Man, I get you. When a woman cries rape, she can bring a man down," the stranger said as if conspiring with McAlister. "Shit, I've been there; spent time in the can over a goddamn lie. But I got my revenge, and now I feel vindicated," he said with a wink.

"Revenge, huh . . ." McAlister muttered through glassy eyes.

"Yeah, made him beg for mercy before getting twenty G's from the guy. It was beautiful."

McAlister opened his eyes and looked at Cooper, "The next thing I knew, I had a plan to work with this stranger and a couple of the guy's buddies. We'd rob the bank—why the hell not—and take care of Thomas at the same time. We were just going to beat him up, teach him a lesson. That's all. I swear."

He swallowed hard before a choking, gagging cough instigated spittle to fly from his mouth and nose. After taking a moment to regain his speech, he said,

"They weren't supposed to take Thomas' wife. Hell, I didn't even know she was going to be there. If that damned alarm hadn't gone off, we would have left her alone. The siren caught us off-guard, and the guy reacted and knocked Thomas out with his gun. Then he, grabbed the woman and drug her out.

"Once we returned to the safe house, the other four took the woman. I swear I tried to stop them, but the thugs ignored me. It made me sick. The men did horrible things to her—and the last man killed the woman by strangling her as he pleasured himself inside her. I'm so sorry."

Thomas closed his eyes, leaned his head down, and cried. Anderson and Cooper recognized his terrible anguish and understood his desire to avenge this horrible act. Hell, who knows what they would have done if they were in his shoes. But they had a job to do. McAllister would go to jail, for a long time, and it was up to them to make sure he stood trial.

"Peter, step back and put your weapon down. They'll try McAllister for the crimes he and his associates have committed. You have witnesses to his confession. Now, move back." Cooper stepped closer.

Thomas raised his head and opened his eyes. He looked at Anderson first, a glance of tormented command and then back at Cooper. The pain and agony of his ordeal emanated so intensely from his face that the image would forever be etched in the detectives' memories. However, Cooper also believed he could see something else, something that he hoped he was wrong about.

Nick turned and looked at Derek. The two seemed to realize what was about to happen simultaneously. They yelled at Thomas not to do it as they urgently headed toward him, but in that slow-motion heart-stopping second, the blade slid across McAllister's neck – slick and swift, with a surgeon's precision.

With eyes bulging from his head and blood spewing down his throat like a freshly opened fire hydrant, the man responsible for the death of Peter Thomas' wife raced toward an unstoppable and eternal dirt nap of his own.

248

Thomas backed away and dropped the knife. He fell to the ground face-first and put his hands behind his back. Cooper rushed over and cuffed him. As soon as they secured the killer, Anderson holstered his gun. Frantic, he tried to stop the torrential blood flow that spewed like a geyser from McAllister's neck, but the effort was futile – McAllister was going to die.

Thomas confessed to the murders of the bank robbers and maintained that the criminal's actions justified the means of his revenge. Each man performed unspeakable acts on his wife. They needed to be punished in a like manner. Regarding the burning out of number four's eyes and the removal of his tongue, Thomas explained that four's blatant disrespect for his wife, and the fact that he laughed and boasted at the things he'd done to her—well, the man pushed Thomas past previous boundaries.

During Thomas' torture of that fourth man, the victim confessed that he waited to take her last on purpose. He crazily boasted that he wanted to watch as each man raped the woman. The scene excited him, but not for the reason some may think. When his turn came, he looked into the woman's eyes and told her that he would be the last thing she would see, the last man that would penetrate her. The last "lover" she would ever have. He laughed as she begged him not to kill her. This pleading only made his vice-like grip tighten on her throat even more.

Thomas said this man had no regard for decency—he'd laughed and bragged of how he assaulted his wife, made her beg for mercy. Thomas knew that he needed to send this man to his grave with those despicable eyes burned out and that twisted tongue ripped from his mouth.

The detectives would discover that victim four was a convicted rapist only recently released from jail.

Thomas had gotten his revenge, but at what cost. He went to jail; his kids were left without a mother or father. There was indeed no justice for anyone.

As Nick Cooper finished reading the last pages of his notes regarding Thomas, he glanced at the clock on his desk, 3:30 a.m. He looked down one more time at his papers, shook his head in disgust, and then went to bed.

The phone rang at 6:30 a.m. and continued to blare off and on until Cooper heard it an hour and a half later. He rolled over and grabbed the receiver from its cradle. In an almost breathless tone, Nancy Bradshaw said, "Coop, are you up?"

"No," the bleary-eyed man responded before adding, "Yes, sort of. What time is it?"

"Eight-ish," she said in a hushed tone. "Coop, turn on the news."

Nick arrived at the crime scene a short while later and saw a circus of law enforcement people scurrying about. He jumped from his car, ducked under the yellow police tape, and raced to the front door.

Captain Lewis noticed him coming. "Nick, wait, I can't let you go in."

"Try to stop me," Cooper shot back, not stopping or even slowing.

He entered the kitchen and jolted to a halt in mid-stride. Stripped down to his undershorts, Derek Anderson was propped up and duct-taped to one of his breakfast room chairs. Gruesome burn marks covered over three-quarters of his body with some wounds being so severe they almost went through the body parts. The sight turned Cooper's stomach and ripped at his heart. His legs wobbled, his mind unable to process the scene.

The scent of burnt flesh hung in the air, a blanketing of stench that attacked his sense of smell with a ferociousness that made him wretch. Cooper swallowed back a gag of bile that caught in his throat.

Making his way unsteadily, he sat down on the couch and stared with unbelieving eyes down the hall to where his ex-partner sat. At that moment, a second in a life of years, Coop felt a part of himself die. The normally rugged and fearless man struggled to hold back the overwhelming grief that pierced his soul.

His eyes filled with tears, and his throat constricted. Nick began to sob into his hands, which now covered his anguished face.

Captain Lewis, knowing all too well that Anderson's ex-partner was drowning in pain, tried to console Cooper by saying how sorry he was, and blah, blah, blah. But all he could think about was catching that motherfucker. Rip the son-of-a-bitch's lungs out of his chest. His mind raged with hate when another horrible thought slammed him back into the moment.

"Where are Barb and the kids? Tell me they weren't the ones that found him," Cooper pleaded with his ex-captain. The mentally drained man just stared at Cooper, unable to answer with the truth.

Chapter 3

THE FRENCHMAN TOPS OUR LIST

With Derek Anderson, the murderer made it obvious from the onset what he was doing. Mimicking the pattern of Cooper's fictional character and Thomas' real-life murders, he tossed random numbers from one to five on the floor and the body. His victim was firmly bound to a chair using duct tape. And the most glaring parallels being the use of a torch as the tool for torture, and the number one etched in Derek's forehead.

Though all these things linked the crimes, some crucial differences surfaced. Unlike the Marshall Kent fictional murders, Derek's mouth and head were taped with complicated wrappings. Cooper realized this intricate way of keeping him in place did two things. The first was obvious. The man wanted to keep Anderson's screams from being heard by the neighbors. Sealing his mouth with the thick grey tape provided an easy fix for that. The second reason, however, was what caught the ex-detective's attention.

Not only had the killer wound the tape around Derek's mouth, but he also continued wrapping the adhesive around his head a few times before looping several strands around the top sides of the chair in a crisscross path. This made it almost impossible for Derek to move his head from side to side or forward, while the back of the chair only gave limited backward movement. The other significant difference in this killing compared to the real murders of Peter Thomas, Derek retained all of his body parts—one in particular.

There would be an additional defining variance explicitly aimed at Cooper; the killer left a poem. The computer-generated note read:

There were five, now just four.

Who's next? You're not sure.

You ruined my life

By taking my wife,

So say your goodbyes

Before the next one dies

OFFICER COOPER—I AM COMING,

Marshall Kent.

Great, a sadistic murderer and a poor-ass excuse for a poet. I am going to kill this fucking asshole.

Cooper got in his car, called Nancy, and asked her to meet him at his home. She arrived about thirty minutes later, and when he opened the door to greet her, she threw herself into his arms.

"I'm so sorry, Coop."

Cooper hadn't had that kind of intimate interaction with anyone in a long time, and he needed it now more than ever.

The two went into his study and sat down on the sofa. The drained man gazed into her eyes for several seconds before finally saying, "Lou, someone is copying the Kent murders from my book. Based on the crime scene today, as well as what I believe is contact from the killer, the entire effort was to exact revenge against *me*. I'm not sure who he is or why he's aiming his insanity toward me, but it is now clear he's targeting those close to me as part of his plan."

While this statement sunk in, Nick discussed what he had seen at Derek's, or at least most of it. He ended the explanation by telling her about the note left behind. The two talked about its contents with Nancy finally asking him what he believed the killer meant about Cooper taking his wife.

He had no idea.

The still shaken man tried to think back to any case he had been involved in where he might have injured someone's spouse, caused a divorce, or possibly even death. Nothing came to mind. "Were you *involved* in any other way," she asked somewhat coyly.

"*Really?*" Cooper answered sarcastically. "And the answer, even if you were remotely serious, is a resounding, NO."

Bradshaw eyed Cooper with just a hint of suspicion but then erased the thought from her mind.

Did Bradshaw ask because of the case or was she fishing to determine if I've dated during our separation? Either way, the answer was still no.

"Do you think that crazy French asshole is behind this?" she asked.

"It appears that way. If nothing else, we have to put him at the top of our list, especially since we don't have any other suspects. We'll talk with Captain Lewis in the morning and recap everything we know about him so far. You know, something about that French guy does seem familiar. I just can't put my finger on it."

The two talked a while longer with Cooper coming to tears several times. Finally, he tried to push aside the emotional pang of Anderson's death and focus on what to do next. It became evident that they needed to come up with a potential hit list of his friends or family.

Their first direction was to look at his family. Cooper's mother and father had died years earlier in a car accident, so no targets there. His younger brother, Henry, lived in Florida, and though he might be a target, the distance seemed to preclude him, but Nick would still call. He had never married, nor did he have any children.

Cooper and Bradshaw both mentioned Reggie and agreed he was high on the list as a potential.

"Don't forget to write my name, we know he's coming after me since he's already made contact," Nancy added.

Cooper looked at Nancy, frowned, and then wrote her name. The action gave him a nauseous feeling, but he knew she was right.

"Lou," Cooper murmured. "You know what's a bit depressing? After Derek, Reggie, and you, I really don't have anyone . . . I mean, I don't have any other close friends. Actually, I don't have many acquaintances of any consequence either."

"Christ, Coop," Nancy said with a look of mock pity in her eyes. She thought for a moment and then added, "Well, I guess in this case that's a positive. We'll have a short list to work from."

"Really, it's a negative," he quickly replied as his mind refocused. "Without any clear-cut choice for those last two spots, the killer could target anyone he believes might be close to me. That's going to make protecting or even alerting the right people almost impossible."

The two spent the next few hours talking about possible targets. In the end, Bradshaw agreed with him that when it came to friends—Nick was a catastrophe.

The need to speak to Reggie became urgent. Nick told Nancy she didn't have to come along, but she insisted.

"Besides," she said, "I haven't seen Reggie in a few years. I'm very anxious to say hello."

Cooper jumped on the phone, he asked Reggie to meet at Benny's, a bar around the corner from his agent's apartment.

"Sure, Coop, that would be great. I'll grab Danielle, and we'll head there. What time?"

"Uh, Reg, I don't think bringing Dani would be a good idea. I've got to talk to *you*, and I think it would be better to tell *just you*. Alone."

"I guess, but what's going on? You're not firing me as your agent, are you?" he asked in a half-joking tone.

"No, it's nothing like that. I'll tell you everything when we meet. Lou and I will be there at . . ." Cooper looked at Nancy and mouthed, "Does 7:30 work?" Nancy nodded in agreement, "How 'bout 7:30?"

"Lou? Are we talking about *that* Lou?" Reggie blurted in surprise.

"Yes, everything will make sense when we meet. See you then." Nick hung up.

Nancy and Nick's eyes locked. It was a strange moment but what happened next stunned him even more. Bradshaw leaned over and gave Cooper a kiss—full on the mouth and thick with passion. The way she used to kiss him when they craved each other's bodies night and day.

"Wow," Cooper muttered when she pulled back. "What was that for?"

"Because you needed it," she answered. "And because I needed it. To be honest, I've needed that for a long while."

Nancy walked over to the liquor cabinet where she found Cooper's supply of Evan Williams bourbon. She made them both a drink—for him, a shot with a splash of water, for her, straight up, which was not how she usually drank it.

"Uh oh . . . This is something serious, and it's not about Derek," Nick said.

Nancy handed him his glass then wandered over to the big bay window that overlooked the front of his property.

"Coop, the other night when you kissed me—it proved to me something that I had long suspected." She paused for a moment, and in that brief hesitation, Cooper saw the woman. *Really* saw her. This vision etched into his mind. He wanted to say something profound, but thought better of it, deciding, for once, to listen. Besides, he didn't want to make a fool of himself saying something way off base.

Nancy took a long sip of her drink. "Back when I broke it off with you, I believed that having a career in law was what I wanted. My entire education revolved around that strategy. To be brutally honest, all I ever dreamt about, almost every minute right up to the second I passed the Bar, was about being a lawyer. I started work at my dad's firm very young and full of ambition, and things seemed to be going as planned. I really believed I was happy. Then I met you and . . ." She turned in his direction. "Damn if I didn't fall head over heels in love.

Most people would be elated, even thankful, to be in my position. For me, our relationship eventually caused confusion. My love for you interfered with my goal in life, and I came to the insane conclusion that I couldn't let that happen. As fate would have it, two significant things transpired right at that time, and I snapped. You know my dad got sick, and then you . . . well . . . you wanted to take our relationship to another level. Jesus, I flat out panicked."

After we split, I put every ounce of energy into running my dad's firm. It was the only way to fulfill the commitment I'd made to myself and survive without you. If I hadn't jumped in, I mean with both feet right up to my neck, I would have folded and come running back. Which, I believed was not what I wanted or should have done."

Nick started to say something, but Nancy stopped him with a pleading glare, "Please, Coop, let me finish. I won't be able to do this without crying if you say anything."

Nick knocked a gulp back and set his now empty glass on the coffee table. "You got it, I'm all ears."

"Look, like I said, I believed that my career was the most important thing in my life. I forced myself to take all my distractions away. It's what I wanted, or thought I wanted. After we split, things seemed to go exactly as planned, which convinced me that I'd made the right decision." She paused, took another long sip of her drink, and looked back out the window as if searching for what to say next.

"Ok, here we go," she said in a resigned whisper, and then she turned back to stare straight at Cooper. "A few months passed, and that's when it happened. I woke up one day and realized nothing in my life seemed right. I felt this huge hole in my heart that felt like a piece of it had been of it ripped out. It left a gaping hole. You know what I mean?"

He did, all too well. Cooper felt that same way since the day Bradshaw broke off their relationship.

She finished her drink, walked over to the bottle, and poured herself another. Cooper started to ask for a refill, but she began speaking again,

"At first, I tried to ignore the feelings, to pretend they didn't exist. With each passing day, I tumbled deeper and deeper into a depressed and withdrawn mood. My father even questioned my disposition. That's when I realized what was wrong. Staring straight at my dad, I knew."

She walked to Cooper and sat, facing him. She gazed longingly into his eyes. "I still loved you. Whether it was a day or a year or ten years that might have passed, I still loved you. Maybe more at that moment than ever before. After this self-proclaimed realization, I couldn't think of anything else. I began to wonder if I had made a mistake—that's not entirely true either. No, I *knew* that I had screwed up. I decided to call you and, you know, see how you were doing. I made up all kinds of things to say."

"Wait, I'm pretty sure that was at least a couple of years ago—if my math is correct. So, what happened? Did you lose my number?" Cooper said, impinged with a smart-ass grin.

Nancy's gaze drilled a hole right through him, and he realized that his sarcasm, though maybe justified, was not good timing. "Sorry, go on," he said sheepishly.

She puffed out a breath and said, "Well, I finally decided just to show up on your doorstep. I resigned myself to take from you what I deserved. When you finished chewing my ass out, I was going to ask you to for forgive me and could we try again. And then dammit, this D.A. thing happened, and I got sucked right back in."

She held her hand up, extending her palm toward the frowning man in a don't-say-a-word gesture. "I know what you're thinking, and I wouldn't blame you if you never wanted to see me or even talk to me again. After everything I just confessed, who in their right mind would want to?" She moved closer. "But I'm going to stick my neck out there. I'm asking; will you give us another try? I promise that my life will be about the two of us and not my job."

Cooper reached for her hand, held it in both of his, and then brought it up to his lips. He gently kissed it and then said, "Lou, I've always loved you. I've thought about you every day."

Without hesitation, he leaned over and passionately kissed her. When he pulled back, she embraced him. Cooper felt her slight trembling and sensed that she was gently weeping. He caressed her back and then kissed her cheek.

Chapter 4

REGGIE

Cooper and Bradshaw arrived at Benny's a few minutes late. As they weaved their way through the tables, they saw Reggie waiting at the bar, his drink half-gone. He looked like a rabbit cornered by a fox as he fidgeted in his seat. The agent would never go to a bar by himself, it wasn't his style, and not knowing why he was there made the situation worse. Any other time, Cooper would take full advantage, making the twitchy Harding sweat and squirm before getting to the point. The circumstances for tonight's visit erased that thought before it even surfaced.

"You look extraordinary, more amazing than I remember—if that's even possible," Reggie gushed, standing and taking Nancy in his arms for a hug and kiss. When they first met, Reggie and Nancy instantly hit it off like lifelong friends. They had a humorous common connection, as they were able to deftly trade moments of teasing Cooper. It often aggravated the gruff and usually unflappable Cooper while delighting Harding and Bradshaw.

"Hello Reg, you always did know how to make a girl blush," Nancy said, as the two embraced.

Reggie pulled back, smiled at Bradshaw, and then turned his attention to Nick. "Um, I think I understand what this is about and Cooper, I can't tell you how sorry I am to hear about Derek. I realize you two hadn't spent much time together the last couple of years, but I know you still had a strong bond with him." At that, Reggie gave his friend an affectionate hug.

The tavern was a small yet beloved neighborhood bar where Cooper and Reggie often went to talk shop. They would review current and new novel ideas and updates intending to stay for no more than one or two drinks, but often found themselves closing the place down. Benny would call Reggie's wife, Danielle, to come and rescue the two inebriated but good-natured clowns. The boys had their favorite spot, a secluded booth in a back corner of the bar, out of harm's way.

"Let's see if our booth is open in the back," Cooper said. He ordered a couple of Evan Williams, and they all headed to the back of the bar.

Just as they reached the booth, a couple grabbed their drinks and vacated. The three slid in and were quiet for several uncomfortable seconds before Nick said, "Reg, what I'm about to tell you is going to be a bit of a shock. It may even scare the crap out of you. But I'm going to do everything I can to make sure that you and Danielle are safe," Cooper promised.

"What the—" The look on Harding's face darkened with confusion and shock. "What do you mean 'make sure we're safe? What have you gotten us into?"

Reggie sat stock-still, almost trance-like as Cooper told his friend all he knew about the situation. When he finished, Harding didn't move. He merely sat there, mouth agape, and eye's wide. He tried to speak, but only a frog-like croak came out. He picked up his drink, took a big gulp, and tried again, "Shit, this is fucked up."

"I know. I'm so sorry to involve you—"

"Revenge for what?"

"I'm not sure what or why, but he has all but admitted in the letter we found at Dere—" Cooper stopped in mid-sentence. It's as if his murdered friend's name had lodged in his throat. Nancy's hand moved to Nick's shoulder as he swallowed a mouthful of bourbon. He took in a deep breath and tried again, "The killer left a note declaring he was out to hurt me. To do that he's targeted the people closest to me."

"You guys need another round?" the waitress asked with a southern drawl.

"For everyone," Nancy muttered.

The perky redhead wrote down everyone's drinks and headed back toward the bar.

"Remember that weird French guy at the book signing?" Nick continued.

"Holy shit, is that who you think is doing this?"

"I think so. The whole scene that day didn't sit well with me, and then someone approached Lou. He did that whole hand gesture gun routine, same as the day of the signing," Cooper said as he nodded in Nancy's direction.

"Same guy?" Reggie asked.

"He called me first and said I was number four. Then, a little after that, I think the same man approached me from behind at a coffee shop. I didn't see his face, but he had the same French accent that the man on the phone had. When I turned around to see his identity, he was walking out the door. He held his hand up and lowered each finger until his hand looked like a gun. Then he walked out," Nancy added. "And now this thing with Derek?"

"No way is this simply a coincidence," Cooper said as he looked at Reggie. "Have you been contacted by anyone unusual?"

"No, nothing. I can't say for sure about Dani but am certain she would have said something to me if some weirdo contacted her." Harding looked at the two faces sitting across from him in disbelief for several painful moments and then said, "Christ, you guys, this is pretty fucking scary."

"Here ya' all go," the waitress interrupted. "Who gets the bourbons?"

Reggie grabbed his glass and quickly downed half. Through throat-constricted words, he asked, "Cooper, what should I do? I could go away—take Danielle and visit my parents in Salt Lake. But I can't be gone forever."

"Actually Reg, that's exactly what you should do, and as soon as possible—tomorrow even. Go home, grab Danielle and get out of town. I'm going to track down this son of a bitch, and I swear to you, I will get him for what he did to Derek. But I need you gone before he can do anything to you or Dani."

With fear radiating from relenting eyes, Harding agreed. "I need to arrange a few things at my office in the morning, and then Danielle and I will head out. I'll call you tomorrow, and let you know when I'm leaving. Who else do you think is on his list?"

"That's a good question," Cooper answered. "There's nobody I'm really close to, not like I am to you, Lou, or Derek . . . fuck, *was* to Derek." A pang of anguish rushed through Cooper. Simply saying Derek's name made him feel like he was sticking a knife in his own gut. He took in a deep breath and let it out. "Lou and I have been going round and round with that, and though a few names come to mind, no one sticks out."

"Being your friend has often had its drawbacks, but this is fricking over the top," Reggie confessed as he looked down at his watch. "I better get home and try to explain to Dani what's going on." The thin man looked gaunt and drawn as he slammed back the rest of his drink. He wiped his mouth then kissed Lou. "I'll be calling you. Take care."

"You too, and don't take any chances. Pack your bags and head out as soon as you can," Cooper said.

Reggie slid out from the table and stood to leave. "Cooper, get this son of a bitch."

Chapter 5

REMODELING - 101

Nick and Nancy rode in a cab back to her apartment. Though they didn't start the ride this way, their hands came together and interlocked. Neither spoke. Thoughts consumed Cooper, circling in his mind like a group of frenzied sharks. The death of one his best friends. The danger Lou faced. The threat to Reggie. The water was treacherous, a roiling bath of acid that ate away at him. Nancy, knowing that Cooper was suffering an incomprehensible emotional hurt, was at a loss for words.

"Lou, for the next few weeks, until we catch this sick bastard, I think you need to stay with your parents. Tonight, you can stay with me, and then I'll take you there in the morning."

"Stay at your place?"

"Yeah. And I know what you're thinking, but just so I can keep an eye on you till we get you set up at your folks."

"Uh huh," Nancy said.

"*I'm not kidding*. Christ, this guy is psychotic. We have to take precautions. Please, pack a few things for tonight. We'll come back tomorrow, and you can grab more. I won't take no for an answer on this so don't argue with me. I have the extra bedroom; I'll put you up there."

Bradshaw smiled, leaned over, and gently kissed his cheek, "You haven't changed—much," she whispered. "Still as chivalrous as always." She leaned over and whispered in his ear, "You know, I don't think either one of us should stay alone tonight. Maybe we could, well, would it be alright if we shared your room?"

"Well, I'd be lying if I said I didn't need the companionship," Nick said. Nancy squeezed his hand.

The cab pulled up to the curb of Nancy's apartment. The two got out, and Nancy went to open the door. Nick told the cabbie to keep the meter running, then bounded up the steps just as Bradshaw opened the door to her apartment. She flipped the light switch and stepped in. As the room lit up, she stopped short.

"Lou, don't move," Cooper demanded as he scanned the room. He pulled his gun from its holster and then pulled her behind him. "Stay here while I check things out." As he walked, Nancy followed right on his ankles. He turned back to admonish her, but the look on her face advised him that he'd be wasting his time.

The first discovery, glaring and leaving no doubt who had been there, were the words painted in thick, dripping red paint on her living room wall: NICK COOPER—I AM COMING.

After several tense moments of searching each room, they realized that no one else was in the apartment, but the place had been ravaged. Furniture turned over with cushions and pillows shredded and thrown. Pictures ripped from the wall and tossed to the floor. Shattered glass everywhere. Cabinets and drawers opened, and their contents spilled. Every room was turned upside down.

"Son of a bitch," Nancy muttered in a low but infuriated voice.

"We can't touch anything," Nick instructed. "I'll call it in."

As they waited for the police, Cooper carefully searched the apartment for other clues. Though he wasn't a forensic expert, he possessed an investigator's eye. Unfortunately, other than the painted note, nothing seemed relevant until he came to the kitchen. Broken plates and glasses covered the floor. Mixed in with this destruction were most, if not all, of her silverware, pots, pans, and dozens of other cooking utensils.

A note in bold font letters hung on her refrigerator door. A sizeable heart-shaped magnet kept the paper in place. "Nick, that's not my note," Nancy said as she nodded at the refrigerator.

Nick carefully walked over for a better look. The message looked similar to the one found at Derek's. It read: "He took my life— my career, my home, my wife, everything I held dear, now I am coming for him through you, and there is nothing he can say or do!"

"What is it with this guy and these moronic notes? This guy is really pushing all my buttons. He is a sick deranged fuck."

The police arrived and were in full investigative mode seconds later. While some of the team worked the apartment, a few blues proceded to knock on every door in the complex. Had anyone heard or seen the intruder? Not one person admitted to seeing or hearing anything. Either they were all deaf, or no one was willing to get involved—more than likely the latter. It would be virtually impossible for someone not to hear the crashing noises of all of Nancy's items as they smashed to the floor.

Once back to his place, Nick secured the house, turned on his alarm, then sat down with Lou to make sense of things. Yet, as time inched near four a.m., they were no closer to an answer than when they started. Calling it a night, they dragged themselves to the bedroom and climbed into bed.

Nancy laid her head on Cooper's shoulder. After a few moments of silence, Nancy murmured, "I know I've already said it, but I have so dearly missed this. Nick, I know that you are dealing with this terrible situation with Derek, but I hope you can take some comfort in the fact that I want to be here more than anywhere else on the planet."

Cooper kissed the top of Nancy's head, took in a deep breath of her flower-scented hair, and let it out slowly. "Having you here with me now means more than you could possibly know. I can't imagine being alone right now."

Beckoning him to kiss her lips, Lou leaned her head back.

He kissed her with sweet tenderness. Her body felt warm and lush on his, and Cooper suddenly recognized a stirring sensation deep within his being. *God, I've missed this.*

After a few moments of silence, Nick whispered, "Are you comfortable?"

No answer.

Her breathing flowed in a constant rhythm. She had dozed off. Cooper smiled, closed his eyes, and thought about the last time Lou had fallen asleep on his shoulder. His mind drifted back to their time together, but the vision quickly blurred as sleep overtook him.

Chapter 6

MY DEAR FRIEND REGGIE

"We'll leave for the airport at noon. You go right to your mom's place. Don't stop anywhere else. I'll head to the office, finish a few signatures, and meet you at your folks. We'll take a cab from there." Reg zipped his suitcase and set it next to Danielle's.

"My mom will want to know what's going on. There's no way she'll believe that at the last minute we dropped everything to go visit your parents," Danielle said. She gathered her purse and jacket. "Reg, I pray to God that Nick grabs this sick bastard before anyone else gets hurt."

"Don't worry." He carried the luggage out of the bedroom. "Nick was a damn good cop. He'll get this guy." He stopped, set down the bags, and faced Danielle. "I know it's not a great reason, but it'll be nice to get away for a few days."

Danielle looked at her husband, saw the twinkle in his eyes, and chuckled. "Uh huh, don't get any big ideas, big boy."

"Who me?"

They both chuckled as they walked out to his wife's car. He put the luggage in her trunk and opened the door. His wife gently grabbed him by the shirt collar and pulled him to her, lightly kissing him on the lips. She smiled again, climbed into the driver's side, and started the car. Reggie hovered above her staring down at the woman.

"What?" She cocked her head to look at him.

Without saying a word, Reggie leaned down and deeply kissed her. As he rose, he whispered, "You get more and more beautiful by the day. I love you," gave her a wink, and closed the door.

Harding watched as his wife backed out of the drive and pulled down the street. He waved as she turned the corner. Once she was gone, he walked back into the house and headed to the laundry room to shut off the washer's water valves. He moved from there to the garage and turned off the water heater. This process became routine each time he and Danielle went away for any length of time. Once, while being out of town for only two days, a hose on the washing machine broke and flooded the house. The water damaged came close to ten thousand dollars. And, without water, the water heater could burn out. He'd done the same process as an "ounce of prevention."

After he was sure the water heater was off, he took a moment more to look around the garage. Confident everything was in order, he turned.

A hulking darkly clad man stood directly in front of him.

Reggie staggered back. A jolt of fright raced through him and grabbed his chest. He looked at the man's face with a solemn glare of purpose, and then at the gun pointed right at his chest.

"Monsieur Harding, I presume? Please come in."

"Jesus Christ, you scared the hell out of me," Reggie stammered, the words barely audible.

"Oh, far from Jesus Christ, I assure you. Now come inside and take a seat in the kitchen. We need to chat a while." He opened the door and motioned with the gun for Harding to go in. Once inside, the man jabbed the weapon in Reggie's back, pushed him toward the kitchen dinette, and demanded he sit down. The imposing man, dressed all in black, went to the opposite side of the table and dragged out a chair of his own. He slid it over and placed it about six feet from Reggie.

"I recognize you. You were the guy at Nick Cooper's recent book signing."

"Oui, *tu as raison*. You've got a real keen eye, my friend."

Reggie broke into a cold sweat. *This was Derek's murderer.* "If it's money you want, I have some cash in my wallet. Here you can take my watch, it's a 1994 Presidential, worth at least $12,000." Reggie took the Rolex off his wrist. "There's jewelry in the other room on top of my dresser. Take anything you want, but please don't harm me, I have a wife," Reggie begged.

The man raised his finger in the air and shook it back and forth, "Come, come now, Mr. Harding, you know that's not why I'm here. I'm aware that you are married. Your lovely wife's name is Danielle, and she's waiting for you at your mother-in-law's." He paused and looked around the kitchen, "This is such a beautiful place. You and Danielle have done a fantastic job. I admire people with the ability to put together the look that you've accomplished here. It's a real talent."

Reggie scanned the room "Yeah, sure," he said, baffled by the odd compliment. He turned his attention back to the intruder. The man was extraordinarily calm. Like Reggie was chatting with a neighbor, which scared Reggie even more. Harding decided that he had to keep the man talking, feeling the longer he distracted him, the better the chance he would have to escape. "How do you know my wife's name?" Reggie demanded.

"I know all I need to Mr. Harding. I've been studying you for some time." He got up, pushed his chair in, and paced around the room. "You see, I have been planning this little game of mine for some time now. And though it wasn't essential, having an intimate understanding of my intended victims has made things, let's say, a little more rewarding."

He stopped walking to admire the cabinetry above the sink, opening and closing the doors, "Nice work, upscale. You can tell by the soft-close European hinges that this is first quality. Solid maple, maybe birch, but I'm betting maple.

The dovetail construction is solid and classic. I guess being an agent has its benefits. Anyway, I digress. Let me see, oh yeah. I'd been gone for some time, and it took me a while to learn my way around the area again. Once I got a good lay of the land again, I started to keep an eye on my prey—from a distance of course. I didn't want to alert anyone. Scare them off, know what I mean?"

The trespasser fidgeted with a loose knob on a cabinet door. He tried to tighten it, but the stripped screw continued to spin. Toying with the knob, he continued, "I've done eight months' worth of homework. I followed all of Nick's friends—getting their routines down. I'm good with the details, you see. You and Danielle for instance, I found out what time the two of you came and went. I followed your wife to her job and the various exercise classes and yoga, and whatever . . . very busy woman, your Danielle, and not at all consistent with her schedule. In time, though, I figured her out.

"Then there is you, Mr. Reginald P. Harding the third. Boy, you're like a finely tuned timepiece. Just like that beautiful Rolex you're trying to barter to save your life. Each morning, you're out of the house at precisely seven thirty. You stop at Starbucks four blocks from here. If that cute little Joanie has your latte ready when you drive up, you're in the office door by 7:44 a.m. When lunchtime rolls around, you either eat at your desk or go to Morta-Delis. Isn't that a great name? I love it! The food is good too. You might also find this amusing. I sometimes ate at the table right next to you.

"But I ramble—a bad habit, *je suise desole,* I am so sorry," the man said with a small chuckle. "Let's see, next you're out of your office every evening at 4:30 p.m. and home by 4:44. That is unless the little woman asks you to stop at the grocery on your way home. But basically, the only time you differ your routine is if you have an event to attend, and those are rare."

The large man leaned against the counter as his narrative went on, "Once I got your habits down, I waited for the call from Nick."

"Wait, how did you—?"

271

"Oh, please . . . Nick's circle of friends is, well, at the very least, somewhat limited. I knew he'd contact you right after Derek's, um . . . unfortunate demise. I was at Pauli's Pizzeria across from Benny's when the three of you got together. By the way, they've got great pizza, and I should know. Their three cheese and pepperoni is sublime," The man glanced at his watch and nodded as if he needed to assure himself that he was on schedule.

"When your wife left yesterday for work, I came by. Let myself in."

"You were in my house?"

"Sure, a bunch of times. You really should have an alarm system installed." He looked at the time and then back at Reggie. Reggie noticed a change in the intruder's expression and was about to say something when the burly man cut him short, "Unfortunately for you, the time to begin my next step toward exacting my revenge on Nick Cooper has arrived." His smile twisted into an evil grin. "And now, as you are number two, we're going to get a little better acquainted."

"What are you going to do to?"

"Oh, my, I'm afraid if I told you, you might not be as cooperative."

Reggie stared at the hulking figure that stood in front of him like a giant evil raven. The agent's mind swirled with terror. *What the fuck am I going to do? Is there any way to get the hell out of here?* The gruesome explanation of Derek Anderson's death popped into his brain, and the vision made him want to puke. His entire body was clammy, and he felt drained of all strength. He put his body's weight on the balls of his feet, with anticipation of jumping up. His legs felt like mush, almost as if they had vanished. He slowly turned his head and looked at the door that led to his backyard and possible freedom.

Reggie turned back toward the man with the gun.

"Don't even think about it," the man said as his grip tightened on the pistol.

"Why are you doing this? What have *I* done to *you*? I don't even know who you are," Reggie pleaded.

"It sucks, doesn't it?' the man said flatly. "But hey, shit happens, and you, *mon ami*, are involved in a big pile of it named Nick Cooper, which by association is not good for you. Reginald, I'm afraid that this just isn't going to be your day." The man got up, opened Reggie's refrigerator and peered in. "Too bad, I planned on sharing a beer with you, you know, to help calm your nerves. But alas, you have none."

"It's eight in the morning?" Reggie said in revulsion. The rummaging figure ignored him.

The man scanned the fridge for several long moments. It was all the time that Reggie needed. The thin but agile man jumped up and went straight toward the unsuspecting figure. As he lunged, his right foot caught up in the leg of his chair, throwing him off line. Instead of hitting the man and possibly knocking him down, Reggie went head first into the refrigerator door. His head bounced off the stainless-steel panel, and he caromed into the wall to the right of where his target had been standing.

In that split second, and with the dexterity of a trained assassin, the man raised his hand and quickly swung the butt of his gun directly into the side of Reggie's head. An explosion of darkness and Reggie fell to the floor, out cold.

Reggie's left eye twitched. After a few seconds more of effort, both of his eyes fluttered, sporadic and without synchronized effort. Finally, both eyes crept open, though only slightly more than slits. At first, Reggie was unsure of where he was and couldn't remember what happened. The excruciating pain in his right temple quickly brought him back to reality, and he found himself in the same spot before his failed attempt to subdue the intruder, though circumstances were now decidedly different.

The Frenchman had tied Harding's arms and legs to the chair, and except for his undershorts, he was naked. His tormentor had also taped his mouth closed and then manipulated the tape around his head and the back of the chair. He found it virtually impossible to move his head more than an inch in any direction.

From behind him, an accented voice said, "Enjoy your nap? I must say I am upset with you, Reginald. You've made my job so much harder than it needed to be. Do you know how difficult it is to move a limp body around and situate it in a chair? Well, let me tell you, it isn't easy, *not at all*. You kept flopping around and sliding up and down. Oh, and I have to confess to something. If your ribs are a little sore, it's because I gave you a quick kick. I got a little annoyed and, well, I guess I took my frustrations out on your midsection. So, I'm sorry about that."

Harding realized that the chair was now in the middle of his kitchen. He faced away from the table. He tried to crane his neck to see where the man stood; he couldn't. The dabble of sweat that coated his face now coursed down his scalp and into his eyes. He could also feel rivulets of the liquid running down his back. He trembled as if he was sitting in frigid temperatures and his muscles were tense like hardened steel.

Several heart-pounding moments passed, and the time grated at every nerve in his body. Not knowing what was happening behind him freaked him out. Suddenly, the man appeared in front of him. He now wore a transparent rain parka, rubber boots, gloves, and an elastic swimmer's cap. "Mr. Harding, sir, I'm afraid the time has come. I hope you have made peace with the world."

Harding began to weep, sobbing like a child, as the man walked behind him and grabbed the top of his chair. With little effort, his assailant spun Reggie so he faced the table. What was on it made Reggie's eyes grows to enormous terror-stricken proportions. *No*! *Fucking no*! *God, save me*!

Sitting on a clean white towel laid three knives of various lengths and blade types. A pair of pliers, a hammer, and a pile of white shop rags—all neatly positioned. The killer picked up the smallest of the blades and then stepped in front of Reggie. He stood there for a moment and tilted his head from side to side with detached resolve. It appeared as though he was a sculptor trying to decide exactly how to start his next masterpiece.

A renewed horror ate through Harding as his mind searched for some saving answers. Though his mouth was taped, his plea for mercy radiated with profound intent from his bloodshot eyes.

"I realize how unfair this seems, and I am genuinely sorry. I, well we, must see this through. If not, the debt Nick Cooper owes me will not be paid in full."

With that, the Frenchman wrapped his arm around Reggie's head, brought the knife to his brow, and carved. A muffled scream like that of a wounded animal emanated from the tape around Reggie's mouth as blood streamed down his face. As if it was acid, the gooey liquid burned his eyes, and the metallic odor fouled his nose. Reggie continued to scream as agonizing pain raced through his being.

The killer patted Reggie's forehead with one of the shop towels and then stepped back to admire his work, "Hey, look at that, not half-bad if I do say so myself. Truth be told, I did much better this time than the last."

Reggie's breath shot from his nose like a raging bull before a bullfight, blood from his forehead mixing with his forced breath and spraying his bare chest in a fine mist. His body wracked and writhed as the pain took over all function.

With blood dripping from the small carving knife, the sculptor moved back to the table. He set the blade down--and then picked up the next knife in line. The instrument was medium sized with a six-inch stainless-steel blade. The intruder looked over at the still bleeding man and confessed with an odd sincerity, "I'm afraid that this is going to hurt a bit more than my last effort.

Chapter 7

A WIFE'S CONCERN

"Captain, I've researched my old cases. I'm looking for answers everywhere I can think of. Who have I arrested or harmed that might go to these lengths to exact revenge on me? I don't recognize this guy, particularly with the French accent; even so, I've come up with six names but . . ."

"But what," Lewis asked.

"Well, I'm pretty certain none of them is our guy."

"Why do you say that? C'mon, there's gotta be several choices when trying to figure who hates you this much," Captain Lewis said with intended levity, but Nick thought he regretted it as soon as the words left his mouth. Lewis quickly added, "Sorry Nick, I shouldn't have said that. Piss poor attempt at humor."

"No problem, Cap," Cooper said before moving on. "The issue is that none of the criminals from my search are French, or at the very least possessed a French accent. The accent could be made up, but I'm pretty sure the guy we're after has some type of French background or connection. I don't want to rule out the list— we need to check them out, but I think the whole exercise is going to turn into a dead end."

"Ok. I'll get with the FBI reps to help you find out where these six are today. We'll do searches on them and then cross-reference their names with anyone else who might show up who could be holding a grudge. Maybe a relative is pissed off enough to kill. Where's the list?"

Cooper pulled out a piece of paper and handed it to the captain, "I'll give your man as much information as I can. I haven't been in contact with any of them since I worked their cases. And then, once we're sure what's happened to these six, we can plan on how we'll track them down."

"Good. Now, who's on the other list?"

Cooper realized what he meant but was not nearly as comfortable discussing that list. He also understood that the potential targets needed reviewing. He sighed slightly and dove in. "Well, Derek, of course, and then Reggie and his wife, Danielle. Oh, and regarding those two, I've asked Reg to take Danielle out of town until we catch this lunatic. They're leaving today."

After glancing at Nancy, Cooper smiled as the two locked eyes for a brief second. He gave her a small knowing wink and said, "Lou, of course, and then after those, I'm at a complete loss. My brother lives in another time zone, and my parents have passed. So, I really can't say who number five might be."

Nancy chimed in, "Could anyone else on the force be a target?"

"Well," Nick moved toward the door. "The only partner I've had as a detective was Derek, and before that, I was a beat cop." That line of thinking brought him to a standstill for a few moments. He then turned back toward Nancy and Captain Lewis and said, "Maybe Patrick O' Leary. The two of us worked together for a while after the Dorsett case, but that's a long shot. I mean, years have passed since we worked together. In fact, if I remember correctly, he retired a year or two after the Dorsett thing. So, I don't know."

"I don't think we should take anything for granted," Lewis commented.

"Your right, of course. I'll find out where O'Leary is, and we'll talk with him," At that, something clicked in Nick's mind.

Nancy immediately noticed the slight hesitation, "Did you think of something?"

"Maybe. There was this guy in the Dorsett case, though I didn't actually have any direct contact with him, but maybe—" Before he finished the thought, his cell buzzed. He pulled the phone from his pocket, "Cooper," he said into the phone.

"Nick, it's Danielle," Reggie's wife said.

"Hey, Dani, what's up?" Cooper glanced at his watch, "Are you guys at the airport yet?"

"No, that's why I'm calling. Reggie was supposed to meet me at my mom's forty-five minutes ago. He hasn't shown up. I tried catching him on his cell phone, but he didn't answer. I even called his office, he was supposed to make a brief stop to sign some papers, but they said he never showed. Nick, I'm worried something happened."

"Ok, Dani, sit tight. I'll head over to the house. If I don't find him there, I'll search the roads he'd take. Maybe he's had car trouble. I'll call you when I catch up with him. I'm sure everything's fine," Cooper said trying to comfort her, even though his stomach began to knot.

"Nick, Reggie would have called if the car failed him. Something bad has happened, I just know it," Dani sobbed, her voice breaking.

"He might be in a dead cell zone, there's plenty of them around the city. I'm leaving right now. I'll call as soon as I find him."

Nancy and Captain Lewis stared at Nick during the entire conversation. Once he got off the phone, Cooper related Danielle's concern.

"Lou, we've got to go."

Lewis called the desk sergeant and told him to dispatch a patrol car to Reggie's address. As Nick and Nancy headed out the captain's door, Lewis instructed Cooper to call him as soon as he found Reggie. He would then direct the patrolman to make sure Harding and his wife made it safely to the airport.

Chapter 8

THE SICKENING TRUTH

Fifteen minutes later, Nick and Nancy turned the corner of Miller's Avenue before racing four blocks to Rush Drive. He steered his vehicle onto the road, barely slowing, and then shot down the block. As they rounded the bend, a few hundred yards after the turn, Reggie and Danielle's house came into view. Parked out front, a police cruiser sat with its emergency lights flashing wildly.

Just as Cooper roared to a screeching stop, an officer came rushing out of the house and onto the lawn. He fell on his hands and knees and vomited.

"Oh Christ," Cooper roared, "REGGIE!" He slammed the car into park and bolted from the vehicle before Nancy could even unbuckle her seatbelt.

As the terrified former detective passed the patrolman, the retching man threw his hand up. Cooper guessed the man was attempting to stop him from going into the house, but the cop's stomach made several involuntary heaves, and all he got out of his mouth was unintelligible gurgling, which Cooper ignored.

Moving through the door, Nick heard a voice coming from the kitchen. He ran down the hall, turned in and froze. The scene was the most horrific thing he had ever seen. In his many years on the force, nothing could have prepared him for the carnage in the Harding's kitchen.

Nancy called out as she came through the front door, and Cooper instinctively put his hand up motioning her to stay back. Not until that moment did he realize that he had fallen to his knees. Nancy ignored his gesture and ran toward him. Nick turned toward her with an expression that jolted her to a dead stop. She slowly raised a hand to her mouth and shook her head back and forth.

Chapter 9

MRS. FLAGSTAFF'S DESCRIPTION

"So, Mrs. Flagstaff, start by telling me the shape of the man's face. For instance, was it oval, like this?" the sketch artist drew an oval form. "Or round like this?" He made another face using a rounded shape.

"No, more like the first," Mrs. Flagstaff said. The elderly lady, dressed as if she was going to a gala affair, pointed at the oval drawing with a glove covered hand.

"Ok, like this? How about the hair? Did this guy have straight, curly, long, or close-cut hair?"

Mrs. Flagstaff contemplated for a moment and then replied, "Short hair on the sides with the top about an inch longer. The color was mostly black with a little graying at the temples. And boy did he have a big schnoz!" she offered with authority.

"We'll do the nose next, Mrs. Flagstaff. How does this look?" the policeman said as he started filling in the hair, first at the top, then the sides.

"More here and here, and gray along the sides— stopping about here. The man also parted his hair on the left side of his head about there." Mrs. Flagstaff traced her finger down the side of the portrait's scalp.

The two worked on the sketch for about twenty minutes until the artist stopped and looked at his work. The two adjusted the nose and ears before starting on the mouth. The sketcher moved his pencil for a moment longer based on the woman's instructions, and then, oddly, drew more—on his own.

"Hey, I didn't tell you anything else yet. The shape of his lips . . ." She stopped as the man continued to sketch without instruction. He finished the mouth and changed the ears. He moved next to the eyes and eyebrows, shading in here and there and adding a few lines and facial features. He worked on the sketch for a while longer and then stopped drawing. He sat back and looked at his creation.

"Yeah, yeah that's him! That's the man I saw go into Nancy's apartment. Except for one other thing. My guy sported a pencil-thin mustache and a little patch of hair below his chin. But other than that, you hit it dead on," Mrs. Flagstaff exclaimed. "How'd you do that?"

The young artist looked at the sketch, hesitated for a second as though searching for an answer, and then up to the woman. "I guess I've been doing this for so long that it just kind of comes naturally, at a certain point." He cleared his throat and averted his eyes from hers and added, "Thank you, Mrs. Flagstaff, you've been very helpful. Now, if you'll give me an overall description of his height, his approximate weight, and a few other details, I'll make sure that everything gets to the appropriate people. You never know about these things, but this might help us find this suspect. Thanks again for coming forward."

After jotting down the rest of the facts, the man held his hand out.

Mrs. Flagstaff vigorously shook it. "Young man," the woman said as she gathered her belongings, "People like this bastard deserve what they get, and he will get his soon enough. I'm sure of that. I'm just glad I could help."

The sketch artist followed Mrs. Flagstaff to the exit. When he knew she was in her car and gone, he walked back to his cube. After picking up the drawing, his cell, and briefcase, he headed out the station's rear door toward his car.

Once outside, the officer opened his phone. He pushed a speed-dial number and waited for the call to connect. Several rings and a woman answered. The man said, "You are not going to believe who I just drew for a murder case. That fucker is back, he's here in Chicago."

Chapter 10

A HORRIBLE DISCOVERY

Nancy stopped short. Her reaction to the grief on his face caused Cooper to snap back to reality. He got up, walked over to her, and they embraced. Nick was not a crier, far from it, but he could feel tears streaming down his face. A large lump formed in his throat and sat there like a wedged rock. He led Nancy into the living room, and they sat on the couch. Nick mumbled, though choking up at times, an explanation of how the killer used a method similar to what his character Marshall Kent used in his second revenge murder, but much worse.

"The killing where Kent cut the man with a knife from head to toe?" she asked.

Cooper nodded.

"My God, Reggie . . ." Nancy said softly.

Nick took a few moments to gather his thoughts and rein in the urge to implode, "It's going to take me a while . . . hours . . . before I'll be able to leave. I can have Lewis arrange for you to have protection—you can go home and relax. Better yet, go to your parents.

"I'm not going anywhere, Nick. Not ever again. Where you go I go."

The woman was stubborn, but he was glad she was staying. He made her agree she wouldn't go in the room where Reggie's body was, no matter what. If she did, the image would haunt her forever. He was sure it would plague him until the day he died.

Staying on the outskirts of where his friend's body, or what was left of it, remained strapped to a chair, he examined the room. The almost surreal scene looked like something from a slasher movie. And though similar in aspect to Derek's murder, with a number cut into his forehead, this time the number two, and paper numbers all around the floor, the message "OFFICER COOPER—I AM COMING" painted on the living room wall in red; things took another path from there.

Cooper found it challenging to look at the lifeless, mangled form. Nothing dampened the pain and anguish of seeing Reggie. He tried to control his emotions, to no avail. Severe slash marks ran from his friend's neck to his waist. Apparently, a surgical-like knife had done the damage. The cuts varied in length and depths and covered almost every conceivable inch of his chest and stomach. On his legs and arms, the skin had been flayed. To Cooper, his skin looked to have been opened and peeled back like a lid on a sardine can. *What kind of sick fuck would do this? He would have had to spend at least an hour carving the flesh. My God, the warped unhinged bastard.*

Along the shoulder and arms and down the thighs and calves, large deep cuts revealed bone and cartilage. Reggie's flesh had a butcher's raw meat look, and a crimson pool of blood covered the floor. Footprints dotted the gooey mass in an almost dance-like pattern. No wonder the patrolman lost his lunch, Cooper felt close to doing the same.

Later, the medical examiner revealed that though the wounds initially caused excruciating pain, the very nature of their effects probably forced unconsciousness not too long after the killer started. In the same report, he also explained how the injuries might not have been what ultimately killed Cooper's friend.

The assailant severed the femoral artery right below the crease where the leg connects to the torso. The M.E. believed Reggie still lived during this phase, for the heart needed to be pumping to drain out the way it did. The organ would have pumped until his veins emptied—and then stopped functioning. Whether he was conscious or not when he died, he suffered. Immensely.

The police found a message pinned to a corkboard positioned above a small desk area in the corner of the kitchen. The note was another written communication from the killer addressed to Cooper. This one read:

"Number two is done, what a sight to see, but just a stepping stone to murder number three. I am paying you back, my old friend Nick, I hope what comes next will do the trick. I AM COMING FOR YOU—NICK COOPER!

"This guy is so totally fucked up," Cooper spit out after reading the diabolical prose.

After he scoured every conceivable aspect of the murder scene, he left the kitchen and walked over to Nancy. Four hours had elapsed since their arrival.

"Hey, I'm sorry. How are you holding up?" Nick caressed Lou's hand.

"I'm ok. How are you? Terrible, right?

"There are no words," Nick said as he sat down next to her. "I think it's time to go. I need to find Danielle; she must be going crazy by now. I can't believe she hasn't been calling me every five minutes." He stood up and looked at Nancy, and repeated those same words in desperation, "I can't believe she hasn't been calling me every FIVE MINUTES! CHRIST, OH CHRIST! Lou, we got to get over to Reggie's in-laws, NOW!"

Cooper yelled for Captain Lewis who had arrived only minutes before. The police team's leader came out of the kitchen as Nancy and Nick hurried to the front door. Cooper turned to him and said, "Its Danielle—Captain, I think she may be number three. Send a car over there, NOW!"

Bradshaw and Cooper ran to Nick's car and jumped in. Trembling and terrified, he started the engine and slammed the pedal down until he thought his foot might go through the floorboard. Bradshaw fastened her seatbelt and held on as he spun the wheel around. The tires screeched as they raced to Danielle's parent's house, about three miles away.

Nick jumped out of the barely stopped car, ran to the porch, and then slowed—fear holding back his pace. Creeping toward the door, Nick saw the first horrifying clue. The door was slightly ajar. He retrieved his gun and crouched down. After motioning with his hand for Nancy to stay put, he pushed the door open and made his way in.

Nick saw it the moment he got through the doorway. On the wall of the living room was the hand-painted sign. "OFFICER COOPER—I AM COMING."

Cooper searched for signs that the demon might still be there. The dining room and kitchen were empty. With a direct view of the family room, Nick watched for a few pulse-racing moments. When he sensed no sign of Danielle nor anyone else, he continued.

As Nick snuck down the hall, he felt his heart pounding in his chest. He inched along, slowly and deliberately. Along the way, Danielle's parents had hung pictures of Reggie and Danielle along the walls. The couple's proud and smiling faces grabbed his heart and squeezed. Gritting his teeth, he sucked back the urge to scream out Danielle's name. Instead, he headed toward the back bedroom doors.

With gun in hand, he sat in place just short of the first door and strained to hear any noise or conversation. Tension raced through his muscles. Wound as tight as the rubber bands inside a golf ball. He moved passed the empty guest bedroom. Except for the floorboards creaking when he shifted his weight, the house was eerily quiet. This, along with the horrifying deaths of Derek and Reggie, stressed the already drained Cooper to the edge of sound reasoning. He swallowed hard and made his way to the next door. It was closed. He slowly reached up, grabbed the doorknob, and twisted, but the handle would not budge.

"Fuck it," Cooper hissed. He bolted upright and stepped back. Raising his leg, he crashed his foot into the door. The hollow-cored entry buckled but didn't give.

"God Damn It!" he bellowed. The adrenalin-driven man reared back and jammed his foot straight into the door with all the effort and strength he could muster. This time, the door crashed open, wood splintered and flew in every direction. With gun raised and finger on the trigger, Cooper burst in.

Chapter 11

SAY IT ISN'T SO

Danielle Harding's naked body hung on the wall above the headboard of her parent's king-sized bed. She was nailed there with large railroad spikes—one in each of her hands and feet and one straight through her throat. The scene was one of a modern-day crucifixion. Nick averted his eyes to hold back the mad rush of fury that jolted his senses. "FUCKING HELL!"

Trying to regain his composure, he turned back and focused on what he had to do. Besides the spikes, nails pierced her flesh from head to toe. The killer sent an additional message by using an abundance of nails in her breasts and genitals. There must have been at least one hundred piercings in her body.

The number three, carved deeply into her forehead, radiated like a beacon. All around the room the numbers one through four—the names of Derek, Reggie, and Danielle on the ones, twos, and threes. The fours and fives possessed no names, but the killer included a question mark on each.

Another sign hung above Danielle's body. "PITY. ONCE AGAIN, YOU'RE TOO LATE."

Nick stood stunned.

Only thirty seconds had passed since he crashed through the door, but it was long enough. A woman's scream spun Cooper around with his gun at the ready. Nancy appeared in the doorway, hands to her face, horror-stricken. Startled, Nick raced over and embraced her before rushing her out of the room and down the hall. Nancy launched into uncontrollable shaking. She sobbed as the two made their way to the kitchen. "NO . . . OH GOD NO!"

Cooper started to speak when a loud thump came from the opposite side of the kitchen. He gently pushed Nancy away and gestured her to stay quiet. Raising his gun toward the noise, he motioned for Nancy to move to the other side of the kitchen. The room contained a door between two rows of cabinets, and something or someone was behind it. With pistol aimed, he leaned against the cabinets opposite the door.

"This is the police. Come out with your hands on top of your head. You have three seconds," Cooper said in a loud and demanding voice. His finger was poised on his gun's trigger. *He would kill this bastard.*

A muffled noise that neither Cooper nor Bradshaw understood came from behind the door. Nick motioned for Nancy to go behind the wall and take cover. Then, with gun clenched in his hand, he pulled the door open. Nothing happened, and no one came out.

"I won't tell you again. Come out, NOW!"

Again, only a muffled noise came from within. Cooper chanced a quick glance into the darkened space. Danielle's mother was balled up in the corner, tied up, a pillowcase over her head. Nick holstered his gun.

Chapter 12

VISITOR IN THE NIGHT

Physically, emotionally, and psychologically spent, Nick and Nancy returned to his apartment around four in the morning. Nick leaned against his kitchen counter and drank a beer. He took a long drink and then pushed off and walked into the bedroom. Nancy was just climbing into bed. He couldn't help but think of the irony. Shaking his head slightly, he sighed and kissed her on the lips. The effort produced a gentle kiss, but one filled with profound sentiment.

The doe-eyed woman opened her eyes after he pulled away. Her eyes met his. A tear rolled out down her cheek. Cooper bent and kissed the wetness and then whispered, "The only positive thing through this entire mess is that you are back in my life, and I am never going to let you go again."

"You couldn't get rid of me if you wanted to. Like I said before, I'm here to stay," Nancy said with a small smile.

"And I am thrilled by that." Nick circled his thumb across the top of her hand. "I still think it would be a good idea if you went to your folks for a few days. It's obvious this maniac has been studying everyone's habits, and he's stayed one step ahead of us. He knows where we both live . . ."

"Coop, that's a smart and logical thing to do. But honestly, I don't think I'm going to feel safe unless I'm with you. Besides, if he knows where I live, he knows where my parents live. I really don't think I would be safer there alone than here with you," Nancy murmured.

Like a butterfly landing on a flower, Cooper's lips touch hers. "Well, I'm still not convinced staying with me is a good idea, but it's late. We'll talk about this in the morning. I'm going to finish my beer. I'll come in soon."

Nick left the bedroom, leaving the door open an inch or two. Once in the living room, he plopped onto his couch. Sighing heavily, he took a deep pull of his beer. He leaned back and closed his beleaguered eyes. Though Cooper made an effort not to do so, he couldn't help but replay all the atrocious things that he'd seen over the few days. The faces of his friends swirled in his head, and though he tried to comprehend the violent events, nothing made any sense.

A soft moan emanated from the other room, and Nick rose up and glanced in that direction. Lou seemed to be having a dream. He hoped the images in her sleep weren't the same visions crashing around in his mind. Taking a deep breath before blowing it out in a long stream, Nick then leaned back into the soft cushion. Sleep came, fast and hard...

"Wake up," the man's voice said. The words were hushed, almost distant in their tone. "Wake up Monsieur Cooper," the voice said again, this time an octave or two louder.

Nick slowly opened his eyes. As sleep left his senses, a startling image emerged. Lou sat across from him in a kitchen chair. She was bound to the seat just as Derek and Reggie had been, with her head and mouth taped. She was naked except for a bra and panties.

Terrified, Lou stared at Cooper, wide-eyed and weepy. Nick realized he was firmly bound to a dinette chair, however neither his head nor his mouth was taped.

"Well, glad you could join us, Nick," the voice said from behind.

Cooper turned his head around as far as he could and yelled, "*Who the fuck are you?*" But stretch as he might, he couldn't see the assailant. Nick turned back around and looked at Nancy. Her pleading look sent a rush of adrenaline racing through his body. *Fuck. I've got to save her*. His heart took off like a racing locomotive. *Fuck. Fuck. Fuck. Where is that fucking bastard?* He struggled with all his strength to free himself, but his bindings held him fast. Anger stormed through him. "Do whatever you want to me, but please, let her go. She's got nothing to do with this."

"*Au contraire*, my dear friend. Don't you see? Miss Bradshaw is number four. It's not good to mess with the beauty of order. Just the thought of it is disrespectful to your other friends and the sacrifices they made for you. *N'est-ce pas?*"

Cooper gritted his teeth as he continued his futile effort to escape. As he struggled, he heard a faint grunting noise. He moved his head back and forth trying to see where it came from when he noticed a piece of paper floating down through the air. Like a group of darting white-winged bats, dozens of pieces wafted around Cooper and drifted to the ground. Each possessed a number.

"God damn it! Why are you doing this?" Cooper screamed at the man. "Who are you? Show yourself." Nick turned his head around so violently that he almost knocked the chair over.

"Nick, I'll give you my name in due time. But first, you need to understand that what *you* did to *me* drove me to do unspeakable things." The man's voice was rife with pain. Laced with a hint of madness, the deep-voiced words came from the shadows. "By now you realize, of course, that I have been following the path of Mr. Marshall Kent, a genius of a man, a legend in fact. Honestly, there were moments where I thought I might not be able to do him justice, but eventually, I followed the script and things worked out great." The man chuckled. "Number one on my list became a bit problematic. Not so much that I had a problem using the torch, or that the tool was awkward to handle. No, the real repulsion was the smell. The odor of burning flesh is no picnic—I can tell you that.

"Number two wasn't nearly as bad as the first. You can't know this, but I had been a fisherman most of my life, so I pretended he was a big fish that needed to be filleted. Kind of funny, huh?"

"You sick fuck. You're insane."

The hidden murderer ignored the insult and continued, "Number three fascinated me, and I'm a bit embarrassed to say, quite a bit of fun. I figured how to hold the body in place by first tying her hands to ropes then securing those to the ceiling. Once I got her in position, I hammered the little lady's feet to the wall with railroad spikes I found on the Internet. You know, you can get anything these days on the Internet. I know. I know. I digress. A fault, I'm sure. So, then I freed one hand from the ropes and nailed it to the wall, and then the other.

"After making sure she wouldn't fall—*and what a hullaballoo that would have been, right*? I used a construction nail gun and a portable air compressor to finish. Those damn guns are *so* cool and remarkably fun. Have you ever used one? To be honest, I didn't have it in me to get rid of it. I know I should have dumped it. I trash everything I've used, but I still have that little beauty."

Cooper heard a shuffling noise behind him and then silence. After a few seconds, the sound of a knife blade on a honing stone filled the air. "As for number four?" the intruder went on, unemotional and detached, "Planning this tryst was the toughest of them all. First, I knew you wouldn't let the lovely Miss Bradshaw out of your sight. Because of that, I needed to include you in tonight's plan. In truth, this made things a tad awkward, but its working out ok. Another issue I toiled with had to be the acid. You remember the acid from the killing of Number four in your book? Of course, you do! Well, it became necessary to take extra precautions because the caustic fluid eats through almost anything. Scary stuff for sure.

"Everything had to be worked out with no room for error. Rubber boots and gloves for my hands and feet were easy to come by. Fishing waders and then a rain jacket—Amazon!"

"Don't do this, please, I'm begging you. Lou hasn't done anything to you."

"Lou? How sweet. I forgot you call her that."

"Leave her alone. She has nothing to do with this."

292

"Oh man, you gotta watch this, this is really something." A stream of fluid shot past Cooper and hit the carpet just to the right of where Nancy sat. The piled matting sizzled and smoked, and within seconds, the liquid had eaten a large spot away. Cement became visible with yellow bubbles roiling up. "Holy shit that's so cool, right?" the voice bellowed.

Cooper sensed someone leaning down behind his head. With a hot, acrid breath, the hidden figure whispered, "I don't want your friend to hear but, times up."

The man walked around and stopped in front of Nancy. He wore a ski mask, black rubber boots, gloves, and an old pair of fishing waders that looked oddly familiar. In his hand, he held a clear glass container filled about three-quarters full. The intruder turned toward Nick and said, "This, my friend, will astound you." He rotated back to Nancy and poured the entire contents on her head. Within seconds, Nancy's head and face dissolved like a melting snowball.

Nick screamed, no words, only a wail of terror. The assailant turned his way and laughed a baritone howl. He grabbed Nick's shoulders and shook him. Nick struggled in his grip, tried to wriggle free. The man continued his malevolent howling. Nick, wrangled to free himself, rocked back and forth, frantic to get to Nancy.

"Coop, Nick, wake up. It's a dream. Honey, wake up," Nancy said, gently shaking Nick's arm. "It's ok, you're fine."

Cooper's eyes bolted open. "Oh my God, I can't believe how real that was. I thought the Frenchman killed you. Christ." Drenched in sweat and sick to his stomach, Nick gasped.

Nancy kissed him on the lips "Well, everything's ok. Please, come to bed and get some rest; it's late."

Chapter 13

THE SKETCH ARTIST'S CONFESSION

Captain Lewis picked up his phone and dialed a three-digit extension.

"Forensics, Peters here, "the voice on the other end answered.

I was under the impression that . . ." Irritated, Lewis looked at his note, ". . . Mrs. Flagstaff came in to give someone in your department a description of the suspect. What's the holdup?"

"I'm not sure," the officer replied. "I know the woman was here as her signature is in the register. I'll do some checking and find out where the sketch is."

"Well, I wanted it ten minutes ago, so somebody better find the damn thing and bring it to me."

A few moments passed, and then a young officer appeared at Captain Lewis' door. Knocking before entering, he walked up to the captain and handed his boss a duplicate of the suspect's sketch. "Captain, sorry this wasn't on your desk when you arrived here this morning. I came in a little late today."

The captain snatched the paper from the man and scanned the drawing. He told the officer to provide a copy of the sketch to all the appropriate channels and then to bring him two additional copies. The artist turned and stepped toward the door when Lewis stopped him. "One more thing. I want you to make another portrait of this man. This time, remove the hair from his face in case he's shaved them," the captain instructed.

Lewis resumed working on the files he had been reading. He looked up and noticed that the officer remained in his doorway. "Was there something else?"

The young officer stood for a second then walked back and sat down in front of the captain's desk. He looked at his boss for a moment and then admitted sheepishly, "Yes sir, there is."

Chapter 14

MARTY'S BAGEL SHOP

In the distance, Cooper heard a persistent noise. The sound kept getting louder, and though he tried to ignore the constant clanging, consciousness took over. The drowsy man reached over to the nightstand, groped around for the phone, and pushed the answer button.

"Cooper," Nick answered groggily.

"Nick, it's Captain Lewis. Wake up."

"I don't want to wake up—what time is it anyway? I feel like I just closed my eyes?"

"Seven-thirty *a.m.*," Lewis stated firmly while emphasizing the a.m., "You know, in the morning. Wake your ass up and get down here. We've got a significant development. I think it will give us the upper hand on this bastard."

Cooper listened as Captain Lewis explained what had transpired.

"No shit," Nick blurted as he popped up from the bed. "I'll be there in thirty minutes."

"What did he want?" Nancy watched Cooper moving around the room, "What's happened? Nick, what's going on?"

"That was Lewis. There's been a break in the case. We've got to head downtown—now."

Cooper and Bradshaw arrived at the precinct in less than thirty minutes. Lewis saw the two heading his way and stood to greet them. A big burly throwback type of cop, the captain was no-nonsense and by the book. He was mostly bald, with just a shaving of hair on the sides and back, but possessed an almost jet black mustache that practically engulfed his face.

"Coop, Miss Bradshaw, thanks for coming. Are you ready to catch this bastard?"

"You're goddamn right!" Nick shot back.

Nick and Bradshaw sat down in the chairs facing Lewis' desk.

The captain reached over, grabbed a large piece of paper, and handed the sheet to Nick. He and Nancy stared at the drawing for several seconds. The sketch was a dead ringer for the Frenchman at the recent book signing.

"Remarkable," Nick said while staring at the portrait. "This is the guy, no doubt about it. Where's the officer that drew this?"

Captain Lewis called out for the man, and within a few seconds, a tall, thin, blond officer entered. The forensic artist appeared to be in his late twenties or early thirties. He had closely cropped red hair and alabaster skin that looked almost translucent. He was a fairly non-descript man. But Cooper noticed one glaring trait. The artist's eyes lacked any sense of life. They were two blank orbs vacant of emotion. Nick, as he typically did after meeting someone, drew a conclusion. Though this was a police officer, the only weapon he would ever pull would be the pencil set he used for his sketches.

"Sit down, Larson," the captain ordered while nodding at one of the empty wooden chairs in his office. "This is Nick Cooper and Miss Nancy Bradshaw. I want you to tell them exactly what you told me," he commanded with a tone of sternness.

The man plopped down, took a deep breath, and then began. "Well, I did the standard things when Mrs. Flagstaff came in to give me her description of the suspect. After the obligatory chitchat, I explained the basics of what we needed, things like hair color, face shapes, eyes, you know, the usual. Then I told her to close her eyes and try to visualize his face more in-depth. I explained that when people did that, sometimes they could remember other features that might make the suspect remarkable. Scars, blemishes, tattoos, and moles. Or maybe crease lines on the forehead, cheekbone structure, or spider wrinkles by the eyes, things like that."

The sketch artist, who had been half-facing the captain for much of the conversation, turned more in toward Cooper and Bradshaw.

"Normally, a person does a pretty adequate job, and we acquire some darn good sketches. We can usually finish things in an hour or less. The time could be longer if the witness gets confused or forgets things, but Mrs. Flagstaff's recollection was spot on.

And then something happened. I began to realize that the face staring back at me started to look very familiar. My memory and instincts took over, and I continued the sketch without Mrs. Flagstaff adding any additional details. She sat in shock when I finished. She said that my drawing was a like a photograph of the man she'd seen."

"The person you drew was someone you knew?" Nick asked.

The young man's lips creased to a thin line and he nodded. "Yes, it is a face I will never, ever, forget."

"If you knew it then, why didn't you come forward yesterday? You should have given the sketch to the captain immediately. And now, two more people are dead!" Nick snapped, the words flying out of his mouth in anger.

The confessor's shoulders sank as he looked at the captain and then back at Cooper. "I understand, and I'm sorry. How could I have known?" the young man muttered in guilt. His demeanor changed somewhat when he added with emphasis, "I needed to warn my mother before this man's picture got plastered all over Chicago. You don't know him like I do. He's got connections and can move around the city like a ghost. I couldn't take any chances. Believe me, I want him captured and put away as badly as you do."

Cooper studied the artist's face for a minute and realized that it was set with grim determination. He sighed, took a deep breath, and then said, "Let's start from the beginning and maybe something else might pop up to help us find this madman."

The four talked for almost an hour, and when they finished, the identity of their tormentor was confirmed. Nick confessed to all that though the sketch was dead on, the killer did not look like the George Dawson he remembered from the Dorsett case.

Only seven years had passed since George had disappeared, but in that time, the man had morphed into the character in the drawing. His hair, once thick, dark, and more in tune with the length of the times, was now cropped with greying at the temples; the goatee and mustache were also new additions. The real change was the gaunt structure of his face. His cheeks, once round and full, were now taut and drawn. His eye sockets appeared sunken with the dark, puffy bags under his eyes giving him an evil, desperate look. The man's facial features, though ingrained in the sketch artist's mind, were a vague remembrance to the slick lawyer he once was.

Now that the group confirmed who they were dealing with, they also understood why he had come after Nick. They believed he'd done the things he'd done because Cooper, as the primary officer involved in the Dorsett case, had caused his demise, as well as others Dawson was closely associated with. The domino effect of arrests that occurred from the files in Dorsett's office had wiped away Dawson's life. In Cooper's mind, it was an insane connection, but all agreed it was the only plausible reason to go on.

As Cooper and Bradshaw were about to leave the police precinct, Captain Lewis explained that he planned to send the drawing to the French authorities. Perhaps they had additional information that could help. He also added that by five o'clock tonight, every cop in Chicago would have the picture, physical description, and real name—George Dawson.

The captain escorted the two to the door, "I have to imagine something will turn up on this asshole, and soon. In the meantime, I'm going to have patrols of unmarked police cruisers watching all of you until this guy is locked up behind bars."

As Cooper and Bradshaw headed back home, Nick suddenly realized that he was starving. "I can't believe that I'm saying this, what with all that's going on, but I'm famished. Are you up for Marty's?" Cooper asked.

"Oh, thank God. I'm so hungry," Nancy replied.

"Marty's it is."

Marty's had been a regular weekend affair for the two while they dated. The baker's fresh bagels and cream cheese were some of the best in Chicago, and the couple rarely skipped a Saturday or Sunday morning there. Unfortunately, after the two stopped seeing each other, Cooper hadn't visited the bagel shop. The two would take heat from Marty when they walked in, but the lambasting would be worth it to eat those incredible rings of dough.

After parking the car directly in front of the bakery's entry, Cooper looked at Nancy and conceded, "This could be a bit painful. I haven't been here for ages. I was always afraid I might run into you and, well, I didn't want meeting up with you here to be awkward."

"You too? Oh boy," Nancy said in response to his confession, "We're in big trouble."

An antique bell hung over the door. When they walked in, the clang caused the man behind the counter to look up. Marty Fielding held a bagel in one hand and a small, flat knife for spreading cream cheese in the other. At first, he put his head back down and continued working.

"Uh-oh," Cooper whispered under his breath. "We're *definitely* in trouble."

Hesitant, the two walked toward the counter, and that's when the memory banks caught up with the eye contact as Marty lifted his head, and a big smile crossed his face.

"Miss Nancy, my beautiful, lovely friend, where have you—" he turned toward Nick. "And you Nicky Cooper, you've got some nerve . . ."

"Crap," Nick mumbled to Nancy. "How come I'm the only one in trouble?"

"Apparently, because you deserve it," Nancy said with a satisfying smirk on her face.

Marty put everything down and wiped his hands on the red and white checkered apron tied around his waist. As the small shop owner walked through the counter opening, he looked at Cooper for a long second before a broad smile formed on his face. He slowly opened his arms wide. "Come give Marty a big hug."

After the small, stocky man finished squeezing the air out of Nick's lungs, he turned his attention to Nancy.

"Miss Nancy, why have you forsaken me? My heart missed you so very much," Marty said with his deep Italian accented voice resonating throughout the room. Nancy passed by Cooper and into Marty's arms.

"Marty I've missed you too. You sure are looking handsome these days," Nancy said as she kissed him on the cheek.

"Oh brother," Cooper feigned in mock disgust.

"You watch your tongue, Nicky Cooper, or there'll be no bagels for you. Miss Nancy, you, on the other hand, may have anything you want."

Cooper grabbed a newspaper from a rack by the door, went over to the counter, and watched the syrupy scene unfold.

Between chatting about things that made Nick's eyes roll and face grimace, Nancy ordered bagels. They got black coffees then Nick sat at a table in front of the shop's big picture window. While the bagels toasted, Nancy and Marty continued their conversation.

Cooper pulled back the tab on the coffee cup lid and took a small sip; the brew was hot but tasty. With empty eyes, he stared at the cars as they passed, one at a time. Memories of Derek jabbed at his heart, and then Reggie and Danielle's mutilated images jolted his psyche. He thought back to the last time he had been with the Harding's as a group. Reggie and Danielle had taken Nick to dinner for his birthday at The Berghoff, the historical Chicago German Beer Tavern, and one of Nick's all-time favorites.

They started the festivities with two great bottles of Cuvaison Pinot Noirs from Napa Valley, and Cooper could remember thinking, as they toasted to the evening, how thankful and lucky he was to be surrounded by such incredible friends.

Danielle wore a beautiful black dress with the heart-shaped diamond necklace Reggie had bought her for their most recent anniversary. The three talked at length about how the success of Cooper's books allowed them all great rewards, including, but not surpassing, their profound and flourishing affections for each other.

As far as Cooper had been concerned, not having Lou there to celebrate was the only negative of the night. He had fallen in love with Bradshaw from the day they met and losing her had left a jagged tear in his heart. If not for people like Reggie and Danielle, Nick would be a lost soul drifting through a meaningless bullshit life. *Christ,* Nick reasoned. *Poor me. What an ass I am.*

There are moments when a person daydreams that they unconsciously notice things in their surroundings. At first, they are rootless in a world where everything around them ceases to exist only to crash back into reality unaware of how they drifted away. That was Nick's current situation, except that as he returned from that never-never land, he found himself focused on a man standing across the street.

The hulking man stared directly at Cooper with familiar brooding eyes. At first, the image didn't register. Then, in that instantaneous moment of recognition, his subconscious mind knew something wasn't right. Nancy set a bagel and cream cheese on the table in front of Cooper diverting him from his trance. Startled, Cooper jumped up and moved around Nancy, and went to the window to check on the man. But in that briefest of seconds that he averted his eyes, the man was gone.

"What's wrong babe?" Nancy asked.

At first, hearing Lou call him "babe" caught Nick off guard. He hadn't heard that nickname for way too long. Shaking free from the memory, he regained his purpose and mumbled, "It was him. That son of a bitch stood right across   the street on that corner. But he's gone."

"Are you sure?" Nancy scanned the area.

The balls on this guy!"

Cooper maneuvered around Bradshaw and ran out the front door going to the edge of the sidewalk. He looked frantically in all directions but saw nothing. "Goddamn it," Cooper spit out, then turned back to the bagel shop. *Where's the patrol car the captain promised?* As he made his way to the door, he noticed Nancy staring at him through the front window. He shrugged his shoulders and mouthed, "He's gone," and started back in. At that moment, something caught his eye. In the reflection of the window, Cooper glimpsed a sedan parked across the street with someone in the driver's seat. He spun around and there sat Dawson— bold-faced and taunting.

The killer's car faced Nick on the opposite side of the intersection a hundred feet or so up the road. Almost like a dare, he stared straight at Nick. Without hesitation, Cooper took off running just as Dawson's car shot forward.

With tires squealing, the maniac turned his car in front of oncoming traffic and headed away from the sprinting Cooper. Nick reached for his weapon, but the Smith and Wesson wasn't there. "Damn it," he fumed. He'd placed the gun under his seat when he'd gone into the police station earlier.

Nick stopped running as the car sped away and tried to memorize the license plate. It read BCS1, and that's when a car backed out of a parking spot blocking his view and causing him to miss the last numbers.

"You got to be kidding me," Cooper yelled as he spun around and headed back toward his car. He saw Nancy standing at Marty's door and shouted, "We gotta go!"

Nancy glanced back at the table of food and grimaced. Once she caught up with Nick, she climbed into the car. Nick started the engine, slammed the transmission into reverse, and jammed down on the gas pedal. The rear wheels screeched with a wail that echoed off the surrounding buildings. The car raced backward, almost hitting a vehicle that had just pulled up on the opposite side of the street. Two men were in the front seat of the car, the cops the captain had promised. Cooper firmly jerked the car in forward and sped off in the killer's direction with the unknowing unmarked cops right behind.

In just a matter of a few blocks, Nick realized their prey had disappeared. Smacking the steering wheel, he glared ahead in frustration, and that's when he noticed it. On the windshield under the wiper blade, was a folded note.

Nick pulled over to the curb, jumped out of the car, and grabbed the paper. The officers pulled up right behind. After getting an earful from Cooper, they explained that after not finding a parking spot, they had circled around the block and missed the entire confrontation.

Cooper grabbed the note from the windshield and climbed back into the car.

"Nick, the time is almost here, so say goodbye to all held dear. Her turn arrives oh so fast, but please don't worry, she's not the last. And when, thank God, we face your turn, all questions asked will then be learned - for years I've been on prison's ice, for that you'll pay the price. NICK COOPER—I AM COMING FOR YOU!

Nick handed the note to Nancy.

After reading the written passages, she looked at Nick. "What's with the poetry, it's so ridiculous."

Nick shrugged his shoulders, "What can I say? He's a deranged asshole."

Cooper called Captain Lewis and gave him an account of what happened, a full description of the car, and in what direction George Dawson went. Lewis apologized for his men's foul-up and agreed to put out an APB, but neither of them held out much hope that the car would be spotted, or that the driver would be apprehended.

Chapter 15

THE FRENCHMAN PREPARES

"Are we having fun yet?" George Dawson mouthed as he watched Nick run back toward his car. "Don't wear yourself out—today's not the day."

He turned the next corner before changing direction. Some of his maneuvers were necessary, some not. Once he was sure no one followed him, he drove casually to his destination. Dawson was staying at a cheap, non-distinct apartment he'd acquired shortly after getting to the United States. He pulled into the lot and parked his rental car. In a detached manner, the lumbering man made his way back to the trunk.

Taking a quick reassuring moment to look around, Dawson opened the lid. He retrieved a large tote bag, a tall glass container carefully positioned in a small case, and then closed the trunk. He made his way to the door directly in front of his parked car. Apartment 4A.

Once inside, he laid the bag on the bed and set the glass jug on a towel in the bathtub. He looked in the mirror and smiled. "The day has come. Payback, Monsieur Cooper."

Dawson opened the satchel, grabbed a rolled-up set of house plans, and spread them on the bed. After reviewing the sketch, he snatched a notebook from his bag. Stashed in the front flap was a folded paper that Dawson opened and placed next to the blueprint of the house. He read a few hand-written passages and scanned the plans. Assured that he had everything memorized, he put the note back in the flap.

Walking to a small storage closet, he pulled out a large army surplus duffle bag. He dropped the camouflaged bag on the bed and removed rubber waders, rubber work boots, a rain parka, and a pair of industrial-grade rubber gloves. As a bead of sweat rolled down his face, he neatly placed them in the satchel and then zipped it up. He checked his watch, nodded once, and walked over to the phone.

Chapter 16

HE'S BACK

The young man paced back and forth, something he had been doing for the better part of ten minutes. Finally, he stopped and looked at his mother on the couch.

"He's crazy, you know that, right? He's killed three people already—tortured them, Mom. And he's planning to kill two more."

"What can *we* do?" the woman said straining to maintain her composure. "I'm scared he's going to come after us."

"He doesn't even know whether we're here in Chicago or not, but . . ." He considered for a moment and then said, "Maybe you should go visit the Bradfords in Florida until he's caught."

"You need to come with me. I don't want you here alone, and I don't want to go to Florida without you."

"Mom, I'm not scared anymore, and I'm not going to leave. Maybe I can help catch him." JJ walked over to his mother and sat down next to her. He looked her in the eyes and then put his arm around her. In his youth, when he needed comforting, she had done the same for him. "Listen, it's only a matter of time before he's caught and put away for good. When that happens, we'll never have to worry about him again."

The frail woman gazed at her son and smiled, but the smile was a sad one. He could tell she was frightened. At that moment, if even possible, he hated George Dawson more than he ever had. He intended to give his mother a hug when the phone rang. The two looked at each other, both stiff from the piercing tone. JJ's mother picked up the phone, "Hello?" JJ stared in sudden awareness as her face drained of all color.

Ten minutes later, another phone rang fifteen miles away, "Cooper," Nick said as he answered his phone.

"Nick, he's contacted his ex-wife in Evergreen Park. He claims he's going to visit her tonight at midnight, and then he's going to leave town."

"Uh yeah, right, Captain. That's not going to happen. He's not going anywhere until he finishes with Nancy and me," Nick said definitively.

"She's pretty sure he's coming. He made her promise not to tell anyone. Kind of attached an 'or else,' to his request. He told her that it wasn't safe for him to stay and decided to leave. He wanted to see her before he did. Do you want to be there, just in case? We can keep an eye on Nancy, so don't worry about that."

Cooper sat for a moment without answering . . .

"Nick, are you still with me," the captain asked.

"Yeah, the whole thing feels off. I'm not believing for a second that he's going to be there. How about this?" Nick said, and then the two talked for several more minutes. As he hung up the phone, he checked his watch. 10:30 p.m. He rubbed his chin for a second or two.

"Lou," Nick called out.

"Yeah," Nancy shouted back from the kitchen.

"Can you come in here? Something's come up."

Nancy came into the room with a perplexed look on her face, "Now what's happened?"

"Dawson phoned his ex-wife and said he is going to come visit her tonight. Says he's stopping by on his way out of town. Lewis suggested I accompany him and a task force to nab him at her house."

"He's going to leave town before he deals with us? I doubt that. Makes no sense. Besides, he couldn't take a chance that his ex might call the cops. He's way smarter than that. No, this is bullshit."

"Yeah, I agree. So, here's what we're going to do."

Chapter 17

THE FLAMES OF JUSTICE

"Well, well, here we go," Dawson said to himself as he watched Cooper leave his house. He stood in the shadows and waited for the white unmarked police cruiser, which he had now discovered was tailing Cooper, followed a few seconds later. "I love it when a plan comes together. Nick, my friend, you and your little entourage are so predictable. And don't worry; I'll be ready for you when you return."

As the taillights from both cars disappeared from view, the killer began the next phase of his plan. Originally, he intended on waiting another half hour before putting things into action, but he got antsy and moved around the block for a better angle of the house. Confident that his ruse with his ex-wife would at least confuse things, he stealthily moved in. However, he still wanted to be sure that his adversary hadn't arranged for an officer to sneak in to keep an eye on Bradshaw. After all, it was the prudent thing to do.

He decided to recheck the rear door of the home before entering. Dawson went through this routine before, a few times, but felt he should look again. He was getting impatient. Though he had been meticulous and tenacious in his planning to get to this point, he also was anxious to get this whole affair over with, for many reasons. He needed closure and justice for all the wrongs done to him and his friends.

Dressed in black, he picked up his bag and strode down the block. He crossed the street and headed toward the next corner. From there, Dawson turned left and moved to the next street where he stopped to look in both directions. Nothing out of the ordinary, so he turned back to his destination.

The lights burned brightly inside the front of the house, and he watched a woman's shadow moved about. *The lovely Bradshaw, just waiting for our little rendezvous.* He considered if she might go to bed before Nick got home, or if she would stay up and wait. It made no difference; he had prepared for either contingency.

As he made his way down the back alley that ran behind the house, he glanced toward the dwelling's rear entrance. No lights here, but he could see down the hallway toward the lit front room. Not ideal to have lights on anywhere in the house, but workable. Dawson walked to the end of the block and looked in both directions. He observed two empty cars parked a few blocks down to his right, though nothing to the left.

The lights went out in Cooper's house. *She's gone to bed.* He waited another ten minutes to give the woman time to fall asleep. After, checking his watch, 11:43 p.m., he took a deep breath and mumbled, "Geronimo" and then chortled at the connotation.

George Dawson, the one-time successful lawyer who had ruled the Chicago legal landscape, walked into the shadows toward the back porch with killing on his mind. Number four was his, number five would be next, and soon.

The ending of Nick Cooper's life would be the ultimate rewarding moment for Dawson, the culmination of all of his planning and efforts; yet he wanted the man to suffer extreme mental anguish before his own demise. When Nick saw his precious Lou, mutilated beyond recognition, he would finally face the degree of pain that George had felt.

Once opposite the house's back entrance, Dawson crept up the steps to the small landing area. From earlier visits, he knew this door gave access to the laundry room. A hallway led from there to the front room where he last noticed movement.

The rear door contained six individual panes of glass in its top half. He opened his bag and pulled out a small, diamond-tipped glass cutter. As he applied the suction cup to the lower left-hand pane, he cocked his head and glanced at the doorknob. *What would be the chances?* He tried the knob. The brass handle rotated slightly and then stopped.

"Was worth the try," he said with a small chuckle.

Suction cup to the window pane, Dawson attached the arm of the cutter to the suction cup spindle. He made a complete circle with the cutter and then, holding firmly to the cup, gently tapped around the cut. The inner section broke free, and he pulled the glass out. A six-inch hole remained. The man put his ear to the opening and listened. Silence. He waited. Listened again. Silence, still. He reached in and unlocked the door.

There was a noise—a faint thud, but Cooper, hidden in the attic, heard it. He slowly moved the panel to the attic back a couple of inches and leaned down. The house possessed two attic access panels, one near the back door of the laundry room, and one in his master closet. Cooper squatted in the darkened area above the laundry room. He believed this to be the logical egress for Dawson.

Nick remained motionless and continued to concentrate on the intruder's entry. After a few heart-pounding moments, a hulking figure passed by below and walked down the hall. Cooper slid the attic panel back and then, with a small flashlight in his mouth for guidance, he stealthily made his way to the bedroom access. He waited in place for the next telltale sign. His house was old, built in the 1940s with oak floors throughout. Like a sentry, ever vigilant, a few boards would creak when stepped on—and they didn't disappoint.

"Mother fuck," Dawson said under his breath. He tensed and stayed in place for a moment and listened. Nothing. His lips tightened in a thin line as he took his next step. Moving as carefully as possible, he continued ahead, but his weight, plus that of the bag, caused the almost eighty-year-old floorboards to moan in protest with each new step. He put the bag down retrieved a dark brown bottle and went the rest of the way with the jar in one hand and a small, white shop rag in the other. His heart thumped in his chest, as it did each time before he subdued a victim. The sensation wasn't fear; it was the sheer energy rushing through his system like pure cocaine. He thrived on the feeling.

Dawson planned his murders to the letter and now stood on the precipice of victory. This moment was the last step before his rendezvous with Nick Cooper, the man that ruined his life. The culmination of an almost seven-year quest for revenge.

Killing the first three people didn't prove to be easy. Taking this woman's life would have its difficulties. Yes, she was innocent, but her death, like the others, was a necessary step, a vital cog in this critical process. *He had to do what he had to do.*

When he reached the door that led to Cooper's bedroom, he lightly took the knob in hand and turned. He tried to go as slow as he could. He didn't want to alert its occupant of his arrival. But the internal workings of the knob were old, and it creaked.

No matter, he reasoned, *I will just overpower Miss Bradshaw. Might be fun.* He smiled as the handle stopped turning and the door opened.

A floorboard squeak broke the silence like a sledgehammer. Cooper had waited for this moment. He moved the panel away from the opening and waited. He didn't need to wait long. That old battered but beautiful doorknob screamed its alarm as the killer turned the handle. Nick waited for him to enter and then lowered himself to the floor and crouched down. Peering through the crack of the closet door, he could clearly see his bed from that vantage point, and with his night vision in sync, he waited.

The intruder went straight to the bed; Cooper watched as the man's hand reached down to the blanket to reveal its sleeping victim. He yanked the blanket and sheet back and then stopped in confusion. "What the fuck?" Dawson said, this time not in a whisper.

He reactively went for the light on the small dresser next to the bed and switched the lamp on. What lay in front of him made his eyes bulge in bewilderment. Positioned under the covers were several pillows forming the shape of a body.

Cooper slid the closet door open and said, "Not exactly what you expected is it?"

Nick aimed his gun squarely at the middle of the large man's back. When Dawson turned toward Cooper, genuine shock was on the ape's face. The reaction made Nick smile.

"Why aren't you at my ex-wife's?" Dawson demanded.

"Hey, no offense, but she's not my type."

Apparently not appreciating his humor, the killer glared at Cooper.

"I'd guessed that the whole ex-wife thing to be crap," Cooper said. "There's no way you would put yourself out there like that. So, I made a few arrangements here and waited."

"To be honest, I didn't really think you'd buy it, so I had plans set for that. But when I saw you go, I went ahead," Dawson said, cheeks shaking with rage.

"No, you watched someone leave, but as you can see, here I am. I had a police officer come to the house. He changed into some of my clothes, put on a jacket and pulled a hat down over his face. I instructed him to walk quickly out the front door to my car and drive down the block. The other car, the unmarked one, followed. I had Nancy hide in the shadows on the side of the house. The officer circled around and picked her up a few houses away. Right now, I'd say that she's safely away and the house is surrounded by officers.

"And for you and me? Well, I prepared a few things for our little rendezvous. I rolled the carpets up so that I would hear you coming down the hall. I then arranged the bed to look like she was asleep. After I turned all the lights off, I climbed up in the attic and waited. I knew it would only be a matter of time before you came."

Cooper moved a little trying to achieve a better angle on the man and then said, "I do have something that has been bugging the shit out of me. What was all that poetry crap? I mean, come on that shit was lame."

"Nick, don't you understand? You ruined my life when things were about to get good. Everything I did, everything I accomplished, you destroyed. So, this, all I have done to you and your so-called friends, the plan was all poetic justice to me."

"Wait, what? You're kidding right?" Cooper said, surprised.

The man only stared back with no change in expression.

"Jesus, that may be the most incredibly asinine thing I have ever heard," Nick said in true bafflement. "That's it, I'm done with you. Put the bottle on the table and lie down on the floor with your hands behind your back. If you attempt to screw with me, I will shoot you more than once. Truth be told—I'm looking for any excuse to kill you."

Dawson glowered at Cooper and for a moment didn't move. Nick's trigger finger tensed as he watched him. He really did just want to kill this bastard. Pay him back for what he had done to his friends. Whatever moral code he had within him, was waning with each passing second.

Without taking his eyes off Cooper, Dawson reached out and sat the bottle on the dresser that stood next to the bedside nightstand. With a quick motion, Dawson knocked the nightstand lamp to the floor. The bulb shattered, and the room went dark. Cooper fired two shots where Dawson had stood, but the bullets slammed into drywall without hitting flesh. Dawson, though a big man, moved with incredible dexterity and anticipation.

With an uncanny sense of the surroundings, Dawson bolted into Cooper and crushed him into the wall. The force of his two hundred and fifty plus pounds almost knocked the breath from Cooper's lungs. Dawson grabbed Cooper's arm and wrenched it backward, into the wall. The gun dropped to the ground.

Gasping for air, Cooper rammed his fists down on Dawson's back as the man gripped him in a bear hug. After several blows, with no apparent effect, Cooper tried to wedge his hands between the man's arms, but his attacker held him in a vice-like stranglehold and nothing Nick attempted affected the man.

Seeing stars and getting dizzy, Cooper spread his hands as far from Dawson's head as he could and with all his remaining strength slammed his palms into his attacker's ears. Dawson released Cooper and reached for his head, screaming in agony. The big slug stumbled backward, his foot kicking Nick's gun into the darkness of the room before catching the corner of Cooper's bedpost. He lost his balance and crashed into the dresser. The bottle of ether flew up into the air, broke against the corner of the solid mahogany furniture, and splashed most of its contents all over Dawson's clothing. Still gasping for breath, Nick fell to one knee by the closet door.

In what seemed like an unnatural move for a man his size, Dawson jumped up and ran toward the bedroom doorway and possible escape. Hearing and sensing the getaway, Cooper dove toward the fleeing man and hit him thigh high. The two men smashed into the doorframe with a hurtling blow, fell into separate heaps, and sat momentarily stunned.

Nick got back to his feet just as Dawson did. Flinging himself at Dawson, the two spilled through the doorway grabbing at each other with neither of them seeming to retain an advantage. Fists flew. Feet kicked, elbows jabbed. As the fight rolled its way into the living room, Nick caught a whiff of the overwhelming odor of ether, and the nauseating sweet scent made him woozy. As stifling as the effects were on him, Nick couldn't believe Dawson, clothes damp from the ether, wasn't down and out himself.

Shaking his head to clear the chemically induced fog, Nick swept his arm down and then rammed it back up between the two. The separation gave Cooper just enough time and room to take a swing. The punch caught Dawson squarely on the jaw, but the lack of range prevented the blow from having any real effect.

As agile as a pro wrestler, Dawson came right back at Cooper. He reached down, grabbed Nick's leg, and with little effort, lifted Nick and tossed him through the air.

Stunned by Dawson's strength, Cooper landed on a coffee table in the middle of the small living room. The table shattered into pieces. Staggered, Cooper tried to regain a sense of the scene around him. His entire right side felt numb, and he couldn't clear his vision. He tasted warm blood that trickled out of his nose into his mouth. The unmistakable metallic flavor fouled his taste buds. Aware enough to know that another attack was imminent, Cooper searched for something to use as a weapon.

Dawson didn't move in as expected, he only stood in place heaving in deep animal-like breaths. He appeared disoriented. The ether was affecting him, though his adrenalin kept him upright and in the moment.

Out of the darkness, a man's voice, monotone in its cadence, said, "Hey, crap sandwich, long time no see."

Dawson spun in the voice's direction, "Whaa . . . ?" he mumbled. "Who the fuck is that?"

Cooper recognized the noise that a flip-top lighter makes when opened and then a clicking sound. A small flame appeared which illuminated the man's face. It was the young sketch artist from the station.

"JJ," Dawson blurted in amazement, his faux French accent no longer there.

"George, so nice of you to recognize me," JJ replied with a smirk on his face.

"What the hell are *you* doing here?"

"George, you have tormented me from the first day you came into my life. My mother has never been the same since you left. What you have done to her is enough of a reason for me to kill you right now." At that, the young man's other hand rose up from his side, and in it, he held a small caliber revolver.

A moment of paralyzing silence filled the room, and then JJ spoke again, though this time with a noticeable change in its tone, "You piece of shit, how about the fact that your friends were responsible for the death of my best friend, Butch?" He paused for effect. "And if all that's not enough, I know you are the one who executed my father."

"Look JJ, this has nothing to do with you," Dawson barked as he moved closer to his one-time stepson.

"You are such an asshole; *everything* you have done involves my mother and me. You ruined our lives, and now I'm here to make sure you don't ruin anyone else's."

Cooper managed to rise back up to his feet, and as he did, he noticed a red and blue reflection bouncing off the wall. "The police have the house surrounded; it's over. Dawson, lie down on the ground face-first with your hands behind your back," Nick demanded trying to end this before the young officer did something stupid.

Dawson turned away from JJ and in the surreal beating of the flashing cop lights; Nick could see the rage of a psychotic man reemerge.

"No, nothing is over until *I* say it's over. I'll kill you with my bare hands." Dawson said, his speech slurred and sluggish. He took a menacing step toward his self-proclaimed nemesis. "And after I'm done with you, I'll find that bitch Bradshaw and kill her—but not before I've had my fun!"

In a moment forever etched in his mind, Cooper watched the flame in the young officer's hand. As if the whole thing happened in slow motion, the lighter JJ held was now sailing through the air turning end over end. It hit Dawson on the hip. The lumbering man's ether-drenched clothes instantly ignited in a raging ball of fire. Dawson went up like a fuel-soaked torch, covered from head to toe in flames.

The human ball of flames screamed in holy terror as the flickering strobes of fire danced up and down his frame. It quickly licked at the soft red tissue of his face, searing his skin and scorching his hair like a magician's flash paper. He wildly swatted at his body in a futile attempt to douse the blaze. Instead of extinguishing the fire, the flames seemed to intensify.

Cooper's mind brought up this odd vision of a Hollywood horror movie as this flaming human form raced toward the front door. He could clearly see Dawson's face as he passed. The man's expression twisted grossly in unimaginable anguish as he tried to outrun the consuming blaze.

Nick grabbed a blanket that lay on his couch and ran after the burning man. He tried to smother the flames, but Dawson's panicked movements made it impossible to maneuver into a position to stop the fire.

Somehow, Dawson yanked the door open and bolted out into the darkened night. The engulfed man's screams sounded surreal, an animalistic roar of horror as they echoed through the neighborhood.

The glow from the running man lit up the walkway allowing Cooper to glimpse the officers standing on the road with guns drawn and looks of horror on their faces. Cooper saw Bradshaw, her hands up to her face in a display of shock as she watched the inferno stumbling down the walk.

Dawson finally fell to his knees, teetered, and then fell forward face first onto the unforgiving concrete. An alert cop retrieved an extinguisher from his trunk, raced to Dawson, and sprayed the flames. As the mist from the red canister evaporated, everyone stood in shock. At their feet was a mass of charred flesh.

Nancy dashed over to Cooper and flung her arms around him. He hugged and kissed her trying to calm the trembling that consumed her body.

"Tell Doris I'm sorry." The murderer's voice barely a whisper. Dawson, though hanging on by a thread, still lived. Cooper and Bradshaw went to the man's side. His breaths came in short random spurts, and though he would soon walk through death's door, he added in confession. "I . . . I killed Dave Larson. Tell Doris I'm sorry."

Chapter 18

THE END SOUNDS LIKE A NEW BEGINNING

After the incident, Captain Lewis questioned JJ Larson about his involvement. A smart man, JJ figured out what Dawson had planned and went to Nick's house hoping to capture his ex-stepdad. The sketch artist didn't know whether Nick would be there or not, but he believed Miss Bradshaw might be in danger and knew he had to try and stop anyone else from getting hurt. He hid himself near Cooper's house and waited. Within forty-five minutes he saw a skulking figure sneak into Cooper's house. He knew it had to be Dawson but was struck by the memory of the tyrannical ogre and his legs felt cemented in place. After getting his nerve up, he followed Dawson into the house.

JJ anxiously made his way down the hall and into the kitchen. He heard the fighting, pulled his gun, and prepared to shoot George Dawson if he needed to. He watched in dumbstruck awe as Cooper came flying past him onto the small wooden table. Seeing the heaving Dawson emerge in front of him snapped him out of his stupor and he stood ready to act. It was at that moment that he smelled the overpowering scent of the ether. Before becoming a cop, he had worked in a lab that used ether as an organic solvent and he'd immediately recognized the odor and knew the compound was highly flammable.

JJ didn't intend on setting Dawson on fire, but when his stepfather turned to attack Cooper, he unwittingly reacted and simply tossed the lighter.

Two weeks after Dawson's death, Captain Lewis informed Cooper that by using his French alias the department had been able to track Dawson's movements over the last several months. This allowed them to trace his steps back to France where the man fled after the Darnell Dorsett case blew up. The killer couldn't risk the connection to the crook, especially with Dorsett knowing he killed Dave

Larson, and took up residence under a fictitious name. He spent almost seven years hiding in the southern part of the country. He learned how to fit in, even becoming fluent in the language.

The investigators also tracked down one of his ex-partners who reported to them that Dawson had been the primary suspect in an embezzlement case involving his firm. Shortly after he went missing, auditors discovered large amounts of money siphoned from the company into a private offshore account. Dawson used that cash to live until he returned to the United States.

Nick and Nancy decided to stay in the Ambassador East Hotel until one of their houses was habitable. There's also talk of them moving into something new, starting fresh, and putting the past where it belongs—in the past.

Oh, and Mr. Bradshaw is still against their relationship, but Nancy has opened her own firm and any threats he might have used, well, case closed…

ABOUT THE AUTHOR

Though born in New Jersey, Dan has been a resident of the Tampa Bay area for the last 58 years. He is married to Nancy and they have seven children between them. They currently reside in Wesley Chapel with their dog Maggie.

Dan is a graduate of Clearwater High School and attended St. Pete College. He has spent the last 40+ years in the foodservice industry, primarily as a broker and purchasing agent for restaurant chains.

Writing for the author, though for years a passion, had been more of a hobby than a vocation. Now, Dan has blended his writing passion with a desire to publish and share.

"I hope you enjoy reading my books as much as I enjoy writing them!"